COWBOY SPELL

LIBERTY VALLEY LOVE: BOOK 2

JOSIE MALONE

Cowboy Spell is dedicated to The Funny Farm in Silver Lake, Washington, the pony farm where I grew up, and to the original Everett Silver Flying A's horse 4-H Club led by Herb and Virginia Weinz. Memories of those bygone days inspired the ponies and horses in this novel, especially my junk-food pony Lucky, who had a predilection for peanut butter sandwiches and soda pop whose name is changed because he's been immortalized before in the Baker City series.

I would also like to acknowledge those trainers who utilize "natural horsemanship" techniques when they work with horses and the horse-shoers I've known, especially Ron Hayden, who so willingly answered all my questions to make this book possible. Any errors are mine.

PART ONE

MARCH 2018

"What you think about, you bring about."

JAKE PRICE

ONE

"COME ON, GUYS. HUSTLE YOUR BUSTLES! WE GOTTA GO!" Elinor yelled on her way in the kitchen door. "You'll be late, and I don't have my pilot's license yet."

Did she have time to change clothes before delivering the kids to their 4-H meeting? She glanced at the kitchen clock and decided against it. She'd just finished mucking the barn and putting fresh pine shavings in the ponies' stalls. Mud splattered her black jeans and there was horse manure on her boots. Hey, she owned and operated a pony farm and the kids were on their way to the Silver Flying A's horse club. If people didn't like horsy poop, they could get over it.

She was still trying to catch up on the farm after two days of substitute teaching at the local high school. Yes, she needed the money, but hell had to be trying to convince sixty seniors that Contemporary World Problems was a graduation requirement if they wanted to get out of Silver Lake High alive, diplomas in hand. She didn't want to even remember trying to teach Washington State History to ninety tenth-graders. Ick!

There was a reason she'd stopped teaching full-time and taken her weekend hobby farm to a real five-days-a-week riding stable. Tonight, she had to get to the grain store in Snohomish, pick up a half-ton of sweet feed, and finish the evening chores, all before collecting the kids from their meeting. Of course, first she had to drop them at the monthly event, hopefully on time.

"Lynn! Jake! Let's go. Move it! Move it!" Elinor grabbed the green and orange baseball cap that proclaimed she was the Silver Lake Pony Ranch Barn Goddess and used it to cover her nasty, black hair. She wanted a shower, but that would have to wait until after 4-H, chores, dinner, baths for the kids, and housework—life in general; hers in particular.

Lynn stormed into the room, all thirteen-year-old angst. "Jake is being a major pain, as usual. Why did you have him?"

"To make your life impossible, sweetheart." Elinor grabbed her light denim jacket and purse. "There could be no other reason why I would have my darling boy and keep him."

"I knew it." Lynn tossed her head, golden-brown curls flying, blue eyes narrowed in fury. "He is your favorite."

"Yup." Elinor snagged her for a quick hug. "And you're my best daughter."

That almost earned a smile before Lynn slipped away and hurried to the bathroom, probably to put on the little bit of mascara and lip gloss she was allowed to wear. Lynn didn't have to say all her friends wore a great deal more—it was obvious at the middle school when Elinor substituted there.

In clean jeans and a navy t-shirt matching his eyes, sandy blond hair slicked back with water, Jake charged in from the living room. "Mom, tell her to leave me alone at 4-H. When she sits by us guys, she pokes me when I ask a question."

"Only when they're stupid," Lynn yelled from the bathroom. "You live to embarrass me."

"Lynn, there's no such thing as a dumb question. You know that." Elinor started for the back door, opting for her best preachy teacher voice, guaranteed to annoy any child in a hundred-mile radius. "Jake has a good point. He needs to develop autonomy, not have his older sister protect him all the time."

The comment brought Lynn squawking protests from the bathroom. She chased behind Elinor to the pickup. Meanwhile, Jake argued that his mother didn't get the point. Lynn wasn't trying to protect him; she just lived to harass him.

Hey, she was the mom of one teen and one tween. Of course, she didn't have a clue about life, but they were all in the Ranger and headed for the meeting on time. Oh yeah, baby. She rocked. She was so cool, she amazed herself every once in a while.

Once she had the truck on the road, she asked, "So, who is your guest speaker tonight?"

"An elf," Jake answered with obvious delight.

"Mo-ther!" Lynn wailed. "Does he have to humiliate me every time he opens his mouth?"

"It's an added bonus. Relax, Lynn. Why would an elf come to your meeting, Jake?"

"Because he's the stupidest kid on the planet. He thinks fairies and elves are real."

"They are. On TV, elves make cookies, but they don't have my favorites anymore—the frosted circus animals. Mom has to get those at the bakery outlet store. Santa's elves only know about toys and reindeer, not horses."

Elinor smiled. Even at eleven, Jake was so innocent. He really did still believe in fairytales, Santa, and fantasy.

"Those are commercials." Lynn heaved a dramatic sigh. "There are no such things as elves, you dork. It's a horse-shoer. He's supposed to lecture us about hoof trims, shoeing, and diseases like thrush."

"I know, Lynnie. That's what I said."

"But he's not an elf, you twit."

"Okay, you two." It was time for parental intervention. Obviously, Jake had mixed up the words. "Lynn, stop calling your brother names. Jake, a horse-shoer is also known as a farrier."

"Not a fairy or an elf. I got it, Mom."

"You'd better. If you act stupid tonight, I'll choke you, Jake Price."

"And I'll ground you for life if you lay a finger on him, Lynette."

"Oh, Mom!" Lynn frumped into the seat. "It's not like I meant it."

"Just checking." Elinor pulled into the parking lot. "Wait inside for me. I'll be here after your meeting, but I could be late."

"Like usual," Jake said. "It's cool, Mom. Marlene will stay with us until you come."

Elinor eyed her boy, but he didn't seem upset by the busy schedule. Before she had time to ask if he was okay with it, Lynn interrupted.

"Mom, Gypsy's feet are too long. She has to have new shoes for the show on Saturday or I won't place in the ribbons. Don't you remember last summer when Gypsy threw a shoe in trail class? I lost all my entry fees because I couldn't ride her for the rest of the day. Can I find out if this shoer has room in his book for more clients?"

Who could forget that equine disaster last year? Lynn had blamed Elinor until Christmas when the flashy palomino mare went lame. The teen did her best silent and sulky martyr routine even though Elinor made up the difference in the show fees. She mentally tallied up the riding students she had before the weekend and the accounts she expected to collect.

"No more than seventy bucks for a set of shoes, and thirty-five for trims, honey. We've got the whole herd to do, not just your horse. If the guy gives you heartburn about how cheap I am, walk away."

"I will." Lynn grabbed her belongings and urged Jake from the truck. "Let's go. Otherwise, we'll be late for the flag salutes and roll call."

Elinor waited until both of them were safe in the red brick building before she drove away. It was fun to be the parent for a change. Since the divorce, the kids tended to act older than their respective ages. They tried so hard not to worry or upset her. Would the world stop turning if they messed up their rooms? If they threw clean laundry on the floor instead of putting it in dresser drawers? If they skipped homework assignments?

She decided she was going too far when she wanted that kind of trouble. Granted it hadn't been her idea to send them to Silver Lake Middle School. There had been so many problems when Jake started at the local elementary shortly after the divorce. He asked too many questions to suit his first-grade teacher who didn't hesitate to label him a troublemaker and insist he be tested for hyperactivity.

As a high school English teacher, Elinor knew all the buzzwords and double-speak used in the education profession. She just hadn't expected those terms to be applied to her boy. Then Lynn started getting in trouble, too. John, their father, and thankfully, Elinor's now ex-husband, was too busy as a high-priced lawyer to even visit the elementary, much less help resolve the problems.

During their marriage, she'd only opened the pony farm on weekends and supported it with her teaching wages the rest of the time. Once the kids fell apart after the divorce, she'd given up trying to work away from home. She left her position at Silver Lake High, homeschooled the kids, and ran the farm full time. They didn't have as much money, but life seemed a great deal smoother, despite John's complaints that she only did it to increase the alimony and child support. The hostilities escalated when he demanded a DNA test for both kids to prove they were his, since they had her cobalt blue eyes, not his brown ones. He'd told the first family court judge that she was forcing the kids on him when he was too busy to entertain them and the judge rained on his parade, telling him to "daddy-up."

The world didn't revolve around one high-priced lawyer, but her ex certainly thought it did. Why wouldn't John simply use his visitation and spend time with their kids? Elinor had suggested shared custody at the time of the divorce, but he refused to consider the idea, so they agreed he'd take them two weekends a month, split the holidays and have them all of July.

He'd pitched a fit the last time they were in court. John had said she wanted the children to slave on the farm, not receive a quality education. The new city-slicker judge agreed and ordered her to enroll them in a public or private school. The kids started at the local middle school last September. Most of the teachers knew their stuff and Mona Craig, the principal, meant well. Jake hated it there and Lynn called the place a party palace.

Elinor pulled in at the Snohomish Co-Op and checked the time. Five forty-five. She had to be back for the kids at seven o'clock, when their meeting ended. She paid for the grain and waited for the fifty-pound sacks of specially mixed COB—corn, oats, and barley—to be loaded. Then she headed for the farm. She parked next to the barn and started to carry the bags of feed into the grain room.

On the tenth bag, she peeled off her flannel shirt and hung it on the stair rail. She was still decent. She had on the tight red T-shirt that advertised her need for a "hard-ridin', straight-talkin', spur-wearin' cowboy." Ten more bags to cart to the feed room. She looked at the barn clock. It was 6:30.

"Come on, Elinor," she told herself. "Get moving!"

She had to be back at the community center in half an hour. And it was a twenty-minute drive. She still needed to put out the night grain and call in the ponies from the pasture. Luckily, they knew coming in meant supper and were usually good sports. It was as if they understood they had to be fed at the same time each day. *Somebody* read her horse magazines before she did, and it had to be the ponies—Lynn always gave her the wide-eyed, innocent teenager look when Elinor asked why the pages were creased. And she definitely wasn't telling her daughter again to quit reading her teacher publications or parenting newsletters.

———

The president adjourned the meeting at 7:02 p.m. and Lynn helped put away the folding chairs. She left the storeroom and spotted

Jake coming toward her. "What's going on? Is Mom here already?"

"No way. She'll be late. She always is." Jake grabbed Lynn's arm. "Come on. He's the one. We gotta talk to him."

"I know. Mom said I could ask about Gypsy."

"Not just that," Jake hissed. "He's our new dad."

"What are you talking about?" Lynn looked around, but it didn't appear anybody had overheard her brother. "Jake, chill."

"Don't worry. I'm not telling him. He has to figure it out for himself. I only want to make sure I'm right."

"How are you going to do it?" Lynn whispered. "If you embarrass me by mentioning what we did last Friday, I'll kill you."

"Be cool, Lynnie." Jake hustled her across the room to the horse-shoer. "Hi, I'm Jake Price and this is my sister, Lynn. We need to ask you some questions."

"About shoeing." Lynn gave Jake an older-sister glare, but wasn't sure it would work. Then she eyed the farrier. Why did Jake think he was so special? The guy wasn't that much taller than their mom. He had graying dark brown hair under his cowboy hat. At least he wore jeans and a regular, western shirt, not a suit like their dad. "There's a show this Saturday and my mare needs new shoes, Mr. Killian."

"My brothers go by Mr. Killian. I'm Sean." Kind gray eyes twinkled at her. "What kind of horse do you have? I usually talk to parents about shoeing."

"Our mom is busy. She told us to see if you have room in your shoer book for more clients," Jake said. "We're supposed to interview you."

Sean chuckled. "Okay, then ask the rest of your questions. I do have room for another horse or two."

"We have thirteen," Jake said. "Will your wife let you have that many new ones?"

Lynn elbowed him. "Maybe his wife doesn't keep his schedule, you dork."

"Yeah, but his fiancée or girlfriend could," Jake paused, "or his boyfriend."

That got them a long look before Sean managed to say with a straight face, "I keep my own schedule since I don't have a wife, or fiancée, or girlfriend, or a boyfriend. Yes, I could do another thirteen horses. How many need shoes and how many are just trims?"

"Ten need trims and three need shoes," Lynn said quickly. "What would you charge us?"

"What's your quantity discount?" Jake asked. "Have you ever quicked a horse? Does a horse ever make you angry or upset? What do you do then? Have you ever hit a horse? Mom freaks out if anybody smacks our horses."

"Good for her." Sean grinned at them, then pushed back his hat a little. "Those aren't easy questions. Let me answer them one at a time."

TWO

Three nights earlier—Ostara eve

"Tell me again." Lynn shivered in her long, white nightgown; bare feet cold in the wet March grass. Rain misted her hair. "Why do we have to do this stupid spell at midnight, Jake? What's so important about the spring equinox?"

"It's the right night and the right time of the year to create perfect balance," her pest of a little brother said, finishing the chalk circle he drew around them. "This is when day and night are equal. They have the same number of hours and it's when this spell will work. I read it in my *magick* book. Come on, Lynnie."

"Mom should censor your reading." Lynn glared at Jake. He wore his Harry Potter costume from last Halloween, complete with the star-splashed, black pointed wizard's hat he got at the county fair. "We tried it last month and it didn't change anything. This spell never will do squat. *Magick* isn't real."

"Your teacher says that today's *magick* is tomorrow's science." Jake took a deep breath. "We just have to do it right, Lynnie. Like Mom always says, 'Third time's the charm.' It'll be great."

"Mom wasn't talking about *magick* spells, Jake."

"How do you know? You've come this far. Do the spell with me again and I know we'll get a good dad."

"All right." Lynn gave up. In truth, she'd known she'd have to help him when he'd come into her room to wake her up tonight, but she'd hoped to talk him out of this stupid stunt. He'd be so upset when the spell didn't do anything. "This is absolutely the last time, Jake. I mean it."

"Thanks, Lynnie. You're the best." His teeth gleamed in a broad smile.

"Yeah, right." Lynn sighed. Since the divorce six years ago, Dad never visited, and she didn't miss him. It wasn't as if Mom kept him away, either. She used to call his office to remind him to come for his scheduled weekends and on summer vacations, but she'd finally stopped that last September. Their 4-H leader, Marlene Dawson, said he'd gotten lost on the way to find himself.

It didn't matter what anyone said about him. Even when everyone else gave up on Dad, Jake wouldn't. He decided a spell would change their father, would make him want to see them. *Magick* always worked in the movies, especially those that Jake watched. There was no problem *magick* couldn't solve in his fantasy books.

Lynn shook her head again. Her brother was supposed to be the smart one. The teachers and librarians at Silver Lake Middle School, the minister at church, Marlene, and even Mom agreed on that. Jake did the multiplication tables faster than anybody else in his sixth-grade class. He read better. Why did someone with such a fantastic brain believe in *magick,* monsters, and miracles?

She was thirteen and this had to be the dumbest thing she'd done to help him get over the divorce. She looked over his three pages of notes. By now, she knew his precisely written spell by heart, but she wouldn't tell him so. "*On this night and in this hour, I call upon the Ancient Power.*" She waved her hand, pointed to the full moon overhead, then dropped a few rose petals in the metal lunchbox at her feet. "*Oh, brave Gods and Goddesses bright; bring us your enchanted light.*"

"*We have a need that must be met,*" Jake chimed in on the chant. "*Help us get the best dad yet.*"

The spell listed all the qualities the perfect dad needed. He'd attend special events at school, church, and 4-H. He'd solve problems, large and small. He'd buy his own holiday gifts. He'd like animals as much as they did. He wouldn't gripe because Mom quit her day job to operate a pony farm, or when she saved a starving horse instead of buying a new dress for a fancy party, or if she walked a colicky gelding all night for old Mrs. Baldusi next door instead of meeting his law partners for dinner.

Their father would laugh at them if he learned *how* they planned to fix him. He'd break Jake's heart all over again. Lynn already knew better than to trust Dad with anything, especially her love. *Keep him away,* she prayed, not for the first time. She'd been thrilled when he moved out, glad when her parents finally split up, not that she was stupid enough to say so

Aloud, she finished the spell with a flourish. "*I now say this spell is done. May it harm none. In no way will this spell reverse or place upon us a curse. As we will it, in days that number three, so must it be.*"

She returned the papers and Jake carefully placed them in the old gray, "working-man's" metal lunchbox he'd used to go fishing with their grandfather. They buried the small container in the garden patch. Of course, if she'd broken Mom's rule about not using matches and allowed Jake to burn the pages, they might only have cast the spell once. Getting rid of the spell wouldn't have worked. Bound and determined to repair the family Dad tried to destroy, Jake would have written another one.

Lynn started toward the old farmhouse. "Don't get your hopes up, Jake. Nothing, not even *magick,* may help our father."

"Who cares about him? In three days, our new *real* dad will arrive. I felt the spell work this time. Didn't you?"

"Wait a second." She grabbed her brother's arm. "What did you say? We were fixing Dad so he'd love us. Right?"

"Lynn, that's evil." Jake's mouth fell open, dark blue eyes shocked. "It's not how *magic*k works. You never use it on people, not unless they ask. Even then, it's bad. Real super-bad. Whatever we do comes back three-fold and we don't want to attract another bad guy when we're getting rid of one."

"Fine." She threw her hands up in the air. "What did we do tonight?"

"We gave our old dad back to the universe." Jake took a deep breath and struggled to explain. "Remember that last Christmas before Dad left?"

"Yeah. It was awful. Mom kept up that fake smiley act like we couldn't hear her crying at night and her eyes weren't all red and swollen."

"Okay," Jake said. "You know that puke-green sweater Dad's sister gave you?"

"Sure. It was so ugly I'd have died before I wore it anywhere."

"That's why you and Mom took it back to Wal-Mart."

"We exchanged it," Lynn said. "Mom let me buy new curtains for my room. She got me a matching comforter, too."

"Yeah, right." Jake hastily changed the subject from that long-ago shopping trip. "Well, that's what we did. We returned our old, yucky dad. We traded him for the one we're supposed to have. Got it?"

"Yeah." A huge weight lifted off her shoulders. She didn't have to worry about Jake missing Dad anymore. Another picture formed in her mind, one of her father in his black lawyer suit being swapped off at a giant Wal-Mart in the sky.

"Your ritual may do the trick." Lynn laughed. "How did you dream this up?"

"Marlene says I'm a realist." Jake grinned at Lynn. "You've gotta grow up, Lynnie. Our old dad never loved us. Wake up and see the dragon before it eats you."

"I know. I know." Lynn hugged him. "I'm crunchy and good with ketchup. Let's keep this a secret. Deal?"

"We have to, or the *magick* will leak out."

Lynn knew better. If she and Jake had been good enough, their father would have loved them. They weren't and he didn't, not that she cared anymore. Getting rid of his relatives was an added bonus to the divorce. They not only lost Dad, they lost his snooty family who thought she and Jake were obnoxious mistakes.

"Jake, how are we gonna get Mom to do her part? She doesn't dress up unless she has to go teach. She hardly ever wears makeup anymore. She grooms all the ponies every day, and their tails look better than her hair. What about when she gets mad? She'll call this guy we find an idiot, and he'll walk."

"Not if he's the right guy." Jake pulled away from Lynn. "I'm working on it. I figure I'll tell her she has to set a proper example for us. She needs to *model* what she wants us to do, like she does for her students when she teaches at school or lessons here. I read it in her educator's magazines."

"You'll be grounded past forever when Mom realizes you're the one who reads her professional journals. We're supposed to stick to kids' stuff, and remember she's the adult, we're not."

"Then she shouldn't have bought me those *Silver Ravenwolf* books," Jake said. "The *magick* in them isn't for babies."

Lynn shrugged, content with the progress she'd made. Jake didn't want their father back. She could deal with whatever came next. For a moment, she wondered if *magick* spells ever worked in real life. It'd be beyond awesome to have a dad who watched her at horseshows, who bought her birthday presents, who listened to her dreams, who didn't say he'd killed her cat.

She shook her head. If she had a dad who loved her…

Not likely. She wasn't the kind of girl a father loved. It was impossible, and she was too savvy to buy into a Disney dream.

———

Sean Killian sat on the front steps of the three-story log house and watched the full moon break through the clouds. Three of his Australian cattle dogs kept him company, steel-gray lumps of fur on the front porch.

The years weighed on him. He'd be forty this summer and he wanted a family, a real one. He'd tried marriage once, but it hadn't worked. His ex-wife hated the farm, his dogs, and eventually him, calling him an 'old stick in the proverbial mud'. He never intended to infuriate her. He just refused to move off the land he'd bought because it was next door to the acreage his great-grandfather homesteaded over a hundred years before in Liberty Valley. Was having someone love him too much to ask?

His engagement last year died as hard as his dreams when he'd realized all she wanted was a steady paycheck. She'd been so sure he'd sell his home for her that she arranged for a realtor to visit and list the property for sale. Of course it hadn't worked since she wasn't a co-owner of the land and he'd had it for years before he met her, but it still led to a major dust-up between them and an embarrassing fight in front of the real estate agent.

He stared up at the black night sky again. As a boy, he'd made wishes on the full moon. He refused to unburden his soul to the moon tonight. That was a boy's fantasy and he was a man grown, no longer a gullible fool. He reached for his beer. He might dream of a soulmate, but no more *Ms. Make-Do,* not after all this time.

THREE

At 7:38 p.m., feeling like a total loser because she was late again, Elinor parked the truck and hurried inside the building to collect her kids. A few parents still lingered, chatting with each other while they waited for their children. She glanced around the room and spotted the older woman who'd volunteered as a 4-H leader for more than forty years. She waved at Marlene, then looked for Lynn and Jake.

They were talking to a lean, broad-shouldered, dark-haired man in a bright red western shirt, and it reminded her of the club song that Lynn and Jake sang around the barn all the time. *"Red and white shall never fight—they're the colors of the best 4-H club in sight!"*

Dark blue jeans encased long legs. He wore battered cowboy boots and held an equally ancient Stetson by the brim. He was a definite switch from the other fathers who came from offices and wore what she thought of as "nineteen-piece" suits. Of course, marriage to John had turned her off doctors, lawyers, and men who were more feminine than she was.

She had to admit she liked this man's strong, angled features and firm jaw. As she approached, she noticed his nose had been broken at least once. He smiled at her. It was a real smile, not a polite one, and she couldn't help it. She grinned back at him.

The impulsive reaction surprised her. As a businesswoman in the community and a substitute schoolteacher, she was courteous to everyone. Mostly it was good business. Customers always talked to each other and complainers drove away potential clients.

She never gushed, so why did he make her want to?

She took a deep breath and adopted the composed mask she used to hide from the world. "Hey, kids. Sorry I'm late. How was the meeting?"

Lynn looked at her with barely concealed disapproval. "Mom, this is Sean Killian. Jake and I hired him to shoe and trim the herd."

"That's right," Jake agreed. "We know everything about Sean. We asked."

"Wonderful." Elinor hoped her sarcasm passed by the children. "Go tell Marlene I'm here. We'll swing by the deli and grab a pizza after you check out with her."

"All right, but I get to fix it up," Lynn said. "And bake it."

"I can cook." Elinor struggled to keep her tone level. "Just because I burned the last one doesn't mean I can't. If there hadn't been a ruckus in the barn, I'd have pulled it out in time."

"You never have before," Lynn said.

"Come on, Lynnie. You know I like my pizzas well-done." Jake headed toward Marlene.

Elinor turned back to the horse-shoer and met his amused gaze. His eyes were gray with a hint of green. They reminded her of the ocean on stormy days. She suddenly felt like a sixth-grader with her first crush. She couldn't let that show, so she lifted her chin to meet his steady look. "What did they tell you?"

"That they're the general manager and foreman of your spread." Sean put on his hat and pushed it back with a thumb. "You have good help."

"It was either give them titles or raises in pay." She struggled to ignore the warmth in her face. "If they're on hourly wages, they'll be after my job. So how good of a farrier are you?"

"Folks say I'm the best in Liberty Valley." He chuckled. "Marlene will give me a good reference. I shoe for Darlene Dawson at the Lazy B, Cascade Equestrian at Mill Creek, Xanadu Arabians in Monroe, and Trails End up past Eagleton."

Those were the largest, most influential stables around. The owners had major bucks and expensive, registered stock. "I can't afford to pay what they must be shelling out. Thanks for listening to my kids, but I don't appreciate you making fun of them."

"What the hell do you mean?"

"You were leading them on. Whatever it was, that wasn't a real offer to shoe my stock."

"Don't flatter yourself, ma'am. You haven't heard the deal yet." His jaw tightened. "Your daughter and I agreed on a year's contract—in writing. Sixty for shoes. Thirty-five for trims. You're lucky I'm a man of my word."

Elinor felt as if her jaw had dropped to the floor. "If you're as competent as you say, that's a hefty discount, at least fifty percent of what you usually charge. What's the catch?"

"Oh, there is one." His gray eyes still held a hint of amusement. "You have to clear any sales with me and keep a minimum of twelve head to get the business discount. It's based on having a quantity of horses at one location. Once you sign a contract with me, none of the reputable farriers around here will touch your stock. I don't share my horses or their owners."

"Like hell." Elinor glared up at him. "I can find a shoer in the classified ads of the weekly shopper."

"None worth a tinker's dam." He folded his arms as he looked her up and down in obvious masculine approval. "Face it, you're stuck with me. You'll grow to like me. I'm downright lovable and I've never quicked a horse in my career. Who was your previous shoer? Did he quit on you?"

"Not willingly. Her reserve unit was called up. Since then, I've tried three others. The first left for divinity school. The second didn't show up on schedule and the third arrived drunk. I wouldn't let him near my animals."

Sean nodded, worry sliding into his eyes. "That first shoer—you must be talking about Mariah Stevens. I've known her since she rode a Shetland pony. She only joined the Army to get education benefits for vet school. She's a good shoer."

"Yes, and when she comes home, she'll be back shoeing my stock," Elinor said, refusing to say that the young woman might not return from serving her country. "You'll be out of a job. This is just temporary, and my kids can't sign a contract with you since they're under eighteen."

"Your daughter and I made a deal and I'm a man of my word. We'll adjust the dates. I'm good with ending the contract when Mariah gets back. Does that suit you?"

Elinor took a deep breath. She probably sounded more immature than her kids and she'd be thirty-five at the end of October. "I'm sorry. I shouldn't be rude to you. When can you fit the stock into your schedule? You must be busy with all those other stables."

"I have an opening the second and fourth Thursday of each month. I'll be at your place at eight a.m., the day after tomorrow."

"No way. It takes weeks to get into a farrier's schedule if he's any good." She eyed him narrowly. Something didn't add up. "Why are you free at such short notice?"

He didn't answer that question. Instead, he repeated. "First thing Thursday. I don't catch horses. If they bite, kick, strike, stomp me, or act out, better be quick to make amends before I start my truck and drive away. If you're not there on time, you pay a penalty plus my mileage."

"Aren't you the cowboy with the mostest?"

He took a step nearer, loomed over her. "I'll audition you and the stock on Thursday. If I like them, I'll bring a contract the next time I shoe. Be at the barn when I get there. I don't wait for owners to come from Timbuktu, or the mall."

"No problem." She shivered, determined not to let him see

how his intimate gaze affected her. "Stop by the house. It's in front of the barn."

"Good." He didn't back down. "Have my coffee ready. I like it hot and sweet, same as you'll be when I get you trained."

She snorted. "In your dreams, cowboy."

"Oh, I'll be in yours, too." He traced a line down her nose with a calloused finger. "I've been looking for you a long time. Should have known you wouldn't be halter-broke. If it weren't for bad luck, I'd have none a-tall."

She gaped up at him, then hastily stepped back. Why didn't his mockery of a western drawl irritate her? She reminded herself to breathe and stop drooling over the broad shoulders emphasized by his western shirt. She wasn't a silly teenager. She had a master's degree in teaching. She couldn't have finished college and grad school without learning a few life lessons.

She'd been married. She had two children. She knew what sex was about. Why him? Why now? "I'm not interested in you."

"Liar. Interrogate your foreman about me. He had at least a hundred questions and I answered all of them."

"I'm surprised you bothered. Or did Marlene make you?"

He smiled. "Nobody makes me do anything." He looked her up and down again. "Just keep running. You'll get tired sooner or later. I'll stand and wait for you to settle down, missy."

"Don't pull that natural horsemanship crap on me. I'm not one of your horses."

"You'll be mine soon enough."

If they hadn't been in a room full of children, she might have cut loose with a few of Grandpa's favorite words. Just because she waited for revenge didn't mean she wouldn't get it. "I guess I should thank you for treating my kids with respect."

"You can later when it doesn't irk you." He rubbed his jaw thoughtfully. "I could teach your boy to trim those ponies. Your girl, too."

"No. They may talk like adults, but Lynn's only thirteen."

Elinor lifted her chin. "You can teach me. Then I won't have to waste good money on you. I'll be able to do the job myself."

"I'll have to get a recipe for that crow so you can cook it before you eat it."

She wouldn't give him the satisfaction of an angry reply. "I'll be calling those other barns to check your references."

"That'll be fine. They'll tell you that I'm not a hard-ridin' or spur-wearin' cowboy, but I do talk straight and I'm a fast learner. You can teach me what you like."

Oh my God! She looked down and realized he'd read her clinging T-shirt with its advertisement wanting a "hard-ridin', straight-talkin', spur-wearin' cowboy," and the offer to train the applicants. She'd forgotten the flannel shirt on the rail back at the grain room. He must think she was majorly desperate—another gal chasing him. She sniffed, as though she'd measured and definitely found him lacking. "Well, at least one out of three isn't bad. Be on time Thursday, Killian."

"You bet, missy." His mockery drifted after her. "I'm never late."

She drew a ragged breath. Just because she liked his smile, the laugh wrinkles around his eyes, his heart-stopping face, amused gray eyes and the way he treated Lynn and Jake didn't mean she planned to fall into his arms. She was through with men, no matter what her T-shirt said. *Been there, done that. And I got the trophy for sucker of the day.*

When she reached Marlene and the kids, she met Lynn's critical gaze. "What? I didn't fire the arrogant son of a biscuit eater."

Jake and Marlene exchanged high fives. "I told you your mom would like him," Marlene said. "Sean's a charmer. He's conned me out of more cookies in the last thirty-plus years than the rest of the boys I raised in the club put together."

"Wow!" Jake's dark blue eyes widened. "He's more awesome than I thought."

"He's a con artist," Elinor informed her son. She eyed his sister. "Okay, spill it. Why are *you* upset?"

Lynn gave her *the look.* "I can't believe you're dressed like that in public. You tracked crud on the floor."

"I forgot to put on my shirt-jac when I finished unloading the grain," Elinor said, trying to defend herself. She glanced at her jeans. The mud had dried, but they still clung tighter than what most of the other moms wore and she did have stuff from the barn on her boots. Lynn was right about the muck getting on the tile. "Oops, guess I'm in the doghouse again, Marlene."

"Working for a living will do it every time." Marlene followed them in the direction of the door. "Call me later. I'll tell you all the down and dirty facts about Sean. He was my favorite mud monster."

"Is he as good a horse-shoer as he claims?"

"Better. He's always been too modest," Marlene said. "He's the only one I allow to touch Roy's old palomino."

"Terrific." Elinor stepped out onto the sidewalk. "Lynn offered him a year's contract. He thinks I'll jump to sign it."

"Everyone else in Liberty Valley has. Having Sean Killian for a farrier is a mark of success."

"No wonder he's so arrogant."

————

Behind her mother, Lynn grabbed Jake's arm. "This doesn't sound good. How do we know he's the one?"

"He answered everything right," Jake said. "He has to be right for Mom, too, not just us. He has to love her and not be scared by her. She frightened our old dad. Our spell is working, Lynnie. Stop worrying."

"Sean didn't quit." The realization struck Lynn. "So, he isn't afraid of her. Come on, Jake. She'll probably gripe about him all the way home and we can find out what she really thinks."

They raced toward the truck.

————

Sean waited until everyone else had left before he ambled toward Marlene. "Take you to dinner, Fearless Leader?"

"Honey, I'd love it." She hooked her arm through his. "I hate going home to an empty house. I still miss Roy so much and it's been two years."

"You and Roy were like parents to us." Sean hugged her. He reflected back on the hours he and his brothers had spent playing poker with the old man who'd been like a father to them. "I miss him, too."

Marlene tilted her head. "So why did you take on Elinor and her place? I thought your shoeing book was full."

"If her stock checks out, I can fire a dozen hard-paying clients who have the horses from hell." Sean guided Marlene to the door. "I prefer professional horse people with big barns to driving all over the place for one or two critters."

Marlene nodded. "You came in the club when you were six. We taught you right from wrong, weak from strong, Sean. I know your good, bad, and ugly sides. Roy said you were the best shoer he'd ever seen. You're wonderful with horses, honey, but you could be more tactful with their owners."

"I could, but then they keep me waiting. They expect me to train their horses. I'm too old and set in my ways to enjoy being stomped on. Now, tell me about my new client. She seems like a real horsewoman. She came straight from the barn to get her kids. A guy has to admire a gal like her."

"If you break her heart, you'll answer to me, Sean Killian."

"Oh, I won't. The third time's the charm, Fearless."

After she sent the kids off to school Wednesday morning and finished her chores, Elinor headed next door to visit Daisy Baldusi. Now in her late sixties, the older woman had been her ninth-grade English teacher. When she applied for college scholarships, Daisy had written numerous reference letters. She'd also guided Elinor through student teaching and mentored her during the first arduous years in the profession. Daisy had taught Elinor to ask open-ended questions and draw people out, skills that were of enormous help in the classroom.

She tapped on the back door, then walked into the kitchen where Daisy brewed coffee. "I have éclairs."

"How did you keep them safe from Lynn and Jake?" Petite with a cap of silver hair, Daisy looked slight and dainty in slacks and a flowered top, not as if she'd been known to make football players quake in their cleats. "Did you threaten them with dire deeds or disguise them as a salad?"

"Of course not, but I did hide them in the 'veggie' drawer in the fridge." Elinor carried the box over to the table. "They each got a doughnut for breakfast. They're up to something, so they didn't touch our evil treats."

"What are they doing now?" Daisy took down two coffee cups from the cupboard. "Anything real creative? Or is it typical kid stuff?"

"They never do anything normal, Daisy. They hired a horse-shoer last night at their 4-H meeting. Sean Killian. There's something else going on, but I haven't figured out what."

Daisy whistled softly. "Honey, if you have Sean to do your horses, count your blessings. I remember him from my time at Snohomish High. He was always a real sweetie, not like his older brothers."

Elinor sniffed and glowered at the checked red and white café curtains. "He wasn't sweet to me. He was a real smart-ass."

"That's my boy." Daisy filled the cups and carried them over to the table. "All the girls used Sean to get to his brothers who were the stars of the high school. Ethan was the football star and Gavin lettered in basketball and track. Another boy might have tried to compete with them, but Sean shone in academics, not that anybody except me knew the class clown had amazing potential."

Elinor opened the plastic lid on the container of four éclairs she'd bought at the bakery last night. "Have I ever mentioned that I hate being conned?"

"Join the club. When he became valedictorian, Sean surprised his parents who thought he majored in sex, drugs and alcohol. His graduation was one of the few times I saw both of them at the high school. Usually, they were too busy with Sean's father's political career." Daisy leaned across the table to pat Elinor's hand. "I have faith in you, my dear. I know you'll make Sean suck eggs."

"Oh, you got that right!"

FOUR

BANG! BANG! BANG!

Elinor jolted up in bed. What was that?

The first reaction of any farmer hit her. *Stock's out!*

She threw the blankets aside as the pounding on the back door grew faster and louder. She leaped from the bed. Grateful for the extra-large T-shirt and sweatpants she slept in, she raced through the kitchen to the door.

Visions of ponies running loose on the country road danced in her mind. How had Bonanza done it? The equine escape artist had never managed to open all three locks on his stall door before, but that didn't mean it was impossible. He could undo snaps, hooks, and the occasional bolt, but ever since she'd added a padlock hasp to the series of catches on his door, he'd remained in the stall.

Had the Welsh pony set free the rest of the stock in the barn this morning? He'd have to get them from the barn through the pasture to the yard to the two-lane blacktop...

Elinor unlocked the back door and jerked it open. "What's wrong? Where are they?" The remaining questions died as she recognized Sean Killian. "Oh no. It can't be eight already. Why didn't the alarm...?"

He looked at his watch. "Actually, it's 8:03." He frowned at her. "I have a schedule, woman."

"Pardon me all to hell." She glanced over her shoulder at the clock on the microwave and saw the numbers flash back: 3:18. "I don't believe it. We must have had a power failure during the night."

"Now it's 8:06." He pushed back his hat. "You should have a wind-up clock for emergencies. Horses need to be fed within five minutes of the same time every day."

"I know that! I'm not a weekend sports rider." Elinor looked past him to the empty yard. "All the noise, was you? The stock's not out playing dodge 'em on the road? They didn't get out?"

"Of course not. If they had, I'd be rounding up and catching horses, not getting you out of bed." He leaned one wide shoulder against the doorframe. "I figured it'd take me a lot longer to get you out of your jeans."

"Dream on!" He must have been up for hours. A blue-checked shirt clung to muscled shoulders and arms. Heavy black jeans and cowboy boots finished the ensemble. Behind him on the porch rail, she saw leather shoeing chaps and gloves. So, he'd come prepared to work.

He'd shaved not that long ago. A scent of lime teased her nose. In one hand, he held a gray cowboy hat that matched his eyes. "It's too early for sexual innuendoes, Killian."

"Really?" He chuckled, put on his hat, and took a step closer. "Does that mean I can't tell you how beautiful you are first thing in the morning?"

"Yes." She hated being bamboozled. It was way too early for this kind of behavior. How could he call her beautiful when she knew how terrible she looked in the sloppy sweatpants and T-shirt? Not only that, she hadn't brushed her teeth, and her hair undoubtedly had more tangles than a horse's mane.

She trembled when he cupped her cheek and slowly trailed his thumb over her lips. Suddenly, she wanted to feel his mouth on hers. That hadn't even been on her list of top ten fantasies. He lowered his head and her pulse kick-started into life.

"What are you doing?" Jake asked.

She jumped, startled by her son's voice. She slipped out of Sean's light hold. What *had* she been thinking?

She glanced at Jake. He didn't seem upset or concerned. "We had a power failure last night, so we overslept. Go wake up Lynn. I'll fix breakfast and pack your lunches."

"What about chores?" Jake asked. "Don't you need our help?"

"I'll take care of the ponies today. School, Jake."

"I'll help your mom," Sean said. "I'd do a lot for a woman who makes good coffee, even if she's twelve minutes late for our appointment."

Elinor tensed; worried Jake might be offended by Sean's flirtatious charm.

Instead, the boy grinned back at him. "My mom's the best at everything."

"Amazing," Sean said. "That was the first thought I had when I met her."

Jake's grin widened. He turned and ran from the room. After a moment, she heard his bedroom door slam.

She eyed Sean warily. Why would he lie to her son? She wasn't the best at anything. She'd been late picking up the kids from their 4-H meeting, argued with him, and dressed like a contestant for a muddy T-shirt contest. Was he just being facetious?

Instead of calling him on it, she opted to change the subject. She went to flip the switch on the coffeemaker, grateful she'd prepped the maker the night before. "That racket should definitely wake up Lynn."

Lynn hurried into the kitchen. She wore faded jeans and an ancient Washington State University sweatshirt. She headed toward the rack of barn boots.

"Lynn, I'll handle it. Get ready for school."

"I'll throw out the hay and grain the ponies." Lynn didn't hesitate as she pulled on her knee-high, muck boots. "Then they'll be ready for Sean and you can do the milking."

"You'll miss your bus," Elinor protested. "I need to get you and Jake to school on time. I don't have time to drive you there and get back here to hold the ponies for shoeing."

"I'm doing the shoeing," Sean said. "I'm not just another pretty face."

"Good. Come help me feed." Lynn opened the back door. "Besides, it's not like we'll do anything new during Power-Time or Social Studies, Mom. The teachers are just babysitting us. You can take us to school at lunchtime and we won't miss anything. Don't stress over it."

"Lynn, it's my job to stress over your education. You can't put a perfect stranger to work in our barns. It's rude."

"Good thing I'm not perfect," Sean drawled. "Besides, Marlene would hang me like a Christmas tree ornament if she found out I stood around watching a woman work, even a young one."

Before Elinor argued the point any further, the two of them vanished in the direction of the barn. A moment later, Jake followed. She shook her head and addressed the coffeemaker. "Someday, I'll be the parent. I swear it." At least, the coffeepot didn't argue the point.

On the way back to her room, she contemplated what Sean had said about loose horses. The only other men she'd known who would chase stock were her grandfather and Marlene's late husband. It came as a nice surprise to hear Sean's priorities matched hers. Horses first, people second. That might sound strange to a non-horse person, but livestock and cars just didn't mix, regardless of how quiet a country road was. If the animal wasn't mortally injured in a wreck, the driver of a vehicle could be.

She hurried to dress, putting on a turquoise striped turtleneck and a denim western shirt over a lacy, dark blue bra. She pulled on tight blue jeans over the matching panties. A black belt with its large western buckle made her waist appear even smaller. She hastily brushed her black curly hair.

A quick glance in the mirror showed she looked slim, trim, and far younger than the appalling birthday that hung over her head. It was hard to believe thirty-five was closer than thirty.

Back in the kitchen, she eyed the dreaded clock. It was 8:20 a.m. and the kids had already missed the bus. Luckily, Daisy was still an early riser. Elinor picked up the phone and arranged for her neighbor to collect the kids in forty minutes and take them to the middle school.

She glanced out the window and saw how wonderful Sean looked in his Levi's. Impulsively, she snagged her Ropers instead of pulling on the muck boots she usually wore to the barn. Okay, so she wanted to be hot today instead of a farmer, and the riding boots made her legs look sexy. What was the matter with that? She wasn't dead yet.

The back door slammed against the wall. "Mom, everything's wrong." Jake skidded to a stop in front of her. "Chipeta has colic. She bites her sides, kicks her stomach, and tries to roll in the stall. The pigs got loose. Lynn can't catch them. Some wild animal or maybe a dog got in the henhouse and killed a bunch of the chickens."

"Let's go deal with the disaster, honey." Elinor grabbed her quilted vest from its hook, determined to act like she was in charge. She couldn't let her son see how overwhelmed she felt. This was a lesson every teacher knew. When the situation couldn't be worse, emotions needed to be checked at the proverbial door. "We'll cope, sweetie. We've been through worse."

The first stop was the barn and Chipeta's stall. The old sorrel mare was down, trying to roll in the confined space. Jake's diagnosis was apparently the correct one. Elinor yanked open the stall door. "Halter and lead, sweetheart."

As Jake ran for the tack room, she hurried into the stall. She caught a handful of chin whiskers on the mare and yanked. "On your feet! Let's go!"

With a moan, Chipeta struggled to rise. Elinor prayed fervently nothing would happen to the horse. She'd found Chipeta starving to death eight months before. She'd paid ten dollars for the pony and fifteen for the young gelding in the same pasture. She'd threatened the owner with Marlene's wrath, a worse fate than anything the law, the county agencies, or equine rescue do-gooders could or would provide in the area. As a longtime 4-H leader, Marlene had been striking fear in the hearts of horse abusers statewide for years. Elinor didn't have the older woman's clout yet, but one day, she hoped she would.

Paragon, the blood bay gelding, had rallied sooner than Chipeta. Granted, he had no knowledge of what a halter, bridle, or saddle was, but he tried hard to please. Meanwhile, Chipeta knew everything, but couldn't seem to gain weight. Though the old mare was wormed, deloused, had her teeth floated, and put on huge quantities of feed, she didn't return to what Elinor considered 'horsey-normal.'

Chipeta remained a constant challenge to her new human family, Dr. Watkins, and of course, Marlene. The few pounds the mare gained went directly to her stomach. Prominent ribs stuck out. So did her backbone. Skin stretched tightly over her thirteen-hand frame and her sickly look wasn't good for business. Elinor was now on a first-name basis with the animal control officers who came to check on Chipeta every month. Granted their favorite was Beth Chambers, who brought treats for the pony and a sixteen-ounce, double-shot mocha for her owner. Unfortunately, Beth had been promoted at Christmas to detective, but she still popped in for the occasional visit and never suggested putting down the sorrel mare.

Jake didn't care what anybody said. He'd fallen in love with Chipeta the moment she arrived. He fed her special treats and groomed her by the hour. He took her for long walks to mow the front yard and orchard. He rarely rode her and when he did, it was at a very slow pace. He even read his fantasy books aloud to her and claimed she understood every word. While he was good to the other ponies, he said that Chipeta needed him more than they did because she had "lonely cobble-wobbles" in her heart, and he did too, sometimes.

Per Dr. Watkins's directives, Elinor locked the mare in her stall with one bale after another of grass hay in the manger. She kept Chipeta confined most of the time, only letting her out when they cleaned the barn or when Jake hand-grazed her. If the pony couldn't trot or gallop with the others, she had to gain weight.

"Here you go, Mom." Jake held out the red halter and lead. "Will she be okay?"

"She'll be fine," Elinor said. "Walk her around the yard for me. It's all right if she lies down, but don't let her roll. Colic is a bad stomachache. Remember, because of their body structure, horses can't throw up. She has to…"

"Poop and she can't because she has a blockage. I read about it on the 4-H website," Jake said. "Besides, Marlene told us that colic is the number-one horse killer."

"That's right. Start walking. I'll check on everything else. Then, I'll come find you. Deal?"

"Yeah." Jake led the mare from the barn. "Nine out of ten horses die when they get colic, but not Chipeta. Right, Mom?"

"We'll take care of her until she's better and I'll call Marlene and Doc Watkins for advice too." Elinor headed for the pigpen, hoping that she was right, and they could save the pony. She arrived in time to see the sows racing toward her. She grabbed the bucket of feed, which had been left near the pen by Lynn. The Berkshires ran through the open gate and to the trough. Elinor poured in the mash. The pigs pushed at each other, grunted, squealed, and fell to eating.

She went around the pen and closed the gate. The hog pen was the remains of a barn that had fallen down long before she had purchased the farm. Six-foot concrete walls of the foundation made the perfect pigpen. She didn't see any holes or weak areas that would have allowed the hogs to escape. The only opening was the wooden door that she'd closed.

"What you need is a good dog." Sean joined her. "I've seen every inch of your place now."

"I have my name down at a couple of breeders of Australian cattle dogs. I should be able to get a pup this summer."

"Heelers are the best," Sean agreed. "I have a few at home, but many horse people have issues with them since they don't want their horses chased."

"It all depends on how you train the dogs." She studied the pen again. "How'd the pigs get out?"

"Broke the latch on the gate," Lynn said, as she came up. "Sean told me he'd fix it."

The latch was supposedly the best on the market, but the metal was bent. It looked as if it'd give way under a small push, much less the hearty shoves the sows gave it. "What did you have in mind?"

"Two horseshoes and a two-by-four," Sean said. "I prefer to keep things super-simple."

"Well, that makes sense," Elinor said.

Sean looked at Lynn. "I have some used horseshoes in the back of my rig. Blue box, left side, halfway to the cab. The canopy's unlocked."

"We have a few in the barn too. I know right where they are." Lynn dashed away.

Elinor waited until her daughter was out of earshot. "You don't have to stay, Sean. Horse-shoers run on tight schedules. My neighbor's coming to drive the kids to school, but it will take another hour for me to finish chores. We can try again in two weeks."

"And Lynn's horse show?" Sean leaned against the wall of the pigpen. He rolled his shoulders in small circles. "Her pony needs shoes for Saturday."

"I know." Elinor sighed. "Today's in the toilet. I can't ask you to wait while I sort out this mess." Meanwhile, she found herself fascinated by the way he continued the motion of his shoulders. "What are you doing? Trying out as a cowboy model?"

"I hear it's better money than working for a living." Sean

smiled. "I have horseman's back. I have to stretch out my muscles and limber up each morning."

She shook her head, determined not to be mesmerized. This had to be the most erotic movement she'd ever seen, but she hadn't had sex since her divorce. Six years of abstinence seemed like an eternity. "Weren't you the guy who told me that if everything wasn't perfect, you'd walk? So far, you haven't seen the ponies, much less started on time. And I don't even wear a watch on farm days."

"It's 8:36. I saw your stock. I fed them. Nice bunch. It'll take more than you stomping and kicking to drive me away."

Lynn arrived with tools, two rusty horseshoes, and a short two-by-four scrap. "Lynn, leave those with Sean," Elinor said. "You need to feed the Angus. Chipeta has colic. Jake's walking her. I'll do the chickens. After the steers, grain the ponies. I'm going to the house and call Doctor Watkins."

"Call him at home. He's on my contact list." Sean handed her his cell phone. "Then he'll come straight here instead of going to the office. As soon as I fix this gate, I'll check the mare."

The veterinarian answered before Elinor could tell Sean what she thought of his take-charge attitude or say she had a cell phone of her own if she'd wanted to use it. She explained the situation and listened to the vet's advice. By the time they agreed on the appropriate actions to take with Chipeta, Sean had finished the repairs to the pigpen.

She returned his phone. "Thanks. I need to get the muscle relaxants from the house for Chipeta. Some animal attacked the chickens last night. That's why I told Lynn I'd look after them."

"I'll come with you." He strode beside her in the direction of the henhouse. "Stop fretting. If I had to be somewhere else, I'd tell you."

She studied him, amazed at his perception. Most people couldn't see through her façade. Had she lost her touch? She tried to be controlled, poised all the time. John claimed he'd never known what she felt, or how often he hurt her feelings. By the end of their marriage, she'd learned to hide her emotions.

In the chicken house, several hens lay dead on the floor. Elinor bent to touch Lynn's favorite Rhode Island Red.

Sean lifted away the bird. "Not dead yet. I'd say a weasel got in and had a killing fit. It's amazing that this hen survived. Do you want to try and save her? It could be a lost cause."

"Let's take her in the house," Elinor said. "I don't want to be responsible for killing my daughter's pet."

Once inside, she scanned the kitchen. As in most farmhouses, it was the largest room. She'd found a cardboard box to hold the hen. Now, she needed somewhere to put the box. The counters, sink, and electric range were on the far wall. The right-hand wall held her desk, file cabinet, and the doors to the bath and her bedroom.

Directly behind them was the outside door. In the left-hand corner of the kitchen were the table and four captain's chairs. The washer, dryer, and refrigerator were on the left wall. She put the box between the dryer and fridge. Now, the hen was safe.

The smell of fresh-brewed coffee filled the air. She crossed to the rack of mugs on the wall and took down two cups. "I'm ready for caffeine. How about you?"

"Sounds great."

She poured coffee into the cups and passed one to him. She pasted on what she hoped was a polite smile, hoping she didn't look as overwhelmed as she felt. "Cream? Sugar?"

"I can handle it." He caught her chin with his free hand. He lowered his head. "Sweeter than sugar."

She tensed despite the fact she really wanted this guy to kiss her. What was she thinking?

"Too soon?" He stopped, his breath warm on her lips. "I can wait." He released her and stepped back.

"You'll wait forever," she said after a moment. "I'm not in the market for another man."

"You're only getting one. Me. I prefer to do my own chasing."

He studied her with an amused gaze. "Just not halter-broke. Go ahead and run, missy. I'll wait right here until you finish kicking up dust."

"I'm not a horse!"

"Still wild as the wind. Most folks would figure otherwise since you have two kids." He shook his head and drank some coffee. "Foolish."

"What?" She felt stupid. "I already told you. I'm not a horse."

"People are more like horses than they admit." He finished his coffee. "I'll check that mare now. It's 8:48. You'd better round up those children if you expect them to go to school today."

"I know my job."

"I'm sure you do." He was out the back door.

FIVE

SHE COUNTED SILENTLY TO TEN BEFORE SHE WENT FOR THE TUBE of *Banamine* in the refrigerator. She'd treat Chipeta and collect Jake at the same time. Sean was right, damn it. If the mare died, she didn't want her kids to see it. School was the perfect place for them, especially if she had to deal with getting rid of a dead pony before they returned.

Sean and Jake stood with Chipeta in the orchard. As Elinor walked toward them, the sorrel began to graze. "What are you doing? The grass will cause more of an impaction."

"Not necessarily," Sean said. "Grass is a natural laxative. We're not dealing with colic. We have plenty of pipe."

"What on earth are you talking about?"

"He means her intestines work fine," Jake said. "Look, Mom. I'll show you." He pressed his ear to the mare's side, directly in front of her back leg, beside Chipeta's flank. "If you hear a sound like water running, it means she's not constipated. Anyhow, she pooped."

Elinor spotted the pile of fresh manure a few feet away. She never thought she'd be glad to see *that*. Of course, the mare could have passed some of it and still have a major blockage. This might be gas colic in which case the mare would need to pass wind, or fart until she felt better.

She inspected the pile, grateful none of the high school students saw her examining manure and studying the consistency. One of them would undoubtedly film it and put it on the Internet. It was the usual amount and the droppings were the same size that Chipeta usually dumped in her stall. None of the turds were over-size, clumped together or overly dry.

The mare groaned and dropped to her knees.

"What's the matter with her now?" Elinor demanded.

"Nothing a few hours of close attention won't cure." Sean looked at his watch. "It's eight fifty-three. When will your neighbor be here?"

"In seven minutes." Elinor gestured to the house. "Jake, get your sister. She should be done with the steers and the graining by now. I'll be right up and fix breakfast."

"I'd rather have Lynn do it. Then my cereal isn't super soggy from too much milk. You'll look after Chipeta for me, won't you, Sean?"

"I said I would and I'm a man of my word. You should go, son."

"I am." Jake started away. "I better like this surprise."

"What surprise?" Elinor scanned Sean's amused features, waiting until Jake was out of earshot. "Spill it, cowboy. What do you know about Chipeta?"

"She's fine for a thirty-year-old pony who's about to have a baby."

"Whoa! Hold it right there. She's not thirty. The previous owner said she was six. Granted, it's hard to tell a horse's age by its teeth, but hers weren't that worn down." Elinor took a deep breath. "She's not in foal. She can't be. I don't have any stallions."

"How long have you had her?"

"Eight months or a little more."

"A mare carries for eleven months, three weeks and one day, give or take a few days either way," Sean said.

"Really? How many hours and minutes?"

"Fifteen hours, forty minutes, and twenty-three seconds." He eyed his watch. "So, I'd say we have about…"

"You're joking."

He laughed. "You bet. But not about her being in foal. I had you going for a while, though, didn't I?"

"Yes," Elinor admitted. Another thought came. "Oh my God! I bought her and Paragon together to keep them from starving. If he lied about Chipeta, he could have lied about Paragon."

"Which one is he? You have ponies of every color, a real rainbow herd."

"The blood bay with white markings." She ran a hand through her hair. "Chipeta will be okay alone for a few minutes, won't she?"

"Sure. We have hours to go before she delivers. Why?"

"I want to know what Paragon really is. I have a feeling he's not a fully trained five-year-old Welsh gelding."

"I saw him in the barn." Sean grinned down at her. "He's a nice, quiet youngster. I'll bet you a nickel he isn't more than two."

"What a high-roller." She led the way to the barn, aware Sean followed her. "If Paragon's a stud, he's probably the sire, isn't he?"

"I'll double my bet and say Chipeta's undoubtedly his dam."

"What?" Elinor wrinkled her nose in disgust, then took a deep breath. "All that matters is this foal is healthy."

"We'll have Art Watkins give the baby a solid once-over when it comes."

"I feel stupid. I should have known better than to take his old owner's word when he complained about the cost of feed and starved the horses. I didn't look to see if Paragon was a gelding."

"You'd have had to look with your hands." Sean adopted a lazy drawl again. "Most colts don't mature before they're a year old. Some take longer, especially those who don't get enough to eat. Anyway, Art wants everything dropped before he gelds. Darlene Dawson had a paint colt with only one testicle. While she waited for his equipment to drop, he sired three fillies, none of whom had any color."

"You're just full of good news," Elinor snapped. "I've been running that damned Paragon with my mares." She frowned as she remembered the previous spring. She'd seen Paragon act a little studly and mount the occasional mare, but her older geldings did the same thing in warm weather. The veterinarian explained that it was normal behavior for what he referred to as "proud-cut" horses.

Art said it happened when the vet didn't cut out all the testicular tissue from the horse during the gelding procedure, and the horse continued to produce a high level of androgen. In real-life terms, Lightning and Bonanza still thought they were stallions. Although they couldn't breed the mares, they still practiced in warm weather, or when the mares were in heat.

The older geldings drove Paragon away from the mares and bullied him whenever they had the chance, so she penned the old-timers away from the herd when they got really rowdy. Elinor heaved a sigh. "I'll bet this means I have more foals coming."

Sean wrapped his arm around her shoulders. "Don't worry, darlin'. I'll teach you to do a ball check after I show you how to mouth a horse and tell its age by the teeth."

———

Two hours later, Elinor felt back in control. She milked the cow while Sean repaired the henhouse and buried the chickens who hadn't survived the weasel's killing spree. The kids were off to school, thanks to Daisy who ignored their complaints and told Sean to be sure to trim her horse, too.

The memory of the stunned expression on his face made Elinor smile. He didn't have a clue who lived next door, and it was equally obvious that Daisy could still intimidate former students with ease. On her way to the chicken yard to see how Sean was doing, Elinor glanced at the orchard to check on Chipeta. The pony lay flat out on her side in the spring grass. What had happened?

Foaling was supposed to be perfectly natural and Chipeta was an experienced mare. Those thoughts didn't comfort Elinor. She ran toward the orchard, praying the pony would live. *Don't let her be dead. Don't let her. Don't let her!*

Chipeta's groan stopped Elinor in her tracks. Okay, the mare was still alive. Now what? The pony strained with each labor pain.

"Looks like everything is going well," Sean said from behind Elinor. "I'm going to need some supplies. I hope you have a horse first-aid kit somewhere."

"She's suffering."

"Not that much. Watch." Sean rested a hand on Elinor's shoulder.

Elinor caught her breath when Chipeta turned her head and cropped at the spring grass between contractions. "Maybe she's doing better than I thought."

"Definitely." Sean chuckled. "Now, I need two buckets of hot water, one with soap and one for rinsing after I wash down Chipeta after the birth. We'll also want a white hand towel, two warm bath towels, sharp scissors, rubbing alcohol, iodine, and strong white thread in case I need to tie off the umbilical cord."

"Anything else?"

"We can wait to bury the placenta after Art sees it, but Chipeta should have a warm bran mash and a bucket of water to drink."

"Okay." Elinor started for the back porch. "How much time do I have?"

"How long did it take you to give birth to your daughter?" Sean asked. "I'll go hang out with Chipeta, but I'm pretty sure nothing major will happen until you return."

It didn't matter what he said or what she knew from personal experience. She'd been in labor for nineteen hours with Lynn. Elinor hurried into the house and found the two buckets she used for equine first aid. She squirted dish soap into one and filled it with hot water. While the second bucket filled, she went into the bathroom to find the towels he wanted.

In fifteen minutes, feeling like a midwife loaded with medical supplies, she hurried back to the orchard paddock. Chipeta was up on her chest, a red foal lying behind her with its head on the extended forelegs. The shoulders had already passed out of the mare, and as Elinor watched, the rest of the baby slid free of its mother.

"That's it?" Elinor stalked to where Sean knelt beside the foal. "She's done?"

"No way. She still has to pass the afterbirth and we have a lot of things to do. If it'd taken more than twenty minutes from the time the water broke, we'd have needed the vet."

"Payback is hell, cowboy, and you're gonna get yours." She couldn't believe he'd sent her off to the house when he knew how fast the mare would deliver.

"I can handle it." He grinned at her. "Besides, this way you didn't upset the horse."

"No, but I'm planning to upset you."

"Do it after we wash down the mare, dip the umbilical cord, get the foal up and nursing, and check out the placenta, along with everything else."

The list surprised her, but she wouldn't admit that he had a point. Her feelings had taken over and she'd lost her usual control. "You've got a deal. I'll do better next time."

"I know you will."

The bright red baby had four white legs. Would they turn into socks? He'd undoubtedly keep the blaze on his face. He was a looker, Elinor thought, and her son would fall in love as soon as Jake saw the new addition.

Later that afternoon, she ran through a mental checklist of all the information she'd learned about Sean. She knew how he'd built his shoeing business from nothing to more than four hundred horses, all the details of his apprenticeship to irascible Buck Green, and how much he loved Marlene and his siblings. He had two older brothers, and two younger sisters.

For a moment, Elinor savored the thrill and triumph of her detective work. She enjoyed interviewing people, learning their secrets so she could help them achieve their innermost dreams. It was the high school teacher in her. Tomorrow morning when she went next door for coffee, she'd entertain Daisy with Sean's post–high school life.

He was kind and patient with the ponies, even when Taffy tried to kick him. It always amazed Elinor that the ponies could be so good with children and hate men so much. Lightning threatened Sean from start to finish. The Arab-Welsh tried to bite, strike, and kick Sean several times. It'd been the longest half-hour of her life, but no matter what the dark blue roan did, Sean never lost his temper. He didn't even swear at the four-legged brat. She'd worried that he'd quit since he'd said he didn't put up with ill-tempered horses. Instead, he just asked who was next on the trim list.

Now it was Rebel's turn. They'd moved to the front yard for shoeing because it was closer to Sean's pickup and his portable forge. Elinor eyed him as he measured a shoe against the chestnut's left front hoof. "Do you think Lightning will get over his attitude?"

"No doubt in my mind that he's getting better." He straightened and went to the back of the truck to put the shoe in the furnace. "When Marlene and I trimmed him right after I got him, he had to be tranquilized. We had Art Watkins standing by. You and I did Lightning by ourselves in less than thirty minutes. The last time I did him, it took me almost three hours."

Elinor almost had to scrape her jaw off the lawn. "What are you talking about? Marlene brought him here two years ago. She said he needed a home. When did you have him?"

"I rescued him just shy of four years ago. The first time I saw Lightning, he was at a dairy farm with three nasty little boys. Whenever they fed him, they'd drop his hay in the muck and then stand on it, so he had to pick through the cow crap to eat. They didn't stop at messing with his feed. They pounded on him, too. Ponies can be mean, but they need some provocation to turn ornery. One visit to that farm convinced me to run interference."

"What did you do?"

"I went back with my trailer that afternoon. I loaded Lightning and told the kids' dad he could deal with me or one of the Dawson gals. Marlene and her sisters have been rescuing mistreated horses for over forty years and they have a rep for being meaner than the animal control guys. I even said his boys should have activities that didn't include animal abuse."

Elinor blinked. "I'll bet you weren't the most popular guy on his farm."

"Well, he didn't try to punch me, which was what I was going for. I wanted to clean his clock."

Using a pair of tongs, Sean shifted the shoe in the portable furnace. "He told me the boys were his step-kids and he'd just married their mom. Their counselor thought the pony would be good for them. They weren't, so I took Lightning to Marlene and Roy. Marlene told me she'd find the perfect home for Lightning, one where he'd be happy, and nobody would ever hurt him again."

Elinor nodded, still astonished. "She did. She made me promise never to sell him. And she only charged me a dollar for him the day he arrived. She said it made giving him to me legal."

"That was all I paid." Sean pulled the shoe out of the furnace, studied it, and then put it back in the forge. "I'm not good about seeing any animal abused. And Lightning wasn't the first I'd taken home to Marlene and Roy."

Elinor studied the man while he worked on the shoe. Her ex had acted as if the desire to save animals was a federal offense. John had demanded she send them to the pound or the slaughterhouse and sell the farm so they could have a luxury home in Seattle.

She'd refused and their marriage died in an avalanche of frozen feelings and broken dreams. He'd wanted the glamorous life of a powerful attorney and she wanted stability in a small town, the safety and security of a rural lifestyle complete with a *real* farm. "So, Lightning likes you better now?"

"Nope. He still hates my guts. He'll probably fear men for the next thirty years. Horses have very long memories, but he trusts you and that's what made the difference. He knew you wouldn't let me hurt him." Sean removed the heated shoe from the forge. He put it on the anvil and began to shape it with the hammer. Sparks flew from the red-hot steel.

His words didn't shock her as much as the praise she heard in his deep voice. John hadn't liked her respect for animals, ridiculing her in front of his friends and co-workers at the law firm. She'd started to avoid social occasions with him. It made it easier for him to cheat on her with his new paralegal, but it also meant less public humiliation.

She waited quietly. Her horse grazed, eagerly cropping spring grass as if nothing could compare. The afternoon sun beat down, the temperature almost like summer, although the official start of the season was at least two months away. Sean had tossed his flannel shirt into the cab of the truck two hours ago. A light blue T-shirt clung damply to his arms, shoulders, and back.

Her gaze wandered over his rippling muscles. She couldn't help but admire the efficient way he moved the shoe from one position to another on the anvil. While she watched him pound on the horseshoe, she wondered how he'd touch a woman.

Could he be as slow in his approach as when he'd convinced Chipeta everything was all right? Would he be as tender with a woman as when he handled the newborn colt?

"Mom!" Jake's shout distracted her from those thoughts and the din of the hammer striking steel. She saw her son running toward them. She pulled up on the rope until she had Rebel under control. Now, the Quarter Horse gelding couldn't spook and injure the boy—not that the stocky sorrel would. He was the calmest, steadiest horse Elinor had ever known. Still, Jake slowed to a walk as he came closer.

"Hi, Sean. How's Chipeta?"

Elinor laughed. When she met Sean's gaze, she noticed he shared her amusement at Jake's single-minded concern for his pony. "Chipeta's fine, honey. She's out in the second pasture."

"Is she all over her colic?" Jake asked, dropping his backpack on the ground.

"It wasn't colic. You can always check on that by listening to the horse's side for gut sounds," Sean reminded him.

"Bobby says that's an old wives' tale."

"Is Bobby a horse-shoer with more than twenty years of experience and thirteen-plus years in the Silver Flying As before that?" Sean stopped shaping the shoe as he waited for the answer.

"No. He's my best friend. His grandpa breeds ponies." Jake stopped to think. "Wait a minute. He can't know as much as you do, not when you get paid to work with horses. Besides, Lynnie and I—"

"I promise Chipeta never had colic. At least not this morning." Sean returned his attention to the shoe on the anvil.

"Okay." Jake grabbed his backpack and ran in the direction of the porch. He dropped the pack and his jacket on the steps and vanished around the corner in the direction of the paddock. In a moment, he was back. "If it wasn't colic, Sean, what was it?"

Elinor leaned against Rebel's shoulder, shaking with laughter. Trust her son to think of that before going to find his pony. He always wanted to know the reasons for everything. His favorite hobby had to be asking questions.

"Well, are you gonna answer him?" She mimicked Sean's lazy drawl to perfection.

He shook his head. "Why don't you?"

"You're the one who promised to look after his pony." She tried to control her giggles. "It's your job to give him a response he can understand."

"I'm not dumb," Jake interjected. "You two are being silly. Will you answer me, Sean?"

"Nope." Sean strolled toward Elinor, a teasing light in his gray eyes. "I'm gonna kiss your mom. If you want to know about Chipeta, go find her. She can show you what was wrong."

"Kissing's pretty sappy, Sean. Are you sure you don't want to come with me and see Chipeta?"

"Positive."

"I will." Elinor started to lead Rebel to the hitch rail in the front yard. She stopped when Sean's hand closed over her arm.

Sean looked at Jake. "You'd better go before your mom sends you to change your school clothes."

"Yeah!" Jake raced toward the barn and the field behind it.

She didn't know what amused her more, Jake and his worry about the pony, or Sean and his defense of what he obviously considered his manly honor.

"You really thought that was funny?"

"It was. You should have seen your face when Jake told you Bobby knew more than you did."

Sean leaned closer; his intention obvious. Her voice shook. "You've got to admit it was hilarious." She read the determination in his gray eyes. She wanted to step away, but she couldn't make her feet move. She moistened her suddenly dry lips. "No."

"Mean that?" His mouth brushed her forehead.

"No." She felt her nipples tighten. Did he have to be so slow? She turned her head, tried to catch his lips with hers.

"Wait." He kissed her brows.

She splayed her fingers against the material of his T-shirt. He smelled like man, horses, and faint lime from his aftershave. She shuddered when he dropped a kiss on the tip of her nose. "Just do it."

He chuckled. Then he nipped at her chin. He began to work his way down the side of her neck. "I told you." The words were murmured against her skin. "I want you hot and sweet." He flicked his tongue in her ear. "You're sweet, darlin'. But, you're not hot enough."

She slid her hands up to his shoulders and dug her nails into his skin. "You don't know how to kiss a woman, do you?"

His jaw tightened. "You don't fight fair, do you?" He smiled with scant humor. "But neither do I."

"Prove it."

He gently twisted a hand in her hair and pulled back her head, so their gazes met. "Just remember. You want this, too."

SIX

His mouth claimed hers. The kiss wasn't sweet or slow or innocent, as she'd somehow expected. Instead, he kissed her as if they'd been together for years, as if he was the only man in the world who had ever touched her and ever would. The pressure of his mouth branded her and she enjoyed it. Had she totally lost her mind? *Yes*, she thought. *Yes!*

He pulled her against him. She melted into him, became part of him, and it felt amazing. His tongue dueled with hers, conquered and demanded surrender. *Oh, but wait until next time.*

"Mom!"

Jake's shout broke the spell. She wrenched out of Sean's hold, bewildered. She stared up at him. "You…" She took a deep breath.

He laughed. "Didn't expect to shut you up that quick." His eyes glinted. "Now I know what to do when your mouth overloads your common sense."

She glared back at him, but before she could answer, Jake raced up to them.

"Mom, did you see what Chipeta has? It's awesome. Can we keep it?"

"Of course, we'll keep him. He didn't exactly follow her home."

"How did he get here, then?" Jake asked. "We don't have a stallion."

A blush seeped into her cheeks. She fiddled with Rebel's lead rope. How could she explain the mistake she'd made to Jake?

"*Magick*." Sean touched her shoulder. "Right?"

"Yes. That's it." She looked up at him, flustered by his compassion. Tears stung. She blinked them away. Sean was kinder in this brief instance than she'd anticipated. How could this stranger be so decent?

Jake's dark blue eyes widened. "Wow! I'm getting Lynnie and telling her you can do *magick*, Sean. Isn't he great, Mom?"

Elinor chose not to answer. "Why don't you change your clothes, Jake? You can help Doc Watkins when he comes to check Chipeta and the colt."

"Why is he coming? Is something wrong with her? The foal?"

"No," Sean reassured. "They're fine. I promise."

"You should know. You conjured up the baby," Jake said, smirking at them.

The statement made Sean grin. "It's always a good idea to have a veterinarian look at a newborn foal. Why don't you try to come up with a name for the colt, Jake?"

"Okay. This is great. I always wanted a baby horse to train." Jake glanced down the driveway where Lynn stood by the road with her best friend, Cassie. "I gotta tell them. They'll be stunned. My new colt is awesome. He's a lot better than their dumb ol' horse shows and trips to the mall."

"You could name the baby, Awesome," Elinor suggested. "It's one of your favorite words this week, Jake."

"I like it. Okay, he's Awesome. Mom, Gypsy's not having a foal, is she?"

"No." Elinor shared a look with Sean. After they'd learned the truth about Paragon, they'd discovered that Star and Taffy were both pregnant. She'd explain everything to the children, but later, after Sean left. Then she'd be able to answer all the questions they raised without worrying about an audience. She just didn't want to get into a sex talk with him standing there.

"I knew he'd be excited." Elinor watched Jake race off to join Lynn and Cassie. "So, baby horses come from *magick,* huh?"

"That's what my oldest brother Ethan told me when I was Jake's age." Sean crossed to the anvil. He picked up the shoe he'd altered and brought it over to measure it against Rebel's hoof. Not satisfied with the fit, Sean returned the shoe to the forge. "Are you going to tell me something different about the birds and the bees? Was Ethan wrong?"

"Ask him." Elinor concentrated on straightening Rebel's thick, red forelock. "Isn't he your tutor for sex education? I don't give more than one free class, cowboy. I taught you to kiss. That's all you're getting."

"Want to bet?"

———

"Chipeta foaled!" Jake yelled as he ran toward his sister. "She had a colt. He's awesome and he's mine. They're in the second paddock. Come see."

"What?" Lynn and Cassie shared a look. "Chipeta was pregnant? How did that happen?" Lynn demanded.

"*Magick,*" Jake announced. "Sean did it, and I never even thought to put that on the list."

"What list?" Cassie's big brown eyes widened. She pasted on her sweetest smile as she stepped closer to Jake. "Tell me about it."

"Oh, you know, Cassie," Lynn said quickly. "Jake's always thinking up the things he wants for his birthday months ahead of time."

Jake nodded hastily when his sister stopped beside him. "Yeah, that's right. Come see him. He's really awesome."

"You couldn't keep me away," Lynn said. "Let's go, Cass."

When Cassie led the way toward the pasture, Jake caught his

sister's arm. He took a deep breath and whispered to his sister, "I know he's the right one, Lynnie. I just know it. He kissed Mom and she totally didn't freak out. She kissed him back."

"No way!" Lynn stopped to stare at the adults and Rebel. Their mother and the shoer seemed to be engrossed in their conversation. "You're joking."

"Come on. They'll know I saw and told you." Jake pushed her to take another step up the driveway. "I knew the spell would work. I told you we'd make it happen."

———

It'd been a good day. He'd finally found a woman who didn't fear anything in heaven or hell, a steel rose. He hadn't counted on the kids, but the package was priceless. She apparently thought that sharp tongue would drive him away. Sean grinned. Didn't she know the opposite of love wasn't hate? It was indifference. She wanted him, even if she wasn't ready to admit it.

He parked his rig in front of his old farmhouse. He frowned at the blue Dodge Ram. What was Clancy Dawson doing here? He'd told her that she needed to figure out what made her happy and go for it. Looked like she'd ignored his advice again. Sean swore softly. They'd been friends since they were kids. Why wouldn't she listen to his advice when she asked him for help?

He strolled toward the porch. Three blue-gray dogs scrambled to meet him as usual, not barking. He bent and petted wriggling bodies, tugged gently on the waving tails. A lot of breeders cropped their Australian cattle dogs' tails. He wasn't one of them.

"What have you guys done today?" Sean asked.

Growls and rumbles came from the dogs as if in answer. He tried to pet the third one again. Ruler snarled and backed away. Sean gave up. One day, he'd find the right owner for the grumpy dog.

Now, he headed toward the woman who waited for him on the back porch. "Hey, girl. How are you?"

"Want a beer?" The voluptuous redhead held out an icy bottle. She oozed sex appeal in her tight blue jeans and fringed purple T-shirt. "Okay that I turned loose the Three Musketeers?"

"Sure." Sean sank down on the steps, popped the top, and took a swallow of the beer. *Nothing like a cold one on a hot day when I have to listen to a princess whine.* "You know my routine of happiness better than I do. These guys always go loose as soon as I'm home." The dogs settled on the ground by his feet.

Sitting beside him, Clancy tried to smile and failed. Huge violet eyes filled with tears. "You're not mad at me for showing up?"

"I could never be mad at you." Sean put an arm around her shoulders. The diamond ring that should be on her left hand was still missing. It looked like the serious trouble in paradise hadn't changed. "Did you get your heart broke by a different loser, beautiful?"

"No. It's the same loser." She sniffled. "So, I came to snivel at you. Okay?"

"Anytime," Sean promised. She was gorgeous, but he'd picked up the pieces of her broken heart too many times to ever fall in love with her, and the tight bond of good buddies worked for them. "What else are friends for?"

"You're the best." She wiped at her nose with her sleeve, managing to look gorgeous despite the childish gesture. "So, what did you do on your day off?"

Sean grinned. "Shod some horses, trimmed ponies, and I delivered a colt for this smart, sassy, and spunky gal I just added to my book."

"And she's not a Dawson?" Clancy laughed. "Good for you. Where did you meet this paragon?"

Sean chuckled. "Your aunt Marlene introduced us last night."

"Aren't you a fast worker? I'll bet Aunt Marlene's already organizing your wedding. She's an avid matchmaker except when it comes to me."

The ring of his cell phone saved him from trying to come up with a suitable response. "Hello. Killian here."

"Sean? It's me, Jake Price."

Sean relaxed. "Hi, Jake. Is Awesome all right?"

"Oh, sure. He's great! I forgot to ask you something today."

"What is it?"

"I wanted to invite you to come with us to my school tomorrow night. It's Parents' Night. And my dad is too busy to attend. So, would you have time?" The last question came out in a rush.

"It's a real compliment to be asked." Was this Elinor's way of going on a date with him? Could she be the kind of woman who'd use her kids to get to him? He never would have taken her for that kind of manipulator. Still, it wasn't the boy's fault, and he wouldn't leave Jake in the middle. Sean knew how that felt. His father had only showed up for school activities when it included a media op.

"I'd be honored, Jake," Sean said. "Where shall I meet you? At the farm? Or the school?"

"Could you come here at six? We have to be there at seven-thirty."

"Sure. Where would you like to go for dinner? We can eat first and then go on to the shindig. All right?"

"That's great. Thanks, Sean. I'll see you tomorrow."

"You're welcome. And thanks for thinking of me." Sean put away his phone.

"You look happier than a flea in a doghouse," Clancy said. "So, who was it? Not her?"

"No, her son. He wants me to join them for a school event." Sean grinned. "Isn't that terrific?"

Clancy clucked her tongue and shook her head. "Sean Robert Killian, you should be ashamed. Chasing the calf to catch the cow? Now where did you learn that?"

SEVEN

"MOM, YOU HAVE TO HURRY."

Caught in the middle of working on the pony farm schedule for the weekend, Elinor looked up from the lesson plans on the kitchen table. Jake stood a few feet away. He wore the blue slacks, dress shirt, and tie she insisted on for church. He'd even shined his shoes. He combed his sandy blond hair, slicking it down with water. "Why are you dressed up?"

"We gotta hurry." Jake came closer. "Night chores are done. Lynnie's out of the shower. She says it's your turn for the bathroom."

"Why?" Elinor closed the pony farm's appointment book and stacked the worksheets on top of it. They always did chores early on Friday nights, so they'd have the evenings to spend together. She rose to her feet. What had she forgotten?

Her son rarely nagged her. He'd give that understanding smile and tell her everything was okay, even when it wasn't. They must have important plans for tonight and, once again, she'd forgotten them, but he remembered every promise she made. Now she felt like a worm for disappointing him.

She went to the calendar on the kitchen wall. It couldn't have anything to do with 4-H. Either Marlene, the older teens or one of the other parents would have called for the youth group. With the first horse show of the season tomorrow, Marlene did have a lot to do. She might have forgotten to phone, although that wasn't like her.

The big red letters in her handwriting told the story. "Parents' Night. Oh, honey, we're supposed to go to your school. I'm sorry."

Jake smiled at her. "Don't waste more time, Mom. Get ready or we'll be late."

"I'm going." She hastily put away the paperwork and hurried for the bathroom. Why did he want to attend this school function? He never had anything good to say about most of his teachers or the kids in his class. He preferred to play with the other boys from the 4-H club, most of whom were older than he was.

No matter how many times she and the teachers discussed Jake's test results, it didn't make a difference. Many insisted on treating him as if he was the same as his so-called peers, although he was obviously more advanced. Since he had entered the middle school at the last minute, she wasn't able to enroll him in the advanced placement sixth-grade block because he would have needed to test into it the previous spring.

Jake took the tests for advanced seventh-grade classes, but those wouldn't start until next fall. Of course, the judge hadn't considered any of those details when he'd ordered her to send the kids to school. Damn John and his freaking mind-games! Why did he use their children as pawns on the chessboard of his life?

After her shower, she finished drying off, then found clean lingerie. She opted for a lacy red bra and matching panties, then nylons, a blue denim skirt, and a light blue blouse topped with an embroidered blue and white jean jacket.

She brushed her hair, debating earrings and cosmetics. She needed them for this social occasion, especially since she often substituted at the school for different teachers. A few minutes later, she was ready. She glanced at the radio alarm clock on the night-stand. Five-fifty. They'd be on time.

"I can't believe you did that, Jake." Lynn glared at her brother, and then glanced at her mother. "Mom, you need shoes. Wear the blue dress boots. They'll go with your outfit. You look nice."

"Thanks, sweetheart." Elinor paused in the doorway. "What did Jake do?"

"Called the jerk and asked him to come." Lynn gave her brother another dirty look. "How could you do something so stupid?"

"It's Parents' Night," Jake said calmly. "He's our legal father. He should attend these functions."

"But he won't, and you know it. I thought you wanted—" Lynn shook her head. "I don't get it."

Elinor hugged both her children. "Maybe your dad will make it this time if he's not too busy."

"It's okay, Mom." Jake hugged her back and smiled up at her. "We've just gotta give him enough rope to hang himself."

Lynn stepped back and stared at her brother in astonishment. "You did it on purpose? You knew he wouldn't come? Your feelings aren't hurt?"

"Nope. Why would they be?"

Elinor sighed and looked from her son to her daughter and back again. Sometimes when she talked to her children, she felt like there was a totally different conversation going on and she'd missed it all. "As long as you're okay, Jake. I don't like it when your dad isn't available for these events."

"You and Lynn both gotta grow up, Mom. You can't change other people. Like you always tell us, we're not responsible for what others do. And you aren't responsible for him either."

Elinor eyed her brilliant son suspiciously. That sounded like advice from one of her educational journals. Somebody read them before she did and since Lynn wouldn't admit to it, then her brother had to be the culprit. "Jake, please remember I'm the mom around here. Stop reading my teaching magazines."

"Somebody has to," Jake pointed out. "You only read the classroom management stuff. I learn lots of good things and the psychology articles have great vocabulary words."

Elinor opted to give up the battle over boundaries for a while and turned to her daughter. "Stop calling your father a jerk. Both of you put on your company manners for tonight. Jake, I know your English teacher's not your favorite, but let's hide that tonight. Deal?"

While he contemplated the idea, Elinor escaped to her room. Being a mom called for an occasional, strategic withdrawal when it came to these two rocket scientists. Why did her kids have to be so darned bright?

She found her boots and returned to the kitchen where Lynn was shrugging on her school jacket. Jake, already in his, was opening the back door. Elinor froze in her tracks as she spotted the tall, male silhouette on the porch. Even though she knew John's attendance would be good for the children, she personally didn't want to see him. Taking a deep breath, she headed for the door to greet him.

Then she recognized Sean Killian.

What was he doing here? It couldn't be to do anything with the horses. Instead, he had on a gray, western-cut suit. The jacket emphasized his broad shoulders. She glimpsed a white shirt and red tie under the coat. Gray slacks and brightly shined black cowboy boots completed his outfit. He looked good—too good.

Stop drooling, she ordered herself. "Hello, Sean."

He tipped his *Resistol* hat. "Ma'am." He softened the formality with a quick, intimate wink. "Thanks for inviting me. I've been looking forward to this all day."

She caught her breath. What had her kids done? No, not the two of them. A glance told her that Lynn looked as surprised as Elinor felt. It had to be Jake.

Elinor struggled to sound calm and collected. "I'm glad you could make it. Shall we hit the road?"

"Okay." Sean held the kitchen door for them. "I figured we'd take my truck. It has more room. I even washed it and cleaned out the horsy stuff."

She managed a smile, but she was afraid it didn't look like her usual one. "You can't get much fancier than that." She rested a hand on Jake's shoulder. "Why don't you and Lynn go ahead, Sean? We'll catch up in a minute."

"Sure." Sean and Lynn went. Before the door closed, Elinor heard Lynn chatter all about her hen's miraculous recovery and the fact that the chicken was safely back with the flock in the pen.

"You invited Sean." Elinor hoped her tone didn't sound accusatory. "Why?"

"Because I need a guy to go with us," Jake answered with easy logic. "I like Sean. And he likes me. He talks *to* me, not at me. Besides, he's nice."

"It was nice of him to come tonight," she agreed. "But why do you need a guy? I'm your parent, even when your dad's busy."

"He's *always* too busy for me and Lynnie." Jake sighed. "The other boys make fun of me 'cause I don't have a dad. I wanted them to see I have all I need and 'cause of Sean, I don't need my dad there. And Ms. Collins really doesn't like me."

"I see." Elinor bit her lip, furious at the other teacher and determined not to let her feelings show. She put her arms around him and held her boy tight. "I'd like to do something with that woman."

"You've tried forever, Mom. Like I told you before, you can't change other people."

"You've got to stop reading my parenting magazines, too," she chided, but her heart wasn't in it. At times, he intimidated her with his brilliance. Then she remembered he was only a boy who loved playing with his trucks in the mud, pizza parties, banana splits, his pony, and going fishing whether he caught anything or not. And who read the encyclopedia for fun.

"So, will it help having Sean there?" Elinor swallowed the lump in her throat.

"Oh yeah! That's why I invited him."

"Okay." She took a deep breath and slowly let go of Jake. "Next time you want someone to go somewhere with us, ask me first. All right? It's the same as when you want a friend to stay overnight. You aren't supposed to ask me in front of them and then nobody has hurt feelings. I don't play those kinds of games and neither should you."

"Because it's manipulative," Jake said. "It's not fair to trick other people and it gets me grounded when I outsmart them." He tipped his head as he considered that. "I got to admit, it's worth it sometimes."

She ruffled his hair. "Just remember, smarty. Don't do the crime if you can't do the time."

Jake nodded. "Yeah. Mom, could somebody ground you?"

"Not really," Elinor said. "But I still have to live with it when I make mistakes or hurt others. So, do you."

"And then I have to make amends." Jake headed for the back door. "It's hard to be smarter than everybody else sometimes. Mom, if Ms. Collins says really dumb things about me tonight, will you wait until we get home before we talk about them?"

"Oh, honey, how could she say anything bad about you? You're a hard worker. But we can talk about your classes when we're alone." She followed him. "I'll wait until Sean's left and Lynn's in bed."

"Good. Then it'll be just you and me."

"Right. Do you think Ms. Collins will be a big problem tonight?"

"She's very ineffectual. Like Marlene says, some people just can't tell skunks from house cats."

"I'll keep that in mind."

EIGHT

Elinor turned to face Sean, who stood by the front of the truck. "Sorry. I needed to talk to Jake about something."

Sean glanced toward the children in the pickup. He pushed back his cowboy hat and studied her for a moment. "He didn't tell you I was coming, did he?"

"No." She met Sean's gaze. "But I appreciate you taking the time when his father couldn't."

Or wouldn't, but she wasn't going to say that out loud. Next week when the kids were at school, she would call John and discuss the situation with him again. "I hope Jake's call didn't disrupt your Friday night."

"No, it didn't." Sean framed her face with his hands. "You sure clean up good."

"You're not too bad yourself." She smiled up at him. She tiptoed up to kiss him. "Thanks for being there for Jake, Sean."

"I've got to admit, I intended to tell you not to use the kids to ask me out. I should have known you wouldn't do that."

"How could you? You don't know me."

"I'm looking forward to learning more." He kissed the top of her head. "Let's go, darlin'. I made reservations at the Hong Kong Chinese Palace so we could eat before we went to the school."

"Dinner too?" It surprised her that he'd come when her son called, and it warmed her heart. Sean obviously intended to make the evening a pleasant one for all of them. "I didn't expect that. It sounds fun." She allowed him to help her into the cab of the truck.

The conversation at dinner revolved around horses, training Awesome, the horse show season, and plans for the summer. Sean answered all of Jake's questions about corrective horseshoeing techniques and common reasons for lameness. Elinor hadn't known so many problems resulted from poor hoof care, so she learned a lot from Jake's questions. As Sean said, without good hooves, the horse wasn't usable. He compared it to tires on a car.

When they arrived at Silver Lake Middle School, they went to Lynn's homeroom first. Elinor paused to study the display of math papers on the bulletin board just inside the door. Lynn's paper had five errors, not the worst paper in the class, but she had more mistakes than most of her classmates.

Lynn had learned to multiply and divide fractions years ago—had she hurried through these instead of taking time to answer correctly? Or was there another reason she was making mistakes?

"I guess Lynn still has trouble with fractions." Jake stood next to Elinor.

"Looks like it," Elinor said. "Maybe you could coach her at home." That would make Lynn take her math assignments more seriously, unless she really had trouble understanding the formulas. "She may need your help, but not want to ask for it at school."

"I'd live longer too. She gets mad if I show off how smart I am here."

"Do you blame her?"

"No. It makes me mad when she bosses me around." Jake stepped closer and pressed up against her.

Something was wrong, Elinor thought. While Jake loved her and Lynn, he was usually careful not to act mushy where another child might see and tease him. Elinor guided him to Lynn's desk where she'd stacked her schoolwork.

"Let's see it, honey." Elinor smiled at her daughter.

"You already saw my best math paper." Lynn kept a file in her hand. "I don't have to show you the rest, do I?"

"Not until we get home. What about science?" That was Lynn's favorite subject.

"I'll show you." Eagerness replaced concern on Lynn's face. "Mr. Sievers says that we'll get to choose extra projects soon." She passed the folder of math papers to Jake. "Here, shrimp. You may as well play with these."

"I think you're choosing not to do the math to the best of your ability," Elinor reminded her. "I'll be happy to re-teach you fractions this summer if that's what it takes."

Jake sat and began to go through Lynn's papers. "Summers are really busy on the farm, so I'll do it, Mom."

"You don't need to. I can do them when I feel like it." Lynn pulled out another stack of reports. "I'm doing great in science. I got an A on my paper about the Pacific Ring of Fire."

"Let's see." Out of the corner of Elinor's eye, she saw Sean move toward Jake. Was she the only one who realized how nervous the boy was? No, Lynn had been the one to give him the math assignments to settle his nerves.

Elinor leaned closer to the girl. "Thanks, sweetie. He's a wreck tonight."

"Not really." Lynn flipped over a paper. It was marked with a red A. "He hasn't hurled yet. I keep him with me during advisory period. At lunchtime, he comes here for science and then goes to the cafeteria with my class."

"Why doesn't he eat with the other sixth-graders?"

"Because the vice-principal supervises the lunchroom then and she doesn't like Jake. She says he's a troublemaker, but Mrs. Craig takes over for eighth-grade lunch and she's okay."

Elinor caught her breath. "Your brother is very well behaved."

"Not when people throw food at him or call him names." Lynn shook her head. "Mr. Sievers wants to talk to you about it tonight. He's fine with Jake here. And after lunch, Jake goes to the library and hangs out with Mrs. Harrison. She lets him play on the computer."

"Does he go outside at all?"

"Sure. Like I told you, he hangs with me during advisory and with Bobby and Jeff in the afternoon when the seventh-graders have their breaks. But we're all older than he is, and Ms. Collins has fits. She wants Jake to stay with the boys in his class, but they treat him like a pariah because he's major smart."

"It isn't your brother's fault that he has a very high IQ."

"I know, Mom. He's just way too smart to be in this school." Lynn held up her hand as a short, older man hurried in. "Be cool, Mom. Here's Mr. Sievers." She left.

Elinor walked toward the teacher. "Hey, Reese. How are you doing?"

"You have two terrific kids." Reese Sievers gave her a quick sideways hug. "Lynn's a real pleasure to have in class and when Jake comes, it encourages the other eighth-graders to get on task. If he can do their assignments better than they can, they feel challenged."

"I appreciate you letting Lynn look out for him."

"It's a stop-gap, not a solution. Have you considered a school for gifted children? Many offer scholarships if cost is an issue."

"I'm thinking about it. I know Jake needs more advanced work." Elinor paused as Sean came to stand behind her.

"Not just Jake." Reese opened a file and handed her three papers. "These are the last math quizzes I gave. You'll notice Lynn aced them."

Elinor scanned the tests. "Then why does she have mistakes on her daily work?"

"She's opted for acceptance by her peers." Reese frowned. "She doesn't want to be ostracized for her intelligence, so she hides it. The girls here are criticized when they succeed in math and science, so Lynn acts out. She pulls the same stunt in her other core classes. Jake doesn't play the dumb card and he gets hassled for it."

"Doesn't this school have any classes for gifted children?" Sean asked.

"Yes," Elinor said, "but the kids weren't able to test into them and there wasn't room in the fall, so they're in regular block classes."

"For Lynn and Jake, it's an unfortunate experience," Reese said.

"Not for Lynn," Elinor corrected. "For her, it's party time."

Reese chuckled. "She'll have straight A's come report card time. She only blows off an assignment when her classmates might see it."

"What am I going to do with her?"

"You could homeschool again," Sean suggested.

Reese grinned. "We could do something even more vile, Elinor. There's a math conference I want to attend in a few weeks."

"You are a very evil man, and you're playing my song. It's why I like you." Elinor pulled out the small, leather-bound calendar she used for her substitute teaching schedule. "When? How many days?"

Luckily, she wasn't already booked for the three days of the conference. Reese agreed to make the needed arrangements with the school district and to email the lesson plans to her. "Lynn won't dare play dumb with me in the room and maybe she won't go back to it when you return."

"We can only hope," Reese said. "She could actually lead the other girls to change their behavior, too."

Elinor nodded. If she supported Reese, then Lynn might work up to her potential. "We'd better head for the sixth-grade class-room. I still have to talk to Jake's teachers."

"I've tried to arrange for him to do his math here, but I haven't talked Mona into it yet," he said, referring to the principal. "It was hard enough getting her to agree to him coming here for science."

"Really?" Sean pushed back his hat. "What if his mother called the office? It seems to me the boy could use the extra tutoring."

"That's a fine case of double-speak if ever I've heard one," Elinor said. "Jake doesn't need tutoring. He needs a challenge." She risked a look at her children. Lynn appeared to be long-suffering while Jake happily lectured her about math.

"Yes, but administrators are generally politicians like my father. He doesn't want to hear that people need challenging," Sean drawled. "Discipline, yes. Tutoring, definitely."

"I'm willing if you can facilitate it." Reese rubbed his hands. "Do you know how much fun it is teaching children who breathe math like Lynn and Jake?"

"I know how much I love it," Elinor said. "Lynn's like that for me when I have her in the riding arena. It's as if she and her horse become a centaur. They can do everything, poetry in motion. It looks perfectly natural."

"It takes a *real* rider to do that," Sean said. "We'd better get moving, darlin'. She has to be up by six to have Gypsy ready for that show tomorrow."

Elinor nodded agreement, exchanged goodbyes with the teacher and they left the eighth-grade wing. "Let's go, kids. Jake, I'll pop in and visit Mrs. Craig. We'll see if you can join Lynn's class for math. I'm sure your teachers will be willing to let you come to Mr. Sievers's room."

"Perfect," Jake whispered. "Mom, you're the best. Lynn's math book has great problems."

"My expectation is that you'll finish your sixth-grade work before you play in the eighth-grade pool of math knowledge."

"I could have that done in ten minutes," Jake said.

"Right, but I expect straight A's," Elinor told him. "Take fifteen and show your work."

"This is gonna be so much fun, isn't it, Lynnie?" Jake asked.

"If I were you, I'd keep it under my hat." Sean patted Jake's back while Lynn rolled her eyes. "A man should never miss a good chance to shut up."

"Really?" Elinor asked. "I've never found a guy who didn't love the sound of his own voice."

Laughing, Sean wrapped an arm around her shoulders. "You're as amazing as these kids. I had no idea you're a teacher. What else am I going to learn tonight?"

"Not much if you're waiting for me to share." She caught her breath when he hugged her for an instant, then released her. "You're different."

"How?" Sean stopped outside the eighth-grade building. "Go ahead, kids. We'll catch up."

"Okay." Jake headed off, Lynn beside him. "Don't take a long time. We're not going in there without you."

"We'll be along." Elinor met Sean's gaze. "What's it going to take to drive you off? I'm not interested."

"Is that why you keep challenging me?"

"Not here and not now." She used the strict tone she adopted when kids acted inappropriately in the classroom and wasn't surprised when he stopped.

He chuckled. "We'll have so much fun when we finally get together."

Just the idea terrified her. She'd only met him three days ago. If she didn't slow down, she'd be in bed with him before Monday. She'd learned not to trust men a long time ago, not to risk her heart. It'd only get broken. So why did she want to jump him? "It's not happening, cowboy."

"Want to bet?"

NINE

Jake and Lynn waited outside the main hall that held the sixth-grade classrooms. They'd never seen her, and John show a lot of affection. Had she already embarrassed them? Thankfully, she hadn't allowed Sean to kiss her here, but still, their behavior was too intimate for a school setting.

Jake hurried to her. "Remember, Mom. Don't lose it with Ms. Collins."

Elinor took a deep breath. "I'll be nice, honey."

She led the way into the wide hall that opened onto the classrooms. Before she entered Jake's class, three boys tried to shove past her. Sean's bulk stopped them.

One of the boys, a blond in baggy shorts and a sloppy T-shirt, sneered at Jake. "Hey, guys. It's the freak."

"Don't you mean the nerd?" his buddy in fashionably torn jeans and a designer T-shirt asked.

"Or Egghead?" That came from the freckled redhead.

Elinor caught her breath. Jake spoke before she could. "Mom, these are three of the Four Moronic Cretins."

"Sort of like the Four Musketeers?" Lynn's voice dripped sarcasm. "Are they missing the head of their little club, or the tail? Do they even know?"

Lynn and Jake's insults didn't seem to faze the boys. The slender blond woman behind them was a different story. "That was uncalled for."

"I couldn't agree more," Elinor said. "Courtesy doesn't seem to be a priority here. You correct yours. I'll correct mine."

"Fine." The blonde shivered despite the cardigan she had around her shoulders. "I'm Debbie Walker."

"Elinor Talbot." She glanced to Sean. "And this is…"

But Sean was already smiling at the other woman. "Debbie and I grew up together." His voice was gentle. "How's it going? Fearless asked about you the other night."

"Really?" Debbie managed a smile. "I'll have to take the kids and visit her on my day off."

Elinor glanced at them. Did Sean have a history with this woman or were they just friends? She'd wait and see what she learned from watching them.

Debbie eyed Elinor again. "I'm sorry for George's manners. He knows better, but ever since his dad and I split…" She shrugged. "It's a poor excuse. His friends' mothers will agree the name-calling stops."

"Mom!" The redhead appeared stunned by her betrayal. "You can't do that." George pointed at Jake. "And he is weird. He uses words nobody knows."

"I do." Debbie's voice was firm. "I don't like it when he calls you stupid either."

"He didn't say we were dumb, Mrs. Walker." This time it was the towhead. "He calls us morons, or cretins, or imbeciles."

"Only because you are," Jake said.

"Enough." Elinor frowned at her son. "We've discussed your tendency to embellish your vocabulary. Rudeness when someone else starts it is forgivable, but redundancy?" She shook her head. "You can do better, Jake."

"What?" Sean asked. "Name-calling isn't as big a deal as repetition? What's up with that, Elinor?"

"Jake likes to expand his vocabulary and I'm usually fine with that," Elinor said, "but I can't stand superfluous language and he knows it."

"It's because our dad's a lawyer," Lynn finished up. "He always has to make the same point at least three times in every document and uses twenty-five cent words that only Jake understands."

"Okay, I'm sorry for calling them names," Jake said, "but, I still think ganging up on somebody different is moronic, cretinous and imbecilic."

"Next time it happens, tell your mom right away and she can call me," Debbie said. "I'll take care of George."

"Good idea." Elinor smoothed Jake's hair. "It's not tattling, honey." She watched comprehension dawn on the faces of the other boys. Sneaking or telling on one another was a serious offense to sixth-graders.

She rested a hand on her son's shoulder. "Go show Lynn your work."

"And me." Sean winked at Jake.

The adoration in Jake's eyes as the three of them walked away touched Elinor's heart. She hoped Sean was worthy of the emotion.

She took a deep breath as two other women joined her and Debbie. One was a tall, heavy-set brunette in a long, flowered dress. She had a baby on her hip and a toddler swinging from one hand. Her companion was a slender young woman with black curling hair falling to her hips. In jeans and a Saddle Up for St. Jude's T-shirt, she didn't look old enough to be anyone's mother, but obviously she was.

The brunette smiled at Elinor. "I'm Bonnie Fitzwilliams. It looked like all the serious talk was going on over here, so we came to join you."

"I'm Christy." The other dark-haired woman held out her hand to Elinor, brown eyes friendly. "Did you and Debbie solve the world's problems?"

"Not yet," Debbie said. "This is Elinor Talbot who arrived with

Sean, my long-ago crush back when we were in 4-H together. I was apologizing for George calling their boy names and I was sure the two of you would agree that Frank and Oscar should stop bullying him, too."

"What?" Christy stiffened as she stared at the blond boy. "What were you thinking, Oscar?"

"It's no big deal." Oscar tried to defend himself. "And Jake calls us names back."

"We just didn't know what they meant before," the brown-haired boy in torn jeans said hastily. "Now we do. It's cool, Mom."

"Not to me." Bonnie released her hold on Elinor's hand. "The bullying stops now, Frank Junior."

The boy looked down, picking at a hole in his jeans. "Mom, we're not bullying. It's only names."

"Name-calling is bullying," Bonnie said. "You can think about it instead of spending the weekend with your PlayStation."

"Nick started it. How come he's not in trouble?" Frank demanded.

"Because I haven't called *his* parents yet. I will when I get home." The comment silenced all three boys, and Bonnie turned her attention back to Elinor. "I'm sorry. If I'd volunteered like I usually do in Frank Junior's classes, he wouldn't have misplaced his manners. I always put a stop to name-calling the first time I hear it, even if the teacher's not bothered by it."

Elinor caught her breath. "That's a terrific solution, but Ms. Collins would probably freak out if I did it. She'd think I was after her job."

When the other women looked confused, Elinor explained. "I substitute teach in the district, but I haven't been in this room all year. When I talk to Mona Craig, I'll offer to come next time Ms. Collins isn't here."

"That would be great," Christy said. "And Bonnie's right about the way we reinforce good manners when we volunteer. We met when we were chaperoning field trips back in first grade." She blushed, then giggled. "I mean when Oscar and Frank were in first grade. I didn't know Bonnie when she was. Or when I was."

Debbie laughed. "Did you homeschool your kids, Elinor? Is that why Jake's so advanced?"

"Not really. He's very intelligent and homeschool meant he worked up to his capacities," Elinor said. "Being with children his age has been hard on him. Lynn's teacher thinks I should arrange for both of my kids to attend a private school with classes for gifted children. I'm going to have them test for Hi-Cap this spring and they'll be in advanced courses next year."

"Private schools are great if you've won the lottery," Bonnie commented. "What about the rest of us? If Frank Junior had challenging schoolwork, he might not have so much time to get in trouble."

"Mom, no! I don't want to do harder work," Frank looked indignant. "We're in the same group for all our blocks. I like this class."

"Me too," Oscar concurred. "If we'd known this was Jake's first year in school, we'd have taught him how to do stuff, not picked on him."

"But, he's weird," George griped. He yelped when Frank elbowed him. "I guess he can't help it if he thinks learning's fun. We can teach him better."

Elinor shared a look with the other mothers. "God, I hope not." She saw Bonnie's amusement. "Okay, I will admit it's hard having a kid who's going to be smarter than I am by the time he's twelve."

"You still want him to work up to his full potential," Debbie said. "And it's what we want for our boys too. I think you're right about volunteering. I just don't know how I'm going to manage it, Bonnie."

"Me either. You're already working over-time at the casino. You only get one day off a week and you're exhausted by then." Bonnie frowned thoughtfully. The baby babbled and tangled fingers in her mother's hair while the toddler twirled around her. "What if I drop off my girls and you baby-sit? You don't have to get dressed for that. I can cover both Wednesdays and Thursdays here, and I might regain my sanity, with kids who can talk."

Elinor admired the way Bonnie arranged it, *so* it sounded as if Debbie were doing her the favor, rather than the opposite.

"Are you sure you don't mind?" Debbie rubbed her cheek wearily. "It's really not fair when George has been causing trouble too."

Elinor watched shame ease into George's eyes. "I could cover the occasional Thursday morning if I'm not subbing and if Sean isn't there to shoe horses. I don't have lessons until noon."

Christy exclaimed, "Wait a minute. You have that pony farm. I bring my daughter pony riding all the time. She just adores Galaxy." She sighed. "Of course, it's all I can do to get there before you close. I've been getting a lot of extra hours at work too. Don't waste that eagle eye on me, Bonnie. I've got Fridays off. I'll come then."

"Fine. That leaves Tuesdays for one of Nick's parents. His mom's in the Navy and at sea a lot." Bonnie shifted the baby to the other hip and the toddler to her right hand. "But I'll bet his dad would love to volunteer."

"He will by the time you finish with him," Christy giggled. "Oh God, here comes Ms. Collins. I'll see you at church. Let's go, Oscar. Thanks for taking the initiative, Bonnie."

"Didn't I see you with Sean Killian?" Bonnie asked Elinor, then continued before getting an answer. "Considering how hard it is to find a decent shoer and how long it took Clancy to convince Sean to add my Warmbloods to his book, I don't want Frank Junior calling anyone names, especially Sean's kid."

"Sean's not Jake's father," Elinor said.

"In these days, who stays married to their kids' dad?" Debbie smiled and glanced past Elinor. "Make your escape while you can. The woman who gives blondes a bad name really has found us. She's been making me crazy since school started, but they wouldn't let me switch George out of her class." Putting a hand on her son's shoulder, she urged him out of the room.

Elinor looked and saw the teacher approaching. She heard Debbie scolding her son as they headed down the hall, but there was no way to tell these women that Sean was practically a stranger. Meanwhile, Frank tried to convince Bonnie she didn't need to volunteer in the classroom as they waited for Ms. Collins to arrive.

Elinor figured his arguments were a lost cause. Bonnie seemed like the kind of person who never changed her mind. When Ms. Collins joined them, Elinor slipped away, leaving Bonnie and the teacher to chat. It didn't take long to join Jake, Lynn, and Sean at the far end of the room, between the two sets of windows.

Jake's desk was in one of the corners, providing a perfect view of the grassy school-yard, swings and baseball diamonds. She didn't ask how much time he spent dreaming. It wouldn't do any good. Her son never measured time in hours or minutes, only in segments of forever. She glanced through the stack of assignments piled neatly on his desk. Each page sported an A or 100% with zero errors. Under the schoolwork was a notebook. She picked it up. "What's this?"

"My stories." Jake took the binder. He returned it to the inside of his desk. "They're not ready to be shared."

"I see," Sean said. "A guy might want to take them home, son. You didn't put them out for sharing, did you?"

"Of course not!" Jake took out the notebook and looked up at Sean. "I'll ask Mrs. Harrison if she has a special place I can keep it in the library. She lets me write my stories on the computer at lunchtime."

"Sounds like an awesome teacher to me." Sean put his hand on Jake's shoulder. "Do we have time to meet her?"

"We do," Elinor said. "Do you have time to write stories in class, Jake?"

"Mostly I edit them then." Jake scowled as Ms. Collins approached. "Remember, Mom."

"I will."

Ms. Collins was a pretty young blonde, tall and slender in a blue pinstriped jacket and skirt. White teeth gleamed in a brilliant smile. She always reminded Elinor of a *Barbie* doll.

"It's nice to see you again, Mrs. Talbot." Ms. Collins beamed at all of them. "Jake's been such a joy to have in class this quarter. His behavior has improved so much since progress reports. I really appreciate you talking to him about it."

"Really?" Elinor pasted on the professional smile she saved for obnoxious customers or arrogant vice principals. She saw a muscle begin to pulse in Sean's jaw and realized he was irritated, too. "I never have trouble with Jake. How has his conduct changed here?"

"Oh, a thousand different ways. He doesn't disrupt class by answering all the questions."

"Were they the right answers?" Sean asked, his gaze narrowed.

"That has nothing to do with it." Ms. Collins's bright smile didn't fade.

"Does he raise his hand? Or is he passed over because he knows the material?"

"Well, really." Ms. Collins's cheerfulness started to fade. "I'm afraid you don't understand the situation. It doesn't matter how much Jake knows if he lacks patience when he's waiting for his classmates to understand. He's working on that. He sits quietly back here. He doesn't argue with the other children."

Elinor nodded. "What else does Jake do that makes you believe he's changed for the better?"

"He's stopped making trouble in the library. When the class goes to visit, he sits by himself and doesn't try to pick out books that are too old for him." Ms. Collins sobered. "I'm concerned about him downloading those stories on the school's computer. I don't think Mrs. Harrison understands what Jake's doing."

"I didn't download anything," Jake said, indignant. "I *wrote* these." He glared at the teacher.

Ms. Collins shook her head. "He's so touchy. He needs to work on accepting criticism. I don't think spending so much time in the library is appropriate."

Jake's jaw dropped. "Mom, no! Don't let her stop that, too. It's the only thing I have that makes this school…" His voice trailed away.

"Bearable?" Sean asked. When Jake nodded, Sean continued. "The boy likes his classes with Mr. Sievers, and his mother will arrange for him to do math there, too."

"Mr. Talbot, you simply don't understand," Ms. Collins tried again. "Jake isn't an easy child to have here. You must back up my authority."

Sean held up his hand. "The boy will do math with the eighth grade after his mother arranges it with the office. At lunch and when he has free time, he will go to the library. I saw Bonnie Fitzwilliams here. I know she'll put a stop to the name-calling and harassment her son inflicted on Jake."

"She's *afraid* you'll stop shoeing her horses," Elinor said, unwilling to intervene, although she ought to stop Sean from expressing his opinion. For the first time since the kids started at this school, the teacher was listening to another adult.

"But I don't like the kids in this class," Jake complained.

"You could change your mind when they start being nice instead of picking on you, Jake." Sean's tone gentled. "I know you'll try, son."

"Okay. If I still don't like it, can I spend afternoon study time with Mrs. Harrison and the computer?" Jake asked.

Elinor nodded. "All right. But I want a good try." She eyed the teacher again. "Anything else you want to tell us before we visit Mrs. Harrison?"

"I don't think you're giving him enough time to work on his social skills with his classmates," Ms. Collins said. "You're taking the other boys' teasing far too seriously."

"So were the rest of the mothers," Elinor said, struggling not to ask if the woman even paid attention in the latest professional development classes. Bullying was a big deal and the school had policies to prevent it.

"Nobody calls the boy anything, or I'll start phoning school board members." Sean rested his arm on Elinor's shoulders. "Let's mosey, people."

"I never thought of going to the school board," Elinor said. "It seemed like tattling. I thought it was enough if I talked to the teachers, the counselor, or the administrators."

"I'll teach you how to play the game with bureaucrats." Sean's anger eased. "You have to go up the chain of command until you find someone who takes responsibility, honey." He glanced at the teacher. "Do you have anything positive to say about Jake?"

"He has such lovely manners. He uses them all the time. He always says, please, thank you, excuse me." Ms. Collins gestured to the schoolwork on the desk. "He finishes his assignments and doesn't read ahead anymore in his textbooks since he got marked down for it six weeks ago."

Elinor counted to twenty. "I'm happy you see an improvement, Ms. Collins."

"It sounds to me like he's marking time," Sean commented. "It's too bad he can't get an education here."

Elinor took a step toward the door. "Let's go. I'm sure Bonnie explained her volunteer schedule with you, Ms. Collins."

"As I told her, anything like that would have to be approved by the administration," Ms. Collins said.

"And as I'm sure Bonnie reminded you, Frank Fitzwilliams, her husband, is the head of the school board this year." Sean started with Elinor toward the classroom door. "Plan on seeing your volunteers next week until school ends. Let's go. We've made enough points here, and I want to meet the fabulous Mrs. Harrison. Where is she, Jake?"

"In the library." Jake danced ahead of them, down the hall.

"This was great," Lynn said, and she followed him, dignity personified.

Elinor tipped her head back to see Sean's face. "Thanks for riding to the rescue, cowboy. I could have done it myself. I have to admit it was nice to have that teacher listen to someone."

Sean chuckled. "It's something Marlene told me about. It

annoyed her big-time when people didn't pay attention to her because she's a woman, but they always listened to her husband. Roy used to say she'd have a foot-stomping hissy fit when he intervened and he worried he'd have to sleep on the couch until our Fearless Leader called the game, *The Man Says,* and began laughing about it instead of swearing."

TEN

THE REST OF THE VISIT PASSED SMOOTHLY. MRS. HARRISON WAS an older woman who seemed to think the sun rose and set with Jake. When they left the school, they still had time to stop for ice cream on the way home.

Instead of discussing lameness in horses, Jake brought up fishing. He and Sean talked about the best places in the county for close to an hour. Finally, Elinor suggested Jake take off from school on Thursday and go fishing with Sean. The idea met with quick approval from him and her son.

Jake bombarded Sean with more questions on their way back to the pony farm. Sean patiently answered them, his amusement apparent. Jake continued to bounce up and down as they walked into the house. The conversation became background noise as Elinor checked for phone messages.

There were six. Three concerned riding the next day. Two were for riding on Sunday. The last was from Penny, her riding instructor. Once again, the sixteen-year-old had called in sick for Saturday.

"I don't need this," Elinor murmured, knowing the manufactured emergency wasn't real. If it was, the teenager would have called Elinor's cell phone, not the landline.

"What's the matter?" Lynn asked.

"Penny called in. She can't work tomorrow." Elinor studied the reservation book. How many lessons were there? How could she teach the classes, send out the trail rides, and take care of walk-in customers?

"I don't have to go to the show. I'll cover the front and the office while you teach." Disappointment colored the girl's tone.

"Let me try to come up with another solution first, honey. Thanks for volunteering."

"What's the problem?" Sean asked. "Call someone else. Do what any other business would do. Hire a replacement and cut Penny's hours."

"Great strategy, cowboy," Elinor mocked. "There's only one problem. I trained Penny to teach my way. I don't believe in whips or spurs for beginning or intermediate-level students."

"Sounds like Marlene struck again." Sean chuckled. "Get someone our fearless leader taught to ride."

"But who?" Elinor asked again. "Most instructors don't insist students use natural aids. Plus, I make the students groom and saddle their own horses."

"I'd better stay home and work," Lynn said, blinking hard to hold back the tears swimming in her dark blue eyes.

"You'll lose your show fees," Sean said. "And I'll bet you paid them yourself, didn't you?"

"Out of her chore money," Jake agreed. "How are you going to fix it, Sean?"

"It isn't his problem," Elinor said, putting a comforting hand on Lynn's shoulder. "And you and I can cope, Jake. We did last summer."

Sean took out his cell phone. "I'll call Clancy Dawson. She owes me. She'll do this."

"Really? Why does she owe you?" Elinor asked, eager to get some information without being too nosy.

"Because I've been letting her cry on my shoulder since she broke off her engagement right before the wedding." Sean punched in a number. "Guy's an idiot. I told him that and then I knocked him on his tail."

"There's a reasonable way to cope with a problem." Elinor gestured toward the living room. "Bedtime, you two. And better a broken engagement than a broken marriage. Don't you ever let me hear that you hit someone. Violence doesn't solve problems."

"Made me feel better," Sean said from behind her. "And Clancy's ex has five inches on me and more muscle."

"What a hero," Elinor lightly mocked. "Lynn, we'll feed at five. It'll give Gypsy time to eat before Marlene arrives with the trailer. With Sean's friend teaching, we'll do fine without you."

"Are you sure?" Lynn asked.

"We'll be fine," Elinor repeated.

"Sean was a good friend to her, Mom," Jake said, heading for his room. "That counts even if he did hit her boyfriend."

Elinor suppressed a sigh. Her son had a point. If someone like Sean had punched her ex-husband, she probably would have enjoyed the sight.

She didn't know how she'd pay an instructor of Clancy Dawson's caliber, but there had to be a way. It wasn't fair to expect Lynn or Jake to sacrifice their childhoods. And she wasn't the kind of mother who used her kids for cheap farm labor, regardless of what John had told the judge. She'd talk to her lawyer about private schools. Let Harold go after John for more money. If her ex had to pay for tuition, he'd back off on whether the kids were homeschooled.

It didn't take long to tuck Lynn and Jake into bed. Elinor agreed they could read for fifteen minutes before lights out. She smiled when she saw Jake's choice, a *Terry Brooks* novel. Ms. Collins would have a hissy fit because he was reading beyond his grade level again.

Elinor returned to the kitchen in time to see Sean put away his phone. "How'd it go?"

"She'll be here bright and early." He removed his hat and placed it on the table. "An interesting first date."

"I really didn't ask Jake to call you."

"I know. We already covered the subject." He took a step toward her.

She took a step back. "I'm not chasing you now."

"Good. I'm old fashioned. I prefer to do the chasing." He pulled her into his arms. "Wow, I like you." He kissed her ear. "Did Debbie tell tales out of school?"

"Only that the two of you were close friends, eons ago." Elinor rested her hands on his chest.

She should push him away. She couldn't make herself do it. She surrendered to the long, slow *magick* of his kiss. It was different from yesterday. He still kissed her as if he wanted her body and soul, but this wasn't a fierce possession.

She could walk away whenever she chose. She just didn't choose. She put her arms around his neck and clung to him. The taste, the feel of his lips on hers was what she'd dreamed of all day.

Slowly, he lifted his head.

She looked up at him. "Are the rest of your ex-girlfriends going to praise you to the skies, too?"

"Denise won't. She wanted a meal ticket and I told her to get a job." Sean glowered at her. "What is it with you, woman? I've told you more in the last couple days than I ever tell anyone."

Elinor laughed. "Call it survival, cowboy. Knowing what makes people tick gives me an edge. And I'm good at getting info."

"Better than Marlene," Sean grumbled. "The two of you should go work for the cops. You just make folks spill their guts."

Elinor brought his head down for a leisurely kiss. "I'll tell you a secret, handsome. I haven't wanted to jump a guy's bones in ages. But you're different."

"I knew that already." This time he controlled the kiss.

Afterward, he released her and backed away. "Clancy says she'll come early so you can show her what to do. Then you can go with Lynn."

Elinor stared at him. "Sean, *I* don't go with her. I have a business to run. Marlene looks after Lynn and Gypsy."

"But she has a whole crew of kids and horses," Sean said. "Who helps groom Gypsy? Who helps Lynn dress? Who finds out what the judge wants? Who checks out the trail course? Or the jumps? Horse shows are hazardous places."

Elinor struggled to dismiss her guilt. She couldn't be in two places at one time and she had to be sure the children and ponies ate.

"Lynn's been showing for three years. I don't push her to do this. She can stay home and ride here."

"No wonder she acts like an adult." Sean jammed his hat on his head. "I'll juggle my schedule and go with her."

———

Elinor tossed and turned for hours, switching her pillow to the cool side time and again. She wished Sean had remained until they'd come to some kind of agreement.

Finally, she got out of bed. She went to the kitchen and made a cup of herbal tea. Maybe this would help her sleep. If not, she could rehearse a speech for the next time she saw him. She *was* a good mother, damn it!

I don't hit my children. I can't even remember the last time I yelled at them. Granted, they were good kids to start with. Her personal, albeit prejudiced, opinion was that they were the best on the planet. She discussed their actions with them when they did something wrong, and they responded to it.

The only thing people have over animals is the ability to reason and that's what I teach my children to do. Okay, so I don't attend Lynn's horse shows. But my children don't go hungry. They have good clothes to wear, even if I shop at thrift stores and don't buy name brands.

The last time the electricity had been turned off for nonpayment was when John hadn't bothered to mail the check. The telephone hadn't been shut off since the divorce. Her credit rating was better now than it had been during their marriage. Of course, it helped that she only had one credit card for emergencies and insisted upon paying cash or by debit card for almost everything. She kept a landline at the farm and only used her cell phone for emergencies, but that saved money too.

Her kids had physical, emotional and psychological stability. She might not be the best mother in the world. She certainly wasn't the worst. As a teacher, she'd seen the gamut of parenting styles and hers ranked in the top ten.

She added more hot water to her cup and waited for the bag to steep again. The only way she could continue to keep them solvent was by working, and the prime hours on the pony farm were on the weekends during the school year.

Lynn shuffled into the kitchen, snugging the belt on her bathrobe. "What's the matter, Mom?"

"What are you doing up?" Elinor asked.

"I saw the light and came to see what was wrong. Are you sick?"

"No, honey. I'm just feeling horribly guilty." Elinor leaned across the table and brushed a lock of her daughter's golden-brown hair from her forehead. "I wish I could be there to help you at the show."

Lynn rubbed her cheek against Elinor's hand. "Yeah, but it can't happen unless we want to take up starving. It's okay, Mom."

"You're such a good rider. Is getting Gypsy into the ring too much for you?"

"I can do it. Marlene always helps me. So do the older kids."

Elinor stroked her daughter's hair once more. "Well, Sean says he's coming tomorrow. He'll help you, too."

"Really?" Lynn's eyes widened. "Dad never wanted to watch me ride. This is so great!"

"What's great?" Jake yawned as he wandered in and joined them.

"Sean's coming to my show." Lynn jumped up and whirled in a small circle. She stopped and hugged Jake. "You were right."

"It's 'cause I'm so smart." Jake wriggled away from Lynn. He padded to Elinor and leaned against her chair. "Are you having bad dreams, Mom?"

"No. I couldn't sleep." Elinor checked the clock. Two in the morning. "Shall I make hot chocolate, or do you want more ice cream?"

"Ice cream!" Lynn headed for the refrigerator. "I'll get it."

"Thanks, honey." Elinor wrapped her arms around Jake. "Did you have a nightmare, sweetie?" She felt his nod. "About what?"

"Monsters," Jake whispered. "Bad ones. They're still in my room."

Elinor knew there was nothing wrong in Jake's room. She'd checked it every night since Christmas, but these dreams continued. She didn't know what caused them. She didn't let him watch scary movies or read horror novels.

How long would the fear continue? He'd seemed so secure before last Christmas and now – monsters. "Do you want to sleep in my room? Those monsters won't dare set their scaly feet in there or bug Lynn."

"I know." Jake relaxed; his terror gone. "They don't like Lynn."

"Who doesn't?" Lynn carried over two servings of ice cream topped with chocolate syrup and set them down before bringing over her own.

"The monsters."

Lynn sniffed. "There's no such thing." She brought over spoons before she sat back down. "Honestly, Jake. Just tell them they're only pretend."

"See, Mom." Jake shook his head. "She makes 'em disappear for good 'cause she's an unbeliever. They're scared of her."

"Well, you could do the same thing," Lynn said.

"It wouldn't work. They know *I* know they're real."

Elinor shared a look with Lynn. "Well, until we figure out what else to do with the monsters, you can sleep in my room. Okay?"

"Only when they visit me. Is Sean's friend coming to teach?"

"Yes." Elinor studied her sundae. "It'll be nice to meet her."

"I bet you'll like her." Jake spooned up ice cream. "She comes to our 4-H meetings and talks about how to present your horse in the best way to the judge. She was even nice when Bobby told her we liked games better than classes."

"She's cool," Lynn agreed. "And now I know why she's hardly judging any shows this summer. Maybe if we get back in time, she could tell me why I don't win."

"You get ribbons at every show," Elinor said.

"They're 4-H shows, Mother. Every kid who rides gets a ribbon. I want firsts and seconds. The highest I've ever gotten is a third."

"Sean could tell you after he sees you ride," Jake said.

"If he really comes." Lynn looked downcast.

"He will. He's not an oath-breaker. Like he says, he keeps his word." Jake scraped his bowl. "You'll be fine, Lynnie."

Elinor frowned. On the one hand, she wanted to reassure her daughter, but on the other, she wanted to tell Lynn not to get her hopes up. "I don't remember Sean using that term, Jake. Where did you find it?"

"It's in my *Mercedes Lackey* books. She's pretty smart about horses even if she hasn't figured out that all horses can talk to people, but not all people listen."

"I see." Elinor smiled. "If you're right, I should have a talk with Lightning."

"You can't. He's too full of hate to hear. You gotta do what I do, Mom. Keep thinking love at him. One day, he'll believe in it again."

"Not a bad idea," Elinor mused. "Now, tell me about oath-breakers. What are they?"

"Bad people who break promises and try to hurt you. They get in trouble with the *Rule of Three*. It's what'll happen to our old dad."

Elinor decided to let the disrespectful reference to John go by. "What's the rule, Jake? I've never heard it."

"Sure, you have, Mom. You say it all the time." Lynn finished her ice cream. "What goes around, comes around. Reverend Bill talks about it, too. 'As you sow, so shall you reap.' It's the same thing."

"It's a little different in *magick*. Whatever you do, good or evil, comes back on you threefold," Jake said. "So, a guy has to be careful."

ELEVEN

Music from the clock radio woke her. She hastily switched it off so Jake could continue to sleep. She dressed, put on the coffee, and headed for the barn. Turning on the lights awakened the ponies and Rebel who promptly whinnied at her. She went through the early morning routine of watering, feeding the hay, and measuring out grain. Once they were eating, she moved on to the steers and pigs.

Let the kids wake up on their own. They hadn't gotten back to bed until almost two-thirty and Marlene wouldn't arrive with the trailer before eight. Lynn had her alarm set for six-thirty.

Elinor collected buckets, a clean white washcloth, and a small pail of warm water. She'd milk the cow before she went into the house and organized the day's activities. A half hour later, she'd finished the milking when she saw Sean's truck, towing a two-horse trailer, pull into the drive.

She went to meet him. "Good morning." He wore a denim jacket over a red and white checked western shirt, blue jeans, and boots. A real cowboy hunk. "So, what's with the silent treatment?"

He looked worried. "I know the best way to eat crow is while it's still warm. The colder it gets, the harder it is to swallow."

She curbed her amusement. "Is that a cowboy's apology?"

"Yes, ma'am." He pushed back his hat and she saw the sincerity in his eyes.

Rising on her tiptoes, she kissed his cheek. "Come on. The coffee should be ready by now."

They entered the kitchen and she poured coffee into two mugs. She glanced over her shoulder as Lynn came in. "Your horse is eating. I left on her stable-sheet so she'd stay clean. You only used instant shampoo on her, right? It's still too cold to bathe her completely."

"Yeah. I know." Lynn smiled at Sean. "Hi. Mom said you were coming along to help me today. I appreciate it."

"I'm looking forward to it. How can I help now?"

Elinor passed him a cup of coffee. "Is Gypsy trimmed enough for today?"

Lynn shook her head. "No, not really. I smoothed out her bridle path, fetlocks, ears, and the whiskers on her face. I still have to shave her nose and chin again."

"I'll do that." Sean sipped his coffee. "I've got practical experience. I shave every morning. Didn't even cut myself today."

Elinor smiled, but Lynn obviously wasn't in the mood for humor. Showing was serious business for her daughter.

Lynn eyed Sean speculatively. "It'd be more help if you put the new silver on my saddle. You can use a screwdriver, can't you? I couldn't get the horn-cap to stay or the pieces for the stirrups."

"I'm an expert. Where's your saddle?"

"In the living-room. I'll get it." Lynn brought in her cleaned and oiled western saddle. "You don't mind, do you?"

"Not worth beans, according to our fearless leader, Marlene," Sean said with a quick smile. "Where's the silver?"

"Coming right up." Lynn vanished again.

Elinor added cream to her coffee. She wouldn't say it aloud, but she was surprised Lynn was so calm today. Maybe Sean was right. Lynn might need her and resent not having her at the show. It made their discussion in the wee hours even more important.

Lynn returned with the pieces of German silver she'd been

collecting all winter. There were pieces for the sudaderos, as well as the stirrups, the new horn cap, and an engraved nameplate for the cantle.

Sean laid out the various pieces on the table. "I brought my trailer so we can take Gypsy ourselves and I've already called Marlene to let her know we'd meet her there. We have plenty of time. Go ahead and eat breakfast while I do this, Lynn."

"There's too much to do. I'll grab something later. I still have to finish Gypsy, get my stuff out to the truck, and shine both pairs of boots again."

Sean took the screwdriver. "You're not going to have time to eat at the show, Lynn. You won't win any blue ribbons if you're a nervous wreck, or a hungry one. If we're going to argue, I won't be able to put on the silver and hold up my end of the battle."

Elinor waited for Lynn to explode with nervous rage. It didn't happen. Instead, she turned to the cupboard. While Lynn made herself some instant oatmeal, Elinor went to the washer to take out the load her daughter put in the night before. Pulling out a pillow-case with the ends tied in a knot, Elinor glanced at the teen. "What's this? I thought you washed your halter and lead line days ago."

"I did. Green clashes with my outfit." While the oatmeal cooked in the microwave, Lynn poured cold cereal into another bowl. "Jake let me borrow his and he only agreed yesterday. I had to sell my soul to get it."

"Did not." Jake came in from Elinor's room, rubbing his eyes. "You had to promise to help me next time I want to do a..." His voice faded at the stern look his older sister gave him. "Will you make me some cereal, too, Lynnie?"

"I just did." Lynn added milk to the bowl and then retrieved her oatmeal from the microwave. "Want to eat yours in the living room so you can watch cartoons?"

Jake shook his head. "No. In here is good."

"All right. But don't spill anything on my silver. I don't have time to polish it again this morning."

"I'll be careful." Jake carried two glasses of orange juice to the table.

Elinor opened the pillowcase. She removed the red nylon halter and cotton lead rope. She took them into the bathroom and turned the baseboard heater on high so the tack would finish drying. Coming back into the kitchen, she said, "I'll pack a lunch for you, Lynn. I don't want you eating a lot of junk food from the snack bar."

"I never do." Lynn was indignant. "Jake's the one who pigs out at the fairgrounds. I have to watch my weight."

"Do not!"

"Do too."

"Cool it." Sean didn't look up from the horn cap. "I've got to concentrate to do this right."

The squabble ended as quickly as it started. Elinor brought over the pot of coffee and topped his cup. She smiled at him. "Thanks for helping."

"Any time." His grin warmed her and made her yearn to kiss him. She controlled the impulse. She had a lunch to pack.

Elinor replaced the coffee pot on the warmer and went in search of peanut butter and jelly to make Lynn's favorite sandwich. At some point, they would have to discuss the teen's new concern with her weight. If it wasn't one thing, it was another with her kids. "What are your plans today, Jake? I know you're spending the night at Bobby's."

"I'm playing with Chipeta and Awesome. I've got to teach him to wear a halter and be brushed and have his hooves picked. Marlene brought me a baby halter when she stopped by to see him because we didn't have one."

"You mean a colt halter," Lynn said.

"Actually, it's a foal halter." Jake drank some of his orange juice. "It's only a colt halter because Awesome's a boy. But I like calling him a baby. Besides, Sandy's gonna help me in between trail rides."

Elinor spread peanut butter on slices of bread. "Honey, I think Awesome's too young. He's only two days old."

"Perfect age, darlin'," Sean drawled. "He's too little to know he's got a choice. If Jake starts working him now, Awesome will never learn he's bigger and stronger than people. When I get back from the show, I'll help you teach him to lead, Jake. Wait for me so you don't get hurt. Okay, partner?"

Jake nodded. "Sure."

Elinor realized that her son seemed happier when he had an opportunity to interact with Sean. She hadn't realized he was so lonely for a man's attention.

"I'm going to the barn." Lynn hesitated at the back door. "Sean, did you mean it when you said you'd finish trimming Gypsy?"

"Yes, I did. Remember, we've already talked about piecrust promises? No 'easily made and easily broken ones' for either of us. Right?"

Lynn smiled. "Okay. I'll just get my stuff out to the truck. Sometimes when I'm nervous, I forget something important. Then poor Gypsy looks awful in halter class."

"She won't today, not with both of us putting a shine on her. Do you have detangler for her mane and tail? Instant shampoo? Whitener for her socks? Hoof polish?"

Lynn nodded. "I'll add them to my groom kit. You mean it's okay to take that stuff with me?"

"It sure is." Sean's attention appeared to be on the nameplate he was fastening to the cantle. "You need to give your pony a final going-over before she enters the show ring."

"I hope this judge isn't a stickler for conformation," Elinor said. "Some judges forget all 4-H kids don't have parents with unlimited money."

"Good point." Sean finished screwing down the nameplate. "Who is the judge, Lynn?"

"Brigid Dawson. I got a third from her in trail class at the Monroe fair. I think she's good," Lynn said.

"Is she related to Clancy?" Elinor asked.

Sean nodded. "Clancy's older sister and one of the better 4-H judges. If you perform well, she'll give you the high ribbon."

"Yeah," Jake agreed. "There was a kid in blue jeans in Lynn's class at the fair. He rode great, but he didn't have a silver saddle or fancy chaps, and he still got Grand Champion."

"I forgot about that." Elinor tucked a sandwich into a plastic baggie. "I admired the judge for having the courage of her convictions. She caught hell from a lot of the parents when their kids didn't perform well. She told them that disposable income didn't make good riders. Practice on the horses did."

Jake drained the last of his juice. "But you were the one who told that kid's mom where to look for outgrown show gear. Then if he got to the state fair, he'd have a better shot with the other kind of judges. That was great, too, Mom."

"I'm glad you think so," Elinor said. "It was the right thing to do." She glanced at the clock—almost seven. She eyed her daughter. "Better hustle."

"Okay." Finishing her oatmeal, Lynn headed back toward her room. "Jake, you've got carrot duty today. Sandy's bringing ice, but you're the one who has to put out the carrots in the cooler."

"What's with the carrots?" Sean asked.

"The kids sell them to customers," Elinor said. "Three carrots for a dollar, or one for fifty cents. The farm provides the ice, which Sandy picks up on her way to work, and I buy a 25-pound sack of carrots every week at the grocery, or the produce stand until we have fresh ones from the garden."

"And that comes out of the sales?" Sean asked.

"No way," Jake said. "Mom says our chores cover that, but since we still get paid for those, I'm amazed at her bookkeeping skills."

"Come on, smarty," Elinor said, "Lynn needs your help. And I'm the mom. I can do what I want."

Sean chuckled. "I just hope we both want the same thing." He winked at her

The heat in her cheeks intensified, and she urged Jake out of the kitchen. She followed him to his room. She switched on the lights, drew back the curtains, and checked out the closet. "No monsters, honey."

Jake sighed with relief. "Thanks, Mom. They usually leave at daylight, but I still worry."

She hugged him. "Hey, it's my job to drive off monsters. Now, get dressed. You can help me send Lynn and Sean off to the show. Then we've got a pony farm to run."

"Can I boss people around?" Jake asked.

"Only if they forget how we do things here," Elinor said, grateful Sandy and Marcie, the teenage guides, were so patient. "But I get to boss around Clancy, okay?"

"Yeah. It's her first day. I'll only straighten her out if she does something dangerous and you're not there to fix it."

"Works for me." Elinor dropped a kiss on top of his hair and returned to the kitchen. She refilled Sean's coffee cup and topped her own. "What time will Clancy be here?"

"Between seven-thirty and eight. She has to help feed the stock and do her share to get the Lazy B organized before she drives down from eastern Liberty Valley." Sean tightened the last screw on the stirrup. "She wanted you to make some notes for her, the names of the students, where they are in their lessons, and their horses' names."

Elinor nodded. "Already done. I do that for Penny, so she knows what to cover in the lessons. I teach several of our riders during the week. I can look at a student and see what's needed to improve his or her skills." She took a deep breath and met his gaze. "I understand why you think I need to be at the show for Lynn, but I have to be here, too. Otherwise, I won't take in any money. Supporting my children comes first."

He stood and came toward her. He gently slipped his hands along the sides of her neck and stroked her cheekbones with his thumbs. "I talked when I should have listened last night. I'm not perfect."

She rose on tiptoe to touch her mouth to his. "Neither am I. Do you think two not-perfect people can be friends?"

"More than that, darlin'." He lowered his head.

The kiss took on new passion. He tangled one hand in her hair and pulled her head back. This kiss was hungrier than any that had come before. Her curves melted into his lean, muscled strength. She'd never dreamed a kiss could cause so much excitement inside her. She'd only known him since Tuesday night. It was too soon to want to get him naked. She shouldn't obsess over him. He was a man. That was all.

She moaned, tipped her head back further so the angle changed on the kiss. She tasted the coffee he'd drunk and the faint mint of toothpaste. She put her arms around his neck, tried to get closer. She yearned to crawl inside him. The sharp tang of his lime aftershave made her dizzy.

One of his large hands cupped her breast. His thumb stroked her nipple into aching life. As the kisses continued, each one drew her further into the spell he cast. When he finally lifted his head, she let her hands slide down his chest. His heart thudded against her palm and she realized he wanted her as much as she desired him.

"I've got to go." His voice sounded as if it was dragged out of him. "But I want to take you to bed."

"Yes." She shook her head. "No. It's too soon."

"I'll change your mind."

TWELVE

THE MEMORY OF HIS KISSES HAUNTED HER THROUGH THE DAY. SHE sent out the trail rides, doing the mini-lessons that started each ride by rote. Luckily, nobody seemed aware of her distraction.

She liked Sean, but she hadn't expected this kind of physical attraction. Sex never had been important in her marriage. From early on, John seemed on a mission to destroy her self-esteem, pride, and ego. No, she was being dramatic. She'd lost herself in their marriage and only recently completed the journey back.

At least she had Lynn and Jake. She shuddered as she recalled the long-ago fight she had with John when he'd learned she was pregnant with Lynn. He demanded she get an abortion. His sister had come to Elinor's rescue and told John's parents about the pregnancy. They insisted he marry her if he wanted them to pay for law school.

As for Jake – Elinor refused to remember her son's conception. The last trail ride was out, but all the ponies weren't working.

She went into Lightning's stall. The gray Arab-Welsh nosed his manger as he searched for leftover scraps from lunch. "Don't worry... dinner's coming." She stroked his neck. "You won't miss a meal again, not here."

Stepping to his left side, she began to unfasten the latigo that tied on the western saddle. She glanced up as Clancy came into the barn, leading Rebel and Bonanza.

"How did the last lesson go?" Elinor was still stunned by the tall redhead's friendliness. In contrast, the women John dated before, during and after their marriage always treated Elinor as if she were Public Enemy Number One. She supposed it should have been expected. Was she as frigid as he'd said? Would Sean think so, too?

Suddenly, she realized she hadn't heard Clancy's response. "I'm sorry. Did you have any trouble with the students?"

"Nope." Clancy moved with a slow, languorous grace. "And I didn't say anything." She locked Rebel into his stall with an affectionate pat on the bay's neck. "Nice kids, for the most part. The last girl, Natalie, tried some attitude. It didn't get her anywhere. She stopped."

Elinor blinked. Since the kid had been turned away by six other instructors, Elinor had decided to give Natalie a chance. But the girl and Penny were at loggerheads most Saturdays, and Elinor ended up teaching Natalie herself rather than send her to a different stable.

"The girl's born-again rude," Elinor agreed. "But she has good hands, the lightest I've seen since Lynn's. Natalie never kicks her horse and she told me flat-out she wouldn't ride with a crop or spurs on the first day. She always remembers her carrots. Of course, she also told Jake his carrot prices were a rip-off."

"He likes her, too." Clancy grinned. "He took her into the stall to meet Awesome and he told the rest of the students they could look but not touch the colt. Your son is going to be a good rider once he learns to focus."

"I'm glad you can teach him." Elinor swung Lightning's saddle and pads onto the half-door. "He distracts me with questions. I get so busy telling him how things work, I forget he's supposed to learn equitation."

"I noticed." Clancy led Bonanza to his stall and began to untack the strawberry roan, frequently stopping to pet the stocky,

Welsh gelding. "I told him to save his questions for the end of class and I'd answer them all at once."

"Did it work?"

"Hey, I've been teaching kids to ride since I was twelve. I must have learned something in the last sixteen years." Clancy was quiet for a moment. "I like the cards you have on your stalls. I'm going to do the same thing at our place. Our horses know where they live, but it confuses the customers who don't know their names or places."

Elinor smiled. "Help yourself to any of my ideas. If I get a chance to visit your place, I'll probably borrow a ton of yours. You know how horse people are. We steal from each other to make our barns better."

"You're welcome to anything you can use," Clancy said. "Your stud's a little sweetheart. Most pony stallions are obnoxious, but Paragon's a dream."

"I didn't know he was a stud." Elinor shrugged. "I taught him to lead, stand, stop on whoa, be groomed, saddled, clipped, wormed, the works. I didn't take any crap from him. If I'd known he was a stallion, he'd have frightened me, and I wouldn't have taught him manners."

"Well, as Jake would say, Paragon's awesome." Clancy straightened Bonanza's thick, golden forelock. "You're a good trainer. I wanted to ask if you'd lend me Paragon for the summer. I could breed him to our pony mares and break him to ride for you."

Elinor opened her mouth, but Clancy held up her hand. "With a kid, not me. And I'll lend you a couple well-trained geldings for the season in return. Star and Taffy are close to foaling, aren't they?"

"Yes, sometime within the next month." Elinor considered the offer. "Why not? Doctor Art doesn't want to geld Paragon before September when it cools off."

"There's less chance of infection then." Clancy paused, then added, "Sean's like a brother to me. I hope he told you that. Did he tell you about my fiancé?"

Elinor hesitated. "He said the guy broke your engagement."

"It was mutual. We had a big fight, but I want him back." Clancy eyed Elinor hopefully. "If you tell Sean I've started to date, he'll pass the word."

Elinor felt an immense pity for the younger woman. "On one condition, Clancy. You've got to actually date and look for a good guy. It's better to have a broken engagement than a broken marriage. I should know."

"You sound like my mom." Clancy sighed. "All right. But you've got to come with me and my sisters tonight. We're going line dancing and checking out the weekend cowboys. Maybe I'll find a replacement for the loser."

"That's the spirit." Elinor carried Lightning's saddle to the tack room. "I'll talk to Sandy and see if she'll stay with Lynn. Jake's going to his buddy's place for the night."

"I forgot to ask if you and Sean had plans. Do you?"

"We haven't made any. We just met Tuesday night. It's not a real relationship yet."

"He wants more." Clancy followed with Bonanza's gear. "And unlike my loser, Sean doesn't want to hear he's rushing it."

"He'll have to get used to it."

———

When they finished the evening stock chores, she and Clancy headed for the house. "I do appreciate you filling in today."

"You've already said that three times." Clancy smiled. "I'll talk to Mom and Audra about buying the other half of the steer when you butcher. You can call me to teach again, but your students are ready for a schooling show. I'll even judge it, especially since you're helping me get back the zombie."

"Did I say that?" Elinor teased, waving goodbye to Sandy as the college student headed for her car. "Or did I tell you to get your act together?"

An empty red horse-hauler pulled into the parking lot and Elinor went to meet Marlene. "Hi. Where's Lynn and Sean?"

"They'll be along." Marlene turned off the truck engine. "Sean helped Lynn all day. They were stopping for pizza and ice cream. Wait till you see how well Lynn did. She deserves to be proud of herself."

Climbing down from the rig, Marlene headed over to hug Clancy. "How are you doing, honey? How's Kate?"

"She's fine, Aunt Marlene." Clancy hugged the older woman back. "So am I. Elinor's going to help us get back the loser and the quitter."

Marlene rumpled Clancy's red hair. "Both those boys have names. Now, you and Katie stop picking on them, and teach them to suck eggs. They shouldn't have dumped either of you, especially so close to the wedding. It's hard enough arranging one ceremony, but your momma and Audra worked their tails off to make a double wedding happen on Valentines' Day at the Lazy B."

"You helped them a lot," Clancy said. "I know you're right. Audra and Brigid are upset, too."

"How many Dawson girls are there? Four?" Elinor asked.

"Six. The twins are in college. And we all look alike," Clancy said. "All red-haired with big boobs, bigger butts and taller than most of the guys in the county."

"Quit griping about your hourglass figure." Elinor said. "You've never had to shop in the pre-teen section when you're a grown woman."

Marlene laughed. "Sounds like she has your number. What are you girls going to do to get back the boys?"

"I'll tell you the same thing I told Clancy." Elinor gave Marlene a stern look. "Men are like buses. Another will be along in a half-hour. She won't go after the loser. She'll find somebody decent. And we're starting tonight. All of us are going line-dancing and checking out the available hunks."

Marlene whistled softly. "That should do it." She patted Clancy's shoulder. "Honey, you'd better head for home and get dolled up if you're going hunting. Tell Kate I agree with Elinor. Best cure for one man is another, especially if you've got somebody to help you rub the first guy's nose in it."

Elinor stamped her boot in the gravel. "Marlene, don't encourage her. It's much better to break your engagement than to lose your husband to some bimbo lawyer in his office."

Marlene adopted her wise-woman look. "Especially when you don't care about your husband?"

"Oh, stuff it!" Elinor headed back to the barn. She'd been grateful when John finally left. As for the bimbo, the woman had the influence John wanted to advance him in his career. If she hadn't, he'd have played it safe and remained in his marriage.

And made me and the kids miserable for another eight years until I got the guts to throw him out.

Marlene came into the barn. "I shouldn't have said that. I never liked John Price. I didn't think he was good enough for you or the kids."

Elinor went inside Lightning's stall to groom the pony. "Knowing you, it was Lynn and Jake who influenced you the most, Marlene."

"And you." Marlene checked the feed in the manger. "I get attached to my kids' parents, Elinor. Roy used to say it was because we weren't blessed with chicks of our own, so I had to mother the world. And I want my nieces to be happy, with good men."

Elinor nodded. "What about Clancy's ex-fiancé?"

"He loves her. He's being stupid. He's got sixteen years on her and worries he's too old for her. He doesn't think Clancy knows what's best for her. But that child was born knowing it."

"And Kate?" Elinor moved to brush Lightning's right side. "What's her story?"

"She has her mother's and my temper. We tend to throw fits first and think later."

"Maybe they'll still work things out." Elinor hoped she sounded positive. "My grandparents didn't let me have friends my own age. I couldn't do the things they did like slumber parties or dances at school."

"Little wonder you ran off with Price." Marlene picked up the dandy brush and started on Lightning's left side, ignoring the pony's attempts to bite her. "Was he your first boyfriend?"

Elinor grimaced. "I wouldn't call him that. I slept with him because I thought it'd make him love me. He said I got pregnant to trap him."

"I always thought he was a jackass."

Jake hurried into the barn. "Marlene, guess what? Sandy helped me train Awesome today. We brushed him and everything. We even picked his hooves."

"Now, I call that awesome," Marlene teased. "You're going to have a great horse there."

"And guess what else? Clancy says we're having two more baby horses. Is that *magick* or what?"

"I'd say so," Marlene agreed with a grin.

"Clancy and I have a plan for Paragon." Elinor glanced at the corner stall and the flashy young bay.

"Sounds like he had a plan of his own."

Elinor glowered at the 4-H leader and tried to hide her own amusement while she continued brushing Lightning. It was humorous. Instant ponies. Just add Paragon to the pasture, stir in a mare or two and wait eleven months.

"Where is Clancy?" Jake asked, looking around.

"She went home," Marlene answered. "She and your mom are going out tonight, and Clancy didn't want to look like she'd been working all day."

"Mom, you're going to get dressed up, too, aren't you?"

"Yes, honey." Elinor waited for the next question, sure there would be one.

"You're going to let Lynn choose your dress-up clothes, aren't you?" Jake rested his arms on the top of the stall door.

"I can dress myself," Elinor said firmly. "I did last night when we went to Parents' Night, didn't I?"

"Yes, but if you're going out with Clancy, you've gotta look hot," Jake said. "And you dressed like a mom last night."

"I *am* a mom. And I'm proud to be one. But I'll dress up tonight, okay?"

"Yes," Jake said, satisfied. "You have to play hard to get with Sean, Mom. Otherwise, he won't think he's lucky to have us."

"Oh, really? And what are you, young man? The matchmaker of the universe?"

"No, I am." Marlene laughed. "Scoot, Jake. Thanks for the help."

"You're welcome." Jake turned away, going to check on Chipeta and Awesome. "This was my idea, too, you know, Marlene."

"We know," Elinor said, glaring after her son. "Believe me, *I* know."

THIRTEEN

TEN MINUTES LATER, AS THEY WALKED TOWARD THE HOUSE, Sean's truck pulled into the drive. Elinor saw Lynn waving a blue ribbon through the windshield. Sudden guilt mixed with self-pity.

I should have been there.

She hurried to the pickup. Lynn tumbled out, chattering about halter class, doing the perfect pattern, and having the cleanest pony at the show according to the judge. Elinor listened to the story repeatedly while they took care of Gypsy. Lynn told it again while they ate pizza and then twice more through dessert, homemade banana splits.

When her excitement faded for a moment, Jake spoke up. "Clancy says we're having two more foals. She's nice. She taught me to trot. She says only dudes or people riding English trot fast. Cowboys trot slow. Me and Galaxy did it perfect."

"I'm impressed." Lynn beamed at her brother. "Soon, you'll be going to shows with me. Who else is pregnant?"

"Star and Taffy. Clancy says you can help me train their foals."

"Great." Lynn's smile widened. "I'm glad you had a good day, too."

"It's not over yet." Jake jumped to his feet. "I gotta get ready.

Bobby's dad will be here soon." He started toward his room, then stopped. "Mom, I brought in the mail. I put it on your desk."

"Thanks, honey." She flicked a glance toward Sean. She felt as if she might drown in the warmth of his gray eyes. *Take it nice and easy*, she thought. She eyed Lynn and saw the girl yawn. "Looks like your day wore you out, too."

Lynn nodded, eyelids drooping. "I forgot to give Gypsy her extra carrots."

"Jake did it for you." Elinor stood. "Lynn, will you be okay if Sandy stays with you this evening?"

Lynn shrugged. "Sure. Are you and Sean going out?"

He leaned back in the chair. "Are we?"

Elinor enjoyed his lazy smile. "Well, I am. I don't know about you. Clancy invited me to go line-dancing with her and her sisters. I understand we're on a mission to find cute guys."

"That will raise hell on the home-front," Sean warned. "The Dawson girls aren't supposed to date other guys."

"They aren't nuns."

"Elinor's right. It's time for those boys to grow up." Marlene began to help clear the table. "I'll stick around until Sandy gets here. Why don't you get ready?"

Elinor hesitated. "I hate to take advantage."

"I'll tell you when you do. Scoot, honey."

Before Elinor could leave, Sean stepped in front of her. "What is it?" she asked.

"I can do cute better than some drugstore cowboy and I'm a good dancer." His jaw tightened. "I'll show you next Saturday."

She choked back an appreciative grin. "Say please."

"Don't push it, girl." He bent down and kissed her quickly. "I'm trying to give you time. I'm not losing what's mine."

She tossed her head. "I'm not yours."

"Not yet."

He sat on the porch and contemplated the sunset. It'd been a damn good day until she told him she was going out with the girls. He'd hoped to get her into bed tonight. Now, he'd have to settle for another cold shower.

A familiar car stopped in the drive. Three men piled out, his two older brothers and Art Watkins.

"Get 'em," Sean ordered his dogs. "Go earn your dog food."

The five blue heelers on the porch leaped to obey. In silent threat, they raced toward the intruders.

"Figured we'd bring the poker game to you." Ethan strolled toward Sean, ignoring the two blue heelers nipping at his ankles. "What's up? You look like you lost your best friend."

"Can't be much." Gavin glanced up from where he was petting the other dogs. "Boy's home."

"I wouldn't be if it weren't for you." Sean stood. He idly debated which one he wanted to punch first.

"Simmer down." Art opened a brown paper sack and handed over an ice-cold beer. "What'd they do?"

"They didn't get married."

"Does that still have your tail feathers on fire?" Ethan took a beer. "You already tried beating me up, boy. It's my business. And Gavin's."

"Not anymore," Sean said. "I met a gal last week. She's funny, sweet, and spunky as hell. I figured on spending tonight with her and her kids."

"Why don't you?" In blue jeans, a flannel shirt, and hiking boots, Gavin didn't look much like a university professor who taught reluctant freshman the joys of Shakespeare. "Go already. We won't miss you when you're in one of your snarly moods."

Art sat down on the porch steps. "When I was there to examine the colt, I thought she was interested. Her boy seems stuck on you. What happened?"

"The Dawsons." Sean popped his beer. He watched Gavin straighten, worry seeping into his eyes. "Kate got a job breaking rodeo rejects in Montana and she's leaving tomorrow. Clancy hauled my gal Elinor off with them to go honky-tonking. I offered to go along, but Kate turned me down. Says they can't find cute cowboys if I'm around."

Fury turned Ethan's silver eyes to ice. "Say what, boy?"

"You heard me. Clancy says she's looking for a young guy with a libido. What happened last Thursday?"

"None of your business," Ethan rumbled.

"Yeah, right." Sean concentrated on the beer. "The Dawson women are laughing about it. You're a joke all over Liberty Valley, big brother."

"Sounds like we both are." Gavin came to join them on the porch. He leaned against the porch rail. "Kate knows how I feel about her training the rough ones. She's button-pushing."

"Yup." Art studied his beer bottle and began to peel the label. "You boys don't have to stand up now. Be like me. Let your pride rule your lives the way I did after my first wife died. Keep your mouths shut and allow the second woman you love to marry a no-good, rat bastard. Then when he leaves her with four little girls while she's pregnant with two more, you can try to pick up the pieces. And damn near twenty years later, I'm still trying, and she still won't take the risk."

"Where are they?" Ethan asked.

"I don't know," Sean said. "They wouldn't tell me. Fearless is ticked. She says my brothers are afraid to get hitched. And my track record's not much better. How do I convince Elinor I can keep a commitment?"

"Early to be thinking along those lines, isn't it?" Art asked. "You haven't known the gal long."

"Some things don't need all the thought folks want to give them."

"Well, be sure the goin' up is worth the comin' down," Ethan advised.

"With her, it will be," Sean said.

"Good." Art ran a hand through his thick, white hair. "Love can be a rocky trail, but it's always a pretty ride."

Sunday morning, Elinor woke in time to meet Lynn and Sandy at the breakfast table. While she drank her first cup of coffee, she described the decor and music at the country western bar. "I learned to two-step. It was fun."

Sandy giggled. "Did Clancy find a new guy?"

"I don't think she's serious," Elinor admitted. "But she attracted a lot of attention. So did Kate."

"Good. Tell Sean next time you see him." Sandy finished her muffin. "I've got to go. I promised the folks I'd meet them for brunch. Be back later for trail rides."

"We'll have to hustle, too," Elinor said. "Lynn, will you call Viv and tell her we'll meet them at church?"

"She'll remember. We always get Jake there when he spends the night with Bobby."

"I know. Call anyway. It's courteous."

As soon as they arrived at the church, Elinor spotted her son and Bobby. She waved at Vivian and Harold, who were behind the boys. Vivian wore a blue skirt and jacket. She'd coiled her blond hair into a neat bun. Elinor admired the way the other woman carried herself, grace on high heels.

Vivian looked like the perfect example of the professional woman. It never surprised anyone to learn she was considered the best child psychologist in western Washington.

In contrast, Harold, who was a divorce attorney, opted for beige walking shorts, a brightly patterned Hawaiian shirt, socks, and sandals. Waist-length graying black hair was confined in a ponytail.

John hadn't had much respect for Harold until they went to court. During the divorce proceedings, the aging hippie proved his own abilities as a lawyer, taking John for every cent he hated to pay.

Elinor smiled as Bobby raced over, followed by Jake. "How are you guys today? Did you sleep at all?"

"Sure," Bobby said.

At the same time, Jake said, "A little."

Elinor smoothed her son's sandy cowlick. "Well, you can rest today."

"Maybe, if I get too tired," Jake agreed and pulled her aside. "Can Bobby stay over next Saturday?"

Elinor began to agree in automatic reflex, then recalled she had a date with Sean. She didn't like to leave more than her two kids with a babysitter, although Bobby was a sweetheart.

"How about the one after that?" Elinor murmured softly. "Will it fit into your schedules?"

Jake nodded and hurried back to his best friend. "Come on. Let's go ask your mom."

The two were gone in the next heartbeat and Elinor followed with Lynn. They joined Harold and Vivian on the steps.

"Sounds like they had a good night," Elinor said.

"Jake's sharp," Harold agreed. "Only kid I know who likes to read my law books."

"Penny's rebelling again." Vivian shook her head, amusement in her eyes. "This week's she decided she's not going to college."

"She'll change her mind." Elinor considered mentioning that the teenager had cancelled on her job at the last minute and decided to wait. "Penny told me she wants to be a veterinarian and specialize in large animals. She always helps me take care of the ponies when they're sick. Art Watkins says she's a bright kid."

"I hope he doesn't call her a kid," Harold said. "She's almost seventeen and all grown up. I've heard that a lot this past week."

"I said that when I was her age." Elinor paused, remembering the way she'd failed most of her classes. Her maternal grandparents sent her to live with her father's side of the family for the last two years of high school to keep her away from John Price. It hadn't worked. She went back to him as soon as she returned home. "I made some big mistakes when I was sixteen."

"Who doesn't? It takes too long to learn how much we don't know," Vivian said. "And our parents really aren't stupid."

"Speak for yourself." Harold winked. "I have it on Penny's authority that I'm as dumb as a rock."

Lynn giggled. "Yeah, but she's lucky to have a dad who cares."

"That's it." Harold draped his arm around Lynn's shoulders. "I'm keeping this girl. Your mom can have Penny. Even trade."

Elinor smiled. She followed the two with Vivian. "He's a good man."

"I think so, but I've spent twenty-five years training him." Vivian elbowed Elinor. "I heard you found a guy, too. One who kisses you? I'm shocked."

Heat flooded into Elinor's cheeks. "That's it. You can have both my kids forever and put them through college."

Vivian laughed. "Now, tell me all about it. You and Sean Killian? I drool whenever he comes to shoe the horses. All those muscles. And is he flexible! He could give a dancer lessons. Girl, you're so lucky."

"We're in church." Elinor choked out the protest.

Vivian leaned close and whispered, "Honey, who do you think created love? And sex?"

FOURTEEN

WHEN THEY RETURNED TO THE FARM, A BOUQUET OF GOLDEN daffodils and a box of chocolate covered nuts waited for Elinor on the kitchen table. "What's this?"

"It's for you!" Jake danced around her. "Did we really surprise you? Didn't you understand what Reverend Bill said about showing people how you feel all the time and not waiting for special occasions?"

"I'm amazed." Elinor touched one of the yellow blooms, wondering what had prompted the gift. Was it because of the horse show yesterday, or the colt, or even Sean Killian's arrival in their lives? While she didn't doubt her children's love, they rarely showered her with gifts. "How did you arrange this?"

"Sean helped us," Lynn said. "He had to buy Marlene a birthday present yesterday, so I shopped when we went to the store. It was my best horseshow day ever and you're always doing stuff for us."

"And we hid the flowers and candy in my room and Lynn told me she brought them out when you went to start the truck today," Jake told her. "Are you happy, Mom?"

"Thrilled." Elinor hugged both kids. "This is the best surprise ever."

"Mom, you say that every time we give you anything," Lynn scolded. "But this is the first time we could buy you presents in ages."

"Before, we never had anyone to take us to the store. And we couldn't ask you to drive us or it wouldn't be really from us."

"Well, I think all of you are awesome." Elinor held them tight and tried not to cry. "Let's break into the chocolate and spoil our lunches."

"It's for you, Mom." Lynn's tone was stern. "You don't have to share."

"Unless you want," Jake added.

———

The telephone rang late that evening while she folded laundry. Elinor answered it, praying none of the ponies were loose on the highway again. "Silver Lake Pony Ranch."

"Relax, darlin'. It's me, Sean."

"Sorry, I thought it was an emergency."

"Only if missing you counts." He chuckled. "How was your day? Did the kids surprise you? It meant a lot to them."

"I was flabbergasted," Elinor admitted. "Thanks for helping them. What about you? Did you visit Marlene today?"

"Actually, I just got home from taking her to dinner," Sean said. "I made reservations at the Space Needle. It's her favorite place."

"I'll bet she loved it. Do you take your mom to her favorite restaurant on her birthday too?" The silence grew, lengthened, until she had to break it. "Come on, Sean. What about your mother? What do you do for her?"

"Okay, you win. I'll tell you if you tell me. I give my biological mother what she wants, peace, quiet, and distance, which isn't that hard since my father's career is what she lives for. Now, where's yours?"

"Dead. She died of a drug overdose when I was six. What about your father?" Elinor asked. "Do you avoid him, too?"

"I don't have to since he's a Senator and he spends most of the year back in the other Washington. He's always been too busy with his political career to have kids. Lucky for me, I had Ethan. What about your dad? Where is he?"

"He was a soldier. He died in Grenada," Elinor said. "My mother's parents raised me for the most part. What does your mom do?"

"My mother is a politician's wife and does whatever she needs to do to keep the old man serving this wonderful state of Washington. Marlene Dawson is more of a mom to me than mine."

"Sounds like you have some issues," Elinor said.

"And you don't?" Sean changed the subject. "I called to see if you wanted me to go with you to the Lazy B to choose those ponies Clancy wants to lend you."

"I'd like that." Elinor said, "but as friends, nothing more."

"You're scared. You can't kiss me like you do and then yell *Whoa*."

"Oh, yes I can." She struggled to sound disdainful. "It's not like I haven't been with a man before. I was married."

"To a guy who couldn't teach you the difference between geldings and stallions."

Her face warmed and she was grateful he couldn't see it. "I haven't even known you for a week. And I won't fall into bed with you."

"Good. If you were that kind of woman, I wouldn't want you. Now, what about an answer to my question? Shall we go to the Dawsons' on Friday night?"

"Only if it's not a date. It's two friends looking at horses."

"Not a problem, darlin'. I can do nice and easy. Can you?"

It would be hard to keep her hands off the man. No way would she tell him that. Before she admitted it, she heard a child crying. "Call me tomorrow. I've got to go! Jake's having a nightmare."

She hung up and ran into Jake's room, switching on the light. "Wake up, honey. Mom's here." She shook him awake.

At her touch, Jake opened his eyes. He threw himself into her arms. "It was awful."

"What?" She sat on the edge of the bed, stroking his hair. "Monsters again?"

"Worse. I dreamed Awesome died. Don't let him, Mom."

"I won't." Now wasn't the time for a discussion about all the things that killed horses, who were surprisingly fragile animals despite their size. Her son didn't need a dose of reality right now.

"You're silly, Jake."

Elinor turned to see Lynn in the doorway, leaning on the door-jamb. "Nothing's happening to your colt." The girl sat down on the bed. "Unless the two of you beat me when you start showing him. Then I'll have to thump both of you."

"If you hurt Awesome, I'll put frogs and snakes in your bed."

Elinor hugged her daughter, too. "Let's go out to the barn and check on the ponies. Then Jake will know both Chipeta and Awesome are safe."

"Good idea." Lynn put her arm around Jake. "I'd never really hurt your horses." Then she got to her feet. "I'll be right back," she called over her shoulder.

Elinor waited while he dressed. "Sometimes, your mind can pick up messages."

"Like an answering machine?"

"Sort of," she said. "If something is wrong, you may have a feeling you need to be somewhere else. One night, your father and I were at a party. Suddenly, I knew I had to get home. When I got here, I discovered Lynn had broken her arm. The babysitter couldn't get through to me on the phone."

"I remember that. The cab driver took us to the emergency room because you didn't know how to drive. After that, you took classes and got your license and bought the truck. Boy, was *he* mad."

She knew she should correct the use of the pronoun where John was concerned, but somehow, she lacked the strength. "I always thought it was good I came home early. After you check on Awesome, and know he's okay, you'll be able to sleep."

"I think Lynnie was more upset because *he* didn't come. I mean *he* always acted like she was the most important one in the family. I knew *he* was faking, but she didn't."

Why did her son understand people so easily? She still had a difficult time grasping motivations. She'd just gained more insight into her daughter's character in the last five minutes than she had in the past six years.

"I know you miss your father, Jake. Why are you calling him 'he,' and not 'Dad'?"

"*He* isn't my dad, not anymore. I gave *him* away."

A son couldn't give away his father like a rejected toy. Reluctantly, she chose to postpone the issue. If she brought it up now, Jake would have a thousand questions.

The trip to the barn proved successful. Chipeta quietly munched hay while Awesome slept in the back of the stall. The chestnut mare stamped a warning hoof and pinned her ears back when she saw Elinor and Lynn, greeting Jake with a low nicker before nuzzling him.

Once the boy was convinced, she and Awesome were all right, Jake was ready to return to his own bed. Elinor smiled when he fell asleep on top of the blankets. Shifting the covers, she tucked her son in. She brushed a kiss over his forehead.

Turning on the small lamp on the nightstand, she left the room. Maybe the light would prevent more nightmares. She'd get a nightlight for him the next time she went shopping.

Lynn had just climbed back into bed when Elinor came into her room. "Thank you, honey. I think you helped your brother cope with his fears."

"Someone has to. Otherwise, he'll move out to the barn and live with his ponies."

Elinor smiled and smoothed the blankets over her daughter.

"Don't suggest that to him." She paused. "Sean called. He wants to take me up to see the Dawsons' ponies next Friday. We're going to borrow two of them to get through the season since Star and Taffy are in foal. Maybe you and Jake could come along. I'll need someone to ride the ponies."

"We can't. I have another show on Saturday. Marlene will pick up me and Gypsy."

"Oh, I'm sorry. I forgot about the show. I'll reschedule with Sean. I wasn't much help for you this week getting ready, not when there was Parents' Night and Penny cancelled."

"You don't need to reschedule, Mom. Just call Sandy. She'll stay with us and help me with Gypsy. Go with Sean. By yourself."

Elinor kissed her daughter's forehead. "Okay, I'll show you and your brother I'm not a total wimp. I will go out with Sean by myself."

"Good for you, Mom. We'll be proud of you. He's a fun guy. I had the best horse show ever with him yesterday."

———

The telephone rang while Elinor was getting the kids off to school. "Silver Lake Pony Ranch. Can I help you?"

"Good morning. How's Jake? All over his bad dream?"

"He's fine today. Thanks for asking." She grinned at the kids. "It's Sean."

"Tell him hi," Jake said. "Are we still going fishing on Thursday?"

"I'll check," Elinor promised. "The fishing trip? Is it still on? Jake wants to know."

"You bet. Jake and I will catch something for dinner. It may turn out to be pizza." Sean chuckled. "Are you arranging for him to do math with Lynn's teacher today?"

"Yes. I'm taking them to school so I can do that and start volunteering in his class when I'm not substituting."

"Great. He'll love it. On a different subject, I was out shoeing for Bonnie Fitzwilliams yesterday. She said to tell you the office staff would be ready to give you a pass and help in any way you needed. She said she sicced Frank Senior on them."

Elinor laughed. "She seemed very *take charge* when I met her."

"That's Bonnie." Sean sounded cheerful. "She and Ethan dated for a while. It was a match made in hell. They're both complete control freaks, and they couldn't figure out which of them was going to be boss. I was glad when our Fearless Leader put Bonnie and Frank together."

"Are Bonnie and Frank really happy? Debbie seemed to think so on Friday night."

"Oh, Frank's a good guy. He lets Bonnie think she's the head honcho and then he runs his whole family, his construction company, the school board and the local Scout group."

"I thought I'd call and arrange to meet with her after I volunteered today," Elinor said.

"That was her idea, too." Sean chuckled. "Just don't get so busy with Bonnie and Clancy that you forget about me."

"It'd be impossible." Elinor felt her cheeks burn at his sexy laugh. How did she handle this? *By striking back.* "Good horseshoers are hard to find, even if they do have egos bigger than indoor arenas."

"Spitfire." He sounded amused. "I'll bring along a year's contract for you to sign. I don't want another man touching what's mine."

"My horses belong to me."

"I wasn't talking about them," Sean said. "Fuss and stomp all you like, missy. You'll be mine when the dust settles."

"No way." Her voice trembled. What was wrong with her? All she could think of was his touch, his kiss and she'd told him she didn't want that. *Liar.*

"Catch you later. Start thinking of all the nasty things you want to say. They turn me on."

She shivered but managed an icy tone. "As if I care what interests you." She sniffed. "You're replaceable."

"Good start, darlin'. I can't wait to hear more."

FIFTEEN

When he arrived that afternoon, Elinor was unloading groceries. Jake and Lynn were off at their friends' houses and she didn't know whether to be glad or upset.

Despite his leisurely stroll, Sean was able to take the grocery bags from her before she moved away from the pickup. She drew a ragged breath. "What are you doing here?"

"I told you." He stroked his thumb over her lips. "I brought the contract for you to sign. Now, ask me to kiss you."

"Go to hell."

He grinned. "Close enough." His mouth teased hers.

She tangled her arms around his neck and found his lips with hers. The kiss seemed to set her body on fire.

When he lifted his head, she met his gaze. "How many ways do I have to tell you I'm not interested?" Her question was meant as an insult, at odds with her behavior. "I may want you, but it's just physical."

He nipped her ear. "Wait till you see what I can do with physical." He nibbled his way down the line of her jaw.

If he'd put his hands on her instead of holding the bags of groceries, it would have been difficult to leave. She grabbed the last two sacks. "Come on. I'll look at your contract in the house."

She glanced over her shoulder as he followed her. "Can't you keep up with me?"

"Then I'd miss the way you fill out a pair of jeans. I can't wait to get you in bed." He whistled softly. "Of course, it doesn't have to be a bed. I'll take you anywhere I can get you."

"You aren't original. John and I had sex in his car."

"Fair enough." Sean's tone darkened. "But we're not having sex, baby." He put down the bags he carried on the kitchen table.

That jolted her. "What?"

"When I have you, we'll make love." He caught up with her and threaded his hand into her hair. "And you'll enjoy it."

She moistened suddenly dry lips. "You must think you're something."

"I know I am." He kissed her. "And you'll know it, too." His mouth captured hers again.

She still tasted his kiss a few minutes later as she brewed coffee and put out store-bought cookies. He'd insisted on putting away the groceries for her. John always ignored household chores as if they were done by an assortment of Jake's elves. Little wonder Sean fascinated her. He was the opposite of every man she'd known.

No, he wasn't. A sudden memory hit. When she stayed with the Talbots, her father's family, her grandfather had always jumped in to help with chores and insisted everyone else do so. He'd said teamwork was part of being a family.

Elinor shifted her gaze from Sean as he slid a box of cereal into the cupboard. She eyed the paperwork he'd left on the table. "Okay. Let's see what you think I'll sign."

His quick grin made her pulse jump. She sat down at the table and reached for the first page.

She wasn't stupid. She knew her ponies' and horses' welfare depended on consistent hoof care. She kept their hooves clean, fed supplements and vitamins to promote good hoof growth and applied pine-tar dressing when needed. If they had infections, she used bleach the way Mariah taught to clear it up.

Sean Killian was the best shoer she'd seen since she opened the pony farm, but she wouldn't tell him so. He was already too arrogant.

The first clause in the contract about not switching shoers made sense. A series of hoof-related disasters could close her business. She knew other stable owners worked lame animals, but not the reputable ones.

Sean had found a half-inch difference in Lightning's front hooves, and the gelding's angles were ten degrees apart. Sore feet didn't improve the pony's nasty attitude. All she could see was that he stumbled and tripped a lot. She hadn't known why until Sean had measured the hooves. A different shoer might undo all the good Sean had already done.

The second paragraph described the relationship she ought to have with her veterinarian, and Sean had to approve of the doctor. "Who do you think you are?" Elinor demanded. "I decide who treats my horses for medical problems. You don't."

"Why are you pitching a fit?" Sean poured two cups of coffee and brought her one. "Art's on my list. His associates aren't. By the time he slaps some horse knowledge into them, they leave."

She had to agree with that assessment. The last time Flicka had choke, one of the younger vets had recommended euthanizing the little Welsh mare before he had even tried treating her. The pony made a full recovery, but only because Elinor called Art and insisted he come to the farm. From that point on, she refused to allow his junior colleagues on her place.

She continued onto the next section of the contract. This one detailed the cleanliness of the animals. "No mud or dirt on the bellies, legs, or hooves? How could you shoe them if you can't see their feet? Who'd be stupid enough to expect you to shoe dirty horses?"

"The owner of Xanadu Arabians, for one. I had to take towels with me to dry the horses' legs every time. It was ridiculous considering he spends thousands of dollars for each one." Sean sipped his coffee. "It's better now that Audra Dawson manages the place."

"I'll bet." Elinor kept reading. "Lice? I keep chickens for the eggs and meat, but you won't find one louse on my ponies. My kids never had lice until they started public school. Mona told me lice were a normal part of childhood and I told her...."

"A lot," Sean said. "You'll never suffer fools in silence. I'll bet she felt like she'd been in an avalanche."

Elinor eyed Sean. He didn't sound intimidated by her tactics. She dismissed him with cool disdain. "Don't get any of *your* lice on *my* horses."

He howled with laughter. "Do it again. Say something snooty."

"I'm serious." She glared at him. "You visit all sorts of places. Don't bring lice or contagious diseases from those horses onto my farm."

He laughed harder. "I can't bear it." He strode to her. "I'll never make it through the whole contract."

"So, leave." She gestured to the door. "If I decide to sign this manifesto, I'll call you."

"No, you won't." She trembled when he brought her down on his lap. "How am I going to finish your silly paperwork now?"

"I'll tell you what it says. Trust me." He shifted and drew her closer.

Her thighs were on either side of his hips. She felt him harden against her. She sniffed. "So, talk. What else do I have to promise?"

One hand slipped up her back. With the other, he began to unfasten the pearl snaps of her blouse. "A clean, level, well-lit place to work."

"I can do that. If it rains, I have lights in the barn." Her nipples tightened. She bit back a moan when his hands cupped her breasts. "What else?"

"You're ready when I get here." He explored the tops of her breasts with slow kisses. "And you tell me what you want."

She squirmed. She ached with sudden longing. She whimpered. "Please."

"If you want shoes on a horse, say so. And if your stock needs training, tell me before I get started." He rubbed her nipples with his thumbs. "And…"

"Damn it." She unhooked the front closure of her bra. "Is everything else difficult for you, cowboy?"

He chuckled and flicked his tongue over one nipple. "You've got to tell me what you need, darlin'."

"Your hands on me." She couldn't believe she'd said the words.

"Where?"

"You know."

His fingers trailed across her hips. "Here?"

"No." She sighed, frustrated when he stopped. She grabbed his wrist and put his hand on her belt buckle. "Now do you have a clue? God, you're slow."

He grinned. "You'll like it my way. I want you on fire, not pretending."

How did he know so much about her? He brushed a kiss over her nipple, then took it into his mouth. She tangled her fingers into his thick brown hair, tried to bring him nearer.

Dimly, she heard the slam of the front door. "Mom, I'm home! Did Sean come to see Awesome?"

Elinor scrambled off Sean's lap. She managed to fasten her bra and button her shirt by the time Jake gained the kitchen, pretending to stare at the contract.

"I wanted to go over the shoeing contract with your mom. But I'd love to see Awesome."

"Don't you have a schedule to keep?" Elinor taunted. "I seem to remember timeframes being a big part of your contract."

Sean glanced at her, the look as intimate as a kiss. "We didn't finish, darlin'. We never got to what I'll provide."

She struggled to ignore the warmth in her face. "Spell it out."

"Later." Sean tousled Jake's sandy hair. "Let's go see Awesome. Your mom can wait."

She tried to breathe normally. "You'll wait, too."

On the way to the back door, Sean leaned down and whispered, "Hotter and sweeter. You're not ready yet, but soon." And then he was gone.

She was grateful Jake hadn't overheard. When Sean returned to the house, she'd take him aside and let him know she didn't want him. The last thing she needed in her life was a man. Especially a control freak like him.

No other shoer she had ever heard of had a five-page written contract. Who did Sean Killian think he was? She picked up the document. She'd let him have it when he came back. She could find another farrier.

It flustered her when Sean didn't return to the house. Instead, he apparently headed off for another shoeing appointment. He would come back the next night to continue the discussion.

"We'll see about that," Elinor said. "What if we have plans?"

"But we don't," Jake said. "I already knew that, so I told him to come." Distress filtered into the boy's face. "Was that wrong?"

"Of course not." Elinor hugged him. "I'm just in a crabby mood, honey. Sean teased me and I'm not good at jokes. Okay?"

"Yeah, but you like him. Right?" Jake asked. "He really likes you."

Elinor sighed. She murmured a soft agreement, relieved when her son accepted it. She wished her emotions were as simple to understand. She'd never craved a man's touch the way she did Sean's. And when he kissed her, she longed for more.

She'd be poised and nonchalant tomorrow. She'd freeze out Sean Killian whether he shod her horses or not.

———

She didn't get a chance. Sean arrived the next night with a bucket of fried chicken from the local fast food place for dinner. He was all business as he went over his part of the shoeing contract afterward.

"I'm already knowledgeable about hoof and leg anatomy," Sean said in answer to her question about one section of the contract. "I attend clinics and seminars to stay on top of new techniques."

"And I thought you knew it all." Elinor loaded the dishwasher. She glimpsed his barely suppressed grin. "What else?"

"Fair rates." He held out the salad bowl to her. "Good treatment of the horses. I won't ever hit, kick, or beat them."

"You'll live longer that way." Her tone glacial, she continued. "The hell with being wary of my horses. You'd better beware of their owner."

"Got it." He began to wipe off the counters with a clean dishrag. "I also answer all my clients' questions. I'm polite and I'll listen to your opinions even if I believe you're wrong."

"What about when I'm right?" She studied him as he washed off the kitchen table. "Will you admit it?"

"Sure. But I expect the same from you. And I want you to trust my judgment when it comes to the horses."

She nodded. "I can do that."

"I also guarantee to use gauges and measure each and every horse's hooves so the ponies can work right after their trims, and shoes are fitted as perfectly as possible," Sean said.

"Are you serious?" She closed the dishwasher and turned to stare at him. "I don't expect that. I know you did it the first time you worked on my stock. Once you get to know them, it's okay if you tell by looking."

"I've got news for you, darlin'. Nobody can tell if a horse's hooves are even to the correct degree without measuring." He came to join her. "And I take pride in knowing that the horses I shoe are level. If the hooves don't match, you'll end up with lameness or permanent injuries. And some owners can't tell if or when a horse favors one leg."

She gaped at him. She hadn't expected him to be so fussy.

"You've been shoeing for what? More than ten years? And you still don't have an eye for it?"

"Oh, I can guess." He tilted her chin with one hand. "But I want the exact, ideal result each and every time."

Despite her initial intentions, she tried to reach his mouth, but he held back. "What? Don't you want to kiss me?"

"Thought I had to guess, missy. We may not fit."

His mockery infuriated her. She wrenched away. "I have to put the kids to bed. I'll sign your damned contract and then you can leave."

"Works for me." He followed her to the desk. "By next week, you may be ready for me. We'll see."

She scrawled her name on the last page of the contract. "I want a copy of this mailed to me. And I don't want to see you before you come to shoe the horses in six weeks."

He chuckled. "We don't always get what we want. It's why I've got to wait for you to heat up." He caught her hand. "Walk me out, darlin'."

When they arrived at his truck, he gave her a huge teddy bear dressed as a cowboy from his front seat.

"What's this for?"

"Our one-week anniversary." Sean pushed back his hat with his thumb and winked at her. "I figure you can sleep with him until you sleep with me."

Tears stung. She took a ragged breath. "He's my kind of cowboy. He won't hog the covers."

"You'll change your mind. It's worth the wait."

He'd gotten to her, but she couldn't tell him. She started toward the house. Behind her, she heard a low whistle of admiration.

"Damn you," she muttered.

A tear fell onto the soft gray fur of the bear, but at least the toy wouldn't tell anyone. Another tear escaped.

———

Elinor went to greet Jake and Sean when the truck pulled into the drive the next afternoon. "How was the fishing?"

"We didn't catch anything today." Jake gathered up his pole and tackle box. "We got pizza at the deli. Sean says he'll fix it, so you don't burn it and Lynn doesn't have a fit."

"I don't burn everything." Elinor glowered with mock sternness at her son.

Sean came around the pickup. He wrapped an arm around her shoulders. "Burn me, missy. I'm still waiting for you to get hot."

A blush scorched her cheeks. She glanced at Jake, but he hadn't heard. "Behave," she whispered.

"Well or badly?" Sean kissed the side of her neck. "You'll like both ways."

SIXTEEN

"Time to get ready for bed, guys," Elinor said.

Lynn gathered up the cards from the game. To her brother's dismay, she'd won every hand.

"I'm not tired," Jake protested with a yawn. "And I deserve to get my revenge."

"Honey, it doesn't matter how many games you play when you're tired," Elinor said. "You can't figure out good strategy."

"He never beats me when he's awake either," Lynn pointed out.

"Manners, Lynn. Pick on your brother when we don't have company."

Sean sat on the couch. "Is that what I am?" he teased. "Company? And I was hoping you were used to me by now."

"Live in hopes, die in despair," Elinor told him.

Lynn and Jake shared a look. "Come on, Jake. Let's get ready for bed. Mom will tuck you in when you call her. Okay?"

"Yeah. Good night, Sean." The kids headed off.

"Night, kids." Sean caught Elinor's hand and pulled her down on the couch next to him. "Is this the *later* you had in mind?"

She stared into the smoky depths of his eyes. He pulled her closer and dropped a kiss on her forehead.

"They'll see us." The protest sounded weak even to her ears. "I'm not ready."

"Then we'll wait." He kissed the tip of her nose, then let her go. "Tell me about your morning in Jake's class. How'd that go?"

She struggled to ignore her disappointment. She'd wanted him to kiss her, but she didn't want a big, steamy scene in front of her kids. She took a deep breath. "Well, Ms. Collins—Cindy—was nicer than I expected when I arrived. She asked after Jake and I told her he'd be back tomorrow. I think she assumed he was sick, and I didn't tell her he'd gone fishing."

"So, what did you teach?"

"Greek mythology." Elinor wrinkled her nose. "The story of Arachne, the girl who is turned into a spider by an angry goddess. I was supposed to help a group of kids read it. I made them read it to me instead and then find the answers for their worksheets. It wasn't what Cindy had in mind and she told me I was making them work too hard."

"Did you give her the lecture about high expectations?" Sean asked. "Jake told me that you think kids either live up or down to what teachers expect."

"I told her that, but I waited until the kids went to lunch," Elinor said. "I wasn't getting into an argument with her in front of the class. And I also said the students didn't have any trouble doing the work by themselves and peer teaching each other."

Sean chuckled. "I'll bet she can't wait to see you next week."

"Oh, I'm sure." Elinor looked at the clock over the fireplace. *Time to go tuck in the kids*. She pressed her mouth against Sean's throat, then lifted her head. "I've got to check on Lynn and Jake. I must make sure he really brushed his teeth. Otherwise, he rinses with the mouthwash and pretends."

"Don't forget me."

It didn't take long to usher the children to bed. Jake didn't even want her to read one of his favorite fantasy stories. He was almost asleep by the time she adjusted his blankets and kissed his forehead. As for Lynn, she was content with *Album of Horses*, studying the classic equine manual when Elinor came into the room.

"Mom, what color do you think Star's baby will be? She's a liver chestnut and Paragon's a bay. Last time she was bred to a palomino and Galaxy looks just like his sire."

"I have no idea. We'll have to wait and see." She kissed her daughter's cheek. "Only read until nine-thirty. Then it's lights out."

"Okay." Lynn snuggled further back on the pillows. "I love you, Mom."

"I love you, too." Elinor closed the door partway behind her. "Sleep tight, honey."

She crossed the living room to the couch where Sean waited. He caught her hand and pulled her down beside him. "Do you remember where we left off?"

"You may have to remind me."

"Liar." He wrapped his hand in her hair. "You want me." His mouth claimed hers in a series of long, hungry kisses. Slowly, he lifted his head. "I've wanted you for so long."

"Are you seducing me?" She leaned against his broad shoulder, shivering as he planted soft kisses on her skin, her hair, and eyebrows.

His whispered compliments warmed her when he kissed her ear and the side of her neck. He pulled her onto his lap.

"I'm too heavy," she told him.

"You're as light as a bale of hay."

"Alfalfa or grass?" She didn't have to be much of a farmer to know that Eastern Washington hay came in heavier bales than the local grass. "I'm waiting, cowboy."

"I haven't decided yet."

Before she could object, his mouth claimed hers. Dimly, she felt his fingers on the front of her blouse. Then her mind faded out when instinct took over.

She wound her arms around his neck. She felt the hardness of his thighs beneath her, and the rise of his erection. For once the idea of intimacy didn't make her uncomfortable. She yearned for his possession, but knew he'd take his time.

When he finally lifted his head, he had the detachable, ruffled bib from her shirt in his hand. Slowly, he set it aside, as if it were a decoration or a trophy. She raised her head, caught his mouth with hers, and kissed him with the same fierce hunger he'd brought to her moments before.

One of his hands tangled in her hair again. He plundered her mouth with his tongue. Suddenly, the edges of her blouse parted under his free hand. She gasped and pulled away.

"Let me go." She heard the ragged sound of her voice. She'd never dreamed she could sound so sensual.

"Are you sure?" He trailed a finger over her cheek to her lips. "I'm here for the duration. What about you?"

"I've never felt this way in my life," she admitted, flustered.

He lifted her into his arms. With a moan, she buried her face against his tanned throat. She felt as though she were flying. He carried her through the house and then lowered her onto her bed.

She debated sending him away, but she couldn't. Before her brain formed a thought, his mouth captured hers. He drew her on top of him. The idea of waiting faded away.

When the kiss ended, she wanted more. She sat up and eyed him. He was perfectly still beneath her, but his arms were still around her waist. She began to unsnap the pearl buttons on his shirt.

She peeled back the material. She studied the broad expanse of his chest. Dark brown hair swirled down to his narrow waist. It curled around her fingers. She bent to kiss one of his nipples. Then she heard a child's muffled sobbing.

"Jake," she said. She rolled away and leaped to her feet, fastening her shirt on the way. She switched on the light as she stepped into her son's room, "I'm here, honey." She pulled her son into a hug. "What was it? Awesome again?"

"No." Jake shuddered. "Monsters. Are they still here?"

She tried to smile as he hid his face in her shirt. "Do you know what's wrong with you? Too much junk food tonight. First, we had pizza and sodas for dinner. Then it was ice cream in front of the boob tube during your favorite show."

"Don't forget the popcorn," Sean reminded them from the doorway.

Jake looked up, tears in his eyes. "Was that it?"

"It has to be. Come on. I'll fix some hot milk for you." She stood, allowing her son to get out of bed. He wouldn't thank her for treating him like a baby in front of Sean.

She felt her tension ease when she realized Sean had fastened his shirt, too. She tried to ignore the warmth in his gaze as she and Jake passed by. She wished she was more successful at hiding her emotions. Instead, Sean only had to look at her.

Once they were in the kitchen, she directed her attention to warming a mug of milk in the microwave.

She took a deep breath. She had to take charge of her turbulent emotions. The man was almost a stranger to her.

Sean finally spoke. "It's getting late."

"Yes." Elinor opened the microwave door when it dinged. "You'd better go." She carried the mug over to Jake, who sat at the table, disheveled and looking tired.

"If you want to kiss her good night, it's okay with me," Jake said.

"Thank you," Elinor retorted. "I didn't know we needed permission."

Sean chuckled. "Calm down, darlin'."

He placed his hat on his head before he cupped her elbow. "You have to close the highway gates behind me anyway."

Once outside, Sean led her into the yard. "Stop fretting." He rested his hands on her shoulders. "Your kids don't worry me."

"I'm concerned about them, not you. I haven't dated since the divorce. I don't want Lynn or Jake to have unreasonable expecta-tions. I don't even know where we're going."

"I have hopes of my own." His hold tightened. "I'm not a

drifter. Your ex ran from the responsibilities of a family. I'm not him."

She caught her breath and tried to read Sean's face in the moonlight. "What if it all goes wrong?"

"We deal with it." He pulled her against him. His hand smoothed her hair. "We're adults."

"Like that'll make life easier." She pulled away. "You're a fool, Sean Killian. This will never work."

"And you're scared." He shrugged. "Keep running in circles, darlin'. Soon you'll get tired and come to me. That's what fillies do."

She lifted her chin. "I've got two kids. I'm no filly."

"Want to bet? You're the one who didn't know how to tell a stud from a gelding."

———

A tray of assorted frosted brownies in her hand, Elinor headed over to Daisy Baldusi's for their usual Friday morning get-together. As always, her mentor had the coffee ready.

Daisy filled two cups. "So, how's your love life?"

Elinor struggled to ignore the blush warming her cheeks. "Going way too fast, too soon. And I have a date with Sean tonight. I don't know how that's going to end up."

"Bull." Daisy laughed. "You know exactly what might happen. You just have to decide."

"That's true." Elinor pulled out a chair at the kitchen table. She proceeded to bring Daisy up to date on everything that had happened this week, from volunteering in Jake's classroom to line dancing with the Dawson girls.

"I'm glad to hear you're making friends," Daisy said. "Are you planning to contact those two teachers in your graduate school class that you really liked sometime soon? The three of you went riding together during your breaks."

"I don't know." Elinor grabbed the coffee pot to refill their mugs. "We've drifted apart since I left teaching full time."

Daisy frowned, concern on her face. "Teachers take time out for real life, Elinor. It's what keeps us sane. Think about touching base with Ann and Margo. Doesn't your entire cohort still get together for picnics during the summer?"

Elinor nodded, staring into her cup. She hadn't been to one of the celebrations since John had thrown a fit in front of the other women. He always chose to list her defects when there was an audience.

"I'll think about taking the kids this year." She deliberately changed the subject and opened the plastic lid on the brownies. "What kind do you want? We have chocolate with and without walnuts, pecan-coconut frosted brownies, and white chocolate."

"I'm getting a knife and cutting them into little pieces so we can have one of each," Daisy said.

———

The rest of the day passed all too quickly. With no students scheduled, she put the ponies out in the paddocks. Chipeta and Awesome had the two other pregnant mares for company and Paragon was by himself grazing in the round pen. Of course, a lot of horse trainers would pitch a fit about letting a pony play in the training ring, but she didn't see the need to waste the grass. She spent the rest of the morning cleaning the barns.

In the afternoon, she painted the wooden fence that bordered the road. When the kids got home from school, they hurried to change clothes so they could help. At five, Elinor organized a cleanup. "We'll have to hurry with chores. Sean and I are going to the Dawsons' place to look at ponies. Jake, do you want to come and ride them?"

"Nope. Mr. Sievers gave me a neat book about geometry. I'm going to study angles tonight."

"I think you already know them." Elinor eyed her daughter. "Lynn, what about you?"

"Mom, you'll be fine. Jake and I had great times with Sean. If he acts obnoxious, threaten to tell Marlene. Everybody's scared of her."

"Did you two do that?" Elinor asked, suspicious.

Jake shook his head. "It's what Marlene tells us to do. Nobody's allowed to hurt our feelings, or say bad stuff to us, or bully us."

"Or touch us without permission," Lynn said. "Didn't you go out with other guys besides our dad?"

"No. Your dad was my first boyfriend." Elinor ran a hand through the hair pasted to her scalp. Her shirt clung damply to her skin and the Levis felt glued to her legs. "Okay, let's hit it. Or I won't be ready on time."

Lynn beamed at her. "Come on, Jake. Race you to the barn."

Elinor started to follow but stopped when she heard the crunch of gravel and turned to see Sean's truck. He parked and stepped out.

Brown slacks hugged his long legs. A patterned western shirt emphasized his broad shoulders. He'd left the collar open to expose his tanned throat.

"You're early." Her tone was accusatory, but a man who arrived two hours before she expected him, when she looked this awful should be staked out for the slugs. "And I still have chores to do before I can get ready. Go away."

He laughed. "Not in a million years." He bent to kiss her. "I like the fence. Come paint mine when you have time. Then I can chase your body."

"I have news for you, cowboy. That's called sexual harassment." She smiled. He was good for her ego. Now she felt like a supermodel, not hot, tired, and sweaty.

"I'll go help the kids," Sean said. "And you can get ready. Deal?"

"Okay." Elinor smiled. "Don't get dirty." She used the same

prissy teacher's tone that irritated Lynn so much. "I have stan-
dards. If you're messy, I'll have to go to the Dawsons' place by
myself. Of course, then Clancy and I could go look for cute
cowboys after we see the ponies."

"Your cowboy hunting days are over," Sean drawled. "You've
got one. Me."

SEVENTEEN

ELINOR SHOWERED AND DRESSED, DELIBERATELY CHOOSING A DARK blue teddy to wear under her navy striped western blouse and dress jeans. She put on her high-heeled boots, the ones she wore to dance in, not ride.

Sean's eyes widened when he saw her. He escorted her to his gleaming pickup, which he had obviously cleaned out and washed for the occasion. "I made reservations at Mexicali Rose. Lynn said it was one of your favorite places to eat."

The restaurant, across from the Everett Mall, proved to be a popular choice. As soon as they walked through the carved wooden doors, Elinor felt the ambience. She hadn't been there since Marlene had brought her to celebrate her birthday last year. She looked around at the arched doorways that led to the dining rooms, the brightly colored murals of rural Mexico, and the pottery decorations.

Sean smiled. "You look like a kid who just discovered Disneyland is real."

"Isn't it?" Elinor asked, trying to sound naive. "I didn't know that."

He kissed her. "Watch it. I know how to deal with smart-mouthed cowgirls."

The hostess, a young girl in a white peasant blouse and gaily flounced skirt, guided them to a high-backed booth. She placed menus on the table in front of them and left, shortly replaced with a young man who delivered water, a basket of warmed tortilla chips, and a bowl of salsa. "Your waiter will be here in a few minutes," he said before he left.

Elinor opened the menu and examined the list of entrees. As always, it seemed to go on forever and she knew she'd debate over several entrees before choosing her favorite rice and chicken dish. "Have you decided?"

"Let's start with strawberry margaritas," Sean suggested. "We'll have them without tequila." He winked at her. "Virgins."

Elinor narrowed her gaze. "Are you trying to embarrass me?"

"It's so much fun," Sean drawled, unabashed. He lowered his voice. "And I keep wondering how easy it will be to make you blush after I take you to bed."

That did it. Elinor shot him a final glare before she buried her face in the menu. She knew her face was fiery red.

Sean ordered drinks along with a large order of nachos as an appetizer. After the waiter had left, Sean asked, "Do you know what you want?"

"Yes." She paused. "Oh, were you talking about dinner?"

He grinned. "You are so due to get lucky."

Smiling, she looked around the restaurant. It was hard to see the other patrons. Suddenly, she realized she didn't mind. One of her favorite occupations had always been people-watching. Was that because John wouldn't talk to her when they went out?

She didn't know. It wasn't a problem with Sean. He liked being with her. *Obviously*. No man would go to this much trouble to simply get a woman in the sack.

"I always like eating here," Elinor said. John wouldn't come with her and the adventure wasn't worth dealing with his tantrums when she came alone, or brought the kids, or hung out with the other teachers on a professional development day.

But...she was divorced. Why was she still allowing John to control her life? "I wish I came here more often."

"We'll add it to our list of places to eat," Sean said. "We'll have to bring Lynn and Jake next time."

The elaborate order of supreme nachos arrived at the table along with their drinks, and she bit into some, enjoying herself. They were halfway through the appetizer when a big, dark-haired man stopped at their table.

"Go away," Sean said, the grin vanishing from his face.

"It's what I love about you, boy. Your charm." The stranger smiled, an oddly familiar gesture. Equally familiar gray eyes under heavy lids and dark brows returned Elinor's curious gaze. "I'm Ethan." He glanced back at Sean. "Saw your truck in the lot."

"Next time I'll rent a car," Sean murmured as he reached across the table to hold Elinor's hand. "What do you want?"

"An introduction. Where are your manners? I know you've got them. I raised you right."

"Elinor, this is my big brother Ethan. This is Elinor Talbot, Ethan. Now, will you go away?"

"In a minute." Ethan studied Elinor.

She returned the once-over. He didn't dress like a Boeing engineer. He wore jeans, a flannel shirt, and cowboy boots. He carried a denim jacket over one big arm. Where was the pocket protector? The nerdy glasses?

There was a similarity to his brother in the fierce angles of his handsome face and square jaw. Silver threaded his dark brown hair and the lines around his mouth and eyes showed he had a few years on Sean.

Elinor decided she liked the way he made her feel safe, a reaction she rarely had with Sean. She smiled at Ethan. "It's nice to meet you. Sean's told me a lot about you."

Amusement warmed his gray eyes. "I hope some of it was good. He told me you made the sun rise and set."

"Now you've met Elinor. We'd like to be alone," Sean tried again. "Go bother Gavin."

"Can't. He went to Montana to check out those rodeo broncs of Kate's."

"It ought to make his life exciting," Sean said. "How many pieces will she send him home in? Inquiring minds want to know."

"It's a personal problem. His." Ethan narrowed his eyes. "Where is she?"

"Who?" Sean asked. "Be specific, big brother."

"The two of you have been in cahoots since she was born. She wouldn't do anything to irritate me without asking you first."

"Sounds interesting." Elinor tried to free her fingers from Sean's, but his grip tightened. So, who was the *she* the two of them meant?

"Clancy comes and cries on my shoulder about what a loser you are," Sean said, "and I agree."

Elinor relaxed. "So, *you're* the guy who dumped her?"

"I didn't dump her," Ethan said. "We argued."

"Take my word for it," Elinor said. "You're wrong. Go apologize. Then she will."

"Nope. She's a Dawson from a long line of strong-willed women. They don't apologize."

"But they like it when others grovel." Sean pretended to zip his lips when Elinor glared at him. "You could lecture her, too, darlin'."

"Provided Ethan calls to apologize first."

"Fine." Ethan glowered at her. "I don't like it."

"You don't have to." Elinor used the same tone of reason that worked on unruly teens when they only wanted to harass the substitute teacher. "Now, stop by the florist and send her flowers, too. The one at the mall will deliver tonight."

"Man alive. Flowers?" Ethan's frown deepened, but there was a glint of humor too. "I'm leaving before you make me buy her something else. She threw her ring at me, you know. Barely missed my eye."

"Don't whine. Man up. And Sean's right. You should plan to grovel."

Ethan glanced at Sean. "It would be easier to just thump you. I'm outta here. I can't wait to see what this woman does to the girls and Gavin."

"I'm holding out for the Senator and his wife. That will be fun to watch."

"It might get you to their place without me dragging you," Ethan agreed before he turned and headed for the door of the restaurant.

Sean watched his older brother leave and then turned back to Elinor, a smile in his eyes. "Well, I didn't expect him to show up."

"Talk about first impressions," Elinor said. "I'm surprised he liked me."

"Ethan always admires strength and courage."

"I'm surprised Clancy didn't tell me who she was engaged to," Elinor said. "She just calls him 'the loser.'"

"She probably thought you already knew. She's been crazy about Ethan since she was tiny." The memory softened Sean's face. "Roy told him they couldn't date until she finished college and tried out a few boys. Nobody breaks Roy Dawson's rules. Ethan always said he was too old for her and they've been on a real rollercoaster these past two years."

"How old is he?"

"Forty-five. Sixteen years older than Clancy. He says he broke it off because of the age difference and she says she did because he's a major loser."

"She's twenty-nine. She's more than old enough to know what she wants."

"Our families have known each other forever. If her aunt Marlene was the mother we never had, then her husband Roy was the father. Mine was so busy being the star of his political party, he never had time for us kids. Ethan took over being a dad to me, Gavin, and my sisters."

She took a deep breath. "My grandpa Talbot was a father after mine didn't make it home from Grenada. My dad was a Ranger and the Army always came first with him."

"And your mom? Where was she?"

"Gone. She didn't want a kid. She dropped me off with her parents after I was born." Elinor stopped there. Her maternal grandparents were more involved in real estate than they ever were with her, although they kept a roof over her head. Whenever she inconvenienced them, they packed her off to her father's family in Eastern Washington.

Much to her relief, their entrees arrived. After a few bites of her *arroz con pollo*, she asked, "Should I call the Dawsons to confirm our appointment?"

"No need," Sean said. "I called before I picked you up. Darlene would have told me if something changed. Clancy's been at a conference on handicapped riding, but she'll meet us there."

"You could have told your brother."

"Nope. Clancy told me not to." Sean sipped at his margarita. "Now I know why. She wanted him to fret about whether she had another guy."

He didn't sound perturbed by the idea that he'd been manipulated. Finally, Elinor asked, "Why aren't you mad about the games she's playing?"

"Because she's cried her heart out for the past month. There's nothing I could do before. Ethan's a stubborn jackass once he makes a decision. He's my brother and I love him, but this time, he's wrong."

After a dessert of cinnamon-dusted fried ice cream, they headed for the Lazy B, the Dawson ranch in east Liberty Valley. While he parked the truck, Elinor looked in the direction of the indoor arena. Clancy waved from the doorway.

The redhead sported a purple T-shirt that proclaimed *Horses are the Goddess's apology for men!* When they reached her, she grabbed Elinor in a hug, then Sean. "Guess what? Ethan called. He left three messages while I was at the conference."

"Really?" Sean laughed and hugged Clancy back. "I told you he'd get his brain working."

Clancy hugged Elinor again. "You should welcome the respite, Sean. I won't be whining at you every day now."

"Have you talked to Ethan yet?" Elinor asked.

"No, but I will." Clancy frowned. "I haven't figured out what to say. If he does his macho routine…" Her voice trailed off.

"You need to think about what you want," Elinor said. "If you're gracious and apologize, you can make Ethan feel like a real worm."

Clancy tilted her head. "Wow, I never thought of that."

"Good." Elinor elbowed Sean in the ribs when he snickered. "Now, show me the ponies."

"Okay. I've picked six for you to look at." Clancy started toward the double row of stalls, Elinor and Sean following.

The discussion for the next hour centered on the ponies. Sean contributed what he knew about their legs and hooves. Elinor finally settled on Musketeer, a small bay gelding with four white socks and a blaze. His best buddy was another trustworthy mount, a slightly larger Welsh called Midnight who was as black as his name deserved. One white sock, a star, and snip added some flash.

"Let's go do the paperwork for you to borrow them," Clancy said. "There's coffee and Brigid baked a cake."

"Great. I love her cakes," Sean said. "My ice cream wore off as soon as I heard the word cake."

"Yeah, well the only reason Kate and I are still among the living is that she hadn't bought the ingredients for our wedding cakes." Clancy glanced at Elinor. "Brigid makes gorgeous specialty cakes. She's into the creative side of things, so she only works part-time at the local bakery, and we get to eat her experiments and mistakes."

"Not that she has a lot of mistakes," Sean added, "but if the cakes aren't perfect, she won't let her clients buy them. Do you want to bring the ponies down tomorrow, Clancy? Or shall I come by with my trailer? Either works for me."

Elinor frowned at Sean. "I don't want to take advantage of

either one of you. I can arrange for a hauler to come pick up the ponies."

"No worries, darlin'," Sean said. "I've got your back on this. Darlene would have a fit and fall in it if somebody other than the Dawsons or the Killians hauled her stock. Believe me, you don't want to cross her."

"That's really true," Clancy agreed. "My mom can give Aunt Marlene lessons in ornery. But Aunt Marlene has our trailer and she's hauling to the 4-H shows. I can bring the ponies in when I get it back and pick up Paragon at the same time or vice versa."

Clancy started toward the door, then stopped in mid-stride. "Elinor, come on up to the hayloft. I'll show you the kittens I was telling Jake about. If you want a couple, I'll bring them when I bring the ponies."

"Sounds wonderful." The kids constantly talked about pets, but her ex-husband hated cats in the house and had constantly threatened to dump their Siamese at the pound. Finally, she'd given away the cat so she wouldn't have to worry about it being poisoned or run over by John. Lynn had cried for weeks afterward, making Elinor feel even worse.

John had strutted around the house until Elinor told him that breaking a little girl's heart didn't make him a hero. The argument ended when he slammed the door on his way out and stayed away for three days. It was the beginning of the end of their marriage since she discovered she enjoyed the peace and quiet of his absence and found herself wanting more of it.

A big calico trailed by four roly-poly kittens came to greet them. Elinor dropped to one knee to make friends. "How many do you have?"

"Two darned many right now," Clancy said. "We missed a litter last fall and by the time we figured out the twins hadn't taken them to the vet clinic to get fixed, four of the cats were pregnant. Vonnie said we could do 'kitty abortions,' and Mom lost it. Anyway, we ended up with twenty-two kittens. I've been giving them away all spring. If it was summer, it'd be easier to find homes."

The mother cat rested a paw on Elinor's thigh and purred. A fluffy gray kitten attacked an orange sibling and the pair rolled and tumbled across the floor. "I bet you don't have any mice."

"Not a one." Speculation filled Clancy's face. "You could take them all."

Elinor thought. They were outside cats so if she parked them in the barn, they'd take care of any mice who got into the grain. The kids would love having cats again and so would she. It'd been six years since the divorce, damn it, and it was past time to start living again. "Okay. Works for me."

"Wonderful. I'll bring the whole batch with me next week."

"The kids will be thrilled." Elinor accepted the hand Sean offered and rose to her feet. "I'll have to tell Lynn she can't sleep with them."

The three of them headed to the old three-story house situated in the middle of rolling lawns. Clancy led the way into the kitchen where four other women sat around the long, oak dining table. Elinor greeted Brigid with a smile, remembering her from the previous Saturday night when they met at Billy's Wild West Bar and Grille. She'd dressed down for a night at home in green sweats that matched her eyes. A book of updated 4-H horseshow rules lay on the table in front of her.

"Mom, do you remember Elinor?" Clancy asked. "She owns Silver Lake Pony Ranch. I told you about her cutest little stud - - -."

"Thank you. Thank you very much." Sean bowed elegantly. "And I thought you never noticed."

"Shut up, Sean. I was talking about Paragon and you're not one."

"Could have fooled me." Elinor smiled at Darlene. "We've met before at your sister's."

"Yes." She wasn't as tall as her daughters, but like them, Darlene wore blue jeans and a western blouse. Silver streaked her fading red hair. "You helped me with the dishes at the kids' holiday party."

"Definitely the perfect time to bond," Brigid said. "Aunt Marlene had me clean up the garbage and mop floors."

"That's why we don't do her parties." One of the younger women spoke up and Elinor recognized Yvonne. Clancy had been right in the description of her siblings. All the girls were tall, voluptuous, and did have bright red hair that they wore in a variety of styles. Tonight, Vonnie wore a red and white striped blouse with her tight-fitting jeans while her twin, Wendy had on a turquoise and white shirt with hers.

"Your daughter was a credit to you at the show last week," Brigid went on. "She needs to relax in her riding classes and not try so hard. When she gets nervous, she tenses up and her pony blows its leads on the gallop."

"I've noticed the same thing in lessons," Elinor agreed, "so I have her stop and start over. Lynn knows Gypsy needs to lead off with the left or right front leg, but it depends on the track the class takes. Does she cue for it correctly?"

"Yes, and she gets her lope right away. She just doesn't keep it for more than half the ring."

"Spurs and a whip would help," Vonnie suggested. "If she taught the pony who was boss, it wouldn't dare break a stride or change the lead."

Elinor stiffened, outraged at the idea. She knew other instructors and trainers did that, taught the horse to hold gaits regardless of what the rider did, but it wasn't her style. The notion that beating an animal was the perfect solution when the human made the mistake just seemed wrong on so many levels.

"I don't think so," Elinor said firmly. "I may not have as many riding students as other instructors do, but I use horsemanship as a vehicle to teach life lessons and I especially want my daughter to emulate me and my morality."

Wow, she sounded like a smug bitch. She glanced toward Sean and caught the admiring look he didn't try to hide. Elinor took a deep breath and tried to calm down, determined not to apologize. "That's my philosophy for my barn, but it may not suit everyone."

"It does here too. Whips and spurs don't belong with beginning riders," Clancy said. "They promote lazy habits. Lynn should be a good horsewoman, not an incompetent passenger." She eyed her sister with obvious concern. "Vonnie, are you okay? Why would you say such a horrible thing?"

Vonnie scowled but didn't answer. Brigid intervened again. "Elinor, why don't you suggest to Lynn that she do the same thing in the ring that she does at home? Stopping and starting over would show any judge that she's aware of the problem and wants to fix it. Sure, some sticklers would continue to count her down, but a lot of 4-H judges would appreciate the effort Lynn makes."

"She wouldn't lose points and would place higher in the riding classes," Sean said. "It'd be great for her self-esteem. Do you want to tell her, or shall I at tomorrow's show?"

"I still think if the pony was fully trained, the girl would achieve more," Vonnie insisted. "When a pony balks or refuses to perform to the highest standard, laying into it with a whip or jabbing its sides with spurs does wonders."

Elinor bit her lip and counted to ten, determined not to let her mouth run away with her manners.

"Like your Uncle Will says, 'when you give a lesson in meanness to an animal or a child, don't be surprised when they learn it', Yvonne," Darlene said. "Maybe if I'd smacked you and your sister instead of just talking to you, it would have 'done wonders' and the two of you would be better people."

"Come on, Mom. It's not a big deal," Wendy jumped into the conversation.

"I thought you two were headed for Billy's for the line-dancing contest." Clancy put down her papers on the counter at the back of the room, obviously thinking that a change of subject could lighten the tension in the room. "What happened?"

"We were. We are," Wendy said. "Mom wanted to talk to us first."

"Lecture, you mean." Vonnie tossed her long, curly red mane. "Gavin called and told her that we're failing his stupid class before he left town. He shouldn't have done it. Our grades are our business and I'm going to file a complaint against him with the university."

"Try it and Kate will have your guts for garters," Brigid said in an even tone. "I don't know what they're arguing about or why she broke her engagement, but she won't let you ruin his career."

"And I'm grateful he told me what you two are doing down there," Darlene added. "Or rather what you're not doing. This isn't high school, ladies. You can't cut your college classes or avoid doing the work without wrecking your futures."

"Why you listen to him after what he did to Kate, I don't know," Yvonne retorted. "And I can pass his class if I ace the midterm."

"Barely pass it. You're failing," Wendy said. "I have a D."

"The Dawson family isn't paying tuition at the U-Dub for you two to party and blow off your classes and your futures." Darlene stood up. "You are smart girls, just as smart as your sisters and I expect you both to be on the honor roll by the end of spring quarter. Now, you have choices. You two snots can get upstairs and do the work for that class and the rest of them, or you can pack, get out and pay your own way."

Wow, that was not what she expected. Elinor wondered if it would be better if she and Sean made a discreet exit. She and Clancy could do the paperwork at another time. "We can do this later, Darlene."

"There's no need for that." Darlene glared at her youngest daughters. "What's it gonna be, ladies? My way or the highway?"

Wendy and Vonnie shared a look. Then, Wendy said, "Your way, Mom."

"Good. We'll be discussing this at Sunday dinner and your attendance is mandatory, ladies." Darlene didn't budge until the twins stormed from the room. Then, she slumped against the table. "Oh, *God*. I'm so sorry. That was embarrassing."

"What's wrong, Darlene?" Sean's tone was sympathetic. "I've known you forever. You don't slap your girls down when you have company. It's not your style. How can I help?"

Tears filled Darlene's eyes, and one trickled down her cheek. Elinor wasn't surprised when Sean drew the older woman against him and tried to comfort her. His kindness and understanding touched Elinor's heart.

"I spoiled them," Darlene choked out the words.

"Mom, we all did." Clancy began to fill cups with coffee while Brigid produced an elaborately decorated cake from the refrigerator. "They aren't that bad."

Darlene cried harder. Clancy looked at her older sister, puzzled. "Brigid, what's up?"

"We had a couple calls while you guys were in the barn," Brigid said. "One was from Sandy, Elinor. Your kids and the ponies are fine."

"That's a relief," Elinor said. "But then why did she call? Oh, I bet I can guess. Penny called in and won't work tomorrow. So, my two farm managers tried to arrange for Clancy to cover again. Is it okay with you, Clancy?"

"Sure." Clancy carried coffee cups to the table. "Who else called?"

"Ethan." Brigid passed napkins and forks to Elinor. "Here. Make yourself useful. Set the table."

Glad to have a task, no matter how mundane, Elinor complied. Why hadn't the kids called on her cell phone to bring her up to speed? Because they didn't want to interfere with her date, she thought, and decided to remind them that she was the mom when she got home. "Why would Ethan call you or your mother? He should be calling Clancy."

"Yeah, that's right. He's a loser."

"No, he's not." Brigid sliced large pieces from the carousel pony shaped cake. "He was angry because the twins called and told him that he wasn't welcome here and to stop bothering you.

He seemed to think they were calling for Mom, Audra and me. He had a rigging fit and a half."

"How appalling!" Elinor said, annoyed at the lack of manners. "When I see him, I'm giving him a piece of my mind. I told him to call Clancy and apologize for being a man."

"You said I had to apologize and make him feel like a worm." Clancy widened her eyes, acting shocked. "Talk about a match-maker. You're as bad as Aunt Marlene."

"Not yet, but she's working on it." Sean patted Darlene's back. "All better?" He passed her a napkin to wipe away the residue from her tears. "I'm sure the girls were just trying to show their loyalty to Clancy."

"Well, that's their story and they're sticking to it," Brigid said. "Personally, I doubt their veracity. They are totally pissed at Gavin for telling them to stop the party times at the university this quarter, weeks before he talked to Mom. I'll bet pay-back was starting World War Three between Kate and Gavin. Clancy and Ethan just caught the fall-out."

"That's what the family meeting is about on Sunday." Darlene blew her nose and went to wash her face at the kitchen sink. "Will you tell your brothers, Sean? I don't want them to think I didn't mean it when I gave them my blessing. They were the first boys who ever came to me and asked for my daughters' hands."

"How lovely," Elinor said. "Of course, he will."

Sean winked at Darlene. "Of course, I will. Now, can I have some of Brighty's cake? I've been sensitive and caring for too long. It's bad for my reputation as a macho cowboy."

EIGHTEEN

"I don't believe this." Lynn walked with Jake toward the barn. "What do you think is wrong with Chipeta and Awesome? Why don't you want Sandy to call Mom or Dr. Watkins?"

"Because nothing is really wrong with them. I just wanted you out here," Jake said, "and I wanted Sandy to stay in the house. We gotta do something about Mom and Sean."

"What?" Lynn stopped and stared at him. "They're on a date. I don't think we have to do anything. This will work."

"I've only seen them kissing once," Jake said. "It'll take a lot more than one kiss to get them married, Lynn."

"What do you want to do?" Lynn eyed the papers he pulled out with dread. "Oh no. Tell me you didn't dig them up out of the garden."

"I had to. We gotta do the spell again." Jake held out the pages. "And don't skip over the new part I added about the kissing and hugging. They have to really love each other if Sean's right for our family."

"I thought you said it was wrong to use *magick* to *make* people do stuff."

"I'm not making them do anything," Jake said. "I just put in that if they're right for each other to let their hearts know it and show it. And if they're not going to make each other happy, then it's okay if they drift apart."

Lynn caught her breath. "But I really like him. And he's coming to help at my show tomorrow."

"Yeah. I finally got to use the fishing gear Santa brought me." Jake shook his head. "I know Sean's right for you and me, but he hasta be right for Mom, too."

Lynn sighed. "Okay, here goes." She took a deep breath. "*On this night and in this hour...*"

———

"Shall we stop for a nightcap?" Sean asked on the way back.

Elinor pondered the question. She wasn't ready to go home. Sandy planned to sleep over, so there wasn't a reason to rush. "Where did you have in mind?"

"My place." Sean took the exit for Snohomish. "Don't worry. I don't have any etchings I want to show you."

"Really?" Elinor mocked. "Then why are we here, cowboy?"

"Because I have something better to share with you. I don't like the idea of you and your kids not having protection. You need a stock dog to work the animals on your farm. I told you that after I chased your pigs last week."

"I can't afford one right now, Sean. I have my name in at a couple of the breeders. I'll buy a puppy when I have two hundred dollars to spare."

"You don't need a damned puppy, Elinor. You should have a fully trained, mature dog."

"I haven't won the lottery. And I am not waiting while I save a thousand bucks for an adult dog."

"Fine." He switched off the engine. "Come see my dogs. You can help me find the right one for Lynn. Her birthday's coming up and I want to give her one if it's okay with you."

Tears burned her eyes. "That'd be great, Sean. That's so—

nice." How could he be so kind to her children when their own father didn't want them?

"Hey, I'm a nice guy." He pulled her close. "Nice doesn't mean weak, babe." Sean stroked her hair. "And I'm gonna teach you to trust me. Okay?"

She nodded. "I'm trying. The last man I trusted was Grandpa Talbot and he died on me."

"I can't promise to live forever." Sean kissed her forehead. "Neither can you. We just do our best to be together for as many years as we've got. Deal?"

"It's too early to make promises like that."

"Not for us. Don't be scared, darlin'. I won't rush you." He kissed her left eyebrow, then her right. He chuckled softly. "I have two litters of puppies right now. Eight border collie mixes and six Australian cattle dogs, blue heelers."

She let him help her out of the truck. She landed in the circle of his arms as he held the door. He leaned over her. "You promised," she reminded him. "Slow."

He dropped a kiss on her hair. "And I'm a man of my word. You like that about me."

"You're right." She ducked under his arm and started up the driveway. "I do."

"Soon, I'm going to make you say that for keeps."

Her face warmed. "Don't hold your breath, cowboy."

"I never could resist a challenge." He caught her elbow. "I'm going to kiss you. I can't wait."

"Good. Neither can I." When his mouth touched hers, her trembling increased. He cradled her head, sliding his fingers into her hair.

His kiss became slower as his tongue probed her mouth. She pulled him closer, pressing against his body. Her desire astonished her.

Sensation filled her mind. His lips burned a path to the pulse that thudded in her throat. She wanted him, but where would all this take them?

She twisted free. "The dogs?" she managed a whisper. "Where are they?"

He trailed a line of kisses to her ear. "Do I scare you that bad, babe?"

"Yes," she admitted.

"Good." He kissed the side of her neck, the top of her shoulder under the collar of her blouse. "Then we're both taking this seriously."

She shuddered. *Am I ready to get involved?* She wasn't sure of the answer to the question. She pulled from his embrace and backed away.

She wouldn't tell him how special he made her feel. She couldn't decide if she was melting or bursting into flame at his lightest touch. All she knew was she lost herself.

Instead, she was a mindless creature who longed to cling to him. As he strode toward her, she continued to retreat. "Don't."

He shook his head. "Come on, Elinor. You can't possibly mean it. As soon as I kiss you, you'll change your mind."

"I know," she agreed. "It's why I don't want you to kiss me again, not right now."

"Tell me why."

"Sean Killian!" She hesitated.

He took two steps closer.

She moistened her lips. "I've never felt like this before." Anger gave her the courage to continue. "I don't want to explain all my emotions to you. I haven't come to terms with them myself."

"Okay, we'll go look at the dogs. I shouldn't have pushed you."

She measured his sincerity and decided it was genuine. His willingness to follow her lead increased her admiration for him.

Her knees weakened when his arm curved around her waist. He guided her to the barn door. She heard furious barking when he opened the door and turned on the overhead lights.

The stalls were the kind found in most board stables. The wooden walls were built of planks four feet high, topped with vertical wrought-iron bars. Heavy sliding doors could have contained huge horses, much less the medium-sized dogs that were barking up a storm. She peered into the first stall and found a purple-gray dog staring back at her. He was silent compared to the boisterous greetings of the others. His brown ears and the white stripe up the middle of his mottled face gave him a sober look.

She smiled and wriggled her hand through the bars for him to smell it and get acquainted with her. He approached, sniffed. Then he stood on his back feet, propped his front paws on the wall and deigned to let her pet him. "Aren't you pretty?" She glanced at Sean. "What's his name?"

"Ruler." Sean approached.

When he did, the dog curled his lip and revealed his teeth. "He's never been fond of me for some reason, but his parents love me. I haven't found the right person for him yet."

"He's a beauty." She petted the dog again, and wished she had the money to buy him. "What kind of training does he have?"

"Works cattle, horses, sheep, and pigs. I've even let him round up chickens. He's good with cats, too. Some heelers try to kill them. Not Ruler. He tolerates kids, but it's definitely noblesse oblige."

"Well, let's see the puppies." Elinor reluctantly left Ruler. When she glanced over her shoulder at him, the dog was still watching her. "My old heeler used to do that. Just sit and keep an eye on me."

"It's typical of the breed. Even the puppies do it. They'll watch me for hours. I think they understand almost everything I say."

She glanced at Ruler once more, then started down the aisle, which was wide enough for a pickup to drive in. She liked the barn, although she preferred her own stalls, which allowed the ponies to socialize with each other. "This works great for keeping dogs."

"The indoor arena comes in handy for training them." Sean stopped halfway down and gestured to a sixteen-foot gate on the right. "The stalls on the other side weren't finished. The couple who put this place together planned to open a stable, but they split up nearly twenty-some years ago." He shrugged. "The property was adjacent to the Killian homestead, so I bought it for me and my dogs."

She was charmed with his concern for his animals. "You know, cowboy. I like you. I really do." She stepped over and kissed his cheek. "You're pretty special."

He feathered a finger down her nose. "You only like me because we have so much in common, girl."

She slid her arms around his neck and brought his mouth to hers. She kissed him, a quick, light pressure. "Is it okay if I admire your compassion, too?"

"Are you trying to seduce me? Are you ready?"

She considered the question. "I think I am." She fitted her mouth to his and outlined his lips with her tongue. "Is that all right with you?"

"Works for me." He swung her up in his arms. "Shall we look at puppies in the morning?"

"Works for me."

Turning off the lights, he left the barn and carried her toward the house. The path was lit by a row of overhead lights that seemed to come on by themselves. She realized there had to be motion sensors. What an elaborate operation.

Before she could see more, his head lowered. His mouth captured hers. She was dimly aware when he unlocked the back door. They went through the mud porch into a large country kitchen.

He carried her through what had to be the living room and up a staircase. He flipped a switch as they went into his bedroom.

The spacious area was twice the size of a normal bedroom and at least three times the size of her own small bedroom. There was a rock-faced fireplace on one wall and across from it a king-size bed with a massive oak headboard.

She looked around, noting every detail. There were two oak

dressers, a matching antique oak wardrobe, and two beautiful oak nightstands on either side of the bed.

Heavy flowered drapes blocked the windows, picking up the maroon in the comforter and the carpet. There was something about the room that bothered her, and she realized what it was. It had been done professionally, or by someone with an artist's eye. She didn't think it was Clancy. What woman had decorated and furnished the house?

"Who was she? Who designed this room?"

He chuckled and dropped her on the bed. "My sister, green eyes."

Elinor sniffed. "My eyes are blue, cowboy."

"Not tonight, sweetheart." He followed her.

He kissed her. At the touch of his lips, the battle was over, and she didn't protest. She twined her hands in his hair and drew him closer. She gasped when his tongue eased between her lips.

His muscles tightened under her fingers. She slowly unsnapped his shirt. She wanted him as much as he wanted her. All at once, she yearned to feel his weight on her body.

She longed for him to finish what he'd started. "I need you."

His hand cupped her chin. "Be patient, babe." His lips traced her forehead. He kissed her eyelids. "We have all the time in the world. We'll do this your way, nice and easy."

"No, we're not!" She'd made up her mind and she wasn't going to wait any longer. She pushed him down and lowered her lips to his. Her tongue claimed his mouth, warring with his.

As the depth of the kiss intensified, she felt his fingers tighten on her waist. He rolled over on top of her.

She caught her breath. He was heavy, but it felt so good. His hands were on her shirt, unfastening the pearl snaps.

She slid the cloth away from his shoulders. The warmth of his skin seared her fingertips. She explored the strength of his broad back. His muscles rippled. She moved her hands over his arms, easing off the shirt.

He lifted his head, his lips a breath away. His fingers touched her breast through her blouse. "You're the most ravishing woman I've ever seen."

"You probably say that to all your women."

"No. Only to you." He peeled away her blouse to reveal the blue teddy with its coffee-colored lace. "And this must have been for me."

She shuddered when he slipped the satiny material off her breasts, fumbling with the cloth. Her excitement grew as she realized he wasn't an expert where women's lingerie was concerned. His thumb found her nipple. She couldn't stop the moan of pleasure.

Her head moved restlessly. His legs pinned hers to the bed. She shifted her fingers to the buckle of his belt. She had to feel his skin.

"Easy, babe." His mouth trailed along her neck to her collarbone. "Quit trying to hurry me."

She unbuckled his belt and unsnapped his pants. "I want you, and I'm not going to be patient."

"I can see that." He sat up. One hand rested on her stomach.

He took off his boots, then stood to remove his slacks and shorts.

She admired the wide, tanned chest. His narrow waist and lean hips caught her attention next. Then her gaze dropped lower. He did want her.

She drew a ragged breath. She sat up, unfastening her jeans.

He shook his head. "Don't, babe. That's my pleasure."

She rose and pulled off the comforter and the blankets. She sat back down on the edge of the bed to take off her dress boots.

He went down on one knee to help her. When he stood and held out his hand, she took it, standing as he unzipped her jeans. He caressed her hips and slid his hands toward her legs, taking the Levis along. She hadn't known getting out of a pair of jeans could be so erotic.

His hands curved around her rump and he was back on his knees. She groaned when he strung a line of kisses down her thigh while he pushed her jeans to the floor. She almost screamed when he started on the teddy. "I can't bear it."

She felt his smile through the clingy material.

She wasn't sure how he unsnapped the teddy, but his lips were on the inside of her leg before she knew it. This time, she did scream when his mouth found her. Somehow, she was on the bed again. His tongue teased and tormented her. Waves of passion swept through her until she exploded in rapture, shouting.

She floated back to reality. Her eyes opened to find him looking down at her. "I never knew…"

"You still don't." His features were a fierce mask of planes and angles as he gazed down at her. "We've barely started, babe. This time, you'll really scream in delight."

"No way. It can't get any better."

He laughed. "Just wait and see."

He flicked her nipple with his tongue. She took a deep breath.

It seemed like a lifetime later when she stirred, her head nestled in the hollow of his shoulder, her arm across his chest. "I think we skipped past awesome."

"Definitely," Sean agreed. He stroked her hair. "Do you want to talk?"

"Not particularly." Elinor kissed his throat. "Except for one question. Is making love always that good?" She ran a finger down his muscled arm.

"I don't think it could be better." He caught her hand. "Are you going to sleep or not?"

She contemplated the idea. "I'm curious." She propped herself up on an elbow and studied him.

A lock of brown hair fell across his forehead, and she pushed it back. She tasted his mouth in a quick kiss. "I want to do an experiment and see if sex is always this good."

He opened his eyes. "No sex, girl. We decided we'd only make love."

"Okay." She nipped at his ear, then his jaw. "I'll check out my theory."

His hands tangled in her hair. She melted against him. Her fingers traced his face. "I thought you told me you never went all the way on the first date."

"Anything for science," he mocked with a lift of his eyebrow. "I'm all yours."

He brushed her mouth with his. "And you're all mine, too."

She smiled. "Works for me."

———

The sound of country music woke her.

She promptly opened her eyes. The melody came from the radio on the nightstand. She leaned over Sean to turn off the music. She frowned as she noticed the time on the clock. It was after four.

When he gripped her waist and pulled her close, she smiled. "We can't."

She placed her hand on his cheek and felt the beard stubble. "I've got to get home. Lynn has a horse show today. She'll be in the barn before six."

"Not even one kiss?"

"We've been through that," she said. She smoothed his hair. "One kiss leads to a second. Then we make love. There simply isn't time. I've got to be home to feed the stock. You're supposed to pick up Lynn and Gypsy at seven-thirty."

A mischievous gleam entered his gaze. She tried to wriggle free. It was too late.

He pulled her mouth down onto his. She felt herself flowing into him. All her doubts dissolved.

"You're mine," he rumbled. His mouth roved down her neck. "I won't ever let you go."

An hour later, she rose shakily to her feet. When he followed her, she backed away. "It's after five. I've really got to get home."

"One kiss."

She considered arguing. Then she saw the determination on his face. She stood on tiptoe and planted a swift kiss on his lips.

Before he caught her, she scurried into the bathroom and locked the door.

It didn't take long to shower and brush her hair. Wrapped in a giant towel, she returned to the bedroom to find it empty. Her discarded teddy and other clothes were on the bed. It'd already been made. She smiled.

She put on her teddy and followed it with the blouse. As she snapped the pearl buttons on her shirt, the door opened behind her. She turned to meet Sean's admiring gaze. "No leering."

He grinned and held out a cup of coffee. "For you." He put the mug on the dresser, then stepped back. "If I touch you, we'll never get out of here. I still have to feed the dogs. When is Lynn's birthday?"

"Next month."

"That will work out well. The border collie pups will be about ten weeks old and ready for new homes. Would she like a black and white one, a tri-color, or a gold and white? They may look like rough-coated collies, but they're working dogs. Their father is one of my champion heelers."

"I don't think she'd care about the color, but I'll find out in the next couple of days." Elinor picked up her jeans. "And a working dog will make my life easier."

"If it's okay with you, I thought I'd also give a heeler pup to Jake. If you had two puppies, they could play with each other. They wouldn't get in so much trouble."

"That makes sense." She reached for her socks and sat on the edge of the bed to put them on. "But your dogs are bound to be expensive. Stock dogs are."

He held up his hand. "Your kids are worth it. And I damn sure wouldn't sell you any of my dogs." He swung around and left the room.

"Arrogant, stubborn, and a real pain at times." Elinor drew on her boots and picked up the cup of coffee. The hot brew was wonderful, even better than what she made at home.

He was a definite keeper. A guy who would make a bed, and bring her coffee, should be cut some slack. Besides, the little smile that flickered at the edges of his mouth and shone in his eyes was enough to thrill her.

She stopped in the kitchen to leave the empty cup on the counter and headed for the barn to help with the chores. He was measuring dry kibble into pans when she approached. "I guess it's my turn to eat crow. I'm sorry. I didn't mean to hurt your feelings."

He studied her with narrowed gray eyes, then nodded. "Okay. It'd help if you'd tell me when I do something that reminds you of your ex."

"All right." She sauntered to Sean, feeling like the sexiest woman on the planet. She laced her arms around his neck and kissed him. "I will." She tipped her head, so their gazes met. Her tone was calm. "My grandpa Talbot was the last man who gave me anything. I'm not good at accepting presents."

Sean slipped his hand into her hair. "We'll work on it together."

NINETEEN

As they pulled into Elinor's driveway, she realized that the barns were still dark. She checked her watch. It was 6:10. The house appeared still, too.

"That's strange." Elinor opened her door as soon as Sean turned off the engine. "I'm going to start chores. Gypsy needs to finish eating before you and Lynn leave."

"I'll help you," Sean said. "What do you want me to do?"

"Feed the steers and the pigs. I'll get the ponies squared away. Then I'll do the chickens. Once everybody's eating, I can see what the story is with the kids. They've probably overslept, and as busy as Lynn gets with Gypsy, she ought to have more rest."

Elinor hurried into the old two-story barn. She turned on the overhead fluorescent lights.

Like the rest of the ponies, Gypsy was in her stall. However, the palomino mare wasn't blanketed. Her tail wasn't wrapped in a long bandage the way Lynn always did the night before a show. She hadn't been clipped again or had her muzzle shaved.

What's going on? Elinor hastily fed the ponies. She made sure everyone had water, gave Bonanza and Rebel their extra vitamins, then headed for the house. The chickens could wait and so could the cow. Whatever was wrong with Lynn wouldn't…

Guilt and terror overwhelmed Elinor. *What was I thinking? I never should have spent the night with Sean. If she's sick, I'll never forgive myself.*

The lights were on in the kitchen as she hurried up the back steps. She opened the door. Sandy sat at the table, tying the laces on her boots. Elinor took a deep breath. "Where's Lynn? Is she all right?"

"Of course." Sandy looked confused. "Why wouldn't she be? I'd have called you if something happened."

"I didn't leave you a number for Sean's," Elinor said.

The blond college student grinned. "Marlene has it. Besides, I had the number for your cell. Lynn's fine. So's Jake. Honest, Elinor. Breathe. You can trust me."

The fear slowly seeped out of her body, and Elinor relaxed. "Sean's here to take Lynn and her horse to the show in less than an hour. Why isn't Gypsy ready?"

"Because Lynn refused to do any prep work last night after Penny telephoned." Sandy sighed. "I must have told Lynn a hundred times that we could cope without her. We did last week. Clancy's mom said it'd be okay if she came in to teach and that Clancy would call back if she had a conflict. But Lynn wouldn't work on the pony."

Elinor shook her head. "I'm the mom. I've said it so many times. Either the girl still doesn't believe me, or she's setting herself up for failure."

"What do you want me to do?" Sandy asked.

"Go groom Gypsy. Wash her tail and get Sean to help you trim her if she needs it." Elinor headed toward the coffeemaker and started to prepare a pot. "I'll wake up Lynn and get her moving."

On the way to her daughter's room, she checked on Jake. He was still sound asleep, and she adjusted his covers. Then she went to wake her daughter.

Lynn was already dressing when she entered the room. She closed the door behind her. "We've got to talk."

"About what?" Lynn asked, dragging on a clean T-shirt. "Did you have fun last night?"

"Yes." Elinor sat down at her daughter's desk. "Honey, I appreciate the fact that you want to help me. But showing Gypsy's very important to you."

Lynn shrugged. "You need me here. Penny's not coming again." She took out a pair of socks. "It doesn't matter, Mom. It's no big deal."

"It is to me. Get your act together. You've saved your allowance for months to pay your show fees. You're going today."

"No, I'm not." Lynn took her work boots from the closet. "You're the first one to say we can't impose on other people. It's not fair to Clancy to ask her to work here when we can't afford to pay her."

Elinor stood and crossed the room. She hugged Lynn. "All right, Miss Thirteen Going on Thirty, you listen up. I'm the mom. For once, you're going to do what I say."

"But you're wrong." Lynn's voice was muffled against her.

Elinor stroked the girl's golden-brown hair. "No, I'm not. I made a deal with Clancy. She wants to use Paragon for stud service. She's taking him to her place next week. The Dawsons will board him, break him to ride, and when they're finished using him for stud, arrange to have Dr. Watkins geld him. Then he'll come home to us. Clancy will work out part of the stud fees."

"What about Penny?" Lynn's shoulders shook.

"She's going to have to find another job." Elinor cuddled Lynn. "Don't cry, sweetie. It's enough when we save the four-legged people in this world. We don't have to rescue the two-legged ones."

"Okay." Lynn returned the hug. "I do love you."

"I love you, too," Elinor promised. "Now, get ready to go. Sean's here with his trailer. He and Sandy are getting Gypsy ready. I'll go make breakfast and pack your lunch."

Elinor hugged her daughter once more. She released Lynn and started toward the door. "Once Clancy gets used to being here and can manage the place, I'll find another riding instructor. Then I'll be able to see you ride in the shows." She paused. "I talked to Brigid last night and she gave me a tip for you about your gallop. It's not cheating. It's something I didn't know was okay to do in your show classes."

"What is it?" Lynn wiped her face.

"She says that when you gallop and Gypsy goes off on the wrong lead, it's all right if you stop and start over. It shows you know that you lost your balance…"

"And I made Gypsy lose hers, so she got on the outside front leg." Lynn blew her nose. "Marlene says in dressage they call it a counter canter and if I'm not careful when Gypsy leads on the wrong foot, she could fall."

"That's right. And where would you be if your pony fell?"

"Squashed underneath her like a bug." Lynn sounded cheerful. "That's why Marlene taught me to vault free of the saddle. But it doesn't always work." She sounded unperturbed by the idea of a serious accident.

Typical kid, Elinor thought as she left the room. *She doesn't think she could get hurt. At least Sean will be there to watch over her.* Was trusting him the smart thing to do? *Yes.* He cared about Lynn and could be counted on where the child was concerned.

Should I trust him? That was the question. She'd never been able to rely on a man before. She always survived because she didn't take the risk of loving anyone except Lynn and Jake.

Grandpa Talbot said that my father wanted me, but his country needed him more than I did. My mother's parents never wanted me. John didn't love me. I was convenient. I just wanted someone to hold me, to care about me, and I pretended he did.

What am I going to do about Sean? How do I know I can trust him?

———

With Sandy's, Jake's, and Sean's help, Gypsy was ready and loaded in the trailer on time. Next came Lynn. Elinor breathed a sigh of relief as she carefully placed the Western and English saddles in the back seat of the Sean's super-cab pickup.

"What do you think?" Sean asked. "Do we have everything?" He pushed back his hat to study her. She looked back.

All she could think about was the hours in his bed and he knew it. She saw the barely suppressed smirk. "Stop it," she hissed.

"I haven't done anything yet," he pointed out. "Wait until tonight." He tipped up her chin.

She quivered as his calloused fingers rubbed against the softness of her throat. His touch reminded her of the way he'd caressed her when they were in bed. Her nipples hardened. He hadn't even kissed her. A low moan escaped her lips.

"Okay, Sean. Let's go." Lynn raced past them to the truck. "Come on. I'm ready."

"So am I." Sean dropped his voice. He feathered a thumb over Elinor's mouth. "And so are you."

"Aren't you going to kiss me?" The husky note in her voice embarrassed her.

He shook his head. "Nope. I plan to wait and make you beg me for it tonight, babe."

She lifted her chin. "In your dreams, cowboy."

He chuckled. "And you'll be fantasizing about me all day." His fingers slipped down to the open collar of her shirt and pressed softly on the pulse beating in her throat. "Won't you, sweetheart?"

"No." She took a step back from him. She bit her lip as his hand cupped her breast for a moment, his thumb on her nipple. What was she doing? "Go away, Sean."

"Tell me you'll miss me first." He smiled down at her.

She glared up at him. "All right. I'll miss you, but I'll make you pay for it later." She spun and started away. She jumped when he patted her rear.

His low laugh caused her head to spin. She'd never wanted a man the way she desired him. She hadn't played these kinds of sexual games before, but she enjoyed every moment of the flirtatious foreplay, especially when she anticipated what would happen tonight.

She swung back around to wave goodbye to Lynn. Sean tooted the horn and Elinor felt her smile widen. She headed for the house to collect the buckets and warm water she needed to milk the cow, humming a classic Charlie Rich country song as she walked.

———

Like the previous Saturday, this one went well. Jake helped Sandy and Marcie tack up the ponies for trail rides. Clancy taught the lessons and jumped in wherever she was needed with a cheerful attitude. Elinor hadn't realized how tense everyone became when Penny sulked like a spoiled princess and refused to groom, saddle, feed, or water the ponies. It was time for the teen to work somewhere else and learn a few life lessons about taking responsibility.

The local hamburger place might be a good option for her. Next time I run into Vivian, I'll suggest it.

Nobody seemed to realize Elinor didn't have her brain totally on the business. She didn't call Penny or her parents right away. Firing the girl required finesse since her mother was a friend and her father was Elinor's attorney. Besides, she couldn't forget Sean and his erotic promises. Waiting until tonight seemed an impossible dream.

I haven't had sex in six years. No wonder I can't focus on anything else.

Meanwhile, the customers came and went, perfectly happy with the new instructor. Several parents signed up their kids for more lessons when Clancy announced she'd be teaching at Silver Lake Pony Ranch for the next six months. Elinor collected deposits, scheduled birthday trail parties, and led little ones on pony rides through the afternoon. Toward the end of the day, she found Clancy in the barn grooming Bonanza.

"Thanks a lot for coming in today. I don't know what I'd have done without you," Elinor said. "I don't like pulling Lynn away from her shows."

"No worries." Clancy used the body brush in sharp strokes, taking off the dirt and loose hair. Bonanza leaned into it, obviously enjoying the thorough brushing, nuzzling the other woman whenever she paused. "You should go to some of her classes. Maybe we could free you up in the mornings before things get hectic this summer."

"I'd hoped to have you manage the place for me," Elinor agreed, "but I hadn't planned on losing Penny. If she's going to be unreliable, I can't keep her."

"Talk to her parents." Clancy switched to the dandy brush and began to put a shine on the strawberry roan. "Have you considered a leasing program? If you leased out all your ponies, we could shut down on Saturdays and take your students to the 4-H shows. Kids just need horses to use…"

"Which makes them eligible for 4-H," Elinor said, "but I don't have time to run a club."

"Of course not. They could join Aunt Marlene's. She's been running it forever and has a good reputation which makes her the perfect selling tool."

"She told me she wasn't accepting any new members, that she was overloaded with kids."

"Yes, but that was before you started dating her favorite cookie monster, Sean. She'll take on your students, and we won't lease to any snots, so she won't have to deal with behavior problems. Jake could show Awesome in the colt classes this summer."

"I don't know, Clancy." Elinor picked up a groom kit and walked into Lightning's stall to prepare the pony for the next lesson. "I've heard some of the other stables do it, but their programs have always seemed too costly to me."

They continued to talk about how Elinor could restructure her business to allow more spare time for her to spend with her kids. And then Clancy brought out Lightning's saddle and pads from the tack room. "Have you ever thought of doing a summer riding camp? You've got a terrific location for it. Your place is surrounded by housing developments. Downtown Everett is only fifteen minutes north and Lynnwood is fifteen minutes south. You could make some major bucks."

"Marlene said your mother's been doing horse camp for years. I don't want to take any of her business."

"You wouldn't be. We're already booked full for our camp. We could refer our overflow customers to you. Mom said you remind her of herself twenty-some years ago. Nobody except the Dawson relatives helped her. They did their version of an intervention and arranged for us to move to the Lazy B when she couldn't work, and my father was between jobs. When they divorced, my dad never contributed one red cent, not even when the court ordered him to pay child support."

"But she made it." Elinor cleaned Lightning's hooves. "I will, too. Marlene's been a big help to me."

"Other people will be, too. Mom says it's time for us to return the favors we received." Clancy eased the blankets onto Bonanza's back.

"Well, tell me." Elinor eyed the younger woman. "Are you and Ethan back together? I've been dying of curiosity."

Clancy snorted. "Not hardly."

"What are you going to do?" Elinor asked, trying to suppress her amusement. "Trade him in for two twenty-some bucks?"

"Not a bad idea. At least they have libidos." Clancy put on the saddle. "Let me think about it."

"About what?" Sandy asked, entering the barn. Marcie followed her. "The last lesson students are here. So is the trail ride party. They're signing in at the back porch with Jake."

"What are you two discussing?" Marcie shook back her brown hair. She put a bridle on Tonka. "Can you tell us?"

"Sure. We're just talking about my love life." Clancy widened her eyes and added, "Or what passes for one if you date the only zombie outside of that TV show. Who is the latest single hunk around here?"

"You were checking out the cute guys at Billy's Western Bar last week," Elinor reminded her.

"I want a real man, not one from the drugstore cowboy set."

"Doctor Art." Sandy bridled Galaxy. The palomino gelding's golden coat matched her hair. "If Marcie and I called all the older girls in the Flying As and we started passing the word you had a thing for the vet, Extinct Ethan would certainly notice."

"'Extinct Ethan'?" Elinor eyed Clancy. "Now, who would give the poor man a nickname like that?"

"Me." Clancy contemplated the two college students. "You'd have to do it in strict confidence."

"Yeah." Marcie led Tonka from his stall. "Otherwise, it'd take too long for the gossip to get rocking."

"We'll start tonight. We're still Marlene's official callers. You take the first half of the alphabet, Marce. I'll take the last." Sandy opened Galaxy's door. "Clancy, call Art and get a date with him. Make sure it's for tonight. Then you'll be out with him when Ethan calls."

"How do you know Ethan will phone?" Elinor asked.

"That's your job." Sandy continued to delegate. "Tell Sean to make Ethan do it. Sean will know how. He's made Ethan jump through hoops for ages."

"Why aren't I surprised?" Elinor felt her knees weaken at the mention of Sean's name. She glanced at her watch. He'd be back soon. She couldn't wait. She had plans for tonight and they started with ripping his clothes off, but she could talk to him, too. "Okay, you've got a deal. I'll get Sean involved."

PART TWO

APRIL 2018

"*Magick* happens if you let it."

LYNN PRICE

TWENTY

Lynn finished the chart detailing the qualities of sedimentary rocks and began to color in the different layers of the hills on the worksheet. Mr. Sievers had said this assignment would count as a makeup for one of their tests, so he didn't want the students to work together. That meant she could do her best and not stress over what the others thought of her.

She heard the classroom door open and ignored it until Jake came to stand next to her desk, George beside him.

"What's going on?" Lynn said, glaring at the redheaded demon who'd plagued her brother since last September. "Why are you two here?"

"Because Jake's in trouble again," George told her. "And I didn't do anything to him, so stop looking at me like that."

"He's right," Jake agreed, tears swimming in his eyes. "Ms. Collins says I'm bad again and she's going to take away my new book."

"Oh, Jake." Lynn sighed. She stood and urged the boys in the direction of the door. "Come on." Out in the hall, she eyeballed her brother. "Why on earth did you bring it here?"

"I was at a good part and we have to read all period today, so I thought it'd be okay. Things have been better since Parents' Night last month." Jake caught his breath. "But I don't want to lose my book and have her call or e-mail Mom or get more demerits 'cause I'd have to go to Saturday school. I need to train Awesome then."

Lynn nodded. Other people might not understand Jake's worry about their mother. She wouldn't be angry at him or even yell at either of them. She had enough to do on the farm. She didn't need to deal with a twit like Jake's stupid English teacher.

"What do you need me to do?" Lynn asked.

"We told her that Jake took your book by mistake," George said. "So, he brings it to you and then you back us up if she asks you."

Lynn blinked. "There's no way Jake came up with that. He's super honest."

"Yeah, but me and the guys are teaching him better," George said. "Will you help?"

"Of course." Lynn took the hardcover from Jake. "Wait here."

"For what?" George asked.

"Well, if he had my book, I must have his," Lynn said. "Right?"

"Oh, man." Disgust filled Jake's face, and he wrinkled his nose. "Lynnie, I don't want to read one of your baby books. They suck."

"No, they don't. They've won all sorts of awards and teachers just love 'em." Lynn went back in the classroom to her desk. She opened her backpack and pulled out the thin paperback she'd brought for her own reading period. She stuffed Jake's book into her backpack, carefully arranging her textbooks around it.

She returned to Jake and George, handing her brother the other book. "Here. This should make your teacher happy."

"*Surviving the Applewhites*." Jake rolled his eyes. "I read this ages ago. It's good, but it's a kids' book."

"That's what Collins thinks we are," George told him. "Come on, Jake. If we don't get back, she'll call security on us."

"If she does that, I'll be stuck in Saturday school for sure and then Mom won't let me go with Sean…" His voice trailed away.

Lynn caught on. If her brother was in trouble at school, he couldn't take Thursday off to go fishing with Sean. She supposed she should be jealous of his special times with Sean, but she wasn't. She liked hanging out with her friends at school and goofing around. Besides, Sean came on Saturdays to help her at horse shows and they had their own special times.

"Go." She pointed toward the sixth-grade wing. "I'll see you in Math class later and you can tell me how things went."

"Okay." The two boys hurried down the hall, talking like friends.

Weird. Maybe, her brother's *magick* spell had worked on more people than Mom and Sean.

That afternoon, Lynn wasn't as happy or pleased with Jake and George's scheme. Her English teacher gave her a big smile and asked to see the new book Lynn was reading. It seemed that Ms. Collins had talked about it in the staff lounge. With a sigh, she pulled out the hardcover.

"I'm so glad to see you reading something suitable for the ninth-grader you'll be in the fall," Ms. Porter gushed. "This is such a wonderful series, Lynn. Which one do you like best?"

"Oh, the one I'm reading now," Lynn said, hoping she didn't get any more questions. She headed for her seat and opened the book. A princess? A magic kingdom? Couldn't her brother do better than that?

However, the heroine wasn't the typical princess. Any girl who got suspended for bringing a dragon to school was pretty awesome, as Jake would say, and Lynn found herself enthralled by the story. No wonder Jake couldn't leave the book at home.

———

Elinor had spent her morning overwhelmed with a list of tasks she hoped would keep her mind off Sean, but it hadn't worked. While she watered and fed the livestock, she remembered his cheerful attitude when he pitched in to help with chores.

She'd gone to coffee with Daisy and the two of them talked about everything under the sun from the reading list Daisy made for Jake every month to Lynn's latest research project. This one was on border collies, a topic that Daisy had suggested to help Lynn get ready to train a puppy.

Working with the retired teacher allowed the kids to continue their education from where they'd left off the previous fall and it made all of them happy. It also filled an emotional niche for the three of them, providing Lynn and Jake with the grandmother they didn't have and giving Daisy surrogate grandkids.

Finally, Daisy brought up the latest political scandal. The subject brought Sean to mind again. He'd mentioned his father's annual Memorial Day barbecue and asked her to mark the date on the calendar so she and the kids could attend with him.

It wasn't a real problem. She closed the pony farm on major holidays, but how did she tell the guy that meeting his parents terrified her? It wasn't something she wanted to share with Daisy, who'd tell her to "woman up" and go for it.

After coffee, Elinor returned home and used the next hour to muck out her kitchen. The cluttered counters, the double sink full of dirty dishes, overflowing laundry baskets, and stacks of paperwork on the table always amazed her. How did the house get beyond her like this?

Clancy would be here this afternoon so they could plan summer day camp. Elinor smiled when she recalled the way that Sean had agreed to let his brother know who Clancy dated. He said it'd be fun to torment Ethan. Of course, Sean hadn't thought it was fun when she'd sent him home again after their heavy necking session.

They hadn't slept together since their first time at his house. It wasn't that she didn't want him. She did. She just didn't feel comfortable having sex with him—okay, making love to him—while her kids were in the house. Besides, she could just imagine how her ex would use it against her in court. He might claim not to want their children, but he lived for power plays and her new relationship would provide far too much ammunition.

An afternoon cup of coffee in front of her on the kitchen table, she considered her options. She was attracted to Sean Killian. No, it went deeper. She was in love with him, even if she didn't have the confidence to tell him.

Lynn and Jake adored Sean. In barely three weeks, he'd spent more time with them than their father had since they were born. Sean gave her children more love and affection, too.

Puppies, for heaven's sake. She couldn't turn that down, not when it was the kids' dream to own one. He attended their activities. He listened to them. He let them hang out with him.

She buried her face in her hands. What was she going to do?

I've been rejected and abandoned all my life. What if Sean's trying to rescue me?

If he thought she didn't need him, he might leave. What if he stayed?

Love was a trap. She could survive pain, abuse, hatred. She had before. What had Grandpa Talbot said? *Your enemies will make you strong.*

A tap on the back door startled her. She snapped to attention. She never showed her vulnerability. That was a life lesson she'd learned as a child.

"Relax, Elinor." Marlene came into the room. "It's me. I came to join the brainstorming session you and Clancy have planned for today. I promised to return the trailer so she could use it to haul Paragon up to their place. Is the coffee on? Shall I make a pot?"

Elinor jerked her head toward the counter. "It's ready." She stood. "I'll pour you a cup."

"I haven't broken either arm." Marlene walked across the kitchen and took a mug off the rack on the wall. "How's it going? Do I get in trouble for asking?"

"You should." Elinor shook her head. "You're the one who played matchmaker between Sean and me. Lynn and Jake think he's the greatest. He realized Chipeta was pregnant. He brought

Lynn's favorite chicken back from the dead. He's helped her take a first and two seconds this show season, the best she's ever done. And the fish in the local streams and rivers have been in jeopardy ever since he and Jake threatened to bring them home."

Marlene ran a hand through a patch of gray streaks in her black hair. "All that?" A grin came to life on her lips. "Does he walk on water, too?"

"The kids say you do. Maybe you taught him." Elinor sighed. "If he'd done it last week when he and Jake were fishing, I'm sure I'd have heard about it by now." She wasn't sharing Sean's other miracle. He made her enjoy sex and she'd abhorred it with John.

"I'm scared, Marlene. I'm a failure when it comes to relationships. I'll blow this. I know it."

"You won't." Marlene sat next to Elinor. "It takes two people to make or break a marriage. Or a relationship. Both you and John Price screwed up. It wasn't a hundred and ten percent your fault. Stop blaming yourself."

Elinor stared into her coffee cup. It was as dark as her future looked without Sean. "I'm afraid. How can I trust him?"

"Wait a while. Trust comes on its own time," Marlene said. "Trust me if you're not ready to trust him. Have I ever steered you wrong?"

"No." Elinor studied the older woman's careworn features and gripped Marlene's hand. "You're closer to me than my grandmother who raised me. When I married John, she told me I could suffer in the bed I'd made. And I did."

"Oh, honey. I'm sure she didn't mean it."

"Oh, yes she did. I haven't heard from her since I left home. She and my grandfather have never visited Lynn and Jake since they were born. John's family feels the way he does, that I only got pregnant to trap him. I haven't heard from any of them since the divorce."

"So, write them off. No loss. If you marry Sean, you'll have his family."

"I haven't even met his parents yet. Sean wants to take us to this picnic at his folks' place on Memorial Day. What if they hate me? I can't put my kids in that kind of situation."

Marlene pursed her lips. "Okay. Tell him that you need a written invitation from his mother."

"I'll sound like a total—a total dweeb, as Jake would say," Elinor protested. "I'm not that formal."

"I'll admit they aren't the greatest parents or the best people I ever dealt with, but the Killians aren't evil, Elinor. They just have the wrong priorities and it's starting to come home to them. Fish or cut bait, girl. How do you feel about Sean?"

"I've only known him three weeks, Marlene."

"Time doesn't enter into it, Elinor. I loved Roy the instant I met him. I was never sorry I married him. I'm glad we had our forty years together. I wanted more, like his children. It wasn't meant to be, so we spoiled my sisters' girls. And we had the club."

"What happened to Darlene's husband?"

"Roy's cousin was a jerk. I told Darlene that when she dated him, and she didn't speak to me for six months after the wedding." Marlene sipped her coffee. "He ran off with another woman while she was expecting Audra. Darlene had to move in with Roy and me."

"But she took him back. Why?"

"Because nobody in our family had ever divorced and she was a good Catholic girl. She hung in there a lot longer than I would have."

"Maybe she was scared to be alone." Tears bubbled in Elinor's throat. "I know how I felt after Grandpa Talbot died."

"Honey, don't you think that's your problem?" Marlene softened. "You don't trust your feelings about Sean. How can you? You never knew an adult who was safe to love. Your parents abandoned you. So did your grandparents. John Price. His family. Even your grandfather."

"He died, damn it." Tears trickled down Elinor's cheeks. "It wasn't his fault. And it wasn't mine. I love the farm he bought me, but I still needed him."

"No one was ever there for you, Elinor. Don't dump Sean because you're terrified."

"I don't want to be alone for the rest of my life." Elinor cried harder. She suddenly realized Marlene held her as if she were a child. "I don't know what to do."

"Grieve." Marlene stroked Elinor's hair. "Cry for the girl you were, the child left to raise herself by the two people who should have been there for you. Then grow up. You can change. All you have to do is want to, and we both know you do."

A half hour later, when they went to turn out the ponies, Elinor felt emotionally hung over. Star, Taffy, Bonanza, Chipeta, and Awesome went to their paddock while the rest of the herd grazed together. Paragon was locked in the round pen to mow the grass by himself.

Together, Elinor and Marlene cleaned the barn. They put out the night hay and grain. With the grass in the pastures, the ponies wouldn't need lunch.

Clancy strolled into the barn as they finished. "Did I time it right?"

"Don't you always?" Marlene gave Clancy a quick hug. "Are you and Ethan engaged again?"

"He wants to be," Clancy said. "I haven't decided yet."

"What are you waiting for?" Marlene hung the plastic manure forks on the stable wall. "I thought the whole idea was for the two of you to reconcile. That's what you said."

"We will eventually," Clancy assured her. "You know how the twins are and the kind of fits they have when they actually end up doing chores. This is the first one Mom's caught since Vonnie sold Bonanza the day she was pissed at me. I want Ethan to choose me over them."

Marlene nodded. "That makes sense, honey. I wish it didn't."

"Wait a minute." Elinor held up a hand, then pointed out to the field where Bonanza grazed. "He actually belonged to the Dawsons?"

"All his life," Clancy said. "I couldn't believe it when Sean said he found him. I looked all over the county for him."

"I bought him for Jake three years ago because I wanted a reliable mount for him to start on when he was eight." Elinor took a deep breath. "And to think I envied you for having sisters. Maybe not so much now."

"That's family for you." Clancy said. "I'm keeping Audra, Brigid and Kate, but I'll give you the twins."

"No way. I don't want them." Elinor laughed. "Well, let's go plan the summer. When do you want to start day-camp?"

As they headed for the house, Clancy gestured to the loft over top of the garage. "What's up there? Can we use it for the camp?"

"A studio apartment," Elinor said. "John used it for an office."

"Maybe we could use it as a lunchroom on rainy days."

In the kitchen, Elinor read the schedule that Clancy had prepared. The camp would run from nine in the morning until four in the afternoon, Mondays through Fridays. The kids would have riding lessons and classes in grooming and saddling. There would be trail rides and games on horseback. Friday's camp would culminate in a horse show for parents and friends.

"How many children a week do you think we can handle?" Elinor asked.

"Two kids to a pony." Clancy brought cups of coffee over to the table. "Sixteen campers. Sandy and Marcie need to ride. So do Lynn and Jake. We'll use them as senior students to show the campers what to do. When camp's over for the day, we'll do trail rides, lessons and lead-around ponies in the afternoon."

"How much do you think we can charge?" Elinor tapped a pen against her chin. "We've got to cover payroll."

"Lunch for the ponies, and an after-camp snack," Marlene said. "You'll have to feed them extra if you expect them to work such long days. You won't be able to turn them out to pasture for three or four hours in the afternoons."

Over the next two hours, they designed the camp brochures. Elinor found her old insurance waivers. The forms always included addresses as well as names. The information would provide the nucleus of a mailing list.

"What about your leasing idea?" Marlene asked Clancy. "Did you bring a flyer for Elinor? If she changes the program, it'd work for her pony farm."

"Right here." Clancy passed over a triple-fold brochure. "We can talk about it when we send out camp stuff, along with a website. You really need one. I've got to go. I'm meeting Art so he can give Paragon his shots. And then I have a date with Jack Abbott tonight."

"Whoa." Marlene blinked. "How does your mother feel?"

"Oh, she's totally miffed about Art pretending to chase me." Clancy stood. "But Art and I made a deal. We go out long enough to convince Mom to rescue me from him."

"And Jack?" Marlene tilted her head to one side. "That boy's a rambler. He'll never stick and stay."

"I know." Clancy winked. "And he irritates Ethan, too. That makes Jack a double winner."

"Poor Ethan." Marlene glanced at Elinor. "We've been trying to get Darlene and Art together for the past twenty years."

"Is that a hint for me?" Elinor asked. "Do you plan to hassle me about Sean for that long?"

"I won't have to," Marlene said smugly. "He knows the time to dance is when the music plays."

TWENTY-ONE

When she walked into the front yard, she saw Jake standing by the truck, peering into the cab of Clancy's pickup. Elinor headed that way. "What's going on?"

"Kittens and a mom cat," Jake said, blue eyes wide. "Clancy says they belong to us and I'm taking them to the barn."

"Not till you change your clothes," Elinor told him. "Hustle and you can cuddle them before they get busy hunting mice."

He was running for the house before she finished speaking. She laughed and turned at the sound of gravel crunching under tires. She recognized Sean's pickup and the trailer behind it. "Hey, cowboy."

"Hi, sweetheart." He shut the driver's door behind him. "Finished up a little early today so I brought Midnight and Musketeer." He caught Elinor's hand. "Come here, you."

"Me?" She tried to look innocent. "Why?" She stepped close and slipped her hands over his chest. She felt the thud of his heartbeat.

He pulled her against him. "I've wanted you all day. If life didn't get in the way, I'd take you to bed now."

"I'm shocked," she teased, sliding her hands up to his shoulders. The feel of his fingers on her back, the strong, muscled arms holding her tight made her ache with longing. She groaned. "Oh, God. Sean."

"I know." He lowered his head. "Kiss me."

She touched her mouth to his, a light pressure that didn't satisfy either of them. "Like this?"

"Witch." His hands clamped around her waist and he picked her up.

She squealed and laced her arms around his neck. He turned and carried her toward the truck. What was he doing? He put her down on the hood of the pickup.

She felt the warmth of the engine through her jeans. "It's hot." She started to squirm her way down.

He stopped her. He parted her legs and stepped between them. "I'm hot, too, witch. Now, kiss me. And make it good."

She threaded her fingers in his hair. She leaned forward to trace his lips with her tongue. "Don't you like bad better?"

"I can go either way." His fist clenched in her hair. His mouth seized hers and his tongue laid claim.

He kissed her as if he owned her. She clung to him, her lips yielding to his, granting him possession.

Strange, she mused when he lifted his head. As much as he made her feel that she belonged to him, she felt he was hers. Despite the heavy denim of her jeans, his hands on her thighs made her moan. She knew where she wanted him to touch her. He was so close, but he didn't move his fingers where the heat coiled inside her.

She tried to wriggle closer. "Please." Her voice trembled. "Please, Sean."

He smiled and kissed her neck. "Oh no, babe. You'll just have to wait and burn like I am." He nipped at the cord in her throat. "Are you hot?"

"You know it." She leaned forward to catch his lips with hers. The kiss lasted barely a moment before he lifted his head. She saw Lynn standing a few feet away, a paper in her hand. "What's the matter, honey?" Elinor asked, hoping she didn't look embarrassed.

"You were kissing Sean." Lynn didn't sound angry or upset, but baffled. "And he was kissing you."

"You're almost fourteen," Sean drawled. "You're a smart girl. You know adults kiss all the time, especially when they're falling in love."

"Not my mother," Lynn said in a matter-of-fact tone. "She never kissed my father and he sure didn't touch or kiss her that I can remember."

She tilted her head. Her face scrunched in thought. "He didn't hug or kiss me or Jake either."

"Oh, honey." Elinor tried to push past Sean, but his body prevented her from getting off the pickup hood. "Your dad wasn't demonstrative, but I know he loves you."

Lynn sighed. "Oh, Mom. It's like Jake says. He's a jerk and he didn't love any of us."

Sean nodded. "Well, in a way, that's good."

His insensitivity astonished Elinor. "How can you say that?"

Sean shrugged one broad shoulder. "Think about it, girl. You're a loyal little cuss. If he'd loved his kids even a smidgen, you'd still be married. I might be shoeing your horses, but I sure as hell wouldn't be chasing you or your kids. And when I fell in love with you, I'd be damned sure not to let you know."

Elinor gasped. She'd never thought of her divorce as being a blessing before. She'd figured it was a case of being abandoned one more time. Her lips trembled. She took a deep breath and glanced at her daughter.

Lynn gazed at Sean with approval. "You're a good guy. I like you a lot."

"The feeling's mutual." Sean grinned at her. Then he helped Elinor down from the hood of the pickup. "What's going on, Lynn?"

"You wanted to see my schedule for the rest of the showing season," Lynn replied.

"All right," Sean said. "Let's see."

"I marked the ones I want to attend. I've signed up for the

show on Memorial Day weekend. It's on Saturday. Is that okay?" Lynn asked, worry seeping into her face.

"Sounds good. Most people go out of town then and I don't do much shoeing." Sean took the list. "I have to go to my folks' place that Monday, but the weekend is open."

Elinor stood next to him. One of his hands rested on her hip and she luxuriated in his touch. It reminded her of the hours they'd spent making love at his place and she wished they could do it again. She forced herself to listen to the conversation.

"Okay." Lynn took the list of dates back from Sean. "I'll go mark the calendar in the kitchen. Then you can have this list for your schedule." She started away. "And you two can go back to kissing." She giggled and ran back to the house.

———

It didn't take long to mark the calendar with the remaining spring 4-H horse shows. Lynn hesitated and then wrote down the two in June. She wanted to earn enough points to be in the medal classes this year at the county fair, but who knew if Sean would still be around.

Yes, he and Mom had been kissing in the front yard and that was different. Mom didn't date. She never even went for coffee with the teachers or principals who asked her. That meant she thought Sean was special. Who knew if it was Jake's *magick* or not, but Sean made Mom smile.

When Lynn returned to the yard, she saw her mother and Sean standing by the rear of the trailer while he unlatched the doors. "What's going on?"

"Sean brought the ponies that we're borrowing from the Dawson's Lazy B ranch and I think we'll put them in the round pen for now until we have stalls for them," her mom said. "Would you like to lead one of them while I bring the other?"

"Sure." Lynn watched while Sean led a small bay gelding with four white socks and a blaze out of the stock trailer. "He's so cute. What's his name?"

"Musketeer," Sean said. "And his best friend is Midnight."

"Cool." Lynn headed toward the round pen, keeping the appropriate distance from the black Welsh pony that her mother led.

After the ponies were secured, Lynn grabbed the barn broom and went to sweep out the livestock hauler. She passed him the show schedule and he glanced over it, nodded, and tucked the paper in his shirt pocket.

"When the next 4-H bulletin comes in the mail, let me know about the shows in July, August, and September," Sean said. "Does that work for you?"

"Yeah." Lynn concentrated on cleaning the corners, staring hard so the tears didn't escape. He sounded like he'd be here all summer, not as if he couldn't wait to get away from her because she sucked as a daughter and a person.

"Nice job cleaning." Clancy arrived with a bale of shavings. "Aunt Marlene and I swapped rigs when your mom said I could take Paragon with me tonight, Lynn. Did you want to help Jake with the cat and the kittens? We just took the crate to the barn loft."

Lynn stopped and stared, her breath catching in her throat. She'd nearly let the truth escape. They couldn't have small animals because her father hated them. He'd killed her cat, then laughed when she cried. She asked him where he'd buried Pyewacket and he said he threw the body in the trash.

When she tried talking to her mother, Mom said she gave the cat away, but wouldn't share any other details about where Pye had gone. So, Lynn knew the truth. Her cat was dead, and her mom wanted to keep the peace in the family regardless of the cost.

"Do we really get to keep them?" The question escaped before Lynn could stop it.

"They're all yours now," Clancy said. "Your mom agreed to take them last week. The bag of cat food is on the back porch."

Sean came over and took the broom. "Go see them but promise me one thing."

Lynn eyed him warily. She wasn't a little kid anymore. She wouldn't let him, or any other guy hurt the kittens. "What?"

"Leave them in the barn until after your birthday. If you move them into the house and then you get a puppy, he'll think the kittens are chew toys. It can be hard to teach a puppy to respect cats."

"Not a good idea with Baby," Clancy said. "That's the mom and she's very protective. She chases dogs out of her barn. She'll have puppy fricassee."

Lynn felt a giggle form. "I won't take the kittens away from their mother. How did you get Mom to say we could have cats again? Our dad…"

Clancy looked at Sean, then said, "Oh, it was *magick*, honey."

"It had to be." Lynn hurried out of the trailer. Behind her, she heard Clancy say, "Now, if you don't find the guy and kick his tail, Sean, I will. Nobody has the right to put a look like that on a little girl's face."

Lynn didn't hear Sean's response but, for a moment, she wished that he would find her father and do just that. That hadn't been part of the spell she and Jake cast, and she knew her younger brother wouldn't approve of the idea. He'd said they couldn't do anything to hurt their dad. But the idea of Sean punching her dad made her happy.

———

Elinor put Paragon's favorite snack of chopped apples and carrots into a freezer bag. Tears stung her eyes and she bit her lip. *Oh, come on. This isn't for keeps. I'll have him back in September and he'll have a great spring making babies.* She stopped in the tack room and gathered up his brushes, then went to his stall where she found Clancy haltering the little stud.

"I have his stuff here, Clancy. Whenever I want him to do something and he does it right, I give him a treat."

"Sounds good. Come visit him whenever you have time," Clancy said. "Believe me, I'll be checking up on Midnight and Musketeer."

"Okay." Elinor led the way toward the trailer where Sean waited. She smiled at him. "Now, let's change the subject. What's on the agenda for Saturday night? You suggested we take the kids out with us. Where did you have in mind?"

"It wasn't really a suggestion. It was my strategy for keeping you away from Clancy's mission of hunting down cute guys." Sean put an arm around Elinor's shoulders. "What if we take in a movie? The drive-in up north opens this weekend with a Disney double feature. You, me, the kids, the stars, and a G-rated flick or two."

"We could do that," Elinor agreed. "Personally, I hoped you had other plans."

"Yeah," Clancy led Paragon forward. "And I bet I know what. Why don't you pass up Disney and come with me to the Arabian auction at Xanadu? They have some great horses and the prices are dirt cheap, which makes Audra crazy, but the owners use the place as a tax write off. Anyway, there will be some cute cowboys and we can bid on those."

"I'm the cute cowboy, not one of the drugstore set." Sean chuckled. "Come on, darlin'. You'll love the movies. We can always neck during the intermission."

"In front of my kids?" Elinor shook her head. "I don't think so, cowboy."

"We'll send them to the playground during the break."

"Maybe." Elinor brushed a quick kiss over his mouth. "I'd better get on the chores then."

"Me, too. I need to head home and take care of my dogs. I must exercise them. They need more time out than my pet sitter gives them." Sean waited until Clancy tied in Paragon and climbed out of the trailer, then he closed and latched the doors. "I'll be here first thing tomorrow to take Jake fishing with me."

"He'll love it." Elinor sighed. "And I'll be in his classroom exercising patience with that silly teacher and trying to convince her to raise her level of expectations."

"If anyone can do it, darlin', you can." After a quick, soft kiss that left both of them breathless, he was gone.

"I'll see you Saturday," Clancy said. "Are you really okay if I take off early to go help Audra with her auction?"

"Yes," Elinor said. "And now, I'll go have a quick cup of coffee with Marlene and then send the woman home so she doesn't help me finish my chores. Where are my kids?"

"In the barn loft with the kittens." Clancy headed for the pickup, then paused. "A few years ago, Aunt Marlene gave us a Siamese cat. Did it start life here?"

"Yes, but my ex wasn't good with animals," Elinor said. "He kept threatening to hurt Pyewacket and I couldn't let him, so your aunt and I agreed we needed somewhere else for Pye to live. How is he?"

"Fine. He's getting up there, but he still bosses Audra around. You should tell Lynn that she can visit him when she goes up to Xanadu for the Memorial Day show."

Elinor nodded. "I will."

She waited until the younger woman pulled out of the yard before going to the house to join Marlene.

"Did you get everybody off okay?" the older woman asked.

"Yes," Elinor said. "Now I just have to drag the kids away from the kittens before bedtime." She filled her own cup and brought over the pot to top Marlene's mug.

The older woman glanced at the clock and shook her head. "No more for me, honey." She hastily finished her coffee and stood. "I've got to go. I'll be late to feed Pryde and he's prone to colic."

"I need to get on my chores, too." Elinor stood and walked Marlene out to her rig.

Marlene hugged Elinor. "Nobody expects you to be perfect, so stop expecting that of yourself."

———

On Friday, Elinor didn't have to teach school, so she went next door for coffee. She and Daisy discussed her substitute schedule for the following week and life in general. When Elinor went home, she saw Sean's pickup parked in front of the house.

He climbed out as soon as he spotted her. "Hey, girl."

"Hey, cowboy. What are you doing here?"

"You. During my lunch break." He feathered calloused thumbs over her cheekbones. "Are you sending me away again, witch?"

"No." She caught her breath on a moan. "The kids are at school." Her pulse beat in excitement. "Come on, handsome."

"In a moment." He tormented her with soft, quick butterfly kisses over her cheeks, lips, and nose. "I'll bet if I make you beg, you'll tell me all the rotten tricks you and Clancy have planned for this weekend."

"Don't count on it." Elinor rose on tiptoe and tried to capture his mouth with hers. "Sean, please."

"That was fast." He swung her up in his arms and carried her toward the back porch. "I want more pleading than that, sweetheart."

"You won't get it."

"Want to bet?"

TWENTY-TWO

WITH MIXED EMOTIONS, ELINOR WATCHED ANOTHER CAR PULL INTO the drive. Another fifteen minutes and she'd have locked the gates. It had been a busy day. Her bank account would love the hefty deposit come Monday, but she hadn't even started chores yet and Sean would be here in less than an hour.

She headed toward the vehicle, recognizing the driver. It was Christy, the young mother from Parents' Night at the school. She helped a small girl out of the back seat of the expensive new automobile. Like her mother, the child wore jeans and a T-shirt. Both had their long black hair in braids.

"Hi, Elinor," Christy said. "I got off late, but we still have time for Ginny to ride Galaxy, don't we?"

"My pony," Ginny announced firmly. "I ride him now! Mommy said. I was good."

Elinor laughed. "Then you deserve to ride Galaxy." She led the way to the house. "Let's have you sign in and find a riding helmet for Ginny. How old are you, Ginny?"

"I'm four." The little girl held up the appropriate number of fingers. "I'm big. I ride by myself."

Christy dropped to her knees, so her and Ginny's gazes were

on the same level. "I hang onto Galaxy's bit. You hold the reins in your left hand and the saddle horn with your right hand, or we go home."

Ginny's lower lip drooped into a pout. "I ride. You said."

"Only if you ride safe," Christy said.

Ginny heaved a huge, dramatic sigh. "Okay, I be good."

"All right." Christy stood and took Ginny's hand. "Let's get carrots for Galaxy and his friends."

"Lots and lots of carrots," Ginny agreed. "I do it. I feed ponies."

It only took a few minutes to do the paperwork, fit a helmet on Ginny's head, feed Galaxy his carrots, and get the ride started on the sturdy palomino. While Christy led the Shetland gelding around the yard, Elinor organized the evening chores. Jake took care of the chickens, the steers, the pigs, and the cow with her. Both he and Lynn were excited about the night at the movies with Sean and pushed everyone to hurry.

Forty minutes later, Elinor checked on Galaxy. He cropped grass in the orchard. Christy and Ginny stood looking through the white board fence at the pasture where Chipeta, her foal Awesome, Star, Taffy, and Bonanza grazed.

Against the green grass and blue sky, the ponies seemed like a painting of a herd with the red of Chipeta and Awesome, the dark brown of Star, Taffy's dapple gray, and the faded strawberry of Bonanza's coat. They were so many different colors it was little wonder Sean called her ponies a rainbow herd.

Elinor walked over to catch Galaxy. She could always claim that she thought Ginny was done with her ride and didn't plan to climb back on after looking at the herd. It was a reasonable expectation. "Come on, buddy. Let's get you ready for supper."

She'd barely reached the barn when Jake pelted in the door. "Mom! Mom! The ponies are out!"

Elinor dropped Galaxy's reins and pushed past the palomino. She raced through the pasture, along the driveway, past the house.

She gasped for breath. Terror kept her running. Out of the corner of her eye, she saw Bonanza climb the back-porch steps of the house. On a carrot mission, he was safe for now.

She went after the mares. Star and Taffy jogged down the drive to the road in front of the farm. Once a peaceful country highway, it now connected two housing developments. The heavy traffic usually exceeded the twenty mile an hour speed limit, particularly on Saturdays.

Star and Taffy didn't seem to care about the cars. Chipeta, with Awesome beside her, followed the heavily pregnant mares. Problems wouldn't end if they reached the hay field. Zane O'Malley across the way, an unpleasant neighbor at best, kept his shotgun loaded with rock salt for dogs, deer, ponies, and any two-legged trespassers.

He shot first and thought later, if at all. Six months ago, Bonanza had let out the herd. When they'd reached the hay field, O'Malley had started shooting at the ponies. They spooked and ran for home, Elinor's old dog at their heels. A car had struck and killed the heeler, narrowly missing the ponies and Lynn.

Fear mounted as Elinor saw her daughter dash across the front yard. Lynn tried to run interference with the ponies and reach the gates first. If the teen could close them, the fence would keep the mares contained on the property. But fast as she was, the girl couldn't outrun a pony. Star trotted through the gates, Taffy behind her. The two were now only twenty-five feet from the paved road.

Do something, Elinor prayed. She ran for Chipeta, hoping she could at least catch the old mare. She'd save the momma and Awesome. She heard the squeal of brakes on the highway. She couldn't look.

The crunch of crushed gravel came to her ears. She stopped as the mares wheeled to race back in her direction, Awesome at his mother's side. A steel gray dog chased them past her.

Elinor realized the mares and colt were headed for the barn. "Lock them in," she yelled to Sandy as the four ponies galloped by her.

"Got it!" Sandy shouted.

Panting, Elinor rested her hands on her knees. When she looked up, she saw Sean. He closed and locked one set of highway gates while Lynn shut the other set of gates, securing the front yard and the farm.

The wooden pallets used as a boundary fence were four feet high, eight feet long, and had one-inch oak boards with two by four supports, impenetrable by ponies, cattle, pigs, and even the dogs. Cats had to climb over them. When Grandpa Talbot brought the oak pallets as a "farm-warming" present, she'd thought he was crazy.

Now, she blessed the day he'd given her the fencing material. It meant the only escape route was through the gates that blocked the two ends of the graveled circular driveway. And the mares were now safe in the barn. Bonanza probably had opened the cooler on the back porch and busily munched on all the carrots. She didn't bother to look. The carrots couldn't hurt the junk food pony.

The purplish-gray dog frisked up to Elinor, wagging his tail. She recognized Ruler. "Yes. You're a very good boy." She petted him and ruffled his short fur. "I don't know what you're doing here, but I was very glad to see you. Those stupid ponies would be dead if you hadn't saved them. You're so good."

Ruler sat down on her booted foot. He leaned against her, growling softly as if he was responding. "You're right." Elinor tugged gently on one ear and then the other. "If a pony was struck by a car, the pony would fly through the windshield and could kill a person. You saved people's lives, too. You're a hero."

She watched Sean stride toward her. A red plaid western shirt did great things for his shoulders. He even polished his cowboy boots. A dark blue bandanna circled his strong neck. She couldn't wait to untie it. "Thank you. I was never so glad to see you and Ruler in my life."

"More him." Sean narrowed his eyes. "I wasn't jumping out the truck window to chase ponies. All I could do was block the end of the driveway and hope they wouldn't get past my rig to the road."

"Thank you," Elinor repeated. She rested her hand on Ruler's head. "You two helped save my ponies."

"Anytime." Sean swung on one heel and studied the cross-fence. "What happened? Did they break the boards?"

"No." Lynn came to join them. "That stupid woman went in to pet Awesome. She and her daughter spooked Chipeta and the mares."

"Makes sense if you're a horse," Sean said. "They wanted to get the foal out of danger." He eyed the dog, then looked at Elinor. "Don't praise him anymore, honey. He missed the pony on the porch."

"No, he didn't." Elinor rumpled Ruler's fur. "He's too smart to chase Bonanza off the porch, aren't you?" She didn't wait for an answer but glanced toward the strawberry roan.

He'd bypassed the cooler of carrots in favor of the sack of dry cat food Clancy left in the corner, happily munching away. "Lynn, go get Bonanza before he eats too much of that and makes himself sick."

"Okay." Lynn eyed the dog with longing. "Mom, keep him with you. I don't want Bonanza to spook and break his legs coming down the stairs. And I don't want him to kick the dog either."

"Very smart girl you got there." Sean grinned at Lynn. "A lot of girls who love dogs as much as you do would think about having the dog with her first rather than what's safest for all the critters."

His praise touched Elinor's heart. She saw a new joy on Lynn's face before the girl hurried off to catch the old pony.

I didn't know she was so desperate for a man's approval. I've got to call John and insist he take a more active role in her life.

She glanced after her daughter once more, then at Jake as he came to join them. Shocked, she realized her son was crying. She left the dog and hurried to hug the boy. "Honey, what's wrong? The ponies are safe. They never even got to the road. It's okay."

"Sean's mad at me." Jake sobbed into her shirt. "I didn't know…"

"What on earth are you talking about?" Elinor asked. "Sean never said he was angry with you." She smoothed Jake's sandy blond hair. His tears soaked her shirt. "Honey, nobody's mad at you."

"It's my fault." Jake cried harder, his body shaking with the force of the sobs. "I didn't know she'd go in the pasture. I'm sorry."

"For what?" Sean rested his hand on Jake's back. "Did you open the gate and leave it so the ponies could get loose?"

"No." Jake kept crying. "I didn't let them out. But it's still my fault."

"No, son." Sean's voice softened. "It isn't." He rubbed Jake's back. "Now, stop crying. You have to let Christy take responsibility for what she did. It's her fault the ponies got loose. And you've got to help us."

Jake choked down his tears. "How?"

"I'll tell you when you stop crying." Sean frowned as Lynn came over, dragging Bonanza along by the chin whiskers. "Now what?"

Lynn's earlier pleasure had faded from her face, replaced by anger. "What are you doing to Jake? Why is he crying? It wasn't his fault that stupid woman let out the ponies."

Elinor took a deep breath. "Lynn, calm down. We all know who opened the gate. It wasn't you or Jake."

"All right." Lynn lowered her voice. "I'm sorry if I was rude, but nobody hurts my brother."

"That's a good rule." Sean said. "Now, put that horse away, Lynn. Jake, go wash your face and then come back to help us chew out Christy for being irresponsible." Sean clapped his hands, gaining both kids' attention. "Hustle, people. We don't want to be late for the movies."

Jake's mouth fell open. The tears stopped. "We're still going?"

"Sure," Elinor said, looking at Sean. "Why not? Our work's almost done. You two really hustled tonight. We just have to straighten out Christy first."

"Lynnie, did you hear?" Astonishment filled Jake's face. "The ponies got out, but we're not in trouble. And we're still going to the drive-in. Is that awesome, or what?"

"It's awesome, all right." Lynn tugged on Bonanza's long chin whiskers. "Come on, pony. You better go wash, Jake. Your face is filthy."

"I'm going." Jake pulled away from Elinor. "Be right back so we can yell at that dumb lady."

"Ignorant lady," Sean corrected. "Christy isn't stupid, son. She just doesn't have horse sense."

He waited until the boy ran off. "When I finally meet your ex-husband, I'm wiping up the ground with him. What he did to those kids is a crime."

Elinor sighed. "Sean, he worried whenever the horses got loose. He's a lawyer. He can't walk down the street without seeing a lawsuit." The overreaction from both kids still shocked her. Ponies wandered. It was their nature. Fences were contrived by people to control livestock, but it didn't mean that the animals always cooperated.

"In an emergency, an adult should take control, not run in circles and scream and shout," Sean said. "Lynn told me that you'll be thirty-five this fall."

"Remind me to thank her for sharing that." Elinor sobered when he still seemed serious. "What's your point?"

"I'll be forty in July; the same age Lynn says your ex is. If I wouldn't act that way because it's immature, why should he?" Sean met her gaze. "As far as I'm concerned, he bullied those kids because they were smaller and weaker than he was."

Elinor knew what Sean left unspoken. John had bullied her, too. Did she want to expose her children to him again? But he was their father. Sean wasn't. Had John truly abused their kids or was Sean just overreacting to the stress of the moment?

Before she decided what action to take, Christy arrived, Ginny in tow.

"Are the ponies all right?" Christy asked. "Your son seemed upset."

Was she serious? What did she think had just happened? She damn near killed the ponies. Elinor took a deep breath and adopted the tone she used for people who were just too stupid to live. "He was scared."

"Sad, too," Ginny announced. She waved the carrot she held in one small fist. "Where the ponies? They run away."

"They're eating dinner," Sean said. "Jake will take you to see them in their stalls as soon as he gets back."

"Mommy see ponies, too?" Ginny asked.

"In a bit, punkin'," Elinor answered. "Too many grownups might scare Awesome and his mom. Jake will show you the colt."

"I give him my carrot," Ginny decided.

Jake arrived in time to hear her. "No. He can't eat carrots yet. He doesn't have teeth. He's a baby. You can give the carrot to his mom. I have a piece of bread for you to give Awesome."

"Okay." Ginny released her mother's hand to grab Jake's. "We go now."

"Good one." Sean gave Jake a man-to-man look. "You see the ponies, all of them, Ginny. Jake will show you the cows, the pigs, and the chickens. Keep her with you for a while, son."

"Can I show her the kittens, too?" Jake asked. "They're in the barn loft, but I'll take her through the grain room, not up the ladder."

"I see kitties," Ginny ordered. "I like kitties."

"If you're careful and mind Jake," Christy said, looking from Elinor to Sean anxiously.

"Okay." Ginny yanked on Jake's hand. "Come on. We go. Now!"

"All right, already." Jake followed along. "Are all girls so bossy?"

TWENTY-THREE

Elinor eyed Christy. "Well, that got my adrenaline going."

"To say the least." Sean pushed back his cowboy hat. His gaze narrowed on Christy. "Two years ago, after your stud colt stomped me, you promised to take some classes and get horse knowledge. Obviously, you haven't."

"Yes, I did," Christy protested. "I took several courses at the University of Washington. I was the top student in those classes the entire year."

Elinor stared at her, then at Sean. He'd said his job could be dangerous, but she hadn't realized he might be seriously injured. "What did your instructor say about the stud, Christy?"

"Professor Iversen said all stallions act like that. They rear and strike at the slightest provocation. He said Sean probably intimidated the colt and my horse fought back," Christy said.

"I see." Elinor watched a muscle twitch in Sean's jaw. "Had you ever seen him abuse one of your horses?"

"Of course not. He babies them too much, according to my trainer. Sean won't even allow a whip near them." Christy scuffed her boot toe in the dust. "Nathan insisted we send the colt for real schooling. He told me we couldn't count on other shoers being as honorable as Sean, who settled for his medical bills, physical therapy, lost wages and refused any more compensation."

"That sounds like a pretty severe stomping," Elinor said. "You're lucky Sean didn't insist you put the colt down or geld him."

"There was nothing wrong with the horse's disposition," Sean said, his tone harsh. "Christy spoiled him from the day he was born and refused to have him trained. He'll be a good horse if she doesn't ruin him. He comes from two great lines of Arabians."

"It's no reason for him to be unruly." Elinor studied Sean, her concern increasing. What if he was injured again? What would she do?

Sean glanced at Christy again. "Or was his mother the one you overfed through her next pregnancy? She died during foaling."

"It wasn't my fault," Christy argued. "Professor Iversen said to follow the directions on the grain sack and that twelve pounds or more of feed wouldn't hurt her. I even checked with the O'Malleys and had their feed mill mix a special ration for her. I spent a fortune on that mare. She cost more than most people's cars. I'm sorry she died, but I'm glad I had her insured."

"Right." Sean's gray eyes glinted with fury. "And was Zane O'Malley drunk or sober when he mixed the feed? Or did you even notice he has a problem with drugs and booze?"

Christy waved a hand as if it was a minor annoyance. "Be serious, Sean. I just called and ordered it from the office."

Elinor grimaced. Christy wasn't doing anything to ease the problem and she didn't seem to understand they even faced one. Sean's scowl grew darker with each moment.

Elinor took a deep breath. "Accidents happen. I'll be the first to admit I don't know everything about horses. I took agriculture classes at the community college before I went to the university for my teaching degree. I had years of riding lessons before I opened this place. I studied to be a veterinary assistant. I read all the books I could find about horses. But I learned more from Sean in one day than I ever had in texts about hooves."

"You listen to me," Sean snapped. "Christy doesn't pay attention to anyone, not me or Art or Marlene. Do you, Christy?"

"I listen." The younger woman flushed. "I just don't think Marlene Dawson walks on water. She's your fearless leader, not mine. I hire the best trainers for my horses. And you're still ticked about the orphaned foal I had. I told you already, Sean. I called Professor Iversen. He said I should socialize the colt with other horses, so I did. It wasn't my fault he got kicked and broke his leg. How was I to know he was so stupid?"

Elinor tried to count to ten and failed. Her voice was deadly sweet. "Did you have him insured?"

Christy stared at her, surprised. "Well, of course. I insure all my horses the moment I get them. Nathan's irritated because the rates went up after Dr. Watkins put down the colt. I don't know what he told my insurance agent."

"The truth," Sean said. "You were negligent. Did Iversen tell you to put out the colt with one horse or a group? Did he tell you to watch the herd and see if the foal was accepted by the others or rejected? Did you even ask?"

"I didn't think of those questions," Christy admitted. "I didn't know it was important."

"You still have tremendous gaps in your horse knowledge." Sean's tone was calm, too calm. "You never should have gone through that pasture gate. You don't enter another horse owner's field without good reason or permission. If you had to go up to those horses, you should have approached from the side, not in front. If the mares had seen you, they might not have spooked."

"How was I supposed to know they'd act like that?" Christy demanded. "They're ponies."

"People always discount ponies and don't treat them like horses," Elinor said. "Would you have expected a herd of yours to stand still?"

"My Arabians aren't as gentle as your ponies," Christy said. "That's why I bring Ginny here to ride."

Sean pulled out his cell phone. "We're never going to get

through to you. I'm calling Felicia. My sister knows how to talk to you and Nathan. I sure don't."

Christy grabbed his arm. "Sean, no! Felicia hates me. You should have heard the names she called me after you got hurt. She lives and breathes lawsuits. And Nathan says if I get in trouble with her again, he'll make me sell all my horses. He hates litigation and his lawyers are terrified of Felicia. She's a shark."

"Too bad." Sean started to punch in a phone number. "I paid for that shark to get through law school. She owes me big time."

A tear streaked down Christy's cheek, followed by a second, then a third. "Please, Sean. Nathan won't let me buy any more horses. I pay for everything out of my own money. And it means I've got to work full time as a web page designer. I hate it. And all Nathan and I do is fight. It's awful. I don't want things to get worse."

Elinor felt sorry for the woman. It didn't sound as if she were mean to her horses out of spite. And Elinor knew what it was like being married to a control freak. "Take it easy, Christy. There's a solution to every problem. We'll work together until we find it."

"I can pay for the damage I almost caused," Christy said eagerly. "How much do you want? I have my check-book in the car, or you can run my credit card."

"That doesn't solve the problem," Elinor said. "You need to learn about horses. Sean, put away the phone. An accident almost happened. Like Marlene says, 'Almost only counts in hand grenades.' Horseshoeing is far too important."

Christy wiped at her tears. "I can't believe you're being so nice to me. I just wanted Ginny to be able to pet the colt. She can't touch any of mine. They're too wild."

"I know." Elinor glowered at Sean. "Put away the phone, cowboy." At her fierce tone, Ruler growled his own threat.

"All right." Sean shoved the phone back in his shirt pocket. "I think you signing Christy up for lessons is the dumbest thing I've ever heard. You'd have to teach her everything from the ground up. She won't pay attention to you."

"Yes, I will," Christy said quickly. "I don't smoke in the barn anymore. Professor Iversen told me it was too dangerous. Hay, grain, and shavings are real flammable, it turns out."

"It's impossible." Sean gave Elinor a steady look. "That poor college professor may know horses, but he didn't know Christy. This is the same woman who feeds grain before hay because it's easier. It doesn't matter if her Arabians colic when they bolt their rations. She has more choking, colics, and dying horses at her place than any other owner in the county. Art's at her barn more often than anywhere else."

"He won't be after Christy takes lessons," Elinor said. "Horse sense has to be acquired, Sean. We'll work out a way to fit into your schedule, Christy."

"Oh, all right," Sean grumbled. "If she's determined to take a year's worth of lessons from you and sign up her kids to boot, I'll talk to Nathan. I'll get him to back off so Christy can have two days a week here to train with you."

Christy's eyes widened. "You will?" She hurled herself against Sean and hugged him. "You're the best. I'll sign a contract with Elinor and do everything she says. I don't mean any harm, Sean. You'll tell Nathan that, won't you?"

"I reckon, but Elinor had better not hear one complaint from you." Sean patted Christy's shoulder as if she were Lynn's age. "If she says one word about your attitude, you're in the web-design business until you die of old age and Felicia will kick your butt to Seattle and back."

"Elinor won't complain at all, Sean. I promise. She won't."

Elinor folded her arms and studied the two of them. She'd been conned, but not by Christy. The girl was so dumb she gave brunettes a bad name. Sean Killian could outfox a politician. He winked at her over the top of Christy's head.

Elinor frowned at him. One of these times, she'd have to tell him how she felt about con artists, but first, she'd have to figure out how to keep a straight face when she scolded him. "When you've finished hanging all over my man, come into the house, Christy. We'll set up a schedule."

The two broke apart, Christy stammering apologies. Elinor ignored them and looked at Sean. "Go find the kids or we'll be late for the movies. They've been thrilled ever since you promised a trip to the drive-in."

"Works for me." Sean sauntered in the direction of the barn.

Elinor led the way into the house. While Christy filled out lesson contracts, she talked about her husband. Nathan had gone to high school with Sean. Today, Nathan ran a chain of grocery stores and didn't have much time for horses. *Or anything else,* Elinor thought.

After everyone left and the kids headed off to change to go to the movies, Elinor turned to Sean. "What game was that?"

Sean chuckled and leaned against the back door. "It was 'Good cop, bad cop.' You caught on fast."

"Next time, I get to be the bad guy." She crossed to him and put her arms around his neck. "Deal?"

"We'll see. I get to be macho occasionally."

"Suffer." She laughed when he pulled her tight against him, then rose to kiss him. Their bodies fit so well against each other, she longed for more. Yesterday seemed like a year ago.

She forgot to think when he took control of the kiss. A lifetime later, he lifted his head. "What's up, Jake?"

She glanced over her shoulder at the boy. Was her son upset because he'd found them kissing? He didn't seem concerned about it, yet he looked worried. "What's wrong, honey?"

"Do you think the ponies will be safe if we're out tonight, Mom?" Jake asked. "What if Bonanza lets them out again?"

Before Elinor could reassure him, Sean did. "I'll call my big brother and ask him to babysit the whole menagerie. How will that be?"

"Great!" Relief shone in Jake's blue eyes. "Thanks, Sean. I knew you'd take care of it."

Resentment flickered in Elinor's mind. It was her job to solve

Jake's problems, not Sean's. She shook her head. His solution worked. She'd talk to him later about not overstepping the boundaries. Still, she should have been the one to reassure her son.

Jake wandered back to his room. She relaxed a little. "Thanks for the dog. I never expected you to give me Ruler."

"You're welcome." Sean lowered his head. "You can really thank me after the movies. If you carry me off to bed now, the kids will be disappointed."

"We can't have that." She smiled up at him. "I'd better get ready and you should call Ethan. He may have plans."

"Not likely. He sits home alone most nights since he and Clancy split." Sean raised a brow. "What are you gals planning to do to him?"

"It's a girl thing," Elinor said. "Marlene calls it rule sixteen. 'Women must stick together and never let men know what's in store for them.' Nobody dares to argue with her."

"Poor Ethan. He's going down, especially if all you gals are ganging up on him and you've enlisted Fearless, too."

Laughing, Elinor headed for the bathroom. She hurried through the shower, quickly washing her hair. She stepped out to towel dry and went into her adjoining bedroom to dress.

She hadn't expected Sean to understand when the ponies got loose. Understand, hell! She hadn't anticipated he'd help catch the stock, or give her a valuable stock dog, or make a giant sale like the one he had with the clueless Christy.

She put on a lacy red bra and matching panties and from her closet she took her newest western blouse. It was a rich ruby with white embroidered stitching around the collar and cuffs. She drew on black jeans. They were tight, but she was able to zip them without too much trouble. She put on her socks, then black dress boots, pulling them over the jeans so the red stitched designs on the leather uppers showed.

It only took a few more minutes to brush her shoulder-length black curls. She added mascara to her dark lashes, a touch of lipstick, and she was ready. She picked up the fringed leather jacket Lynn had convinced her to buy at the local consignment shop.

As she walked into the kitchen, Elinor checked her children's appearances. They'd each put on clean jeans, T-shirts, and the tennis shoes she wouldn't let them wear around the ponies.

"Get your coats," Elinor reminded them. "It'll be cold during intermission. I'm sure you'll want to go up to the playground. Lynn, would you please get the quilt off the cedar chest in the living room?"

"Right." Lynn hurried from the room, Jake at her heels.

"I let Ruler outside." Sean folded the newspaper he'd been reading. "I fed him before I brought him. I have a sack of dog food in the truck. Where do you want it?"

Elinor pointed to the spot beside her desk. "I always kept it there. Would you bring in the cat food, too? I don't want the local raccoons to find it. Or Bonanza." She paused. "I need to buy some dog dishes."

"We'll stop at the grocery on the way to the drive-in," Sean said. "I can talk to Nate at the same time. No problem, honey."

"Is that your other favorite saying, cowboy?"

"Yup." He winked. "I'm sure you'll find new ones to teach me."

She felt her face warm. "It may take a while. You seem to be a slow learner."

He grinned, pure devil in his eyes. "I can show you a lot tonight until you send me home."

TWENTY-FOUR

HE ENJOYED THE GLARE SHE SHOT AT HIM BEFORE SHE ADOPTED the cool mask she usually hid behind. If anyone had ever told him a sharp-tongued woman would steal his heart, he'd have called the person a liar, but he hadn't met Elinor yet.

She sniffed as if he smelled worse than a ticked-off skunk. "Baloney is baloney, no matter how thin you slice it, cowboy."

"Wait and see." He grinned as she blushed.

The dog's bark interrupted. Sean looked out the window and recognized his older brother's late-model Cadillac "Ethan's here. It's time to go."

Elinor opened the door and called Ruler away from the car, greeting Ethan. "Hi. How are you?"

"Fine." Ethan held out his hand to the Australian cattle dog and let Ruler sniff at his fingers. "Didn't think you trained them to guard."

"I don't, but Ruler makes up his own mind about things." Sean watched Elinor fuss over the dog. "He decided Elinor and the kids belonged to him."

Ethan studied Sean with the deceptively sleepy gaze that saw each detail. "It surprised me to see him here." Faint humor trickled into the older man's face. "You fuss worse over homes for your dogs now than you did before Denise stole that litter."

Curiosity showed on Elinor's face. "How could she do it? Sean locks the barn up tight when he's gone, and he says he has a pet-sitter who looks after them when he's going to be gone a long time."

"I trusted her to look after the dogs while I was at a shoeing convention," Sean said. "Gavin should have followed up, checked to see if everything was okay with the dogs. He got busy at the university and didn't get to my place in time."

"I see." Speculation replaced the curiosity. In a burst of hospitality, Elinor began to tell Ethan about the animals, how the TV worked, and what there was to eat.

Sean folded his arms. He leaned against the back door and waited. His brother wasn't easy to charm, but Elinor managed it in a heartbeat. When they entered the room, she introduced the kids to Ethan. Like their mother, the two were perfectly polite and oozed childish appeal. However, neither seemed comfortable despite the appearance of outward sincerity.

Sean wondered if Ethan saw beneath the surface. He must. Hadn't Ethan been the one who'd taught him to look, not just see?

Ethan tossed his keys to Sean. "Take the Caddy. No need for you to be scrunched tight in your truck or to park in the back where the kids can't see the screen."

"It'll get dirty," Elinor warned.

"Already is," Ethan said, amused. "Sean hasn't washed it this week."

"Or last week either." Sean handed over the keys to his truck so his brother would have a vehicle if necessary. "Or any time soon. I told you already."

"Are you sure about him?" Ethan eyed Elinor. "He's cranky, and he pouts when he doesn't get his way. He's more upset about my cancelled wedding than our folks."

"He's sweet, kind, and funny." Elinor smiled at Sean. "Are you sure about changing rigs? The kids and I like your truck just fine."

"I'm sure." Sean crossed to her and put an arm around her shoulders. "Ethan hasn't let me drive any of his rigs since I dinged his classic Mustang twenty years ago."

"Okay." Elinor glanced at Ethan. "Thanks. It's very nice of you."

"No problem. I'll just get my tools and the universal padlocks I brought with me. They all open with the same key and I have several copies of it. When I've finished installing the locks, nobody will be able to let out your stock." Ethan headed for the car.

"I don't think it's necessary..." Elinor's voice trailed away as Ethan closed the door behind him. "He's a bigger control freak than you are. Does he ever listen?"

Sean laughed and dropped a kiss on top of her head. "Sometimes."

Did she really think he was that insecure? He wasn't interested in running her life, or her barn. He only cared that the horses received good hoof care and, of course, that she made room for him in her world. Well, she'd come to know him better. He'd see to it.

Meanwhile, if she fretted over Denise and the puppies, it'd keep Elinor busy. He didn't mind sharing what the other woman had done. He'd allow Elinor to drag the details out of him tonight.

Her subtle, sneaky interrogations were sexy as hell. She seemed to believe she held the reins when she knew all there was to know. She was wrong. He wouldn't tell her so. He'd use Denise's actions to hide the injuries he'd suffered when Christy's Arabian colt almost killed him.

He couldn't mention four broken ribs, a collapsed lung, a busted collarbone and a fractured leg without coming off like a whiner. Or a fool, which was worse. He ought to have paid closer attention to the two-year-old stallion and not let Christy distract him with her complaints about Nathan.

Even now, Sean didn't remember everything that had happened. He'd been half listening to Christy while he worked.

Concern for his buddy made him lose focus. Only for an instant, but it was long enough for the stud to rear and strike him in the head, or so Sean had been told. He'd been knocked unconscious.

Once he was on the ground, the horse had apparently stomped him until the trainer arrived and took control of the young stud. Jack Abbott called for help, and then did CPR until the paramedics arrived. According to Jack, Christy had wrung her hands, run in circles, and screamed. Sean owed Jack a lot. Helping him get a job up at Xanadu training those high-priced Arabians didn't come close to paying the debt.

———

The huge lights over the screen flickered as the first Disney feature ended. Lynn and Jake grabbed their coats and headed for the playground. Elinor reminded them to watch out for each other.

Alone with Sean, she gazed out the windshield. The night sky seemed like a painting. An assortment of white stars decorated the black velvet as if some cosmic artist had run amuck with white paint.

"What are you thinking?" Sean asked.

Elinor studied his calm face. She was curious about the woman who'd stolen his dogs. What had his reaction been? Had he been angry? Hurt? What did he feel? And did she dare bring it up? Or would it ruin the evening?

He leaned back in the driver's seat. "Okay, spit it out. I thought we'd neck during intermission, but you've got other things on your mind."

"I didn't say no," she objected.

"You also aren't over *here*," he pointed out. "You've got half the car seat between us."

"Men." She sighed and made a dramatic gesture of sliding over. "Better?"

He put his arm around her shoulders. "No, I'd feel better if you kept your pretty little nose out of my business. It won't happen, will it?"

She smiled up at him. "I can't make you share your secrets." She rested her cheek against his chest. "Can I?"

"You did before." He dropped a kiss on her hair.

"Why did Denise steal your dogs?" Elinor kissed the line of his firm jaw. "What was she thinking?"

"I knew it." He chuckled. "Sex instead of thumbscrews, right?"

"I prefer to call it seduction." She nipped his ear. "Tell me. I dare you. What did you do?"

"I found the pups missing. Denise claimed she didn't know what happened to them. I called the cops, put an ad in the paper, and Marlene enlisted everyone she knew to look for them. Then a guy who'd gotten one of the pups showed up. He wanted a copy of the papers so he could register the pup. He'd bought the heeler from Denise."

Elinor laced her arms around his neck, pressing close as she heard pain in his deep voice. She wished there was something more she could do. "And then what happened?"

Sean looked past her. "She'd had their tails cropped to make more money. I hate seeing dogs mutilated."

"I'm sorry." Tears stung Elinor's eyes. "How could she do something like that when she knew how you'd feel about it?"

"For the money," Sean said. "I broke off the relationship. I didn't file charges or sue her in civil court. Felicia about had a coronary."

"Revenge may be petty, Sean, but sometimes, it's all the law allows. I've got to admit, it gave me satisfaction when Harold took John for everything he could. Did Denise return the money?"

"Nope. I couldn't take it after what she did to my poor pups. If I'd accepted payment, it would have meant I condoned what she'd had done to their tails. When the vet she used tried to get me to pay the bill, I refused," Sean said. "He threatened to take me to court and I let Felicia have him. She straightened that out."

"I admire your principles, but why didn't you do more to

Denise?" Elinor tried to study his face. "Breaking an engagement doesn't sound like much, Sean. If she loved you, she would have respected your feelings and the way you wanted the puppies treated."

"She was born and raised here," Sean said gently. "Her entire family lives in Snohomish County. She left the state, moved to Oregon after we split. And I didn't do anything to cause it. I just told people things didn't work out for us."

"Then why did she leave?"

"Marlene and the Dawson girls filled in the blanks for every-one. Kate invited Denise to Fist City. I appreciated that. I couldn't fight a girl, but Kate was willing to punch her out for me."

"It sounds to me like Denise took advantage of your decency," Elinor said. "A lot of guys, including my ex, would have sued her sorry butt."

"Not me. Denise figured I was a sucker because of the way my first wife, Connie, and I worked things out when we divorced. I didn't want to sell my share of the Killian farm and she refused to let me give up the land I'd bought next door to the old homestead during our engagement. She said I owned it prior to the marriage. She wouldn't even take money from me for what she'd put into the farm when she renovated the house from top to bottom. She said that just because our marriage was dying, it didn't make us mortal enemies."

Connie sounded like an honorable woman. "Washington's a community property state. Grandpa gave me my inheritance early so I could buy my place and open a pony farm. He insisted I list the land under my name so John couldn't touch it. Which turned out to be a good thing, because when we filed for divorce, he tried."

"Connie didn't. She told her lawyer she made more money as an airline pilot than I ever would as a horse-shoer. I was the one who wanted to be fair to her. She said letting me keep the property was payment enough and if she ever needed a place to live, I'd have to rent her one of the houses I owned."

"Did you agree?"

"Sure. Then we argued about how much rent she'd pay, and the judge told us if we wanted to be that decent to each other, we should stay married. I only asked for a dollar a year, and she threw a fit."

"I don't get it," Elinor said. "She sounds great. Why did the two of you divorce?"

"Because I told her she had to stop flying after 9/11. I was scared to death something would happen to her and she loves being a pilot the way you love teaching," Sean said. "Plus, I wanted kids and she didn't. She was perfectly happy with it being just the two of us. Then she was offered a promotion and it meant flying out of Los Angeles. I didn't want to go."

"Come on, Sean. You could have been a shoer down there. Even if she was flying out of LAX, you didn't have to live in town."

Sean considered that. "You're right, but I was a macho, stupid twenty-three-year old. It took me a while to grow up and come to terms with my mistakes." A smile dawned in his eyes. "Is the interrogation over? Can we move on to the seduction?"

"For now." Elinor brushed her lips over his.

His mouth captured hers in a fierce kiss. His tongue swept into the depths behind her teeth and encouraged her to join the passionate duel.

She reveled in the magic of his touch. She threaded her fingers in his hair. His kisses trailed down her neck. Her western shirt gave way as he unsnapped the first three buttons. She shuddered when his lips found the pulse that hammered in the hollow of her throat. He peeled away her blouse to kiss the tops of her breasts.

Suddenly, he stopped. She moaned a soft protest.

"Later," he promised. "The lights have gone out and the second feature is going to start soon. I'll go meet the kids."

"I'll come with you." She reached for her jacket.

"No. Stay here." Amusement lit his features. "I really did a number on your clothes and you'll want to straighten them. Those kids of yours are sharp."

She fumbled with the snaps on her blouse as he got out and ambled toward the playground.

Funny, she thought. She and John had sex at drive-ins before they got married. She'd never been as excited as she was tonight. She took a deep breath, then another, and a third. She had to calm down. There were at least two hours before she could jump Sean.

When they arrived home two and a half hours later, she still wanted him. She wasn't sure how to arrange the evening from this point. At least Lynn and Jake had fallen asleep in the back of the car. If they stayed asleep, maybe Sean could spend the night and she'd let them assume he'd come by early in the morning. If she ever figured out how to ask him to spend the night.

"If you get the doors, I'll carry them inside," Sean said, switching off the engine.

"They can walk," Elinor said. "They'll still crash as soon as we have them in their rooms. I don't mind waking them up."

"They've each had a long day. It's no problem."

"Okay." She inclined her head. She opened her door and got out of the Cadillac. She held the rear door for him while he unfastened Lynn's seatbelt.

He scooped the girl into his arms and carried her to the porch. Ethan met him and took Lynn into the house. Sean returned to the car for Jake.

Inside the house, Elinor led the way to Lynn's room. "Put her on the bed, please. I'll take care of her and then Jake. Would you tell Sean that?"

"You got it." Ethan left.

Elinor smiled at the remnants of chocolate on Lynn's face. *If I had a photo of her candy-coated mouth and chin, I could blackmail her for the next thirty years.* She headed for the bathroom to get a warm, wet washcloth to clean Lynn's face. Elinor was surprised when Sean met her in the living room with Jake sound asleep in his arms.

"I'll take care of him," Sean said. "Where do I find his PJs?"

"Under his pillow." Elinor stared after Sean as he went to Jake's room. Sean Killian was different, but she felt as if she could grow accustomed to that.

It didn't take long to tuck both children into bed. Elinor returned to the kitchen where Sean and Ethan were chatting in low voices, a bottle of beer in hand for each of them. She opened the fridge and got one for herself. "Anything happen tonight I need to know about?"

"Sandy called," Ethan said. "She told me if Penny didn't want to come in tomorrow to phone her. She'd call Clancy and get her to cover the lessons again."

"I don't know why I think I own this place." Elinor sipped the beer. "If Jake and Lynn don't tell me what to do, it's Sandy and Marcie. So did Penny call to cancel?"

"Yes. I phoned Clancy myself," Ethan said. "I can handle a phone."

Elinor smiled. The situation smacked of a set-up to her. Most Sundays, she taught lessons after church. Lynn covered the office while Sandy and Marcie handled trail rides. How had Sandy arranged for Penny to call? Of course—all the teens were in Marlene's 4-H club and attended the same high school until the older girls had graduated last June.

Before Penny started the teen angst routine, the three girls had been inseparable. It sounded like they still talked to each other, and that was good news. Once Penny passed through this stage, she might want her old friends back in her life.

"So, what did Clancy say?" Elinor asked. "Will she be here in the morning?"

The lines deepened around Ethan's mouth when he frowned. "I don't know. She wasn't home. Her mother said she had a date. And after the third time I called, Darlene said she'd send her and not to phone again."

This time, Elinor managed to hide her smile. "That works. I don't open until after church on Sundays. Anything else?"

Ethan eyed her, then looked at Sean. "I didn't know Zane O'Malley lived across the street. He showed up after you left, complaining about stray ponies on the highway and told me he was contacting the police."

"All that and they never even got on the road." Elinor wrinkled her nose. "I really can't afford a ticket for stock at large."

"Don't worry," Sean said. "I'm sure Ethan handled it, didn't you, bro?"

"Yes. And I didn't break his nose either, unlike some people who punch first and talk second," Ethan said.

"I was fifteen years old," Sean returned. "I didn't like the lying little sneak before he pawed Brigid. When he left her twenty miles from home in the middle of nowhere, he deserved more than a broken nose." Indignation darkened Sean's gray eyes. "I'll go talk to the weasel right now. If he's already gone to bed, too bad."

"No, you won't," Ethan said. "I already told him he'd trespassed by coming here and that Felicia would file a lawsuit against him for sexual harassment on Monday."

"What?" Elinor sputtered into her beer. "How did you know he made a pass at me? I never told anyone."

"Because I'm smart," Ethan drawled. "I guessed he hadn't changed since he was a boy. You won't have any more trouble with him. It scared him half to death when I told him he was messing with Sean's woman."

Elinor tossed her head. "I don't need a rescuer. The district court judge has been more than fair to me whenever O'Malley raises hell."

"Nevertheless," Ethan said. "I also put a call into Beth Chambers. She's a homicide detective now, but she still has connections with the other Animal Control cops and none of them like Zane, so they'll be watching him."

Elinor felt as if her words had fallen like rain on Ethan's head. He'd heard them and ignored them. She spotted a certain smugness in Sean's expression. Obviously, he liked the notion of being her protector. Men, she thought, half amused, half touched.

"I toured your place while you were out. Took a few notes." Ethan walked over to the kitchen table and opened a manila folder. "Those pregnant mares of yours need bigger stalls. I tried to figure out how to remodel your barn, but there isn't room. So, I checked out the garage. I didn't realize how big it was until I went inside."

"John had an office in it," Elinor said. "I haven't used the building for anything since the divorce."

Sean studied her for a slow, silent moment. Then, he said, "Six years is a long time to let a place sit empty."

"It's not empty. It has a ton of bad memories in it."

TWENTY-FIVE

BOTH MEN LOOKED AT HER AS IF SHE'D ESCAPED FROM AN ALIEN spaceship. Sean didn't say anything, and she stared at her beer.

Finally, Ethan said, "It's about time you put that garage to use. That old mare with the colt needs room to lie down. She can't where she is, when the baby is stretched out on the floor, sleeping and she's tired, too. So, she'll get the first stall. I took the liberty of redesigning the place."

Taking her beer, Elinor went to study the papers he'd spread out on the table. Sean stood beside her. The dimensions of the old three-car garage had been drawn neatly on graph paper. Ethan's alterations had the downstairs converted to three large stalls, a hay room, and tack area. Finally, the upstairs studio apartment was now a combination classroom and lunch area.

She pointed to the part of the drawing that showed what had been John's office. "What did you do?"

"Tore out this wall," Ethan said, using his finger to trace a line that showed how he had expanded the space. "It was just a partition. If we double the size of the office area, you'll have a lounge for your customers. Darlene told me about the day camp plan. You'll need an inside lunch spot for the kids. You can use it for craftsy-crap classes, as Clancy calls them. It'll keep the kids busy when they're not riding, and since you're doing shared horses, you need extra activities."

"I see." Elinor focused on the scribbled plans. She felt as if he'd run over the top of her. "Did it ever occur to you that this is my place? Maybe I like things the way they are."

"Fine." Ethan sounded unruffled. "What about the mares? Where are they going to foal? If they don't have enough space to move around in their stalls during contractions, they could die in labor. You can't count on the spring weather. It may be too cold or rainy for them to give birth outdoors. The foals could get hurt if they don't have enough room to stand up or lie down, too."

"Good points." Sean smiled at Elinor. "Now, darlin'…"

"Don't charm me," Elinor snapped. "I know he's right. I know I have to do what's best for the mares. So how much will it cost?"

Ethan grinned at her. The smile reminded her of Sean's. "I'll start tomorrow. The boy will help me. I scrounge lumber all the time for various projects and I'll let you have it at my cost. Family discount."

Elinor nodded. "All right, but I don't want Jake lifting anything heavy and hurting himself."

"Yeah, Jake can help, too." Ethan looked at the clock. "It's after one in the morning. Where's Clancy?"

Sean leaned in to whisper in Elinor's ear. "I'm the boy Ethan mentioned. He always drafts me for his projects."

"I figured that one out."

"Don't whine. I raised you to be a man." Ethan pulled out his cell phone. "I'm calling her, and she better damn well be home by now with a fair to middling excuse."

"Should have thought before you fought with her," Sean said smugly. "She blocked you on her cell phone and now you can only call her at ranch headquarters."

"You two aren't engaged anymore," Elinor reminded Ethan with a touch of satisfaction. "She's free to date whomever she wants. And Darlene will be supremely ticked if you call at this hour. If she's like Marlene when she gets mad, you'll be in big trouble."

"She's worse." Sean chuckled. "Everybody runs for cover when Darlene's pissed. She'll be the mother-in-law from hell."

Elinor frowned at him. He sounded positively gleeful. "You threw Clancy away, Ethan. If you go after her now, she'll think it's because you're like a dog with a bone. You only want her when another man does."

"She's not supposed to date." Ethan swung around to glare out the kitchen window. "We're waiting a while. That's all. And you're right. It's too late to go to the Lazy B. She'll be here tomorrow?"

"So, will you, but I don't like scenes around the customers," Elinor warned. "Bad for business."

"I'll behave until you close," Ethan promised. "What time is that?"

"At six." Elinor finished her beer. "It takes another hour to do chores and she won't leave until the work's done."

"Fine." Ethan studied her. "You know who she's out with, don't you?" He didn't wait for an answer. "You're a witch."

"*My* witch." Sean wrapped his arm around her shoulders. "Yours is at the Lazy B, plotting ways to make you suffer."

Ethan headed for the back door. "You'd better plan to bring her to the Senator's barbecue on Memorial Day. If he crosses swords with her, he's on his own."

"More like *magick* wands." Sean followed his brother to the door. "And I hate those things. I already invited Elinor, but I still don't understand why we have to show up."

"Because I said so," Ethan told him. "And you hate it more when I drag you in by the ear. Man up."

Sean winked at Elinor. "Be right back. I'll get the stuff from the car." The door closed on his complaints about political functions that masqueraded as social events.

Elinor put her beer can in the recycling bin and went to check on Lynn and Jake again. Ruler came out of his den under the kitchen table and followed.

On her way back to the kitchen, Elinor turned off the living room lights. She entered the room just as Sean came through the back door, blankets in hand. "I have to wash those," she said. "They can go in the basket by the machine."

Sean nodded. After he took care of them, he walked toward her, a slow smile playing at the edges of his mouth. "I should have realized you and Clancy were up to no good."

Elinor felt as if she might drown in the fog of his gaze. "I really didn't want to make you choose between us and your brother. I don't honestly know who she's with—it's either Jack Abbott or Doctor Art. Will Ethan be okay?"

"He'll be fine." Sean framed Elinor's face with his hands. "They're miserable without each other. I hate watching that."

"I know." Elinor moistened her lips. She liked the way he didn't rush her, but it frustrated as well as aroused her. "Let's go to bed."

He lowered his head and brushed a kiss over her lips. "Are you sure? I don't have to stay if you're worried about the kids."

"They're both sound asleep." She slipped her hands over his chest up to his shoulders. "I think it'll be okay, just for tonight. Come on."

"In a minute, witch." He feathered his thumbs over her cheekbones. "What incantations do you have in mind for tonight?"

"It's for me to know and for you to worry about." She managed to steady her breathing. "Move it, cowboy."

"Right." He tormented her with quick kisses over her cheeks, lips, and nose. "I bet if I make you beg, you'll tell me all the tricks you and Clancy have planned."

"Don't count on it." Elinor rose on tiptoe and tried to catch his mouth with hers. "Sean, please."

"That was fast." He swung her up into his arms. "I want more pleading than that."

"You won't get it. That was it."

"Sure, I will." He carried her into the bedroom.

An hour later, she lay in his arms, feeling his hand smooth her hair. "Something's bothering you. What is it?" she asked.

He kissed her forehead. "I'm thinking about Christy. Were you angry with her? You didn't show it. I know we were teaching her a lesson, but…"

Elinor put her finger over his mouth. "Shh," she whispered. "When I was growing up, I learned not to let it show when I was angry or hurt. I do confide in Marlene."

His arms tightened around her. "You listen when I'm angry. Let me do that for you. Okay?"

She hesitated. "I don't know if I can. Nobody ever stayed around when I got mad."

"I'll stick and stay. Promise. Trust me."

"I'll try, Sean."

"That's all I want." He chuckled. "Well, that and you one more time."

"Let's see what we can do about that."

———

The next day, she still felt the heat of a blush whenever she remembered the night before. She'd barely slept. Neither had he. It didn't matter.

He'd helped with chores, then gone home to do his own. He'd returned in time to attend church with them and go out for breakfast afterward. Now, he and Jake were locating the tools they'd need to start remodeling the garage.

She'd stayed out of the building when John made it his private place. And even after the divorce, she hadn't wanted to go in there. It was her farm, she reminded herself. It always had been. She could do as she pleased with every inch of it.

She took a deep breath when she saw Clancy's truck pull into the drive and went to meet the other woman. "Hey there."

"Hi. Brigid is in a baking mood, so I brought doughnuts. Is the

226

coffee on?" Clancy slipped out of the Dodge Ram pickup. "What's happening, girlfriend?"

"Ethan will be over to help Sean remodel the garage into a maternity barn," Elinor said. "If you want to avoid him, you'd better go."

"No way. I want to make him feel bad." Clancy gave Elinor a hug. "Don't worry so much. The trick is not to sweat the small stuff." She paused. "Or the big stuff either, for that matter. Now, let's go have a fat pill. I've done enough philosophizing without a maple bar."

Elinor laughed. "All right. But no scenes in front of the customers."

"I was raised with that rule," Clancy said. "Ethan knows it, too. His father was the perfect politician, a master of saying whatever anyone wanted to hear. And the press people were always around, either his own or the media reporters." She climbed the steps to the back porch. "I can't imagine anything worse than living on stage and never having any privacy."

"Neither can I." Elinor felt better since she'd discussed the situation with Clancy. Now, it'd be possible to concentrate on the business.

Later that afternoon, the reservation book reminded Elinor the hay dealer would be in with a truckload of alfalfa-grass bales this evening or early tomorrow morning. She had to clean the loft to prepare for the delivery.

She stopped by the tool room. She heard saws in the garage and hammering. Jake had to be in his element, helping Sean and Ethan fix up a new stall for his horses. She collected the rake, broom, and a pitchfork for her own task. She went to the two-story barn and climbed the stairs into the feed room. She gathered up some empty plastic shavings bags for the garbage she knew she would find.

From the feed room doorway, she could see part of the farm. Clancy was in the arena with the last group of lesson students. Marcie and Sandy had the final trail ride of the day out in the woods. Meanwhile, Chipeta, Awesome, Star, Taffy, and Bonanza were together in the second paddock, safe behind a padlocked gate. Why hadn't she thought of locking the pasture gates with padlocks before? Because it hadn't occurred to her that it would be necessary. Now, no human, or her favorite junk-food pony, could open them by accident.

Next time she went into town, she'd pick up two more padlocks for the highway gates. When she left to do errands or volunteer with Jake's class, she wouldn't have to be concerned about visitors, or whatever mischief Zane O'Malley might have in mind. Of course, with a dog around, she didn't have to fret about trespassers either.

She bent and petted Ruler. He stood guard at her heel, a natural position for him.

She sauntered toward the hayloft. She had an hour before she closed. There was plenty of time to gather up the loose hay, count bales, and organize the loft for the delivery. She needed to rotate the alfalfa-grass hay she had on hand so it would be fed first. The bales due in would be fed next. Ruler followed her.

She was raking the loose hay into piles when Ruler growled.

"I like that," Sean said as he entered the loft. "I'm the one who raised you, dog."

Elinor grinned. "I guess he's figured out I belong to him."

"I reckon," Sean drawled. "Ever make love up here?"

"No. And we're not today. We don't have time." She saw the glint of humor in his eyes. "I mean it. I have a hay delivery due today or early in the morning."

The amusement faded. "Who's going to unload it?" He demanded. "You?"

"Unless Superman shows up." She sighed at the irritation on his face. "I'm the adult here. I'm the one who unloads the hay and the grain. I'm the one who fills the slop barrel and mixes feed for the pigs. I build fences and clean the barn most of the time. The kids are a big help, but I'd never allow them to overwork or hurt themselves."

"I've got a news flash for you, babe. You're not killing your-self putting in the hay, grain, or anything else. Got it?"

Ruler moved in front of her, hackles raised, and emitting a loud growl.

"Oh, for heaven's sake!" Sean stopped and glared at the two of them. "I'm not going to hurt her, dog. Strangle her, yes. Hurt her, no. I'm bigger than both of you. I'm unloading the damn deliveries around here whether you like it or not, Elinor Talbot."

"What am I arguing for?" She shrugged. "I hate unloading and stacking hay. By the time I finish I have to see the chiropractor and have my back adjusted."

"Of course, when I finish muscling around a horse, I need one."

She smiled. "Okay. You can unload anything and everything around here. You can start by tearing down the kids' fort."

"What fort?" He looked around the loft.

She gestured to the stack of hay in the corner. "They play there. There shouldn't be more than ten bales of hay left. I keep track of what I feed so I know when to reorder so the hay stays fresh. Then I don't have problems with moldy feed."

"And you prevent colic. Smart gal."

"Be careful when you move the hay in the corner. You'll find plywood, cardboard, and traps everywhere because Lynn, Jake, and their friends only allow certain people in."

"I should have known." He shook his head. "Ethan always swore I'd end up with kids just like me."

"Did you build forts, too?" She stuffed loose hay into the big plastic sacks so she could deliver it to the steers.

"Yup. Clancy and I built the best ones. We changed the entrances and exits all the time so Ethan couldn't find us and make us do chores. My little sisters used to rat us out so Gavin wouldn't let them in the forts."

Elinor laughed. "Sounds like you had a wonderful childhood."

"Ethan was strict, but fair. And for all his bull about thumping me, he rarely did," Sean said. "Gavin and I talked about it once.

Ethan only has five years on me and two on Gavin. It wouldn't have been right to expect Ethan to be the soul of patience constantly, and he wasn't."

She glanced at Sean. He'd pulled out the bales of hay and stacked the alfalfa-grass mix where it could be fed right away. The squares of plywood were piled against the barn wall. Other scraps of wood were being sorted according to size and type.

She continued to clean up the loose hay. She tossed orange baling twine into the other bag as she found the strings. She worked her way toward Sean.

"What do you do with it?" Sean asked, pointing to the loose hay.

"I used to give it to the ponies, but after Flicka choked on the floor sweep, I started feeding it to the pigs and the chickens. If it's not dusty or moldy, I give it to the steers. Cows have four stomachs, and they can eat a lot of crud horses can't handle."

"At least you're smart enough to know to treat your ponies as if they are horses," Sean said. He reached for her. "What if I show you how to use a pile of loose hay?"

She giggled. "With this audience?" She pointed to Ruler lying nearby and the kittens shadowboxing in the light of the windows. "I don't think so, cowboy."

He threaded his fingers into her hair. "I can change your mind." He kissed the side of her neck.

She arched her head back and sighed with pleasure. "Maybe you can. I've never made love up here. Anything for science."

"Definitely." He nibbled at her ear. "Call this an experiment, or whatever you want."

"Mom. Mom!" The thud of Jake's footsteps on the stairs into the feed room followed his voice. "Come see. We got Chipeta's stall all done."

She wriggled out of Sean's hold. "Later, cowboy."

"I'll remind you." He pretended to twirl an invisible mustache and leered at her.

Jake charged into the loft. "Sean, what are you doing? Ethan said you were s'posed to get Mom ages ago."

"What can I say?" Sean teased. "The woman distracted me. Do you know she thought she could unload a truck full of hay all by herself?"

Jake frowned. "Mom does it all the time. Why can't she keep doing it?"

"Because then she might figure out that she doesn't need me." Sean took the plastic manure fork away from Elinor and leaned it against the wall. "I'll help you finish this later. Come on, beautiful. You've got to ooh and aah about the remodeling."

TWENTY-SIX

THE NEXT MORNING THE TELEPHONE RANG DURING BREAKFAST. Elinor picked it up in the kitchen, where Jake and Lynn were eating breakfast. "Silver Lake Pony…"

"What do you want now?" The angry male voice interrupted her professional greeting. "Why are you hounding me? I called my accountant. You've received child support checks every month and you're quick to cash them, too."

Elinor grimaced. "Hello, John. It's nice to hear your voice, too." The comment stopped him in mid-tirade, as she'd known it would. "I called to ask you to schedule some time for your children."

"No." Jake looked up from his cereal. "I don't want to see him."

"Me either," Lynn agreed. "Mom, don't waste your time."

Elinor held up her hand. "Stop it," she whispered. She waited for a response from their father. "John? They're your children. They need their dad."

"You should have thought of that before you had them." John's tone grew more strident. "You got your damn meal tickets. Now you raise them. Keep them away from me."

Elinor counted silently to ten, then twenty. "John, we've been over this before." She wouldn't let his insults bother her. He'd said worse during their marriage, often in front of the children. "They're your kids. They need you."

Both Lynn and Jake shook their heads. "No, we don't," Jake said. "We've got Sean."

For how long, Elinor wondered. "John, listen to me. I don't want to bring Harold in on this, but I will. You have to visit the kids. It's in their best interests to have a father who takes an active part in their lives."

"It's not me," John shouted. "I never wanted children. You knew it and you had them anyway. I don't know how your lawyer falsified those DNA reports and if I could prove it, I would. Now, leave me the hell alone!"

Elinor heard him slam down the phone and then the buzz of the dial tone. "Damn it!"

"What did he say?" Lynn finally asked, her face white. "Is he coming?"

"No." Elinor replaced the receiver. "He's too busy right now."

"Great." Jake dug back into his cereal. "Breathe, Lynnie. It's okay. I told you he was gone for good."

"Jake, for heaven's sake, he's your father. He'll always be in your life." Elinor eyed her son with rare exasperation.

"No, he won't. I told you. I gave him away. He'll have to ruin some other kid's life, not mine and not Lynnie's." Jake poked his sister. "Hurry, Lynnie. We've got to go." He carried his bowl to the sink. "Come on. The bus will be here in seven minutes."

He headed into the living room and returned with his back-pack. "Sean's coming tonight, right?"

"Yes," Elinor put her hand on Lynn's shoulder. "I'm sorry you're so upset about missing your dad. I'll try harder to get him here for you, honey."

"Don't do it on my account," Lynn said. "I'm just scared he might show up and wreck everything." She slipped out of Elinor's touch. "Stop freaking over him, Mom. We're great without him."

In less than five minutes, the two kids were out the door to catch their bus. Elinor refilled her coffee cup and went to stand on the porch to watch them depart for the school, Ruler a patient escort.

Was Lynn right? Were they okay without John? The kids certainly seemed happier. Elinor took a deep breath. What had she been thinking? He was so mean-spirited. How long had she been like her children today? Afraid?

She'd anticipated a tantrum like the ones he used to throw. She'd tried so hard to keep the farm, the children, and the house perfect, so he wouldn't have any reason to become angry. But it hadn't mattered what she did.

He used to deliberately break her dishes. Once he'd taken the cow-shaped cookie jar off the top of the refrigerator and hurled it onto the floor in a rage. The ceramic container had shattered into tiny pieces. Alone in the shower that night, she'd cried over the cookie jar, a house-warming gift from Grandma Talbot. After that, Elinor had quit attending the Master Livestock Course taught at the County Extension Service. It wasn't worth the trouble at home, the threats and violence.

She had never found another cookie jar like it. She used an old coffee can for store-bought cookies now. She didn't bake anymore. It wasn't as if she were a good cook, after all. John had told her how terrible the meals were for years.

Once, he destroyed the coffee pot by leaving the glass carafe on a live burner with nothing in it. He'd almost set the house on fire one night when he left a skillet on the stove, smiling smugly as she raced to turn off the heat. She'd resigned from the horse-shoeing apprentice class at the community college. She didn't dare leave him alone with the children after that incident.

He'd ruled through terror. Sean was different. He didn't make her feel as if she had to be less for him to be a man.

She took a deep breath and leaned down to pet Ruler. The dog leaned against her, rumbling an affectionate answer to the question she hadn't asked.

Elinor glanced behind her to what had been a three-car garage, now a barn that held Star, Taffy, Chipeta, and Awesome. Why on earth had she allowed her ex-husband to continue to control her life when they'd been divorced for six years? It was past time to let go of him even if she didn't know what would happen next.

———

Sunshine brightened the pastures, turning the grass to emerald green. She watched Awesome dart and dash between the mares, testing his legs. He galloped over to chocolate brown Star, who lifted her head to watch him before the colt bolted back to his mother. Next, he headed toward Taffy, and the light gray mare ignored him. He'd be delighted when the two ponies foaled and he had brothers and sisters to play with, Elinor thought.

Ruler's soft yip warned her, and she turned to see Sean's truck in the drive.

She walked toward him, hoping her excitement didn't show. This was the last day they would have together for the rest of the week. She was scheduled to substitute in Lynn's Science class the next three days. Maybe her daughter would stop playing the dumb card.

"Hey, handsome." Elinor greeted him with a quick kiss. "How's your day going?"

"Good." Sean stopped as his phone warbled out a ring tone, and he answered it. "What's wrong, Marlene?" He listened for a moment, then looked at his watch. "Okay, I'll be there in fifteen minutes. Hold him still until I arrive. Do we need Elinor to help?"

She waited for him to close his phone. "What's wrong?"

"Pryde stepped on a nail and it's stuck in his frog." Sean tucked his phone away. "I'll need you to hold his foot up while I get the nail out and treat the injury."

"Okay. Let me put Ruler inside." She called the dog and ran toward the back door of the house, locking him in the kitchen. She raced back to climb into the passenger side of the truck.

Sean locked the gates behind them. He took a left out of the driveway and headed for the back road to Snohomish. "Look behind the seat and find my nippers. There's a squirt bottle of iodine back there, too. Get that lunchbox on the floor. It's where I keep the tetanus injections."

His instructions continued the rest of the way to Marlene's small farm. Elinor didn't take offense. Instead, his preparation amazed her. How many shoers carried all these medical supplies in their rigs? No wonder most of the big stables used Sean Killian for a farrier.

He brought the truck to a stop in Marlene's driveway, glancing at his watch. "Fourteen minutes." He winked at Elinor as he checked the supplies, he'd told her to gather and place in his plastic tote box. "Not bad. I'm sure glad none of the local cops were out."

Halfway to the barn behind the house, they spotted Marlene and the horse. The pair waited on the circular driveway's concrete apron in between the two structures.

Pryde was a huge palomino quarter horse gelding in his early thirties. He stood with Marlene, his left rear hoof cocked up, most of his weight supported on his other three feet. A white blaze and four white socks added to his glamour. White hairs mixed in with the sunshine gold of his muzzle. He snorted when he saw Sean and nosed Marlene in what had to be a hunt for carrots.

"Hey, buddy." Sean paused to pet the aged horse's neck. "Can you hold him, Fearless? Or do you want to hold the hoof instead?"

"I think he'll stand quieter for me," Marlene said. "You two go ahead."

"Okay." Sean ran his hand across the gelding's neck to his back, and from there to his hip. "Elinor, you'll basically hold the hoof so I can pull the nail out straight. I don't want to bend it or have it cause any further damage. Any questions?"

"No. I can do it." She looked at the hoof and almost instantly saw the nail.

Most likely from a fence or stall board, the nail was a long one. She could tell by the size of its head that it was a sixteen-penny sinker. Two inches of the coated nail protruded from the frog, a triangular piece of flesh in the middle of the hoof. She took a deep breath. "I'm ready."

She slid her hand from the hock to the ankle. It was a signal to Pryde that she wanted the foot. It took two hands to support the hoof. She held it so Sean could grasp the nail with his shoeing nippers.

They looked like a long-handled pair of pliers that could cut hooves, but today, he used them to hold the nail. He nodded at Elinor. "Keep it still."

She did.

He yanked hard.

The nail jerked out.

Blood sprayed from the hoof.

She gagged but kept the foot up. The blood would clean the wound.

"You're doing great, Bubba." Sean put down his nippers, his attention on the horse. He paused to pet Pryde's neck on the way to his shoeing tote box.

"Good job, Elinor. Don't let go of the foot."

He pulled out the bottle of iodine. He splashed it on the inside of the hoof, covering the frog.

"Now what?" She watched the bleeding slowly ease up.

"I'm going to bandage the foot so any infection can drain and the nail hole won't get full of dirt and close up," Sean said. "Then I'll give him a tetanus shot and a dose of antibiotics."

"What about a painkiller?" Elinor asked. "It has to hurt like hell."

"Yes, and if it does, he won't put all his weight on it," Marlene said. "I have some Bute in the house. I'll give it to him in his supper grain so he can rest tonight."

Elinor held the foot while Sean soaked two gauze pads in iodine, then put them over the frog. He followed that with a clean, athletic man's sock, rolling it up over the leg, then two plastic grocery bags to keep the sock clean. Next came strips of flexible bandaging.

Even though the bandaging was made to stick to itself, Sean obviously didn't trust it to hold the bags in place while Pryde walked. He used duct tape to hold the bandages, then wrapped more tape around the hoof and leg until the foot was totally protected.

When he stepped back, Elinor lowered the hoof to the ground and straightened. Her back ached. She flexed her shoulders and stretched. Her neck popped when she turned to meet Marlene's gaze. "I've never seen a bandage like that before."

"You can adapt it for abscesses if you put Epsom salts in the sock," Sean said. He came over to stand behind Elinor. "Let me help you now."

"What are you talking about? I'm fine." She gasped when his hands closed over her shoulders. He rubbed them. Then she felt his thumbs push into her back as he worked his way down her spine. She bit back a moan as the pain subsided. "Oh, wow. That feels so good."

"I'm glad."

She felt forlorn for an instant when he stepped away but knew Pryde still needed his attention. She watched as he prepared the shots and injected the horse. Sean did it exactly the way the veterinarian taught her to do muscle injections, from cleaning the area with alcohol to aspirating blood back into the syringe.

It didn't seem likely that any backyard horseman, even the most experienced farrier, would be able to inject a horse so easily. He did it nearly as well as Dr. Art would have. How had Sean learned to be so professional? The question simmered in her mind on the way back to the pony farm.

"That was amazing," Elinor said once they were in her kitchen. She washed her hands, then pulled the ingredients for roast beef sandwiches from the refrigerator. "You were amazing."

Sean grinned. "Is this when you tell me I'm some kind of hero and give me a big kiss?"

"Only if you tell me how you learned to give shots so well." She left the jar of mayonnaise on the counter and crossed the room to him. She brushed his mouth with hers. "Tell me when I can get that good."

"Go with Art on his rounds for months and you'll learn muscle injections." Sean pulled her against him. "Joe—that's Art's son— and I went everywhere with him when I was in high school. We used to help whenever and wherever he'd let us and, of course, the animal's owner had to agree to it, too."

She tipped back her head to gaze up into his face. "High school would be forever ago. You must have given shots since then."

"I planned to go to vet school with Joe, but my folks weren't supportive, and I couldn't get the scholarships I needed with the old man making as much as he does. So, I started saving money for college." Sean shrugged. "Life got in the way and I never made it."

"That sucks." Someone else might not have heard the pain in his voice or seen the muscle tighten in his jaw, but she'd spent too much time at the high school not to notice when someone packed heartache in their emotional baggage. She put her arms around him and hugged him. "This is when I use my preachy teacher voice and tell you it's never too late and to always follow your dreams."

"Yeah?" Sean feathered his thumb over her lips. "How about if I get that big kiss and a sandwich instead of the lecture?"

"Okay. That works for me." She copied his favorite saying and saw a faint smile tug at the edge of his mouth. This wasn't the end of it for her. If he still wanted to go to vet school, somehow, some way, she'd make that happen for him.

TWENTY-SEVEN

Dᴜʀɪɴɢ ᴛʜᴇ ɴᴇxᴛ ᴛᴡᴏ ᴡᴇᴇᴋs, Eʟɪɴᴏʀ sᴛʀᴜɢɢʟᴇᴅ ᴛᴏ ᴄᴏɴᴛʀᴏʟ her turbulent emotions. She needed to come to terms with her history so she could have a future with Sean. Or without him, for that matter.

He stayed with her the night Star foaled. There weren't any complications, but Dr. Watkins was as far away as a phone call. The newborn filly was a dark reddish brown with a light mane.

"She looks chestnut to me," Elinor commented as she toweled dry the new arrival.

"What's her name?" Sean spread out the afterbirth to see if the mare passed all of it. "I know you have one."

"Comet. Jake picked it. Lynn's still thinking about a name for Taffy's foal." Elinor glanced over into the next stall at the dappled, gray Arabian-Shetland mare. "I've watched her. The milk bag's almost full, but it's not dripping yet."

"You've got a few more days then." Sean scooped up the bloody tissue with a shovel. "I'll bury this unless you need help to dip Comet's umbilical cord in iodine or to squirt the mare and see if she has milk."

"I can handle it." She wouldn't allow herself to depend on him. It would hurt more when he left for good.

In the kitchen a short time later, she made hot chocolate. She glanced at Sean, who was fiddling with the small radio on her desk. "What are you doing?"

"Tuning in the country station. I requested a song tonight during the classics program." Strains of Patsy Cline's "Walking After Midnight" filled the room. A few more country favorites played while they drank the cocoa.

After a commercial break, the announcer introduced the next song. "This is for Elinor from Sean with all his heart."

The mellow, beautiful harmony between Charlie Rich's voice and music combined in "Nice and Easy."

Sean held out his hand. "May I have this dance?"

"Yes." A tear slipped down her cheek as she flowed into his arms. They moved to the music, circling the kitchen floor.

Why did she have to keep questioning every detail of their relationship? What if he didn't break her heart?

―――――

The next day, she still remembered the night of lovemaking. Sean had been so gentle, so sweet and so tender, as if he wanted to restore her soul, heal all the wounds life inflicted.

She smiled as she sorted the stack of mail on her desk. A large envelope caught her attention. She opened it and pulled out a greeting card. It wished her a happy Mother's Day, although the holiday was still two weeks away.

A folded sheet of paper slipped out. Elinor left it for a moment to study the card, signed by Helen. Helen Talbot. That would be one of her cousins, whom she would have met when she stayed with her father's family in high school. Who was that? Had Helen been the tall, dark-haired sophisticate? Or the short, pudgy tag-along?

Elinor didn't recall. The visit had been so long ago and there were a lot of Talbot cousins who had come and gone. She unfolded the letter.

Dear Elly. It's been so long since we saw you.

"Elly?" Elinor shook her head. Who had called her that?

Now she remembered. Grandpa called the short little girl Helen Joy because he said she was both hell and joy. She and Elinor had joined forces to tease and torment the rest of the cousins. How could she have forgotten? It was one of the few good memories she had being shuffled from family to family.

Because I haven't seen any of the Talbot cousins in years, she told herself. Keeping in touch with the other part of her family wasn't encouraged by her mother's parents. The only time she was allowed to visit the Talbots was when they wanted a break from her. When she wrote her cousin after her marriage, Helen hadn't written back.

Elinor returned her attention to the letter. *'We're having a family reunion Fourth of July weekend. Please come. You're all we have left of Owen. Grandma wants to see you and your kids. It's been so long. You can bring your jerk of a husband. I'll even apologize for calling him names. I know he told us to leave you alone. But we're your family. We miss you. We love you. I miss you. If you don't answer this time, I'll visit! So, call me. Collect's okay. Love, Helen.'*

Elinor tried to laugh. She couldn't. She burst into tears instead.

Hours later, she remained distracted. She couldn't focus on the evening's entertainment of dinner, homework, and Scrabble. She'd called Helen, but her cousin hadn't called back yet.

Suddenly, Lynn's squabbling over Jake's choice of words irritated Elinor. She retreated to the living room and a mindless TV sitcom, closing the door behind her. Why had John done it? Had he hated her that much? How could he take away her family, too? Would the Talbots have accepted her so easily if her father had come back alive from Grenada?

"What's going on?" Sean came into the room, closing the door behind him. He passed her a glass of white wine. "You're upset." He sat down on the opposite end of the couch. "Why?"

She appreciated him not crowding her. "I got a note from my

cousin Helen. The Talbots want me to bring the kids to a family reunion this July."

"Nice," Sean commented. "What's the problem?"

She hesitated, eyed the closed door to the kitchen, and then lowered her voice. She poured out the story of John's strategy to separate her from the Talbots. "When Grandpa died seven years ago, I couldn't go to the funeral. I didn't have anyone to look after the animals or the farm. John refused, and I didn't trust him to do it anyway. Of course, the Talbots were upset by my refusal to come, especially since it looked like I didn't have time for any of them because Grandpa had already given me my inheritance. I didn't hear from them again until today."

"How do you know what he did?"

"Because of Helen's card." Elinor put the wine glass on the end table beside the couch. "Which I can't find to show you. Sean, I think I'm going crazy. I had the damned card and letter. I don't know what I did with them. I called Helen again this afternoon. Then I put away the note so the kids wouldn't see it. Helen called John a jerk."

"Good for her." Sean sipped his wine and waited.

Elinor jumped to her feet. "I keep misplacing things and I forget to reprogram the answering machine. I know it's older than the hills, but I like it better than the new ones, but I always need Jake to change out the tapes."

"Machines fascinate the boy. He's probably in hog heaven," Sean said. "Don't be so hard on yourself."

"It's the same with the mail," Elinor continued. "Usually, I leave it for the kids to bring in for me, but the mailman caught me in the driveway today when I was coming in from Daisy's. If it weren't for Lynn and Jake, I swear the envelopes would sit in the mailbox until they died of old age."

Sean chuckled. "Elinor, believe me. It's nothing to worry about."

"How can I be so stupid?" She paced the room again. "Other women don't lose cards and letters."

"Anybody could." He held up a hand. "You were afraid the kids might find the letter. Your cousin undoubtedly wasn't tactful, but honest."

"That's true."

"You put the letter in a safe place." Sean shrugged. "It's even safe from you. It'll show up in a day or two. I'll help you look for it if you want."

"No." His offer touched her heart. "I'll find it when I'm meant to." She returned to the couch, picked up her wine, and curled up next to him. "How are the kids?"

"Fine. I told Lynn to find the dictionary or quit quibbling about Jake's words. I also tallied up his points." Sean put his arm around her. "Jake's ahead by a hundred points. But Lynn's a fighter so I wouldn't rule her out yet."

The telephone rang. Elinor took a deep breath and picked up the cordless. "Silver Lake Pony Ranch."

"Elly? Is that you? It's me, Helen. How are you? I'm so glad you called. Well, say something, Elly. Speak, girl."

Elinor started to laugh, suddenly remembering how fun the girl was. "How can I? You won't let me get a word in edgewise."

"Talk fast," Helen said. "I know you had a baby boy you named after Grandpa and your dad. Grandpa was thrilled, and Grandma said your daughter has Talbot blue eyes."

Elinor smiled. "That's right."

She looked toward Sean as he stood. "Where are you going?"

"To keep the kids occupied with the game. I'm sure you gals have a lot of catching up to do." He made his way to the kitchen.

"Who's that?" Helen demanded. "Your husband? Don't tell me you finally slapped him into shape."

"No. I divorced him. I replaced him with a real man."

"Good for you, Elly. Is he gorgeous? Hard-working? Honest? Nice to you and the kids? Great in the sack?"

"Yes." Elinor smiled. "All of the above."

"Tell me more," Helen squealed.

The conversation lasted for more than an hour. When it ended,

Elinor felt loved, safe, and wanted for the first time in years. Granted, she'd had Lynn and Jake, but now she had an extended family, too. She'd never lose them again.

She strolled into the kitchen. It was past the kids' bedtime, but some things were more important than a schedule.

"Would you like to go to a family reunion over Fourth of July?" Elinor asked her children.

"What family?" Jake demanded.

"The Talbots. I just finished talking to my cousin Helen. They want us to visit."

"Aren't the Talbots your dad's relatives?" Lynn asked.

Elinor nodded.

"I want to meet all of them," Lynn said. "Will they have pictures of him? Will they tell us about him? I remember he died when you were little, but you've always said he'd love us. And Great-Grandpa Jake said our grandpa Owen would, too."

"I'm named after them?" Jake's blue eyes got big. "I didn't know that. That's totally awesome!"

"Why?" Sean asked. "A lot of boys are given family names."

"I was afraid I might be named after somebody in my old dad's family," Jake explained. "Now I know I have a really special name." He jumped up to hug Elinor. "I want to go, too. But who will take care of our animals?"

"We'll ask Clancy and Ethan," Sean said. "Your cousin will tell your family I'm not your ex, won't she? I don't want all your kin coming after me with shotguns."

Elinor knew she must have looked as bewildered as she felt when he continued.

"You came in and asked all of us," Sean pointed out. "So, I'm invited, too. And I am taking all of you to the Senator's picnic. Turnabout's only fair."

"I never thought of going without you," Elinor said gently. At his smug smile, she added. "Of course, it means I'll have to visit another time to look at what Clancy calls real cowboys."

He came around the table toward her. "Say what, girl?"

She backed up a step. "Not in front of the children."

He glanced over his shoulder. "It's time to head for bed, kids."

"All right," Lynn agreed, mischief in her blue eyes. "But you two better not embarrass us by kissing all the time when we're there."

"Yeah," Jake said. "We have to practice company manners in public, Sean."

Laughing, Elinor marveled at the interplay. They'd never dared to tease their father the way they did Sean. "Go on, you monkeys. I'll check on you in a few minutes."

Alone with Sean, she let him pull her into his arms. "Do you have issues if I go cowboy hunting?"

"Not as long as it's me." He kissed the tip of her nose. "I'm not worried. I know how to brand what needs to be branded. And you belong to me."

She rested her hands on his wide chest. "Have I ever said that?"

He kissed her forehead. "Not yet. You will before we go to your family reunion."

"No, I won't." She shook back her hair. "I'm my own person."

"All these challenges make me hot." He pulled her hard against him. "And I think you should admit that you're mine tomorrow at lunch."

God, how she wanted him. She tipped back her head, so their gazes met, clashed. "No way, Killian." She moistened dry lips. "I have to substitute in Lynn's class tomorrow, so you aren't winning."

"Yes, I will." He nipped at her lower lip. "You'll beg for me next time, witch. I won't be satisfied with just one time either. We'll have a wild night."

———

"I don't get it." Lynn dropped her backpack on the floor of the pickup and climbed inside. "Why couldn't we take the bus today?"

"Because I wouldn't be home to meet you," Elinor said patiently. "And this is Friday, so we're going to Dairy Queen because I put up with your class for the last three days."

"I'm good with it, Mom," Jake said, sliding in next to his sister. "Blizzard Friday should be a national holiday."

"Definitely." Elinor drove toward the fast-food restaurant. She wanted to talk to Lynn about her antics at the school. Doing it in a public setting meant less likelihood of a scene and the teen wouldn't feel attacked. Hopefully, she would remember her manners.

Once they ordered their ice cream treats and were seated in a booth, Elinor studied both kids. "We have to talk."

"About what?" Jake asked. "Things are great now that we have Sean. He's not going away, is he?"

"This has nothing to do with Sean. He's fine and he's at the farm starting chores so the three of us can have a sit-down chat," Elinor said. "I promised we'd bring him home a sundae."

"Okay, then everything's cool," Jake said. "What do you want to talk about?"

"School." Elinor glanced at her daughter. "What's going on with you? Why are you playing around?"

"Who says I am?" Lynn eased out of the booth when their number was called to go collect the sundaes in a blatant attempt to escape the interrogation.

Jake stared after her, then turned to Elinor. "Ask her about our old dad. He's the one who made fun of her for thinking she was smart and told her nobody liked her when you weren't there to tell him to stop."

Hurt and anger mingled in Elinor's heart. Why did John feel the need to constantly belittle their kids? There was nothing to gain or prove by doing such a heinous thing.

When Lynn returned, Elinor waited until everyone had tucked into their ice cream. Then she asked, "Is your dad the one who told you to hide your intelligence? To fake your way through your classes because nobody likes smart girls?"

"They don't like smart boys either, Mom." Jake looked at his sister. "Is that how you make so many friends at school? By acting stupid?"

Lynn flushed. "I get A's on all my tests. I just give wrong answers in class discussions to make everybody laugh."

"Weird," Jake decided, digging at the strawberries in his *Blizzard*. "You'd think they'd figure out how smart you are if you *never* get a right answer."

Elinor let the idea sink into Lynn's mind and waited while her daughter ate half of her brownie sundae. Silence reigned until Elinor finished her own *Oreo Blizzard*.

Then she asked, "What do you mean, Jake? They can't know how smart your sister really is since she hides it, right?"

Lynn glared at her younger brother. "He means it's impossible to never get a right answer. The odds are against it. I didn't think of that. No wonder Mr. Sievers just shakes his head and never gets mad at me the way he does with other students."

"More like impatient," Jake said. "He's a real teacher. He wants people to learn and not con him."

Elinor ruffled his hair. "And so, speaks the sage who keeps passing himself off as an eleven-year-old. Eat up, guys. We don't want to stick Sean with all our work."

"I'm not a guy," Lynn protested. "I keep telling you."

Elinor shrugged. "Hey, I'm not a genius like my kids. I'll try to remember."

"Well, we had to get it from somewhere," Jake said. "So, you must be pretty smart. Did you get straight A's in school too, Mom? Lynn said you graduated with honors when you got your master's degree."

"Yes. And I was on the Dean's List in college for my undergraduate work. That's what they called the honor roll," Elinor explained. Discussing her grades brought back another memory of John. She hadn't dared to show them around the house once she began college and took her education seriously. Her grades were always better than his, which infuriated him. "Grandpa Talbot told me my dad was bright, too. He and my mom met at Washington State University in Pullman."

"So, we all come by it naturally," Lynn said. "I guess it's pretty dumb for me to act stupid. I don't know what Mr. Sievers is going to say when I start having the right answers."

"Probably nothing," Jake told her. "He'll just figure Mom got through to you."

Elinor met her daughter's confused gaze. "Your brother means your teacher talked to me about it at Parents' Night. It was the same time he asked if Jake could come for Math class."

Lynn finished her sundae. "I still think Jake should stop reading your teaching magazines. He knows way too much stuff, more than any eleven-year-old should."

"You'll just have to live with it, Lynn. I do."

PART THREE

MAY 2018

"Take back the Power!"

ELINOR TALBOT

TWENTY-EIGHT

"I CAN'T BELIEVE YOU DUG UP THE SPELL AGAIN. THIS IS THE third time, Jake. What is your problem? It's been two months. Mom and Sean are always kissing now."

"I told you before. It's going to take more than a couple kisses to get them married and him as our new dad."

Lynn glared at her younger brother and then at the magick spell in her hand. "Why do I think there's more to all of this than getting Mom a new husband?"

"Nothing except a happy forever after," Jake insisted, but he didn't quite meet her gaze. "All I want is the best for everybody."

"That had better be it." Lynn began to read. *"On this night and in this hour, I call upon the Ancient Power..."*

———

Lynn's birthday fell on the first Saturday in May. She invited six of her friends for a slumber party. Jake planned to stay at his best friend's house for the night since their place would be crowded with what he called a "giggle of girls."

Elinor approved both plans. She walked through the house once more, making sure everything was set. She had potato chips, sodas, frozen pizzas, candy, cookies, the makings for banana splits, and a huge sheet cake designed by Brigid Dawson.

Elinor eyed the pile of brightly wrapped packages on the kitchen table. Would Lynn like the red suede chaps? She'd been dreaming about a pair for horse showing, and Clancy had found these at a tack sale. The puppy stuff would go over well, too. Elinor poured herself a cup of coffee and walked out on the porch to give the farm a quick once-over.

Clancy taught a class in the arena. Marcie and Sandy were out on the trail. In the pasture below the orchard, Awesome and Comet frolicked and raced while Chipeta and Star watched. Taffy was in the stall with her dark gray newborn filly, named Licorice Whip by Lynn.

Sean had stopped rototilling the garden to enjoy the sight of the foals at play. A smile touched Elinor's lips and she returned to the kitchen. He loved horses as much as she did. They had common interests, she told herself again. It could work out.

She carried her coffee and a cup for him to the garden. "Looked like you were ready for a break."

"Definitely." Sean sipped the coffee as he eyed her. "Jake told me he's staying at Bobby's tonight. Is that a good idea? Jake had so many nightmares after the last time."

Elinor frowned. "I wish I knew why."

"I'm telling you what I think. The nightmares seem to get worse before and after a visit to Bobby's. What are the boys doing?"

"Probably the same things the girls plan to do tonight. Talk, play board games, watch movies, and eat me out of house and home. Relax, Sean. I trust Harold and Vivian. They're good people."

"Harold's a friend of mine," Sean said. "I like them, too."

Elinor nodded. "I know you're concerned about Jake's bad dreams."

"Three of them, Elinor. He had three of them last night. Every time we got him back to bed, he woke up screaming."

"Fine." She dumped the rest of her coffee. "I'll go call Vivian right now. Happy, Sean? I make decisions concerning him every day."

"Not always good ones." Sean's tone was measured with deadly patience. "What about Lynn's show next Saturday? Did you arrange to come?"

"I've got a business to run."

"In four years, the girl will be grown and gone to college. Maybe you ought to spend some time with her before then."

"I do the best I can, Sean. If you don't like it, you can hit the road!" She stalked off to the barn, determined not to look behind her. She heard the roar of the rototiller.

Once she checked on the lessons and trail rides, she returned to the house to make the phone call. Vivian answered and assured Elinor that she and Harold would be around to keep an eye on the boys.

"If we go anywhere, we make sure Penny is home. I never leave them with an outside babysitter. It's not a problem to have Jake here. He always asks Harold questions about the lawyers on TV and if real attorneys do things the same way."

Elinor laughed. "That sounds like him. I just wanted to make sure he wasn't overstaying his welcome. I know how much he enjoys his times at your house."

After a few more pleasantries, she replaced the receiver. If Bobby's parents had a handle on it when Jake stayed over, that meant there had to be another reason for the nightmares, and she still had to find it.

Later that afternoon, she was in the middle of untacking ponies when Jake came into the barn. "What's going on, honey?"

"Nothing." Jake took the saddle and pads off the door and carried it to the tack room. "Where's Sean? He said I could help him today."

"He was rototilling the garden. I'm late and we have to get it planted so we'll have vegetables this year." Elinor went to the next stall.

"He's not there now." Jake followed her to carry tack. "I'm ready to go to Bobby's. Sean said he'd take me."

"You're not going to Bobby's until we've had cake, ice cream, and presents. Lynn would be heartbroken if you disappeared on her birthday."

"All right." Jake followed her. "But besides Lynnie, most girls are yucky."

Elinor smiled. "You'll change your mind in a few years." She suspected Sean had gone after the puppy, but she wouldn't say so.

An hour and a half later, they were in the middle of the party when Ruler gave his low bark. She checked the driveway. Sean had returned. She went to meet him.

"We started with cake and ice cream, so we're ready for presents." She looked at the truck. "The puppy?"

"In the cab asleep." Sean put his arm around her shoulders, their mutual short tempers earlier seemingly forgotten. "How's it going?"

Elinor grimaced. "I'd forgotten how loud six girls are. And the only two I recognize are Cassie and Natalie. The other four seem nice, but they look like blond clones."

Sean chuckled. "By morning, you'll know them." They climbed the stairs and entered the kitchen, escorted by Ruler.

"Lynn, look who's here," Elinor said.

Lynn studied Sean's empty hands. "Did you forget today's my birthday?"

Elinor struggled to sound disapproving. "Don't be rude, Lynn. You have better manners than that."

Sean chuckled. "Your gift's in the truck. You can't miss it."

Silence fell. Lynn stared at Sean for a moment before she whirled and raced for the back door. Her friends chased after her, Cassie pushing red-haired Natalie out in front of her. Laughing, Elinor walked after them.

When she reached the porch, Lynn was at the truck. She yanked open the driver's door and almost fell into the pickup cab when a black and white puppy leaped out at her.

"I knew it!" Jake announced, beside Elinor. "I knew you'd get her a collie, especially when you kept asking what colors she liked, Sean."

"He's not all collie. He does look like a blue merle, but he's half blue heeler. He'll grow up and work stock. Ruler can teach him," Sean said.

Elinor gazed at Lynn, who hugged the wriggling puppy tightly while he squirmed and tried to wash her face. "I'll explain that to her, but I don't think she'll care. She finally has a dog."

"I wonder if she'll let me hold it before tomorrow." Jake sighed as the other girls clustered closer to the puppy and Lynn. "Probably not."

"Don't sweat it," Sean told him. "Your mom and I think you're old enough for a puppy of your own. We'll stop by my place tomorrow after fishing and you can choose one."

"Really? You mean it?" Jake held back for an instant before he flung his arms around Sean. "You're the best. I'm so glad we got you."

"Me, too." Sean hugged the boy. "Now, when Lynn gets an extra present on your birthday, no griping. Deal?"

"You bet!" Jake lowered his voice as the troop of girls approached. "Don't tell her. It'd spoil her puppy present. I'll surprise her tomorrow."

Elinor grabbed her son in a quick hug. "You're the best boy I've got. That's so thoughtful, Jake."

Lynn made it back to the porch through her throng of giggling friends. The puppy wriggled in her arms, trying to lick her face. Dark brown ears and tiny gold patches on his face revealed he was more a tri-color than a 'real' blue merle. Lively black eyes filled with mischief seemed to share his new owner's happiness.

"Mom, did you see him?" Lynn demanded, holding the puppy up. "Isn't he perfect? Sean, you're perfect, too."

"I saw." Elinor smiled over Jake's head at Sean. "I couldn't agree more. He is perfect."

"They're gonna get mushy," Jake warned his sister. "They'll be

kissing again before long. And I bet the ice cream is melting, too."
When the group of girls hustled in the kitchen with squeals and
shrieks, he eyed Elinor. "Now can I go to Bobby's?"

Elinor nodded. "Thanks for being such a good sport." As he
ran to get his stuff, she smiled at Sean. "I called Vivian and she
promised to watch the boys as closely as I would."

"I'll drop him off." Sean framed her face with calloused hands
and found her mouth with his. "I'll see you tomorrow. You'll have
your hands full tonight with that crew."

"I'll say." Elinor winced when she heard a crash. "I'd better
go." She caught Jake in a hug as he raced by. "Sean will pick you
up tomorrow morning to take you fishing and I'll see you after
that. Be good."

"I will." Jake wriggled free. "'Night, Mom." He passed his
backpack to Sean and started toward the pickup. "See you later,
alligator."

"In a while, crocodile. Have fun." Elinor waited long enough
to wave good-bye. Then she headed for the kitchen to supervise
the heating of the pizza. She wasn't allowed to touch it since Lynn
was afraid it'd burn.

———

The next three weeks passed quickly. They were the happiest in
Elinor's life. She knew the joy she felt wouldn't last. Sean probably wouldn't stay forever, but she could enjoy each moment with
him. When it all went away, she'd have the memories of his love,
and she'd never forget her first Mother's Day with him. It started
with flowers and champagne for breakfast and ended with dinner
at the Space Needle for her, the kids, and Marlene.

———

"We're like a real family," Jake announced from the back seat of
Sean's pickup. "This place is awesome."

"Not as awesome as Xanadu Arabians," Lynn said. "Did I tell you that Pyewacket has his own room?"

"Only like a million times since you got home on Saturday." Jake let out a yelp. "She elbowed me!"

Elinor turned to glare at the two kids in the back seat and adopted her strictest tone. "Hands to yourselves and put your company manners on now, or we're going straight home."

"Promise?" Sean asked. "I'm so up for that." He winked at Lynn. "I'll pay you to keep hassling him."

"Will you pay me to holler at her?" Jake asked.

"Oh yeah."

"All of you straighten up right now," Elinor ordered. "I'm nervous enough." She stared at the huge, red brick house at the end of the wide driveway. Late-model cars lined each side of the pavement and Sean's truck looked incredibly out of place. She glanced at him. "Did you grow up here?"

"Yes." Sean held her door. "It wasn't a comfortable place. The maids and the housekeeper always gave me a hard time when I tracked in dirt." He guided her to the side yard and pointed. "If you go through those pastures, you eventually get to Marlene's. That's where I really hung out."

"I don't know about this, Sean." Elinor took a deep breath. "What if your folks don't like me?"

"As I've told you for months, I'd be more concerned if Marlene didn't." Sean dropped a kiss on Elinor's lips. "Like Roy used to tell me, don't sweat it. The Senator doesn't pay our bills."

The comment eased the tension in Elinor's mind. She relaxed as Sean escorted them to the front door. He rang the bell and introduced the middle-aged man who answered as his father's aide.

A stunning brunette in tight, low-cut jeans, a clinging bright red tank top, and spike heels came to greet them. She hugged Sean. "Hi. I'm Felicia."

"You're a lawyer?" Elinor's cheeks burned. "I'm sorry. That sounded awful."

"No. It's fine." Felicia held out her hand. "I've got the day off and I dress to irritate my parents when I'm here."

"And me," Sean grumbled, eyeing her outfit with disapproval.

Elinor elbowed him in the ribs. "She looks charming. I'm sure Lynn will want to ask you for fashion tips."

"Over my dead body," Sean said, scowling at his sister. "What's that thing in your belly button?"

"It matches the diamond studs in my ears." Felicia said, grinning. "Again, annoys the parents and can't be seen in my suits. Get over yourself, Sean."

Elinor smiled and shook hands with the younger woman. "I'm glad to meet you. He's very proud of you, but I'm sure you know that."

"Yes, I do." Felicia planted a kiss on his cheek. "Ignore him when he growls at you. It's what Tara and I do." She slipped her arm through Elinor's. "Come on. Let's find Sylvia and the Senator. You'd better meet them right away, or they'll be offended. They're out by the pool. Wait till Sean sees Tara's new bikini. He'll have a stroke."

Her words were close to accurate. A muscle came to life in Sean's jaw when a petite, shapely girl dashed to meet him. She flung her arms around his neck and greeted him with a big kiss. She had dyed blond hair complete with pink and purple streaks that matched her scant swimsuit.

Sean peeled her off and glared at her. "Tara, go put some clothes on."

"No way, big brother." She pasted another kiss on him, then wiped away the bright red lipstick on his cheek. "You know Daddy likes me to provide the entertainment."

Tara winked at Elinor. "You must be the saint who is dating this grump."

"I wouldn't call him a grump." Elinor slid her fingers through his. "He's wonderful."

Tara sobered as her sister came to stand beside her. "Don't you forget it, or you'll have me and Felicia to deal with."

Their loyalty to Sean pleased Elinor and she nodded. "You got it."

"Good. Then we'll get together soon and do lunch," Felicia told her. She glanced over her shoulder as an older woman came to join them.

Sean's mother wasn't the ogress Elinor had dreaded. She was a small, slender woman with short silver hair in the latest style. Her eyes were the same color as Sean's.

Sylvia Killian gripped Elinor's hand between hers. "Thank you for coming. I'm so glad you could make it. Please tell me you plan to stay all day. We'll have fireworks at dark."

Sean stirred beside Elinor. "We have stock to feed, Sylvia."

Hurt flickered in the older woman's eyes. The sight aroused Elinor's pity. "I arranged for someone to babysit my farm. We can stay as long as you want us."

"Really? All day." Sylvia beamed. "Come meet my husband."

Wallace Killian looked familiar. Elinor decided it was because she'd seen him on television and in the newspapers. Then she rethought it. He was tall, lean, and broad-shouldered like his sons. His black salt and pepper hair made him appear distinguished.

He was charming, but it was all façade. She ought to know. She played the same game and hid behind a mask, too.

The afternoon passed. There were activities for the children as well as the adults. After they ate, Elinor helped carry dishes to the kitchen along with Felicia, Tara, and Sylvia.

When Elinor started to go back outside, Sylvia stopped her. "Please wait."

Sylvia waited until they were alone in the large room before she spoke. "I've got so many mistakes to try and atone for, especially with my boys. Two years ago, a reporter was the one who told me that Sean was in the hospital and not expected to survive."

"Good heavens! What happened?" Elinor stopped to think. "That accident with Christy's horse? I didn't know he was hurt so badly."

Sylvia nodded. "Yes. Broken bones, internal injuries, and a

concussion. I didn't know he was in a coma until the middle of that TV interview."

"How on earth could that happen?" Elinor asked. "Why weren't you notified?"

Tears sparkled in Sylvia's gray eyes. "Felicia and Tara were frantic. They called Marlene Dawson, but not me. They didn't think I'd care, much less fly in from the other Washington. After that, I was determined to make amends with my children."

"And your husband?" Elinor asked. "Does he feel the same way?"

"Not yet." Sylvia stared at the pile of dishes on the counter. "He hasn't figured out that stomping on your kids' dreams doesn't make them love you. He told Tara she'd never amount to a hill of beans, so she plays the part of a scatterbrain when she's here and tells everyone that he wants her to be a model for a sleazy reality TV show. He doesn't understand that Sean still bears a grudge because Warren wouldn't let him go to vet school. And he also doesn't grasp that most children don't have to make appointments with their fathers to see them."

"Sean goes the extra mile for my kids. It's why they adore him."

"Good. Out of my children, he needs the most love. He lacks emotional security," Sylvia said. "We never gave it to him. He had to receive it from Marlene and Roy."

"You're lucky they were around," Elinor said. "They raised a good man."

"Lots of them over the years," Sylvia said with a sad smile. "I just wish I'd stepped up and been a mother to my kids instead of putting Warren's political ambitions ahead of them."

TWENTY-NINE

STILL ENJOYING THEMSELVES, ELINOR AND SYLVIA HAD JUST finished their iced tea and conversation when Lynn ran in the back door, her face pale with fear. "Mom, come quick!"

"What's wrong?" Elinor jumped up from her chair. "Is Jake hurt?"

"No. He's fine, but our father just showed up." Lynn trembled. "He'll be rude and nasty. And it was so fun before he got here to wreck everything."

Elinor patted the girl's shoulder. "Honey, it'll be fine. We'll use our company manners and so will he."

"If he doesn't, I'll ask him to leave." Sylvia grimaced. "I'm sorry, Elinor. Wallace uses these events to pay off social debts and to make political alliances. I don't think anyone even thought about there being a conflict."

"It's okay," Elinor lied. She took a deep breath to steady her nerves and went out the back door to the pool area. She saw John.

Big, burly, and running to fat, she thought. The fashionable style didn't hide the fact that his sandy blond hair was receding and thinning. He wore a suit, rather an odd choice for a social event like this picnic. His suit jacket barely hid the start of a paunch.

It was hard to believe she'd ever been married to him.

She glanced toward the far end of the pool where Sean stood with Ethan and Jake. She'd definitely done better since her divorce than she'd realized. Plus, she looked good. She'd chosen a navy dress and added a fancy western silver concho belt. The outfit had impressed Sean so much he offered to leave the kids with Audra. The memory made Elinor smile.

John had seen her. He paced toward her. "What are you doing here? Are you stalking me?"

"What?" Elinor laughed. "Are you serious? Why would I?"

"Because you're crazy. You'll do anything to ruin my political career." Fury mounted in John's brown eyes as he glared at her. "And keep your kids away from me."

"Watch it." Sean eased in front of Elinor. "Don't try to bully my woman."

"Yours?" John snorted. "You're nothing special."

"And you're less than that," Elinor said, finally angered by the insult.

Sean started toward John. Sean's slow movement must have intimidated her ex-husband. He fell back one step, then another.

Finally, he backed to the edge of the pool. At Sean's approach, John reeled and slipped. He landed in the water with a giant splash.

Sylvia came up beside Elinor and put an arm around her waist. "Sean, get that man out of my pool and out of my house."

"Yes, ma'am." Sean smiled in an attempt to comfort Elinor. "Go on inside. I'll be right back. It's okay, Lynn."

Elinor eyed her daughter. The girl had regained her normal healthy glow. "Don't fight with him, Sean," Elinor said. "He isn't worth it."

"Oh, he won't fight with me, darlin'. His type only goes after people who are smaller and weaker than he is, like you and the kids." Sean glanced toward the pool where John was wading toward the ladder on the side of the pool. "It'll be fine. I promise."

"And Jake?" Elinor looked to where her son was jumping up and down next to Ethan. They were watching the proceedings, as were the majority of the other guests. "Well, he seems okay with what you did."

She turned and walked with Sylvia back toward the house.

Wallace Killian came over. "What happened? How did Price fall in the pool? I was just about to endorse the man as a district court judge in the next election."

"You do and you die," Sylvia said. "He thought he could get away with abusing Elinor in my house. Sean stopped him. Now, you help Sean get rid of him."

Wallace blinked and spread out his hands. "Whatever you say, honey. I'm sorry, Elinor. There's no excuse for that kind of behavior. It's unacceptable. I had no idea you were subjected to that in my home."

"It's okay." Elinor escaped to the house as Wallace continued his apologies. She'd heard similar ones from people like him and supposed she might have believed the words if his tone hadn't been so insincere. Once she was inside, she reached for Lynn, who had been watching through a window, and hugged the girl. "Are you all right?"

"I'm cool, Mom." Lynn wriggled free. "Wasn't that major awesome when Sean scared him into the pool?"

Elinor sighed. "How many times do I have to tell you violence doesn't solve problems?"

"Yeah, well he's a lying scumbag who told me he killed my cat," Lynn said. "The only thing better would have been if Sean had hit him."

Elinor held the girl's face with her hands. "Honey, I was worried something might happen to Pyewacket. That's why I sent him to live with Marlene. I told you he was safe again and again, remember? Trust me. I've never lied to you."

"I do trust you." Lynn smiled and leaned against Elinor for a moment. "Next time Audra babysits, can she bring Pye to visit?"

"I don't know about that. Cats like having their own territory.

I'll ask her when we get home and she can decide if she thinks it will work."

Hours later on the way home, Elinor debated how to bring up the subject of her ex-husband with Sean. She waited until Audra left, the children were in bed, and they were alone.

Cuddled next to Sean on the couch, she said. "So, what happened when you and John went to his car?"

"Nothing." Sean dropped a kiss on top of her hair. "I poured him into it, and he left."

"Did you threaten him?" Elinor asked. "He's a lawyer. He could sue you."

"He'll lose. There were at least thirty people who saw him accidentally fall into the pool. Wallace and his aide were there when Ethan and I took him to his car. And Clancy arrived with Jack Abbott then, too," Sean said. "I never laid a hand on him, darlin'. Plenty of witnesses and they all saw and heard him make an ass of himself."

"What if he tries to hurt you?" Elinor measured the calmness in his face. "What will I do?"

Sean held his thumb to her mouth. "Hush. You'll let me do what I need to do." He lowered his head to replace his thumb with his mouth.

The kiss was sweet and warmed her all the way though. "Did your father say anything to you?"

"No, he was too busy telling Ethan that he had a lucky escape when Clancy jilted him. And Ethan told him not to burn his bridges."

Elinor laughed. "You'd think a politician would have more sense than to commit himself to a blunt statement like that."

"Maybe one day he'll figure us out." Sean kissed her again and drew her across his lap. "Come cast a spell on me, witch."

———

Since she didn't have to substitute at one of the local schools that day, she'd decided to use her time to finish renovating the studio apartment over the garage and turning it into a classroom for day camp. They already had ten kids signed into the first week and the other sessions were filling fast. She was going to need the space.

Daisy stirred the gallon of white paint intended for the bathroom. "So, have you contacted those friends of yours from graduate school? The three of you could go riding on the Centennial Trail before school gets out. I'd look after Jake and Lynn for you."

"Riding with them sounds like fun. I sent an email to the dean of the department, but I haven't heard back," Elinor said. "When I called the schools where Ann and Margo teach, the secretaries told me they weren't there anymore."

"How strange. If they'd gone to other schools in Lake Maynard, the secretaries could tell you where and the Baker City School closed a few years back so they're not there." Ruler barked, a short yip of announcement, and Daisy walked over to look out the window where the dog stood with his front paws on the windowsill. "Who do you know that drives a Dodge Ram? The back end is full of furniture. Have you rented this place without telling me?"

Elinor laughed and went to join her mentor at the window. "No, it really is going to be a classroom." She opened the window and waved at Clancy. "Up here. What's going on?"

"I brought stuff to decorate." Clancy slid out the driver's door. "And someone to help paint."

"Sounds good." Elinor closed the window and went to the staircase. "Who is helping?"

"Me," Tara Killian said as she came in from the parking area. Today she wore old, paint-splattered cargo pants, a sleeveless T-shirt, and battered running shoes. Waist-length, cinnamon brown hair gleamed, not a pink or purple streak in sight. Her makeup was light and understated, not the heavy mask of cosmetics she'd worn at the picnic. "Clancy says you're redecorating and that's what I do, so here I am."

Elinor blinked, surprised at both the offer and the young woman's appearance. "I don't mean to be rude, but how did you get that dye out of your hair? Lynn will want to try highlights if they're that easy to change, and I'll be the evil mother from hell when I won't let her."

Tara laughed. "It's a wig and I play with it all the time when I have to go to the Senator's. I'm thinking red, white, and blue streaks for the Fourth of July."

"They still won't step up and act like parents," Daisy said. "Your brother Sean tried all sorts of stunts twenty-five years ago when he was in my freshman English class and none of them worked. You'll have to get input from other folks."

"That's why I'm here," Tara said, her voice light, but tears still glimmered in her green eyes. "Sean's everything to me."

"And me," Elinor said, giving the younger woman a hug. "Thanks for coming, but this is just a low-rent operation. I'm not doing anything as fancy as what you did for Sean at his house." She turned to Daisy. "It's fabulous, every inch of it, but very livable."

"Yeah, but he will bring his dogs inside." Tara leaned down to pet Ruler, who wagged his tail and licked her fingers. "Hi, sweetie. Anyway, I do low budget, Elinor. I'm looking forward to the challenge, especially since Sean won't let me pay him back for college. And my folks didn't pay because they didn't approve of my art courses or the fact that I wanted a degree in home interior design."

"Okay. I'm not shy. I'll put you to work." Elinor turned and introduced Daisy to Tara and Clancy. "So, what's the plan?"

"I cleaned out the attic at Mom's," Clancy said. "We have a desk, filing cabinets, bookshelves, and brackets. Then Tara called me, so we went over to Sylvia's."

"She had tables and folding chairs from the Senator's last campaign headquarters that she wanted to get rid of," Tara said. "So, I grabbed them. She threw in some bulletin boards, too, and a ton of craft supplies."

"She had to go to a big lunch with some of his money men, or she'd have come to help," Clancy added. "If he irritates her anymore today, she may still show up."

"Thanks for the warning," Elinor said. "She was really sweet to me on Monday, but my place isn't clean enough to have Sean's momma visit."

"As long as it's clean enough when Marlene gets here with pizzas and sodas, we're good to go," Tara said.

"Then we'd better get started on our painting," Daisy declared. "Who is bringing in the furniture?"

"Oh, the guys will do that tonight after work," Clancy said, adding, "We just have to get ready for it."

"Then let's get started," Elinor said.

She stood in the middle of the L-shaped classroom and looked around. Three walls gleamed with their new high-gloss coats of school bus yellow paint. The large windows on the east wall had new mini-blinds, too. Tara had painted pictures of galloping ponies in the bathroom and kitchenette, giving a whimsical cowboy look to the area.

"What are you thinking?" Sean asked.

Elinor eyed the two long tables and chairs suitable not only for paperwork but also for lunch. She turned and saw the three study carrels, a gift from Ethan, who'd acquired them from the Boeing surplus store. The computers in the carrels were a donation from Gavin, who'd set them up with the business's own network and then hooked them up to a separate printer. She even had her own teacher corner, cut off from the rest of the room by file cabinets and two bookcases. Her computer sat on the desk where Lynn and Daisy were happily loading necessary software, a gift from Sean.

"I feel like Christmas came early," Elinor finally said. "I love your family."

He chuckled and wrapped an arm around her waist. "I can't wait till you say that to *me*. Come on. Gavin's grilling steaks on your back porch and Ethan wants to put up that big whiteboard on the inside wall. I know he'll make me help."

"Would I be a total teaching fool if I said I wanted to start a year-round private school up here, Sean?"

"You could next fall. With the ponies, you'd have a built-in PE class."

She gaped at him for an instant. Then she kissed him. "You make all my dreams come true."

"Okay, I'll settle for that tonight." He guided her toward the staircase. "I still want you to take the risk of loving me, but I can wait."

She pressed closer to him. She couldn't share what he meant to her. She was too afraid of losing him.

A mural with a dozen ponies cantered along the staircase wall. Elinor smiled as she descended the stairs and they headed toward the house. "I think Tara ran amuck with these," she said, gesturing to the art.

"Wait till she talks you into her next project," Sean said. "She says she wants to create a huge painting of your entire rainbow herd on this side of the building."

"Let me think about it." Elinor glanced toward the driveway and spotted Jake talking to Felicia. "I wonder what he's asking your sister."

"Something to do with those lawyer shows that he watches all the time," Sean said. "He's probably cross-examining her to find out how accurate they are, like he was with Harold."

"Why doesn't that surprise me?" Elinor slipped out of Sean's hold and went to rescue his sister.

Tonight, Felicia wore a tailored black suit and high heels. With her hair neatly coiled in a bun and exquisite but subtle makeup, she looked like a total professional and nothing like the girl whom Elinor had met at the barbecue. "Hey, Felicia. How are you?"

"Good." Felicia tipped back her head and sniffed. "Smells like steak. I got here just in time." She passed a brown envelope to

Elinor. "Your copy of the nasty-gram that I had delivered to your neighbor by the sheriff. Zane won't bother you again."

"How did you arrange that without going to court and suing him?" Jake asked.

"Attorney's secret." Felicia winked at him. "Always make nice with the deputies. Sometimes it's not a case of what you know, it's who you know, and Beth Chambers made sure to introduce me to the ones she thought I'd need when she went to work at the Sheriff's Department after she left the Army. She was in the 4-H club back in the day and we all stick together."

"Wow, I didn't know that." Elinor shook her head, amazed at the idea. "No wonder she was always so nice about Chipeta after I rescued her."

"That's cool." Jake beamed at her. "Do you want to see my horse Awesome?"

"I'd love to." Felicia opened the back door of her BMW. "Let me change my shoes and I'm good to go."

"Wouldn't you rather come to the house and have a drink?" Elinor asked. "You could visit the horses another time."

"Hmm." Felicia considered the idea as she sat on the rear seat, removing her heels and replacing them with running shoes. Then she shook her head. "Nope. I want to see your place and I want Jake to show me around. I bet he knows all the best things about it."

"Yes, I do." Jake agreed. "And afterward, you can see my puppy."

Elinor glanced at the pair as they headed away and wondered why her own lawyer, Harold's mantra rang in her mind. *Be afraid, be very afraid*!

THIRTY

She had high hopes for tonight, a romantic dinner for two. She intended to take a chance and share her feelings for him. The Caesar salad was in the fridge. Spaghetti sauce simmered in the slow cooker and the loaf of garlic bread was ready to pop into the oven. All she had to do was cook the noodles, open the wine, and light some candles once the kids left them alone.

She and Sean could have a leisurely evening together, and she knew where it would end, with the two of them in her bed. The kids had plans of their own. Jake was headed off to Bobby's and Lynn would be at Cassie's slumber party. Right now, the girl was in her room packing all the things a teen needed to spend the night at her best friend's.

Granted, Sean and Elinor would have to puppy sit, but that was easier than trying to have a romantic evening with the kids at home. She slipped red candles into the holders and placed the candelabra in the center of the table. Ruler barked and she crossed to the window to look out.

Had Sean returned from dropping Jake at Bobby's already?

She frowned when she saw Jake in the front seat of the rig. Leaving the dogs behind, she went out to the porch. "What happened? Did we make a mistake about tonight? Weren't they home?"

Jake stopped at the bottom of the porch steps, furious. "I hate him! I wish he'd go away."

"What? But you like Bobby."

"Not Bobby." Jake jerked his head toward Sean. "Him. He ruined everything."

Sean shrugged as he joined them. "You should have realized by now that I'll rain on your parade when I think you're wrong, Jake."

"What's going on?" Elinor said again.

Jake kicked at the step. "He wrecked my night."

"You're responsible for your choices and your actions. Now tell your mother what you've done and stand up for it." Sean's voice remained calm. "A man takes pride in what he does. If he can't take pride in it, he doesn't do it."

Tears spilled down Jake's cheeks. "I had to come home because Bobby and I were watching slasher movies on cable. Penny rented them for us. She lets us read her chop-people-up books, too. She doesn't care what we do as long as we leave her and her boyfriend alone so they can make out in her room."

Elinor winced. She ought to have done more than just make the telephone call to Harold and Vivian, and she should have talked to them about her concerns about Penny. Why hadn't she followed up with the other parents like Sean suggested, instead of throwing a fit because he thought something might be wrong? "What kind of movies? Vampires? Scary monster shows that are funny, too?"

Jake hesitated. Then he looked over his shoulder at Sean, who stood silently holding the backpack and sleeping bag. "The real bloody kind you won't let me or Lynnie see."

"And now you know why." Elinor placed her hands on his shoulders. "And that's why you've been having nightmares." She grimaced. "And you didn't tell me what was going on with Penny, did you? I thought Harold and Vivian were there, too."

"They are lots of times," Jake said. "They think it's okay

because Penny's almost seventeen. But she's not supposed to have her boyfriend over when they're not home."

Elinor took a deep breath. "I'm very disappointed in your behavior, Jake. Go to your room and think about your punishment. I've always trusted you and Lynn. I was wrong, too."

"I'm sorry, Mom." More tears fell. "Maybe I'm not old enough for a puppy. Maybe Sean should take him back."

Elinor hardened her heart. "We'll think about it."

"No." Sean put down Jake's belongings and patted the boy's back. "The puppy's nonnegotiable. I'm not taking him back and he has nothing to do with what you did at Bobby's."

Elinor scowled at Sean. The loss of the puppy for a day or two would have been an easy punishment. She could have let Jake suffer and then allowed the puppy to come home. "All right. Jake, your room. I want to talk to Sean."

Her son started to brush past her, and she stopped him. "Go straight there. I don't want Lynn upset by this."

When her son left, Elinor looked at Sean. "How did you know he was breaking the rules at his friend's house?"

"Because I did the same kind of thing when I was a kid," Sean said, his tone even. "When Ethan learned what I'd done, he kicked my tail all the way home."

"That's what you think I do, not pay attention to my kids." Anger swamped the worry she felt for her son. "It's not."

"You love them, but you expect too much from them, Elinor. You don't step up and act like a mom should." Sean turned and started back to his truck.

Elinor went after him. "I want my kids to have a childhood."

Sean stopped. "Really?" He swung around, steel in his gray eyes. "Then why tell Jake not to upset Lynn? She's not his other parent."

"This place takes a lot of work. I don't have time for Lynn or Jake to misbehave." Elinor stopped, as she heard herself. *Oh my God!* What had she been doing to her children?

Sean gave her a steady look before he headed to the truck. He opened the driver's door, took out a bag of puppy chow, and put it on the ground. Then he removed a battered tin box. "Do you know what this is?"

"It looks like the container I gave Jake when he started collecting fishing lures." She eyed the dirt covering the tin. "What did he do, bury it?"

"In the garden." Sean popped the lid off the box and handed her a sheaf of folded papers that had been crammed into it. "Read these. They'll give you a whole new outlook on your kids. You'll find out what they want. They think it's a dad. I know it's an adult for a parent, someone who lets them be children."

His words stunned her. She looked down at the papers he'd given her, fighting back the tears. In her hand, she held what looked like a school assignment. She recognized Jake's best penmanship, but she'd never asked her son to write a *magick* spell.

When she lifted her gaze from the pages, she saw an empty yard. Sean was gone. She hadn't even heard the truck's engine. She was alone.

Why had she expected anything else? She could handle being alone. She always had. She felt as if her heart had been torn out and handed to her, still beating.

––––––

Elinor studied the spell written out on the papers. Lynn had happily gone off to Cassie's, unaware that anything had happened, and Jake quietly remained in his room, door closed. She had all the time she needed to read through the pages Sean found. It was as if her children had drawn up a blueprint for the man.

He'd done everything on their list. He'd been there for them, as well as her. Was he right? Did she force her children to act older than their ages? Giving them responsibility was good, but had she depended on them too much?

She wanted them to have friends, to play, to belong to all the clubs she'd never been allowed to join. Was she a bad mother? She had to make some changes around here. It wasn't too late, was it?

She continued to think about it while she mucked the stalls the following afternoon. The barn door creaked, and she looked toward the entrance. It was Harold Greer.

She waved at him, then returned to pitching manure. "I was going to call you."

"Figured you were busy. The weekend is when you make money." Harold leaned on the wall. "Sean was at our place when Viv and I got back from the grocery store last night. He told us what's been going on. I'm sorry about Penny's behavior. All of this surprised the hell out of us. Viv says she must be the worst shrink in the world and I feel like the stupidest lawyer."

"You aren't the only ones kicking themselves." Elinor sighed and stopped mucking. "I feel like the dumbest mother alive. Jake's been having nightmares. They escalate before and after he and Bobby spend nights at your place."

"Yeah, that's what Sean told us." Harold scratched his bald spot. "My folks left me home to babysit when I was twelve, and I looked after my brothers and sisters for days, not an hour or two. I can't believe Penny's that irresponsible. I threw out her boyfriend. He's twenty-two. What's he doing with my little girl?"

Elinor didn't answer. They both knew. She propped the plastic pitchfork against the wall. "John was six years older than I was. We dated off and on through high school and things got serious when I was eighteen. I was pregnant with Lynn two years later."

"Tell Penny that when she comes to apologize to you," Harold said. "She told us she had to work late here, and she was sneaking off to be with him. Leave some manure for her *and* Bobby. I can't believe he was dumb enough to cover for her, but Viv says kids are like that."

"I'll let them do the pigpen," Elinor said. "I'm sending the pigs off to be butchered next week. The pen needs to be cleaned before I bring in weaner piglets this summer. It really stinks."

"Fine. I'm good with that, and don't even think of paying them to do it. After all their stunts, shoveling pig poop will be the least of their worries." Harold rested his hands on the wall. "Jake's a smart one. I've started pulling affidavits together. The Talbots were happy to talk to my associate over in Colville. That shark, Felicia, has statements from people who saw Price's behavior at Senator Killian's barbecue."

"What are you talking about, Harold?" Elinor felt as if she were tumbling down the rabbit hole. "What has Jake done now?"

"He called John Price and asked if his dad planned to pick up him and Lynn for the scheduled weekend visitation. Jake's done it every Friday since January. He taped the calls. He has a collection of letters from Price telling Jake to stop harassing him, to leave him alone."

"What?" Astonished, flustered, Elinor stared at Harold. "He doesn't *want* to see his father. Jake was thrilled when John fell in the swimming pool at the Killians' place."

"Price went overboard with insults before that," Harold said. "At Christmas, Jake asked me how to make his dad go away for good. Jake called to thank him for his presents and Price told him he was a monster."

Elinor buried her face in her hands. "I've done that for years, putting his name on their gifts. I wrote it on the packages before our divorce, too. Otherwise, the kids never would have gotten a single thing from him. Why did John want to hurt our son?"

Harold shrugged. "Some guys are like that, Elinor. Anyway, it's over. You've done more to keep Price involved in his kids' lives than my other clients. Now, stop. When Jake told Viv about the letter from your cousin, Viv called it a textbook case of domestic violence, cutting you off from family."

Shame heated Elinor's face. "My God! Jake brought you that? How could he? It was private. My cousin always let her mouth overload her brain."

Harold touched Elinor's shoulder. "Quit covering for your ex. He's a bastard and I'm going to nail him."

Elinor swallowed the lump of tears in her throat. She wouldn't cry. "I wasn't out to use them for revenge or to teach them to hate John."

She pulled away from Harold, wrapped her arms around her stomach. "Why didn't Jake come to me? I wouldn't have been angry with him for wanting to connect with his father."

"He loves you. He explained that you believe that people are mostly good. And he asked me in January if he built a case, would I be able to make John Price go away forever." Harold scratched his bald spot again. "Last time I'll ever underestimate Jake. I figured there was no way he could trap Price, so I said, 'sure'. I never thought he'd manage something like this, but he did."

"Yes, and he suffered for it." Elinor sighed. "I made him choose his punishment for the movies and the books. That was before this. He'll be lucky if he sees his friends before September."

"All he did was give Price the rope. The man didn't have to make like a Christmas tree ornament and hang himself."

"You're right." Elinor relaxed. "I still don't want Jake using his intelligence to manipulate people. Between you and me, setting up John was probably no contest. I doubt Jake gave his plan ten minutes' thought. And he's suffered nightmares for the last five months."

"Those horror movies and true crime books didn't help," Harold said.

"But he and Bobby only spent the night together at your house once or twice a month, Harold. We've always switched around so neither of us feel like we're running a hotel. The nights they were here, they didn't see a single monster movie."

"I never thought of that." Harold looked relieved. "You're right. Most nights when Jake was over, Viv and I were home and we controlled the boys' activities. Thanks, Elinor. I feel better." He fished in his pocket and pulled out a list. "Viv said for me to give you this. She was afraid you wouldn't believe Price was an abuser. She says if you want to talk to her, she's available, or she'll refer you to a head-shrinking friend of hers."

"I don't think it's necessary but thank her for me." Elinor took the small paper. It looked as if it'd been ripped from a grocery list or memo pad. "What's on the agenda with John?"

"I've got an appointment with his lawyer." Harold winked. "She's also his new mother-in-law. I think Price will settle out of court. He won't squabble over this. The last thing a lawyer who's running for election as a judge wants is to have his ex-wife filing for a restraining order."

Elinor choked. "Why would I need one? I never see him now. Neither do the kids."

"And I intend to keep it that way." Whistling, Harold left the barn.

She didn't return to cleaning the stall right away. Instead, Elinor read the list Viv had sent along. Lines jumped out at her.

"Isolate the partner. Degrade the partner. Sexually abuse the partner. Damage the partner's personal property." She shuddered. It read like a plan of her marriage to John. What was she going to do?

Let Harold handle John. She'd focus on healing her family.

She returned to cleaning the barn while she made plans. She'd be a better parent. She'd do what the kids needed a parent to do. She'd be there for them. They had her and, like Sean had told her more than once, it was time to step up. She'd let Clancy manage the farm on Saturdays so she could attend Lynn's shows. They would go to the Talbot family reunion, and there'd be other visits to her relatives after that.

Sean entered the barn. "How's it going? Jake and I were supposed to go fishing today."

"He's in his room." Elinor studied Sean warily. He looked good in black jeans and one of his favorite red western shirts. She didn't see anger or fury on his face, just normal concern for her son. "He decided a good punishment was being grounded. He can't watch television, use the phone, or go anywhere for a month. He can't ride the ponies or play with Awesome for three days."

"Pretty intense."

She nodded and forked another pile of manure into the wheelbarrow. "I don't know how your parents or Ethan handled punishing you. I made up my mind years ago that I wouldn't hit my kids because my maternal grandparents slapped me around and John was uncontrollable when he was angry. Viv says the threat of violence was how he intimidated me and the kids."

A muscle twitched in his jaw. "I guessed as much."

Elinor leveled the shavings in the stall so Lightning would have an even floor. "Jake broke the rules. He chose his punishment. He was a lot harder on himself than I'd have been."

"What if he wasn't?" Sean asked.

"I would have said something." She finished raking the cedar chips and decided the bedding was deep enough. "He can't go fishing for the next two weeks. He doesn't know about that yet, but I'll tell him tonight. I won't cancel your plans for today, though."

"Wait a minute. You said he'd been hard enough on himself."

"He was for what happened at Bobby's." She collected the tools and moved to the next stall. "The horror movies and true crime books, that is. But then I found out that he decided to get rid of John before this magick spell."

"What did he do, hire a hit man? What kind of allowance do you give him?"

"No." Elinor relaxed a little. "It wasn't that bad. He manipulated John into writing down everything from missed visits to how he felt about kids."

"Doesn't sound too bad to me," Sean said. "You can't go to jail for it. My solution would have me locked up in the old Gray-Bar Hotel. Your son's smart."

"Too smart," Elinor said. "Helen's card and letter went with the other stuff he was collecting for his evidence. So, I'm not crazy yet."

"And then what happened?"

"After he built his case, Jake took the paperwork and cassettes from the phone calls he taped to Harold," Elinor said.

Sean whistled softly. "Are you sure he's only eleven?"

"You can admire him. Just because he's brilliant doesn't mean he's allowed to be unethical."

"Your ex-husband can look out for himself and if he's stupid enough to let a kid make a fool of him..."

"Wrong." She started to push the full wheelbarrow from the barn and stopped when he stepped in front of it. "What? Get out of the way."

He took over the handles of the wheelbarrow. "Wrong answer, girl. You pitched. I'll push." On their way to the manure pile, he asked, "Why is it a big deal that Jake made a jackass out of Price? It's the least the man deserves."

"Treating others disrespectfully diminishes my son, Sean"

"Okay, I can live with that." He paused. "And support it."

"You don't have to live with it." She waited while he dumped the load. "I do. And we're done."

THIRTY-ONE

S<small>EAN SLOWLY TURNED AROUND</small>. "S<small>AY THAT AGAIN</small>." H<small>E</small> <small>FOLDED</small> his arms. "I don't get it."

"Fine." She lifted her chin. "You were out of line yesterday. You had no business confronting Harold and Viv about what happened at their house. It was my job. I'm Jake's mother, and I should have been the one who followed up with them, not you."

"We're a team." Sean pushed the wheelbarrow back toward the barn. "You were busy looking over the papers I gave you. I already had plenty of time to think about them. So, I handled it with Harold and Viv. They needed to know what Penny was up to, and deal with her and Bobby. You should thank me."

Elinor glared at him. "Bull. I was married to one control freak and it ruined my life for eight years. I don't want another one."

He swung around and strode to her. "I'm not the kind of man who leaves when the trail gets rocky. I want to take care of you and the kids. You'd better learn how to handle that."

"I won't live in your pocket. I can't let you control me. I'm used to being alone, to surviving. I can do it."

"Damn you, Elinor Talbot." He pulled her against him. "I wish I believed in rough-breaking. I don't. I thought you'd finally learned you could trust me."

Tears stung. "I hate you."

"No, you don't." He smoothed her hair. "Just a little head-shy. You've got to run and kick up dust a while longer. But I'll stand and wait for you to come to me. With enough time, sooner or later, you'll know I'm right. And I'm betting on sooner."

"No, I won't," she repeated. "I've told you before. I hate that natural horsemanship crap when you try to use it on me. We're finished."

———

That night, she served the dinner she'd planned to have with Sean on Saturday. She didn't have much of an appetite, but the kids chowed down on the spaghetti, salad, and garlic bread. When dinner was over and the dishes washed, Elinor called both children back to the table. "Okay, you two. We've got to talk."

"About what?" Lynn asked.

Elinor waved to the chairs at the table. "Sit. Jake, will you tell Lynn what you did to your father?"

Jake dragged out a chair. "I got rid of him."

"I know. Tell us how you did it."

Jake sighed. "It wasn't like he loved or cared about us, Mom. He wasn't ever going to show up."

"Right. How did you learn to build a case against him?"

"There's lots of lawyer shows on TV."

"Okay. No television until September."

"All right. It's reruns till then anyway." Jake propped his chin on his fist. "Are you mad at me, Mom?"

"No. I'm worried about you, sweetie."

"Why?" Lynn asked. "He looks fine to me."

"He's not fine, honey. He's called your dad's office every week since January." Elinor frowned. "Why didn't it show up on the phone bill? Seattle's long distance. I would have noticed the calls."

"I'm not dumb," Jake said, indignant. "I used the toll-free number at his company or else I called Lynnwood and had the receptionist there transfer the call to their Seattle office. Local numbers aren't listed on the phone bill like long distance ones."

"Whoa!" Lynn looked impressed. "Nice. I didn't know that."

"You would have if you thought about it as long as I did." Jake pulled his feet up onto the chair and wrapped his arms around his knees. "It's not my fault. He called me a bunch of mean names when I tried to thank him for my Christmas gifts."

Lynn shook her head. "Why don't you listen to me? I told you, Mom's the one who gets us stuff. He never did."

"You said there was a Santa and an Easter Bunny, too." Jake studied his sister shrewdly. "Our old dad was real. Why couldn't he give me presents?"

"Because he's a jerk!" Lynn glared at her brother.

"Hold it!" Elinor interrupted. "Your father has problems. I tried to protect you from knowing that. I went too far. I shouldn't have put his name on your gifts. I shouldn't have made excuses for him. I wanted you to have a father because I didn't. I couldn't believe what he said was the truth."

"You mean about never wanting us?" Jake turned his attention on her.

"Who told you that?" Elinor demanded.

"He did."

Lynn sighed. "Jake, why did you talk to him if he was so nasty?"

"I needed the letters to make my case," Jake said, logical to the last. "Anyhow, I pretty much talked to his secretary and paralegal. They helped me. I don't think they like him either."

"Honey, don't you think calling him brought on your nightmares?"

"No." Jake blinked. "Why would that happen?"

Lynn jumped to her feet. "Remember what you said about things coming back on you three-fold? It doesn't matter if what you do is good or evil."

"Well, yeah." Jake frowned. "You mean me deciding to make him look bad hurt me, too?"

"Yeah, Sherlock." Lynn patted the top of his head.

"I never thought of that." The boy relaxed. "If I don't ever talk to him again, I won't have bad dreams. I can live without seeing him or hearing his voice."

"Right," Elinor said. "Jake, you're intelligent. Was this a fair contest? You had a battle of wits with someone unarmed."

"What?" Jake stared at her, perplexed. "I don't get it, Mom."

Elinor considered how to make her point. "Do you recall when Christy let Chipeta and Awesome loose? Where were the ponies going?"

"Across the road to the neighbor's hay field. We didn't let them," Jake answered. "Is our old dad like a horse?"

"Maybe a little smarter," Elinor said. "What did you do when the horses were loose?"

"We tried to stop them." Lynn returned to her chair. "If they'd gotten out in the street, they could have gotten killed by a car the way that our other dog did." She leaned down to pet Ruler, who rested quietly under the table. "We won't let that happen to you."

"Because it's your job to look out for the animals since you're smarter than they are. Right, Jake?"

"Sure, Mom. That makes sense. It's like I've gotta look after my puppy, Griffyn. Otherwise, he could do something dumb like when he chased the chickens and the rooster came after him or like when he went in the hayloft and the mom cat got him." Jake scowled. "You mean our old dad is dumb as a stump? And me showing that is wrong?"

Lynn nodded. "It's like when the other boys call you names for being smarter than they are. I get it, Mom."

"Good. I'm glad." Elinor didn't want her children patronizing others, but that was a different lesson. For now, it'd be enough if she taught them, especially Jake, not to treat people like puppets.

"But it's not my fault when the kids in my class aren't as smart as me. It's wrong when they make fun of me," Jake protested.

"Is it right if you make fun of them for being stupid?" Elinor asked. "Two wrongs don't make a right."

Jake looked thoughtful. "I've got to think about this."

"Good. You'll have lots of time to do it," Elinor said. "No fishing for two weeks. No television till September. No going to Bobby's for a month. And no phone calls till July 4."

"Whoa!" Jake's mouth fell open. "Mom, that's real heavy-duty. I was already grounded from Bobby's. I can live with that. But me and Sean were gonna try a new fishing hole this Thursday."

Elinor leaned back in her chair. "Sorry, Jake. I already told Sean. No fishing. How stupid do you think I felt when Harold came and told me what had happened with your dad? I live with you and I didn't know you were calling him."

"You'd have let us talk to him if we wanted," Lynn argued.

"But not without telling me. No secrets in this house, kids."

Jake quickly surrendered. "You're right, Mom. I made a big mistake, actually more than one. No more secrets. Are we done talking? I gotta take out Griffyn." He hastily left the room.

Elinor had to admire his discretion. He'd admitted to the things he'd already done, but he hadn't said a word about the *magick* spell. She glanced at her daughter. "Did you know what he had in mind for your father?"

"Are you kidding? He never said a word except we had to dump our old dad. I didn't know exactly how he planned to do it." Lynn got to her feet. "I better walk King, too. Mom, where's Sean? Why didn't he stay for dinner?"

"Because we talked and decided things were too intense. We've been going too fast. There were problems here and I never noticed what your brother was up to." Elinor took a deep breath. "So, Sean and I decided to call it quits for a while." When the kids were used to him not coming around, she'd say it was permanent.

"Is this some kind of a test?" Lynn asked.

"You could call it that." Elinor stared across the room and blinked back her tears.

"Well, I hope Sean passes." Lynn left the room.

"Me, too," Elinor whispered.

Once she was outside with her puppy, Lynn headed to the orchard where Jake was with his small steel gray heeler. "Are you okay?"

Jake kicked at a clump of grass. "I didn't expect all this stuff, and Mom doesn't even know about the spell."

"If she finds out, we'll both be dead meat." Lynn put her arm around her little brother's shoulders. "I'm sorry you're in so much trouble."

"It's not your fault." Jake hugged her back. "Actually, I feel better knowing about why I was having bad dreams. Now the monsters will go away for keeps."

"Well, we've got more problems." Lynn turned her attention on King. The border collie mix puppy squatted and piddled. She let go of Jake to praise her dog. "Mom sent Sean away. She says they need time apart. She was so busy with him that she didn't pay enough attention to us."

"What? That's not fair. Not after all the work I did on my spell." Jake followed his puppy around a tree. "Man, now I have to write a new spell to get him back. He did everything on the first one. What does she want from a guy?"

"I don't know." Lynn hesitated. "I could call him. I'm not grounded from using the phone."

"Yet." Jake shook his head. "No. We'd better stick to the spells. There's going to be a full moon tomorrow night. We'll do it then, okay?"

"All right. Do you want me to help write it?"

"No. I need you to keep Mom busy." Jake frowned. "I'm gonna miss TV. I learned a lot about how to do magick from the documentaries. I'll just have to use my books."

"At least you're not grounded from going to the library and there's always the Internet." Lynn pointed out. "Do you want me to check out some stuff for you? My English teacher likes us to read everything."

"Maybe. I'll look tomorrow. I'll start the new spell tonight."

Jake scooped up his puppy. "Come on, Griffyn. We got stuff to do."

———

She curled up on the couch, her second glass of wine on the end table beside her. An inane sitcom played on the TV and she kept the sound down so it wouldn't wake the kids. Ruler snoozed on the carpet between the couch and the entertainment center, either in an attempt to provide company or protect her from the insipid dialogue. She wasn't sure which.

She missed Sean and debated calling him. She hadn't shared the truth with him. She was afraid of how much she loved him. Okay, so he thought she was a crappy parent, and in some ways, he was right. No, she didn't hit her kids, but she did expect way too much from them. Their *magick* spell showed her that.

They thought they needed a dad to have good times, puppies and kittens in the barn. They didn't. They had her. They always had her. Why didn't they know that? What could she do to show them how much she loved them?

More, she decided, than she had in the past.

The first thing was to stop letting John ruin her life. She'd stop playing the game that she couldn't cook. She made every effort to provide healthy food, raising her own meat and eggs, keeping a cow for the milk and butter and growing fruit, berries, and vegetables.

It wasn't reasonable for her to expect Lynn to do most of the cooking. Yes, her daughter could cook one night a week and so could Jake. But she would pick up more of the domestic slack. Elinor sipped her wine. *Time to grow up.*

Maybe what angered her about Sean's accusations was the fact that he was right. The only thing worse would be if she had to admit it to him, and that wasn't happening any day soon. She'd told him they were finished and apparently, he believed her. *Bastard!*

She turned off the television. She checked on the kids. Both slept soundly, Griffyn on the foot of Jake's bed and King clutched tightly in Lynn's arms like a living stuffed toy.

Elinor shut off the lights in the living room and softly called Ruler. "Come on, dog. It's time for bed." *And I won't cry myself to sleep over that cowboy. I won't!*

PART FOUR

JUNE 2018

"Be careful what you wish for—you may get it!"

SEAN KILLIAN

THIRTY-TWO

SEAN SAT ON THE FRONT PORCH, THREE GRAY DOGS DOZING ON THE ground in front of the house. They seemed content to have him home, but he wanted to be with Elinor and the kids. Too bad he couldn't go there yet, he mused, and opened a bottle of beer.

He didn't move when a green Ford 150 pulled into the drive covered with the dust of a long road trip. The dogs leaped up, ready to charge the intruder, barking. They stopped when Gavin got out and petted them and headed toward Sean.

"You look like I feel," Gavin said. "You drive to Montana for the weekend, too?" He nodded toward the beer. "Got another one of those?"

"Yeah." Sean pulled a cold one from the sack. "How's Kate? She come back with you?"

"No. She dumped me again." Gavin sat on the porch. "What about Ethan and Clancy? Still on the outs?"

"Yeah."

"Hell." Gavin took a swallow of the beer. "Why are you home?"

"Talked when I should have listened." Sean hesitated, then filled his older brother in on the situation. "Elinor says she's mad because I did something instead of giving her the chance."

"You think that's it?" Gavin toed off one of his boots. "You overstepped the bounds and she kicked you out? That didn't seem to be her style at the Senator's barbecue, even when her ex acted like a jackass."

"I told her she needed to step up and be more of a parent," Sean said. He paused. "What do you think it is?"

"The apple doesn't fall far from the tree. We may be more like the Senator than we think." Gavin toed off the other boot. "You ever tell her you love her? Kate says I never told her. Now, I say it and she doesn't believe me."

"The Senator loves everything. He's always chanting that like it's some kind of political buzzword and it doesn't mean jack shit." Sean stared at his beer and realized that his brother was right.

He never told Elinor how he felt. He figured it was enough to show up, to be there for her and the kids. Obviously, it wasn't, and he needed to man up and share his feelings.

The thought was enough to make him reach for his cell phone. "I'll order in a pizza. You gonna stick around and share it?"

———

That night, she hugged the teddy bear Sean had given her. She should be able to sleep, she told herself sternly. She'd taught English all morning at the high school and had a birthday party come for pony rides in the afternoon. She didn't miss him, even if she'd grown accustomed to sleeping in his arms.

Ruler yipped and nosed her hand.

"What?" Elinor asked the dog. "Do you have to go out?"

Tossing her blankets aside, she rolled out of bed. She picked up her robe and shrugged into it. She stuffed her feet into slippers. "Okay. Let's go."

When she opened the back door, Ruler bolted toward the orchard. Elinor followed. In the grove of fruit trees, she saw Jake and Lynn. "What are you two doing out here? It has to be after midnight."

"Only a bit." Jake looked at Lynn. "We're ready to go inside now unless you want to pretend you didn't see us."

Elinor studied them. Lynn wore her long, flannel nightgown. Jake had on his pajamas, too, but over them, he wore his magician's cape from last Halloween. In one hand, he held the pointed hat from the costume. He tried to hide it behind his back.

"What are you doing out here?" Elinor demanded again. "Lynn?"

"It's not her fault," Jake answered. "I want Sean back. I made Lynn help me cast a spell."

"I wanted to," Lynn said. "It's my fault, too. The first one worked great. We got him in three days."

Elinor pointed to the back door. "Inside. Doesn't this count as manipulating people? Aren't you in enough trouble, Jake?"

"It only works if he wants to come back," Jake said. "And it's not like we got to finish it."

"The *magick's* over." Elinor ushered the two would-be witches to the house. "No more love spells or any spells. Got it?"

"But Mom," Jake whined. "They really do work."

"Don't push it," Elinor said. "You'll be grounded until Halloween if you keep this up."

"It's not fair." Jake stomped toward the house. "You just don't get *magick*."

Lynn tossed her head. "Yeah, Mom. We want Sean, too."

"People don't always get what they want," Elinor said gently. "You're old enough to know that."

"I'm not talking to you until he comes back." Lynn stormed after Jake. "You're just mean!"

———

Tuesday followed the same pattern. She got up early, did her stock chores, and went to substitute teach at the high school. She returned home in time to do a few pony rides and take care of the animals again. That afternoon, she sent the pigs off to the butcher.

It might be immature for the farmer she was supposed to be, but she just couldn't handle having them killed on her place. The butcher would do it on his farm and then take them to his shop in Snohomish where he'd finish processing them into hams, bacon, chops, steaks, and roasts. She'd pick the meat up in neat white packages and load the freezer. Next week, she'd send off the largest steer and the butcher would repeat the pattern.

In a way, she welcomed the fact that Lynn wasn't speaking to her. Every spring when the pigs, steers, and chickens went off to slaughter, the teenager threatened to become a vegetarian. The complaints ended when the freezer was restocked, the new baby pigs arrived to live in the pigpen, the cow calved, and Lynn got to pick out new baby chicks at the feedstore.

As soon as the kids arrived home from school, they changed their clothes and went off to weed the vegetable garden, taking their puppies with them. Elinor counted her blessings. She hadn't caught Lynn and Jake out in the orchard doing spells again, and neither of them mentioned Sean.

The kids seemed to have accepted his absence for the moment, but the longer he stayed away, the more that would change. Sooner or later, they were bound to demand she let him return, but she wasn't ready to deal with that.

A Dodge Ram pulled into the drive and she went to meet Clancy. "What's up? More ideas for day camp?"

"I wish." Clancy sauntered toward her. "Time to spill your guts, girlfriend. What's with you and Sean?"

Elinor sighed. "Do you want the real version or the sanitized one I gave my kids?"

"The truth from your side of things." Clancy sat down on the porch step. "He called to whine at me last night. He's feeling put upon, so I told him to 'man up'.''

"Poor baby." Elinor sat down beside her friend. "Okay. It seems last December, Jake decided to get rid of my ex, whom he calls his 'old dad.' And he wanted a new one."

She went through the way she signed John's name to gifts and continued through Jake's idea to conjure up a new father and burying the spell in the garden where Sean had found it.

Clancy leaned against the porch rail laughing. "I love it."

"I haven't even gotten to the part where Jake built a case against his father. Sean says I should just be glad the boy didn't use his allowance to hire a hit man."

"He probably didn't think of it." Clancy struggled for control, but a smile still lurked in her violet eyes. "Can I ask him to write a spell for me, Audra, and Brigid to use so we can get Mom and Art together?"

"Don't you dare!" Elinor suddenly realized how insane the whole situation was and smiled at her friend. "I'm sure you have a relationship with your dad."

"Not really. His picture is in the dictionary under the term 'deadbeat dad.' My mom struggled to raise us, and he didn't contribute a cent. We only hear from him when he wants money. The four of us have told him where to go over the years. The twins don't even know him."

Elinor frowned. At least John never refused to pay support. The check showed up in her bank account on a regular basis. When she submitted medical and dental bills to his accountant, those were paid, too. "So how did your mom feel about that?"

"Oh, he soured her on men years ago. You should hear some of her jokes. No, maybe not."

"She didn't strike me that way."

"If she learns you and Sean are taking a breather, be prepared to have your guts ripped into garters. She's been giving me hell about Ethan for the past two months."

"Great. That's one more thing to look forward to," Elinor said. "Do you want to stick around a while? I threw a roast and veggies in the slow cooker this morning. There's plenty for dinner."

"Sounds good." Clancy glanced toward the garden. "Shall I round up the kids?"

"Please. I'm on their list because Sean isn't here." Elinor sighed. "I stopped them from casting another spell last night and I have a feeling that when he doesn't show up in three days, I'll be labeled as the worst mother in the county."

"I've got your back," Clancy promised.

———

Sean sat on the front porch of his house. He watched the full moon play hide and seek with the clouds. He missed Elinor. He wanted to pick up the phone and hear her voice. Hell, he wanted to go to her house and take her to bed. He'd be happy just to hold her in his arms.

He didn't want to wait any longer. The two of them could talk to the kids, raise them, and be happy. He found himself thinking about wishing on the moon. Hadn't he done that before? He'd met her so soon afterward, and it'd been worth it. What did Marlene say?

"If you're gonna say no, it's better to say it right away," he quoted. He hadn't told Elinor that he didn't want to do this and stuck to it. Instead, he'd let her convince him that a bad idea was a good one. And that had been a bad decision on his part, one he'd have to do something about.

———

She'd arrived home from the high school, changed her clothes, and turned out the ponies into the various pastures. Now, she could muck the barn without horsy help. She collected the wheelbarrow and pitchfork, then headed for Lightning's stall. By starting with him, she'd work her way around the barn, finishing with Bonanza's roomy box stall.

Elinor had almost filled the wheelbarrow when she saw a shadow at the door. Ruler gave a low yip of greeting.

"In here," Elinor called, expecting a customer. Whoever it was didn't have a reservation, but often folks dropped in for pony rides, and she was happy to take their money. "May I help you?"

"Nope," Sean drawled as he headed across the barn to her. "I came to help you."

"What?" She stopped pitching for a moment. "Why are you here?"

"Because I know your routine almost as well as I know my own, darlin'. You always try to get off early to strip the barns mid-week. I figured you didn't know what Marlene says about that."

Elinor struggled to swallow the lump in her throat. Other than her kids and Sean, no one had ever jumped in to help her with anything, especially shoveling horse manure. "I'm afraid you're going to give me some cowboy words of wisdom."

"Yup." He hung his hat on a nearby wall. "Marlene says everybody gets along when they're picking flowers. When it's time to muck stalls, you find out if your lover is true." He strolled to the wheelbarrow, obviously ready to push it out to the compost pile. "I'm here."

"You sure are." Tears stung. "I could do it myself."

"You could." He turned and took a step toward her. "You don't have to."

She walked into his arms, breathing in the scent of his favorite lime aftershave, horses, and dust. He'd been shoeing all morning. She supposed the fact that he'd worked hard before he came to see her should be a turnoff, but it wasn't. She leaned her head into the hollow of his shoulder. "What will it take to make you leave me?"

"Not until I'm pushing up daisies." His arms tightened around her. "I'll give you all the time you need, girl. Marlene says a body can pretend to care but can't pretend to be there, and I'm not pretending with you."

Elinor took a step back. "It seems like I got you, cowboy, whether I'm ready or not." She ought to send him away, but she didn't want to. Instead, she smiled. "What if we hurry with the barn and I try out my favorite new hobby?"

"Am I gonna like it?"

"Oh, you love it when I give my horse a break and ride a cowboy instead."

THIRTY-THREE

SHE FOUND HERSELF SMILING WHENEVER SHE REMEMBERED THE afternoon. They'd finished the barn in record time, then headed for the shower. They'd ended up in her bed. He'd left before the kids arrived home, promising to call her later. She couldn't tell him that she loved him, but then again, he hadn't told her either.

The phone rang and her heart leapt. Her heart fell as she recognized Harold's voice. Why couldn't it be Sean? Where was he?

She tried to be extra polite and hide her disappointment. "Did you have your meeting with John?"

"Yes, and it went better than I expected," Harold said. "He signed away his parental rights, but I made him pay for the privilege. I got a great settlement and a cashier's check for you. There's some paperwork for you to do and he's out of your lives. That's the good news."

"So, what's the bad news?" Elinor stared at the phone as if it'd bitten her. "I never wanted his money. I wanted him to be a father to his children."

"He's not interested. I think this is the best for you and the kids," Harold said. "The bad news is, when I went to file the papers, the new family court judge decided she wanted to talk to you and the kids. I set it up for tomorrow."

"What time?" Elinor went to her desk to check the reservation book and frowned at the appointment for a birthday party in the afternoon.

"She wants to talk to Lynn and Jake after lunch and then see you and Price immediately afterward, about two-thirty. Will that work for you?"

"The sooner this is over, the better," Elinor said. "I have a birthday party scheduled for tomorrow, but I'll call Clancy and see if she'll cover for me."

"If she's busy, I could pick up the kids at school and take them to the courthouse," Harold offered. "The judge wants to see them alone in her chambers. I can be there as long as I don't talk or keep them from talking to her. If I do, she'll kick me out."

It didn't take long to call the Lazy B. Luckily, Clancy was home. Elinor explained about the birthday party. "I've got to go to court tomorrow afternoon, and I need to be there at one. I'd have to leave here right after lunch, and I wouldn't be back before five."

"That's okay. I'll bring Audra with me. The two of us can handle the party and anything else that happens in the afternoon. Sandy and Marcie told me they planned to drop by since they finished finals today."

"Well, that makes life easy. Thanks, Clancy." Elinor hung up the phone and crossed to the kitchen table where the kids did their homework. "We have to go to court tomorrow. The judge wants to talk to the two of you."

"Why?" Lynn looked up from her math book.

"The judge wants to know how you feel about your dad signing away his rights to you." Elinor focused on Jake. "She may ask if Harold or I put you up to conning your dad."

"But you didn't," Lynn said. "Jake didn't tell anybody, not even me."

"I know why." Jake eyed Elinor. "It's 'cause I'm eleven and I'm not supposed to think for myself. I'm supposed to be like the boys in my class, aren't I, the way Ms. Collins says?"

Elinor hugged him. "I think you're wonderful the way you are. I like being able to talk to you the way I do."

"But you don't like it when I treat other people like they're dumber than stumps. I'm getting it." Jake swung around in his chair and hugged Elinor. "I love you, Mom."

"I love you, too," Elinor said, keeping an arm around the boy. "Will you be scared to talk to the judge by yourself? Harold will be in the room. You can tell him if you want to leave."

"Will our old dad be there?" Jake asked.

"No. And I'll ask Marlene to come with us. Then when I have to talk to the judge, and he is in the courtroom, you don't have to see him. You and Marlene can go get ice cream or walk around town." Elinor smoothed Jake's hair. "Will that work for you?"

"If Lynnie comes, too."

"Oh, I'm definitely coming." Lynn smiled at her brother. "I'd probably kick him or hit him for calling you names or yell at him for saying he killed my cat when he only wanted me to cry."

"No, you won't." Elinor ruffled Lynn's golden-brown hair. "I'm the mom. It's my job to protect you and your brother. Hitting and kicking are very rude."

"Remember the rule of three," Jake advised. "Whatever you do, good or evil, comes back on you three-fold."

"I also recall what you said about oath-breakers. The court will actually nail your *old dad*." She hugged both children one more time, grateful that they allowed it. "Hurry and finish your homework." She straightened. "Then we'll play Scrabble."

———

Elinor strolled down the hall outside the judge's chambers with Marlene while Daisy sat on the nearby bench. All three of them had dressed up for the occasion. Elinor opted for the black jacket and skirt she often wore when she substituted, while Marlene had on a blue chambray dress with a lacy collar and elaborate white stitching. She wore her fanciest cowgirl boots.

Meanwhile, Daisy looked like a saintly grandmother in the gray suit she wore to church and to observe the student teachers she supervised for the university.

Jake and Lynn dressed up, too. Jake opted for the slacks, blue striped shirt, and tie he often wore to church while Lynn chose her favorite red dress. She said it made her feel strong and brave.

"We could walk downstairs to the cafeteria," Marlene suggested. "Harold said it'd be close to an hour. They've only been with the judge for a half hour."

"I promised Jake I'd wait for him," Elinor said. "I told him if he was scared and wanted to leave early, it'd be all right. He wouldn't be alone because I'd be right here."

"Okay." Marlene strolled beside Elinor. "How's the new day camp program? Any takers yet?"

Elinor seized on the subject. "August is full, and July only has a few openings left. Clancy thinks we should have a show for the parents on Friday, so we can sell them on lessons, leasing, and birthday parties."

"That's a good idea," Daisy said. "Like a dance recital or concert where the students show off what they've learned?"

"Yes," Elinor said. "I'll model it after what the Dawsons do at their Friday shows. The campers will take turns barrel racing and pole-bending. Clancy lined me up with her mom's supplier, so I ordered ribbons and trophies for the kids."

Discussing horses, the pony farm programs, and the summer show season made the next forty minutes pass quickly. Elinor looked up in surprise when the door to the judge's chambers opened. Jake was the first to exit, followed by Lynn, then Harold. The boy rushed to hug Elinor.

"It's okay, Mom. Do you know she has some great books with awesome words? I bet I could really whomp Lynnie in Scrabble with some of those."

"Not until I get a dictionary of legal terms." Lynn was adamant. "Otherwise, you'll cheat."

"I don't cheat. I spell creatively."

"Like Sean says, if I always use a dictionary, then I don't need to complain."

Elinor laughed and hugged both kids. "It did go okay, then?"

"We just did like you said and told the truth." Lynn wriggled free, all teen dignity. "Mellow out, Mom. It was no big deal."

"Yeah, but now I'm hungry," Jake complained. "Can we go to McDonald's?"

"Works for me," Marlene gave Elinor a squeeze. "We'll be back in about an hour."

Elinor shook her head. "No. Would you take the kids on home after they eat? There's no reason for them to return, is there, Harold?"

"None at all," Harold agreed, straightening his tie. "Their part's over."

"Then I'll see you at home." Elinor hugged her kids one more time. "Clancy said she'll wait until I get there. Help her and Audra out, will you?"

Once the trio trooped out of the courthouse, Elinor glanced at Harold. "They weren't upset, were they?"

"Nope. They were fine." Harold looked at his watch. "We have time for a cup of coffee. Then we'll come back." He glanced at Daisy. "Did you plan to testify today?"

"No. I'm just here to provide moral support for my girl." She took Elinor's arm. "I've lived next door since she moved out from Seattle so, believe me, that man doesn't want to hear me open my mouth."

When they each had a cup of coffee, Harold led the way outdoors to a landscaped area between the courthouse and the administration buildings. "After the judge talked to them about always telling the truth in court, she asked the children what kind of relationship they had with their biological father."

"What did they say?" Elinor asked.

"They told the truth, that they have no relationship at all. They told her about you putting his name on their presents and never criticizing him until a couple days ago. Jake said it was after you found out what he'd done to 'Get rid of his old dad,' that you weren't happy about him building a case so he got in trouble for making a fool of Price."

"Did she understand that Jake didn't mean any harm?" Elinor tried to keep her voice calm.

"I know that. So does the judge." Harold chuckled. "When Lynn and Jake told her, they'd chosen Sean for their new father already, I think it shocked her."

"Oh my God!" Visions of the spell tormented Elinor. "They didn't tell her *how* they chose him, did they?"

"Yes, they did. They'd already decided what a perfect dad would do. They interviewed him at their 4-H meeting, and he met all their criteria. That was Jake's word. Then they hired him to shoe horses and got you two together." Harold grinned. "Two little cupids, right?"

"Are they ever!" Elinor concentrated on the strong coffee and ignored the smile that twitched at the corners of Daisy's mouth. "What's really going to make them smug is if we get married."

"According to them, it's a done deal." Harold took a swallow of his coffee. "Sean's a great guy. We were in the Flying As together when we were kids. Ethan used to threaten to skin us alive if we didn't behave."

"Sean says that he was a rotten kid who outgrew his bad behavior. Daisy says she helped with that when he was in her English class." Elinor sipped her coffee. "Is he right?"

"Nope. We were mischievous, but we weren't evil. Sean's always been his own worst critic." Harold glanced up at the clock tower. "Time to return to the fray. When you two get hitched, I want an invite for me and Viv."

Elinor smiled, glad for the reprieve. She carefully put her half-full cup of coffee into the nearby garbage container. "Sounds to me like Jake and Lynn have convinced you it's going to happen."

She felt herself relaxing, soothed by his chatter and the comfort of Daisy's presence. When they entered the courtroom, John was already there. Her ex-husband wore an expensive-looking, pinstriped three-piece suit, a white shirt, and a subdued tie. What was left of his sandy blond hair was cut short, close to his head. He glared at her from narrowed brown eyes but didn't speak.

Elinor joined Harold at the table across from John's, facing the judge's podium. *I'm not afraid*, she thought. *It's all going to work out for the best.* She glanced over her shoulder at Daisy and smiled at the older woman.

Like Harold said last weekend, the marriage to John was over and, at long last, Elinor finally agreed. They were finished. Whatever the judge decided would almost be anti-climactic.

They stood when the judge entered. A small woman in a billowing black robe, her red hair streaked with gray, she looked as if she had to be in her fifties. She used the gavel, ordered them to be seated, and then introduced herself as Judge Riley.

"I've already talked to your children and now I'm ready to talk to you," she said. "Are both parties familiar with the petition to end Mr. Price's parental rights? Mr. Price? Are you representing yourself today?"

"Yes, I am." John rose to his feet. "I'll say the same thing I said when we divorced. I never wanted kids. She did. She had them. I've paid support for six years. I'm not seeing them. I don't want them calling and harassing me."

"I see. Do you understand that if you change your mind, we'll be back here revisiting this subject?" Judge Riley asked.

"I won't change my mind," John said.

"Did you send these letters to your son?" Judge Riley held up a two-inch stack of papers. "I believe Mr. Greer forwarded copies of these to you along with the legal papers relinquishing your parental rights. Is that correct?"

"I have a copy of the receipt from his office, Your Honor," Harold spoke for the first time, "and I'm willing to testify that I hand-delivered copies to him during our negotiations."

"I'll stipulate that I sent the letters," John said. "I don't want to see the little monster and I'm sick of his calls."

"Don't call him that!" Elinor jumped to her feet and faced her ex-husband. "He's your son."

"I never wanted kids."

"Well, you should have thought of that before you raped me."

The sound of the gavel banging on the podium caught her attention and Elinor looked at the judge.

"Enough," Judge Riley ordered. "Sit down, Mrs. Price. And I don't want to hear any more name-calling from you, Mr. Price."

"My name's Ms. Talbot." Elinor sat down. Tears swam in her eyes and she blinked them back. When Harold covered her hand with his, she struggled to control the lump in her throat. "I'm sorry."

"Don't be." Harold leaned close and whispered, "Did you file a police report?"

"I called the cops when it happened," Daisy said behind her. "I took her to the hospital, too."

"Good for you." Harold leaned forward to pour a cup of water and pass it to Elinor. "Your Honor, my client just wants Mr. Price to do the right thing. It's in the children's' best interest not to see him."

"Is Jake a child of rape, Ms. Talbot?" Judge Riley asked. "How do you feel about that?"

"Yes, he is." Elinor kept her gaze on the judge. "I've never blamed my son for his conception. I've raised Jake alone from the day he was born, even before my divorce. I love both my kids very much."

"And they made it plain that they adore you," Judge Riley said."

Nothing new came up in the next ten minutes while John filibustered. He didn't mind signing away his parental rights. However, he didn't see why he should pay any more support and griped about the additional money that Harold demanded for Elinor.

"Are you finished?" Judge Riley asked. When he nodded, she turned to Elinor. "What do you have to say about this petition?"

"Your Honor, I think my attorney presented my case very clearly." Elinor struggled to keep her voice steady. "As you said, you spoke to my children. They don't have a relationship with their biological father, nor do they want one."

"Wait a minute," John screamed. "That little monster plagued me for six months. What do you mean he doesn't want me in his life?"

"He built a case to be rid of you, John," Elinor retorted. "Your letters went to Mr. Greer. Your phone calls and insults were taped and forwarded to my attorney. You would know that if you bothered to read the documentation my lawyer provided. How does it feel to be set up by a sixth-grader?"

Before John answered, Harold intervened. "Your Honor, Jake explained his theory of getting rid of his 'old dad' in order to have a new one when we were in chambers."

A smile slipped across Judge Riley's face. "Ms. Talbot, do you have anything else to add?"

"I think my ex-husband summed it up. He doesn't want anything to do with my family and I don't want him around my children." Elinor flicked a glance over her shoulder as the door to the courtroom opened and saw Sean. She wondered why he was here.

Sean came up the aisle and sat next to Daisy. Wearing jeans, a flannel shirt, and boots, he'd obviously come from work. Daisy beamed at him and patted his hand.

"Mr. Killian?" Judge Riley asked.

Sean nodded. "Yes, ma'am."

"I invited Mr. Killian to join us," Judge Riley said. "After hearing all about him and how wonderful he is at horse shows, fishing, and school events, I wanted to meet him."

"And you dropped everything to come here?" Elinor whispered. "Aren't you swamped? The showing season—"

"Nothing that can't wait, darlin'." Sean leaned forward to rest a hand on her shoulder and murmured, "Next time you have to see that jerk, call me. I'll be here."

He always was when she needed him, Elinor thought. She remembered what he'd said the day before. A man could pretend to care, but he couldn't pretend to be there, and when it came to Sean Killian, there wasn't any pretense.

"I heard all about you from Lynn and Jake," Judge Riley went on. "I know how highly they think of you, Mr. Killian. What do you think of them?"

"They're amazing," Sean said. "I have to admit it took a while for them to trust me to keep my word. They aren't used to a man who tells the truth and who doesn't try to bully them or their mother. And the puppies helped."

"Oh yes, I heard all about King and Griffyn." Judge Riley smiled. "I saw pictures, too. Did you know the puppies sleep on their beds with them?"

"I have high hopes that by the time the dogs are full grown, they'll be sleeping on the floors," Sean said with a chuckle. "Once the kids know they have the puppies for keeps, they might give them a little more space."

"We're working on it," Elinor added.

"How long is this soap opera going to continue?" John interrupted. "I have things to do."

"It will continue as long as I want it to," Judge Riley said. "This is my court now. I have the best interest of the children in mind, Mr. Price. I wasn't impressed when your daughter told me about her first cat and what you said you did to it. I've made my decision. Ms. Talbot, you are awarded sole custody and Mr. Price has his wish too. I'm agreeing to his demands with a few conditions."

"Thank you," Elinor said.

"I'm not finished," Judge Riley said. "After talking to the children, I agree with your attorney that they should be attending a private school. Mr. Price will pay for their tuition, books, and uniforms until they are eighteen."

"Wait a minute. I agreed to relinquish my parental rights and pay a lump sum."

"Mr. Greer had the request in his papers, which you should have read and responded to, and since you didn't, I'm ordering it. I'm also increasing the monthly support, Mr. Price. Ms. Talbot will need more money since she will not be able to work full time until Jake is eighteen. Since both children will presumably be attending college, I'm considering extending the support until Jake is twenty-one."

"What if I increase the lump sum, I'm willing to pay to relinquish my rights?" John demanded. "Then will you reconsider your decision?"

"Possibly." Judge Riley turned her attention to Elinor. "What do you think, Ms. Talbot?"

"If he included all the school costs until Jake is eighteen, we could go forward with our original agreement," Elinor said. "To be truthful, Your Honor, I'd really like him out of our lives."

"Sounds like a deal to me. Mr. Greer, will you research those costs and get back to me by Monday? Mr. Price, if your check is in my clerk's hands by Tuesday, we'll be able to finish this matter in a timely manner. Of course, if it isn't, then we'll go with my assessment of the situation and increase the support." When both lawyers agreed to those conditions, the judge used the gavel again, and dismissed them before she left the room.

John stormed toward Elinor. "Well, I hope you're happy."

Elinor stood when Sean pulled out her chair. "Actually, I am." She smiled. "I like this judge much better than the one who insisted the kids go to public school, and I'm perfectly happy having you pay additional support, John. So, I suggest you and Harold do as she said and work things out. He doesn't mind coming back here."

"Not in the least," Harold agreed. "It's what I live for." He picked up his briefcase. "I'll talk to Jake and see what his educational goals are. I know Lynn plans to be an attorney. I think this judge will be receptive to you paying for law school."

John glared at them. "I'm happy to sign away my rights. I don't care about those kids."

"I know." Pity filled Elinor's voice. "That's why I feel so sorry for you, John. You'll never know what you're missing." She allowed Sean to usher her and Daisy away. "Did we really disrupt your day?" she asked him as soon as they had exited the courtroom.

"Not really." Sean cupped her elbow and guided her down the hall. "I finished the horse I was shoeing, got paid, and then came here. I have another five to do. I better head to the next barn and get back to work."

THIRTY-FOUR

HE SHOWERED AND CHANGED HIS CLOTHES BEFORE HE WENT TO the barn to look after the dogs. He turned loose the two females with what remained of their litters to exercise. The border collie pups tumbled and played with their half brothers and sisters in the indoor arena while their mothers watched indulgently.

Suddenly, the two adult dogs charged for the gate, barking. A melee of yipping pups followed. Sean glanced at the main entrance and saw Ethan. "Why do I deserve a visit in the middle of the week?"

"Came to see how long it'd take for you to get your act together." Ethan greeted the two females, then dropped to one knee to pet the pups when they came to investigate. "Do you plan to be like Gavin and me? Alone?"

"I hoped you and Clancy were working out your problems," Sean said. "She didn't sound like she'd finished with you when we talked a couple days ago."

"At the rate we're progressing, we may be married by Christmas a hundred years from now," Ethan agreed. His attention seemed to be totally on the dogs. "I'm not holding my breath."

Sean nodded and wished he knew what to say to solve his older brother's problems. Hell, he had trouble enough with his own. "I saw Elinor today. The judge asked me to come to the hearing. Her ex was as bad today as he was at the Senator's Memorial Day shindig."

"Glad she had you there." Ethan stood as the dogs scrambled to bark at the door again. "You expecting more company?"

"No." Sean started toward the gate and stopped when he saw Elinor's truck in the drive. "Now why is she here?"

"Go find out." Ethan put a hand on Sean's shoulder.

"I owe you, big brother." Sean whistled and the dogs obeyed. "Come on, ladies. Let's go in your pens for now."

———

Elinor almost turned around when she saw Ethan's car parked next to the house, then changed her mind. She didn't dare go home, not after buying three different kinds of gourmet ice cream and two bags of junk food so Daisy would babysit. Of course, the retired teacher and the kids didn't call it that. Daisy said she was spending the night with her two favorite people and Lynn and Jake referred to it as an evening with their adopted grandma.

She pulled in next to Ethan's car and switched off the engine. She felt a smile play at her lips when she saw Sean coming from the barn. He must have been playing with the dogs. She opened the door and slid out of the pickup. She took a moment to adjust her red dress. The skirt fell to the top of her red dress boots. She loved the floral lace overlay with sheer lace sleeves and the satin rose buttons on the bodice. She always felt like a princess in the dress, but tonight she planned a seduction.

She made her way to the passenger side of the vehicle, arriving at the same time Sean did. "Are you hungry? I brought dinner."

He caught her hand and slowly spun her around, the skirt swirling around her knees. "All of you and food, too? What did I do to deserve this?"

"I guess I could say that you're just a good guy." She trailed a finger over his mouth. "But I'd rather you were a bad one tonight."

He laughed and pulled her to him. "That sounds like fun." He kissed her, a quick, teasing touch of his lips. "Should I invite Ethan to stay for dinner?"

"Too kinky." She rose on tiptoe and whispered in his ear. "I left my panties at home."

Sean blinked. A muscle twitched in his jaw. His hand tightened on hers. He glanced over his shoulder to where his brother approached. "Go home, Ethan."

She giggled. "He can stay if you want."

"No, he can't. He's going now."

Ethan paused at his car. "Do I want to know what's going on with you two?"

"It's called make-up sex," she explained. "And as soon as he carries the box of food in the house, I'm attacking your brother."

Sean closed the truck door. "I'll come back later for it." He swung her up in his arms and carried her toward the house. "I desperately need to be attacked right now."

She buried her face against his shoulder. "The lasagna needs to bake for a little over an hour." Dimly, she heard the sound of a car starting and knew that Ethan had opted to leave them alone. "Did you two have something major to discuss?"

"No." Sean kicked the door shut behind them. "He just wanted to make sure that I knew how rare love is and that I wasn't wasting my opportunities."

She slid her arms around his neck. "Neither of us are." She brushed her mouth over his. "I've been so scared, and I really messed things up."

"What scared you?" He stopped and held her tight. "I'd never hurt you."

"I know that now, but loving you is a risk." She took a deep breath. "Loving anyone is a risk, but I'll survive even if you break my heart. I haven't said that in years."

"If you're not ready to say it yet, I can wait." He lowered his head.

Their lips met in a long, slow kiss that was sweet in its innocence. "You've never said it either." She rested her hand on his cheek. "Why not?"

"You've met the Senator. He loves his fleet of cars, his new plane, the newest sound-bite speech from his writers, the huge donation from his latest money man." Sean stared into the distance for a moment. "I've never heard him say that he loves me or my brothers or sisters, or even his wife. And I didn't know I was like him."

"You're not. You're honest, decent, and blunt to a fault, Sean. You don't suck up to anybody, and I'm crazy about you."

"But I haven't told you how I feel. I love you, Elinor, and living without you doesn't work."

"Then take me to bed, cowboy." She nipped at his ear. "Or I'm going to think leaving my panties at home was a big mistake."

He chuckled and headed for the stairs. "Tonight, you have to agree to marry me. I know how to brand what needs to be branded."

"Is that a proposal? I thought you Killian men had a habit of being dashing and romantic. You haven't even dived into a flooding river like Clancy says Ethan did to save one of her horses."

"Nope. I'm not riding any bucking broncs for you like Gavin does for Kate, either."

"Then I'll just drag you off to bed and steal your virtue without benefit of clergy." She rediscovered the fierce line of his jaw with her lips. At the same time, she unsnapped his shirt, and explored his chest with her hands.

"Behave, witch. Promise to make an honest man out of me. Or I'll have to leave you wanting."

"Well, I better get to wear you out," she teased. "I haven't had a man in eons."

"You had me yesterday," he reminded her. "I'll never leave you horny again."

"Okay. Then I'll marry you. Now, take me to bed, cowboy."

"I will, and you'll beg for mercy." He carried her into the bedroom.

"Promises." She clung to his wide shoulders. When he lowered his head, she eagerly met his kiss. His lips were warm and seductive. She moaned as her hands went around his neck.

It felt as if her insides were melting. She dissolved into pure wanting when his hand cupped her breast, his thumb finding her nipple through her dress. The world spun. She turned her face into his shoulder when he put her on the king-size bed and followed her down. His mouth recaptured hers.

She threaded her fingers into his hair. Then she started a new path with her hands tracing over his features. She stroked one finger down his cheek. He'd shaved again, no stubble. Her hands crept along his jaw, and she traced his ears.

He lifted his head. She feathered a line of kisses down the strong column of his neck. She stripped off his shirt, enjoying the sight and feel of his muscles. Her fingers couldn't even meet around his upper arms.

"I missed you," she whispered the words against his skin.

"Good. Now, tell me the truth. Say you love me." He unfastened the first button below the sweetheart neckline of her dress, then the second.

"What if I don't?"

"Oh, you will." He undid the third button, parting the material to reveal her skin. "It's just a case of how much I make you want me."

"Beast."

"Witches do that to men." He unfastened the front clasp of her bra.

She shuddered when he flicked his tongue over her nipple and tangled her fingers in his hair. She drew him closer. "Don't stop."

He lifted his head and smiled. "You haven't said what I want to hear." He pulled out of her embrace and rolled off the bed to unbuckle his belt and undo the top button on his jeans.

She wasn't in the mood to wait. She sat up, unlaced her boots, and took them off along with her nylon socks. She rose to her feet and finished unbuttoning her dress. She skimmed out of it and hung it neatly over the chair in the corner of the bedroom.

He took two steps and was close enough to touch her, caress her, kiss her. She felt the excitement build in her veins. She knew it was the same for him. She could tell by the shudders when she tormented him with her hands, her mouth, and her body.

She stroked the shoulders that fascinated her so much. She explored his broad chest. Each lingering movement of his hands on her breasts, of his mouth as he feasted on her nipples, burned fire into her body.

He lifted his head, then picked her up and carried her to the bed, following her down.

She arched eagerly against him, but he was in no hurry. Instead, his fingers continued to tease her. She shook with wanting as his lips traced warm patterns on her stomach, then on her thighs. How much more did he expect her to bear?

Her impatience grew to an explosive level. She couldn't wait. She rolled on top of him. She pressed him back into the sheets, against the pillows. He chuckled. His hands clasped her waist. He pulled her astride his narrow hips.

She gasped as he claimed her. Despite her position on top of him, he was in control and set their pace. All she could do was respond to his demands and she did. She followed the rhythm he set. His passion filled her senses. All she could think of was him. All she could say was his name, moaning it over and over. "Sean. Sean. Sean!"

She cried out his name one last time as the world exploded, shattering into a million glowing stars. He followed her over the edge of the universe. She collapsed on top of him.

Exhaustion crept up on her. She tried to hold her eyes open for a moment. She pressed her lips against his neck. She tasted the warm salt of his skin. "I love you."

He held her tight as if his body could absorb hers. "I love you, too."

She fell asleep in his arms but woke an hour later to find herself alone in his bed. Sliding into his abandoned shirt, she went to find him.

Elinor found him in the kitchen wearing his jeans and boots. He'd obviously been outside since he carried the box that held their supper.

She smiled. "I missed you."

"I needed to feed the dogs, so I brought in dinner from the truck while I was out there." He put the box on the island counter.

"Thank you." She carried the casserole over to the stove. Once she had it in the oven and the timer set, she returned to the counter. The salad went into the fridge. The garlic bread could be warmed once the lasagna finished baking.

Meanwhile, he opened the bottle of wine, pouring some into two glasses. "I can think of something to do while we wait for dinner."

"So can I." Elinor took the glass he offered. "Maybe we could talk, too."

"About anything in particular?"

She measured his face with her gaze, then shook her head. "No, I guess not. I could tell you that my marriage was awful. I made every mistake in the book and tolerated way too much crap. I'll probably make a whole bunch of new mistakes with you, but I'm willing to try."

"Me, too." He toasted her. "What if we agree to talk about what bugs us? And remember that we like and respect each other all of the time, even when we're both pissed as hell?"

"That might be doable." She sipped her wine. "I need to be straight with you. I appreciated what you did today when you went to court for us, but I wasn't quite ready to fall into your arms and live happily ever after."

"What changed your mind?"

She took a deep breath. "I just found out how short life is again. I've been trying to reconnect with two of the teachers that attended grad school with me. When I didn't find them through the

Lake Maynard school district, I called the dean of my Master's program. She told me they're both in Afghanistan with their reserve units and won't be back till next spring."

"Heavy duty stuff." He put his glass down on the counter and put his arm around her shoulders. "I'm sorry you didn't find them teaching school here."

"Me, too." She sniffed back the tears that threatened to fall. "It made Jake's spell and you trying to step up to help me and me being an ass about it a little trivial. And then I realized I was silly to be so scared to share my feelings."

"I can help with that"—he tipped up her chin with his thumb—""if you let me."

"I'm counting on you." She managed a smile. "If you let me down, I'll kick your butt from here to Tacoma."

"No worries. I won't let you down."

"Good." She picked up his glass. "Since we have almost an hour till dinner, let's go back to bed. I haven't been able to seduce you yet."

She turned the ponies out to graze in the various paddocks for the afternoon, then headed for the house to make her own lunch. Halfway through her grilled cheese sandwich, the phone rang. "Silver Lake Pony Ranch."

"Hi, Elinor. It's me, Audra Dawson. Can we talk?"

"Sure," Elinor said. "What's up?"

"Clancy said you offered her a job as the manager of your farm. I wanted to know if you'd consider me for it instead," Audra said. "She told me I could have it if it's okay with you." Tears clogged the woman's husky voice. "Is it?"

"Only if you tell me what's going on," Elinor said. "You're the manager at Xanadu Arabians. I can't match what they pay. So, what happened?"

"I was the assistant manager and I supervised the entire operation while they looked for someone to take over after the last manager quit. I applied for it and did the job for the last six months. I thought they'd choose me. Only they hired Jack Abbott and I won't work for him, not after I taught him everything he knows about running a breeding, training, and sales barn."

"I see," Elinor said. "Why don't you work at your mom's?"

"Because Liberty Valley isn't that big, and our ranch is too close to Monroe. I signed a non-compete clause contract," Audra explained. "Mom can't afford to take on Xanadu in a lawsuit and neither can I. It doesn't matter the Lazy B doesn't cater to the same clientele as Xanadu and neither do you. Your pony farm is actually beyond the mileage requirement, so it's a safe place for me to work."

"All right," Elinor said. "Why don't you come by this afternoon and we'll see what we can work out? Deal?"

"Sure." Audra took a ragged breath. "Well, something good came of it. Clancy was so pissed when Jack took the job away from me that she dumped him. Tell Sean, will you? He can pass the word to Ethan."

THIRTY-FIVE

THE TELEPHONE RANG WHILE SHE PUT DINNER ON THE TABLE AND she hurried to answer it, hoping it would be Sean.

"Hi, Elinor," Harold said. "It's a done deal. The judge signed the paperwork at close of business today. Price is out of your lives for good."

She shook her head. "All I ever asked was for him to be a father to his children."

"He chose a different path, Elinor and this is best for you and the kids. Shall I bring the papers by tonight?"

"Bring them now. I know you need to send them back to John. Did you arrange for the kids to use my name from now on?"

"Yes, I did." Admiration filled Harold's voice. "You're sharp, Elinor. If you ever get tired of teaching school, you can always come to work for me until you get your law degree. My paralegals couldn't shine your boots. See you soon."

Elinor slowly replaced the receiver. She glanced at Lynn, then at Jake. "This is your last chance. Is this what you really want? We have to sign papers and promise never to contact him again."

"It worked." Jake whooped with joy. "My spell worked. He's gone!" The boy danced around the room, Ruler at his heels. The puppies tagged behind, all three dogs barking.

Lynn appeared dazed. "He's really gone?"

Elinor ignored the circus and focused on her daughter. She put her arms around the girl. "Honey, he never was really here, not in his heart. Okay?"

"Yeah." Lynn turned her face against Elinor's shoulder. "I feel bad because he never loved me." Tears came, followed by a soft keening. "I'd have loved him if he let me."

"I know." Elinor stroked the teen's hair. "It's his problem, not yours or Jake's or mine. Your father can't love anyone. You're a wonderful person, Lynn. When you find someone decent to be a new dad, love him and forget your old dad. Okay?"

Lynn sniffed. "You sound like Jake."

"Occasionally, he's right." Elinor eyed her son who'd danced his way into the living room followed by the entourage of yapping canines. "Do me a favor and don't tell him that. I'd have to buy him a larger wizard's hat."

———

A little after ten that night, Elinor still wasn't tired. She'd listened to the kids' talk about the kind of new school they wanted her to find and telling the judge what they wanted their lives to be like for what seemed a hundred times. Now, they were asleep, worn out by the past two days. The telephone rang, and she grabbed the receiver before it woke the kids. "Hello."

"I miss you, witch. Why don't I come over?"

She struggled to keep her tone firm so he wouldn't realize she was teasing him. "I saw you last night. Don't we need more space?"

"Not me. I need you now."

She sighed. "Okay. Where are you?"

"At your front gate. I called on my cell phone."

She laughed. "And here I thought you were an old-time cowboy. Well, if I have a sexy man at the gate, why should I turn him down?"

"I knew it all along. You're only after my body."

"It's such a sexy body," she pointed out. "I can't help myself. When you showed up at the courthouse yesterday, I almost jumped you."

"I'm shocked. I just came from shoeing. I hadn't cleaned up. I still smelled like horse."

"And very sexy man," she finished. "Well, get in here." She hung up the phone. When she turned, she saw Lynn standing in the doorway, rubbing her eyes. "What is it, honey?"

"I heard the phone. The ponies aren't out, are they?"

"No." Elinor tried to ignore the blush warming her cheeks. "It was Sean. He's coming by."

"It's kind of late, isn't it, Mom?"

"I know his intentions. Go back to bed, Lynn."

"Okay. Don't worry, Mom. I won't wake up Jake and tell him this spell worked, too. I'll wait until morning."

"Good night, Lynn." Elinor waited until her daughter was gone. Then she crossed to the back door, unlocking it. She opened it as Sean came across the porch. He wore a green shirt that made his eyes seem the same color, and dark blue jeans. "What a hunk."

He grinned at her and teased. "Shucks, ma'am. It *ain't* nothing," he teased.

She traced a line down his jaw with her fingertip. "So, when are you going to kiss me, cowboy?"

"Right now." He closed the door behind him and turned the lock. "And then I plan to do a whole lot more."

———

The sound of Jake's muffled sobbing woke her. Elinor slipped from the bed without waking Sean. She grabbed her robe, dragged it on, and hurried to her son's room. "It's all right, honey. I'm here."

She switched on the overhead light and crossed to the bed. She shook him gently awake, pretending not to see the gray lump of snoozing puppy under the covers next to Jake. "It's okay."

Jake shuddered. He flung his body against hers. "Don't let the monsters get me."

"I won't." Elinor held him tight and rocked him. "I hoped we were done with the blasted things."

"Me, too." Jake slowly stopped shaking and clung to her. "Can we sleep with you tonight, Mom? Then the monsters won't get us."

"I'm not sleeping with you and your dog."

"Your mom and I are getting married." Sean stood in the doorway. He wore his jeans, but no shirt or boots. "I'm sleeping with her tonight. Okay?"

"Wow!" Jake pulled back and eyed his mother. Then he glanced at the clock. "See, I told you he'd be back in three days."

"How did you know?" Sean asked. "I wasn't sure how long it'd take for your mom and me to work things out."

"Because me and Lynnie made another spell so you could come back if you wanted to," Jake explained. "But it wasn't to force you if you didn't."

"Good spell. It worked." Sean winked at the boy. "And I really wanted to come home. Nothing could have stopped me."

Jake grinned. "So, when are we getting married?"

"At the end of the summer," Elinor replied. "It'll have to be after day camp, horse shows, and the fair. September, I think."

"I'm not waiting that long," Sean drawled. "At the end of the month, before we go to visit your family over the Fourth of July."

Elinor met his gaze. "All right."

"If we're getting married, do we get to go someplace special for that?" Jake asked.

"Yup." Sean came into the room. He eyed the puppy. "I thought I told you dogs sleep outside and protect the farm."

"He's not a real dog yet," Jake said. "When he is, he will. Right now, he's too little to guard anything, so I have to guard him. Where are we going?"

"Disneyland. But with my schedule and your mom's, that will have to wait till September. Meantime, what if we go to the ocean for a couple of days after we get back from Eastern Washington?"

"Awesome," Jake enthused. "I bet Clancy will take care of the farm for us."

"I'll arrange that," Elinor said. "You and your sister won't. Got it?"

"Okay, Mom." Jake snuggled next to her. "You can be the boss for a while."

"And Sean gets to boss you, too," Elinor added.

"And Lynnie." Jake's grin widened. "We'll be a real family."

"Deal," Sean agreed. "Right now, why don't I show you how to keep monsters out of your room?"

Jake's eyes grew big. "You know how to do that? Lynnie makes 'em go away for good. And Mom won't have 'em in her room. So, they only bug me. But I don't want to hurt 'em."

"We won't." Sean sat on the edge of the bed. "You can send them home. It's pretty easy *magick* for a sorcerer like you."

"I can do it." Jake sat up.

"You've got to follow all the steps," Sean cautioned. "It's very important."

"How do I start?"

"Okay. First," and Sean drew out the word, "you have to remember something very important. Monsters are actually visitors from somewhere else. They don't think they're scary or ugly. They know the real monster is you, and *they're* very frightened."

"Whoa! I never knew that. I'm glad I didn't hurt 'em."

Elinor struggled to curb her impatience as Sean continued the elaborate theory. Talking hadn't really worked. Neither had hot milk. She'd hoped that a permanent solution to John would cause the nightmares to evaporate. She ought to have known better.

"Now, after you tell them to go home, remind them to harm nobody on their journey. Then point your finger at one and order it to disappear. When it vanishes in a puff of smoke, go on to the next one. What do you tell it first, Jake?"

"Go home. Don't hurt anyone on the journey. Then the monster goes." Jake slid under his covers. "After I tell them all it's time to go home, and they do, then I can go back to sleep." He yawned. "I knew it, Sean. I knew you could do *magick*."

"Of course, I can." Sean adjusted the blankets around Jake and the puppy. "That's how you knew I was the guy who was the answer to your spell, right?"

"Uh-huh. It's why me and Lynnie picked you."

"I know." Sean smoothed Jake's hair. "If you have any more trouble with those monsters, let me know. They'll wish they'd left when you told them to go."

"No problem." Jake's lashes drifted shut.

Elinor checked the nightlight. She switched off the overhead lights. She led the way from the room, through the dark living room, and into the kitchen. "So, you do *magick*?" she asked, wrinkling her nose. "Admit it. You made that up as you went along."

"Nope." Sean guided her toward her bedroom. "When a guy plans to marry into a family of witches, he'd better be able to do *magick* as a defense measure."

"I'm sure. Where did you learn that particular spell for monsters?"

"I asked Ethan. He told me how we got rid of the ones that used to visit me. I added a few elements." He winked at her. "Want to see another spell?"

She laughed. "I can't wait. What is it?"

"How to deal with a horny witch."

"I'm not anymore," she lied. All she had to do was look at him and she wanted him.

"My next spell will change your mind." He closed the bedroom door behind them.

———

Elinor leaned against the arena wall next to Marlene and kept her gaze on Lynn. The fourteen-year-old girl managed to remember most of the show techniques she'd been taught. She stood out in her red and black outfit. Gypsy looked beautiful, too. Silver glittered on her black leather bridle and her sunshine gold coat gleamed.

"Here's your coffee." Sean passed over the first cup from the cardboard carrier. "A sixteen-ounce, skinny double-shot mocha, warm not hot, and no whipped cream."

Elinor blinked up at him. "How do you know my favorite coffee?"

"Why wouldn't I when we've been together this long?" Sean glanced past her to Jake and winked at the boy. "*Magick*, right?"

"Yup." Jake beamed at him and took the second cup. "This is my hot chocolate, right?"

"Right." Sean passed the next beverage to Marlene. "Almond Joy with extra almond, extra chocolate, extra whipped cream."

"That's my boy." Marlene beamed at him. "I knew I raised you right and if you're not good to Elinor, I'm gonna get ya."

"Thanks, Marlene, but I think I can handle it," Elinor said. "And Sean." She smiled at him. "I appreciate the caffeine."

"Hey, you've been going since four this morning and I knew you were ready for it. I called the stable. Audra says everything's great on the farm."

Elinor nodded. "I didn't expect her to have any problems. I was thrilled when she said she and Clancy could handle it today, so I'd be able to come watch Lynn. I wish I wasn't so nervous."

"Lynn looks calm," Marlene said. "She was so pleased with the first she got in halter."

"I'm glad I was here to see it." Elinor concentrated on the bareback equitation class now in progress. Lynn seemed to be remembering to keep her back straight and her chin up. Her legs were positioned well, too. When the announcer called for the lope, Lynn signaled Gypsy smoothly. The palomino mare picked up the controlled gallop perfectly on the correct lead.

Elinor breathed a sigh of relief. She glanced at Sean. He seemed to share her feeling of pride. She realized that it was just as important to him when Lynn achieved her goal. Elinor tensed when the judge waved the riders into the center, but Lynn continued the flawless performance.

She executed a good dismount. Then she remounted with practiced grace. Unlike many of the other participants, Lynn did it without any help from the judge or the ring steward. She vaulted onto Gypsy's back, making the jump onto the large pony look effortless. There was a smattering of applause from the audience.

Elinor gripped Sean's hand. She wanted Lynn to do well, but for the first time, Elinor understood how parents could get hooked on the ribbons, too.

"She did great," Jake said.

"I think so, too. I hope the judge agrees." Part of her opinion was a professional one. The rest was strictly maternal.

"She seems so assured this time." Marlene beamed at Elinor. "I'm glad you could make it. You've given her confidence."

Elinor eyed Sean. He smiled at her, and she said, "One of us will be here from now on."

"Guess what, Marlene?" Jake grinned up at his 4-H leader.

"I couldn't possibly," Marlene told him. "Tell me."

"We're moving to Sean's house after we get married. I get to have a computer. And Mom's gonna have two pony farms."

"Wow. I'm impressed." Marlene winked at Elinor. "So how do you plan to pull it off? Run yourself through a copy machine?"

"No." Elinor kept part of her attention on the equitation class. The riders were showing how well they could back their mounts. "Audra is taking over as the manager for the Silver Lake Pony Ranch. Clancy will be the senior instructor and Penny will be her assistant. I've got designs on the indoor arena at Sean's."

"And here I thought she was marrying me for true love," Sean teased. He ruffled Jake's hair. "The truth is out."

"I do love you." Elinor retorted indignantly.

"I know." Sean grinned at her and put an arm around her shoulders. "You have to be able to tease the one you love."

"Or it isn't love," Marlene said. "A day without a shared laugh is a sorry day."

A hush fell on the crowd. Elinor was aware by the sudden silence that the judge had decided the placings. The announcer began to read off the awards. She watched the other children ride out of the arena. Finally, only Lynn and one other girl were left.

Elinor caught her breath when Lynn was pronounced second. "I don't believe it. That's wonderful."

"I thought she deserved a blue," Marlene argued.

"Not another one," Jake disagreed. "There'd be no living with her."

Sean chuckled. "Out of the mouths of babes," he quoted.

"Let's go congratulate her." Elinor led the way toward the huge swing gate at one end of the arena. They arrived at the same moment Lynn did.

"Mom, look!" Lynn held up the huge red rosette. "Didn't Gypsy do great?"

Elinor hugged her daughter, careful not to unbalance her and pull her from the mare's back. "I think she might have had a little help from you, but she definitely deserves a big bag of carrots."

Lynn beamed and looked back at the arena. "There's the girl who took first. I'm going to tell her how well she did." Lynn swung Gypsy around and rode away.

"I'm so proud of her," Elinor said as Sean came to join her. "She's being a very good sport."

"I know." Sean glanced at Jake. "You've got two of the best kids in the world. You've done a great job raising them."

"I'm lucky." Elinor placed a hand on her son's shoulder "I don't know what I did to deserve them, but I'm glad they're mine."

"Actually, I wondered if I could borrow one," Sean said. "If you wouldn't miss him, Jake and I could have a guys' night out."

"Really?" Jake gazed up at Sean with worship in his eyes. "When?"

"Tonight." Sean arched a brow. "I figure your mom and Lynn will be ready to collapse when we get home, but we won't."

"Wow. That'd be awesome. Can I, Mom?"

Elinor smiled. "You bet. I would enjoy the chance to go to bed early. So would Lynn."

Jake looked worried. "I forgot. I'm grounded."

"Yes, but I only said you and Sean couldn't go fishing together. I didn't say you couldn't go other places with him."

"That's definitely awesome," Jake said. "I've gotta go help Lynnie. She needs me to roll up her chaps before she gets off Gypsy." He hurried in the direction of his sister, calling back over his shoulder, "I'll tell her that Sean and I are going out tonight so you can rest."

Elinor giggled. She tiptoed up to kiss Sean. "Now I know why I love you. You're the kindest, nicest man in the world."

"You're not too shabby yourself, ma'am." He pulled her closer for a longer kiss. "I'll wake you up when I get home."

"That better be a real promise, not a piecrust one."

The rest of the day passed in the same golden haze. Lynn continued to place highly in her classes, collecting blue and scarlet rosettes. Elinor carefully stored the ribbons in the cab of her pickup. Along with Sean, Jake, and Marlene, she cheered her daughter's victories. The crowd in the grandstand appeared to be made up of relatives and other horse professionals. They were as quick to applaud the rest of the riders as they were their own children.

The late afternoon sun beat down on them as Elinor loaded Gypsy into Sean's horse trailer. She couldn't hide her pleasure when he made no attempt to take over the task. Instead, he accepted the fact that the mare would trust her first. She tied the palomino securely and gave Gypsy one more loving pat. The four-teen-hand pony had done a good job today.

Sean closed and latched the door behind her. Elinor hesitated as the announcer began to speak. She ought to know what was happening, but this was the first time she'd actually attended a horse show. Her concerns lay with teaching children to ride. She wanted them to know horses were both joy and responsibility. Her lack of knowledge about show ring procedures bothered her. She'd learn.

"It's time for them to announce the high-point trophies." Sean leaned against the two-horse trailer. "Do you know how that works, Lynn?"

"Marlene says there's a certain number of points for each ribbon. First gets more than second and so on. I wonder who won today."

"Listen for your number," Sean advised. "You might win a runner-up trophy when they give out your division's placings."

Elinor caught Sean's arm. She pulled him out of earshot. "How do you know she won anything extra? Don't get her hopes up."

He shook his head. Sean slipped his hands around her neck and into her hair. He touched her lips with his. "I'm not. Lynn took first and second places all day. She stands a good chance of getting one of the awards. If she does, it's because you were here to give her confidence. That's why she did so well."

Elinor managed to nod. She went to her daughter and rested a hand on her shoulder. "Don't be too upset if you don't win this time. There's always the next show."

"It'll be okay, Mom. Gypsy deserves high-point. She worked hard today. Besides, it'd be great for business. We'd get lots more students."

Elinor sighed. "Fourteen going on forty. Enjoy the moment, sweetie." She patted Lynn's shoulder. "Either way, we'll be fine."

"You worked hard, too," Jake pointed out. "Gypsy couldn't have won those ribbons without you."

"I tried. But Sean says a real horsewoman gives the credit to her horse when they win and takes responsibility when she loses. It's because I'm like the adult on this team, and Gypsy's like a kid."

"Will I have to do that when I show Awesome?" Jake asked.

"Definitely," Sean said. "It's not that hard, son. You'll have a great attitude in the show ring. You already do this on the farm when it comes to the animals."

Elinor raised her hand to hush them. The announcer began to give the placings for Lynn's age group. First, the two runners-up were declared. Then the announcer proclaimed the winner of the high-point trophy: Lynn Talbot.

Elinor grabbed her daughter and hugged her tight. "Oh, honey. Congratulations."

"Mom, chill out. Somebody could see you."

"Let them." Elinor hugged Lynn again. "Come on, honey. Let's go get your trophy."

———

Elinor found herself remembering the glorious day when she climbed into bed that night. Why had she played the martyr for so long? She deserved to be happy and to see her children shine. And from now on, she would.

She woke to the light pressure of a kiss and smiled. She opened her eyes and saw Sean's laughter-filled face. "Prince Charming finally got here."

"Nope. Just call me a desperate cowboy."

She giggled. "Well, I'm not scared. What did you do with my son?"

"Put him to bed. Now I can have my wicked way with you." Sean bent closer.

She planted her hand on his broad chest. The warmth of his skin tempted her. She felt a tremor go through her. She slid her fingers into the matted dark hair. "I need to check on Lynn and Jake before you jump my bones."

Sean snagged her wrist and raised her hand to his mouth. "While you do that, I'll lock up. I already walked around the place. The ponies are fine."

"We make a good team." Elinor gathered up her robe.

"I'll say." Sean tipped up her chin and lowered his head.

"Between us, we made everything on the kids' wish list come true. They don't even know it yet." He reached in his shirt pocket and pulled out a jewelry box. "Jake helped me pick out an engagement ring, but if you don't like it, we can exchange it."

"I've never had a ring before." Elinor opened the lid to reveal a simple gold band with a sapphire surrounded by small diamonds. "I love it."

"Good." Sean removed it from the box and slipped it on her finger. It fit perfectly.

"How did you know my size?" Elinor demanded. "How did Jake?"

"He borrowed one of your riding gloves," Sean said. "That boy is sharp. I wouldn't have thought of it, but he had a plan as soon as I said I wanted to surprise you."

"Oh, I'll bet he had a plan before that. I hope we can keep up the good work and give them a little *magick* in their lives." She slipped her arms around his neck and drew him down for a quick kiss. "They need it."

"So do adults," Sean lifted his head for an instant. "Together, we'll make *magick* happen."

"Together has to be the most *magickal* word in the universe," Elinor said, and surrendered to his kiss.

———

"Wake up, Lynnie."

"What?" Lynn opened her eyes. She glanced sideways at the clock on the nightstand. "Do you know what time it is?"

"Almost midnight. We gotta hurry."

"Why?" Lynn closed her eyes. "I'm tired. I'm going back to sleep."

"You can't. Lynnie, you promised. You said if I lent you my halter for shows this summer, you'd help me. I could choose whatever I wanted. What I want is a little brother."

"Two of you?" Lynn's eyes popped wide open. Now she was really awake. "No way!"

"Yes way. We got everything we wanted in our new dad with my first spell. And the second one got him and Mom together. The last one brought Sean back when we almost lost him. I need a little brother."

"No, you don't." Lynn glowered at her own little pest of a brother from the sanctuary of her bed. King was asleep with his gold, black, and white fuzzy head safe on her arm. "Mom told us. No more spells. I can't help you. She'll go ballistic if she finds out about this one."

"She'll never know. We won't tell her," Jake said. "Babies come from *magick* in this family. We have to do another spell."

"No way. You can't make me. This last spell went on forever."

"We could do one for you and one for me," Jake offered. "Mine's ready for tonight, but we could do yours tomorrow."

"What would I want?" Lynn asked. "I got everything I wanted. A puppy. A dad to come watch me ride. I even got Mom there and I never expected that."

"If you help me tonight, I'll write a spell so you can have a little sister."

Lynn hesitated. When it came to looking after Jake, she needed help. "Okay, Jake. But this is it. After these two, no more spells. I mean it."

"Okay, Lynnie. Whatever you say!"

THE END

———

Don't miss out on your next favorite book!

Join the Satin Romance mailing list
www.satinromance.com/mail.html

AFTERWORD

As a child, I loved to dream away the days in an old cherry tree on my family's pony farm. In my imagination, the tree became a beautiful Arabian stallion, a medieval castle and even a pirate ship. On rainy days, I headed for my fort in the hayloft. While the rain thudded on the cedar-shingled roof, I read books, eventually trading Carolyn Keene for Georgette Heyer.

For my book, *Cowboy Spell,* I used the memories of my childhood home as a setting. A pony farm definitely needs an ensemble cast of four-legged critters—in other words, ponies. I drew the fictional ponies in the story from the ones that made *The Funny Farm* so special.

I know that's a rather strange name for a pony farm, but it came from my grandmother who told us our stories about life on the farm could make anyone laugh until they cried. One of my favorite ponies was Luck of The Irish, Lucky for short who inspired Bonanza in this story. He frequently escaped from any stall, pasture or paddock—we called him our "Houdini" pony.

Lucky and I were together until he died of old age, at 40+ years. He still loved junk food, and even after he had cataracts in both eyes, he smelled out the garbage cans and hunted through them for the day camp kids' leftovers from lunch.

However, when I was a kid and rode him, he was young and in his prime. We shared many a picnic lunch on long trail rides with our 4-H Club, the original Everett Silver Flying As led by Herb and Virginia Weinz. Lucky would do anything for a peanut butter sandwich and soda pop, but he didn't pass up dog food, cat food, chicken scratch or the rabbit's alfalfa pellets either. He did eat traditional horsy treats like carrots and apples, but only when he couldn't find more exciting fare.

We rode all over the place, back in the 1960s and 1970s when paradise hadn't yet been paved in Western Washington. Since we got out of school the first week in June, summers lasted forever. Trees and wildlife covered much of Snohomish County and we didn't know that tuna sandwiches and mayonnaise might not be the wisest choice for lunches on hot days, especially after they'd been packed on horses for hours. Crushed potato chips and warm Coca-Cola weren't all that bad, and Lucky got more than his share.

Parades, horse-shows, camping trips at Big Four Mountain with our horses, and the county fair—what child could ask for anything more? The Silver Flying As was as we kids called it, the best "4-H club in sight," thanks to Virginia and Herb Weinz who are gone now, but the memories remain.

And I still have horses. I can't imagine life without them. Today, I live on the family ranch in the Cascade foothills of Washington State in what was once a summer vacation cabin. I usually write at night after a long day on the ranch. Some days are longer and harder than others, so I'm happy when I manage five days of writing in a week. As a substitute schoolteacher, I love the school breaks but I'm just as busy, since there are 24 horses to look after, along with other assorted animals.

I hope you enjoyed this visit to contemporary Liberty Valley and look forward to the next one when Homicide Detective Beth Chambers travels through time to find her true love.

THANK YOU FOR READING

———

Did you enjoy this book?

We invite you to leave a review at your favorite book site, such as Goodreads, Amazon, Barnes & Noble, etc.

DID YOU KNOW THAT LEAVING A REVIEW...

- Helps other readers find books they may enjoy.
- Gives you a chance to let your voice be heard.
- Gives authors recognition for their hard work.
- Doesn't have to be long. A sentence or two about why you liked the book will do.

ABOUT THE AUTHOR

Josie Malone lives and works at her family's riding stable in Washington State. She's taught children to ride and know about horses for so long that she often discovers she's taught three generations of their families. Her life experiences span adventures from dealing cards in a casino, attending graduate school to get her Masters in Teaching degree, being a substitute teacher, and serving in the Army Reserve - all leading to her second career as a published author. Visit her at her website, www.josiemalone.com to learn about her books.

Contact Josie at:
josiemaloneauthor@outlook.com

www.josiemalone.com

f facebook.com/JosieMaloneAuthor